Building Fences

Violet Howe

www.violethowe.com

Cover Design: Elizabeth Mackey Graphics

Published by Charbar Productions, LLC
(p-v3)

BOOKS BY VIOLET HOWE

<u>Tales Behind the Veils</u>

Diary of a Single Wedding Planner

Diary of a Wedding Planner in Love

Diary of an Engaged Wedding Planner

Maggie

<u>Cedar Creek Mysteries</u>

The Ghost in the Curve

The Glow in the Woods

<u>Cedar Creek Families</u>

Building Fences

Crossing Paths

#meetcute

Boy meets girl. It's the way romances usually begin . . . and while we all love a happy ending, it's the #MeetCute that wins our hearts.

How did you two meet?

The #MeetCute Books each have a unique answer to that query. Some might make you swoon, others might make you giggle . . . and some may make you blush.

Twelve authors. Twelve stand-alone contemporary romance novels. Twelve stories that will make your heart beat a little faster.

Because it's all about the #MeetCute.

ACKNOWLEDGMENTS

Bonnie, Sandy, Teresa, & Tawdra – Thank you for your time and your insight. It is a wonderful gift to be able to trust my content with others, knowing they will treat it with the greatest of care but deliver the most valuable honesty.

Christy, Cindy, & Johanna – A huge thank you to my team of nurses who helped me diagnose and treat Caterina and bring her back to her family.

Lisa, Donna, and Melissa – Thanks again for your time in making sure all my T's are crossed and all my I's are dotted. I appreciate you all!

To the staff and crew at Plumley Farms – Thank you for your time and diligence in answering my questions and giving me the grand tour.

CHAPTER 1

It was supposed to be a quiet weekend. I'd planned to clean out closets and start packing non-essentials for our impending move to Orlando. Maybe even put the ferns on the back porch into bigger pots.

An exciting itinerary, to be sure.

If anyone had told me I'd have a weekend filled with a car theft, a coma, two-stepping, and a mare giving birth before driving home in a stranger's clothes, I might have done things differently, but life has a way of being unpredictable.

It all started like any ordinary Friday afternoon on one of Brad's weekends with me dreading his arrival and my kids' subsequent departure, but at the same time praying he'd show up and not disappoint them yet again.

Ethan had a rare Saturday off from soccer, and Eva had arranged to miss ballet so she could join her brother and their father on their camping trip.

I'd been watching for Brad through the front window, checking my phone every few minutes for a missed call or text saying he had to cancel.

"He was supposed to be here ten minutes ago," Eva said behind me.

"He'll be here," I said with more confidence than I felt. "He's running late, that's all."

"He always runs late. When he shows up, he shows up late. Or he doesn't show up at all."

I glanced over my shoulder, already knowing the teenage scowl would be there. It was getting harder to defend their father as she got older and the rose-colored glasses she'd worn faded.

1

"He'll be here. Are you all packed? I put bug spray in the bag with the sunscreen. Make sure Ethan wears both, okay? Have him put it on first thing in the morning, and then reapply it throughout the day. Especially if you go swimming."

"I know, Mom." She rolled her eyes as she ran the emery board across the edge of her thumbnail. "This place better have a pool. I'm not going to ruin a brand-new suit swimming in some nasty river water."

"It has a pool. I showed you pictures online, remember?"

"Mom, you never know what a place actually looks from their website. They show you what they want you to see. You know that."

I watched as she blew the nail dust from her thumb and held her slender hands out to survey them.

She had changed so much since turning fourteen. A growth spurt shortly after her birthday had brought her to my height, but Eva carried herself with an easy gracefulness I'd never quite mastered. She had Brad's dark hair and his deep green eyes, but her lean build was all mine. Tall and slender with willowy limbs and no curves to speak of, but decidedly feminine all the same.

She had her father's darker skin tone as well, with only a sparse splattering of my freckles across the bridge of her nose.

Ethan, on the other hand, had inherited all my freckles and then some; his pale skin burning with even the slightest exposure to the sun. His hair was my same reddish-auburn, but his frame was stocky like Brad's.

It was like Eva's genes had blended the best of our physical attributes, while Ethan had gotten what was left over—the least favorable combination.

What he lacked for in complexion and build, he made up for in his sense of humor, his outgoing personality, and his brilliant blue eyes. Mine were a bluish-gray, rather dull I'd always thought, but Ethan's were the clear blue of a summer sky.

Eva frowned as she inspected some manicure imperfection she'd found, tossing her dark hair over her shoulder where it fell in easy waves down her back as she groaned and started to file again.

My heart longed for the happy-go-lucky girl she'd been a little over eighteen months ago before her father had announced he'd fallen in love with a paralegal in his office and wanted a divorce.

I had no way of knowing how much of Eva's transformation into sullen and cynical was a product of puberty and hormones, and how much was a direct result of the implosion of our family.

"Thanks for going, Eva," I said. "I know camping isn't your thing, but I feel so much better knowing you're there to keep an eye on your brother."

"You mean so Dad doesn't lose him or forget and leave him in the woods like he left me at the ballet studio that day?"

I sighed. "Your father gets distracted easily. He has a lot on his mind."

"So do you. You've never left me waiting outside for hours."

A flash of light caught my eye, and I turned back toward the window, relieved to see Brad getting out of a car but confused as to why he wasn't in his truck.

"Stay here," I said to Eva, stepping out onto the porch and closing the front door behind me.

Brad sprinted up the steps grinning like a teenager who's gotten his first set of wheels, sweeping his arm toward the red sports car in my driveway.

"Isn't she beautiful? Audi TT Roadster. One owner, low miles, and the price was right. She drives like a dream," he exclaimed, staring at the car with beaming pride. "I've always wanted a convertible."

In the seventeen years I'd known the man, I'd never once heard him mention wanting a convertible, but I opted not to bring that up when there was such a bigger issue to address.

"Um, it's nice, but it has two seats. You have a fourteen-year-old and a ten-year-old. Where are you going to put them? And the camping gear?"

His face immediately fell, and he looked at me with his mouth hanging open. "Is that *this* weekend?"

Anger immediately reared its head inside me, but I crossed my arms and tried to remain calm, determined to heed my therapist's directive not to get drawn into arguments during pick-ups or drop-offs.

"I sent you a text on Tuesday confirming you were all set for this trip, Brad. You texted back and asked me to get groceries since you didn't know what the kids wanted. I have all the camping gear and their bags packed and stacked in the garage ready to go. Ethan has been looking forward to this for months. You promised you'd help him get his camping badge for Scouts."

"All right, all right. It just slipped my mind, that's all. I've been busy getting ready for the move. I'm sure we can figure something out. Eva's skinny. They could probably share the front seat, or Eva could hold Ethan in her lap."

"No. Absolutely not. You're not driving our kids around in a convertible without seat belts and without proper seats for both of them."

He frowned. "Maybe Eva can stay home. The campground doesn't have Wi-fi, so she'll probably just sulk all weekend anyway."

"Brad," I said through gritted teeth, "you haven't seen them in over a month. She already arranged to miss ballet to go with you. You need to spend time with *both* your kids."

"Okay, geesh. I was trying to help Eva out since I'm sure she probably doesn't want to go and you talked her into it. She acts like she can't wait to get back here every time she's with me anyway."

The therapist's advice went out the window and anger took the wheel. "Then maybe you should put a bit more effort into connecting with her. Do you ever call her? Text her? See how her week's going? When's the last time you made a recital performance? Did you know she got a part in the school play?"

"I work long hours, Caroline. I'm still responsible for my position here, but I'm already working the position in Orlando, which was a promotion, remember? More responsibility? And more money, thank God. Someone has to pay for the bills and the ballet, the Scouts, and all these other activities they're in. I mean, between child support and alimony, I'm barely able to have any life of my own."

"Oh, don't even go there. I wanted to get a job. You were the one who was so damned adamant that I stay home with them. That's why only one of us finished our degree and got to have a career, remember? You didn't want the kids in daycare, and you didn't want me working outside the home. It was your idea to pay alimony and keep me home with them so they didn't have more to adjust to after the divorce, which was also your idea, so don't start with me about that."

"And here we go again. This is why I don't like to come here, you know?"

"Daddy!" Ethan swung the front door wide open and jumped into Brad's arms, hugging his father tightly around the neck.

"Hey, buddy!" Brad exclaimed, twirling around with Ethan attached to him.

"I tried to tell him you and Dad were talking, but he didn't listen," Eva whispered behind me as she stepped out onto the porch and pulled the door closed.

"It's okay," I told her.

"Eva Marie!" Brad said. "I swear you've gotten taller! Soon you're gonna pass your mom and you might be as tall as your old man someday."

"Doubtful," Eva sneered, and my heart hurt to think of the pain she was masking behind the glare she shot toward her father. "What's with the convertible?"

Brad set Ethan down on the porch and gazed out at his car. "That's my new ride! Go check it out."

"It's got two seats, Dad. How are we all going to fit?" Eva asked as she walked past him and down the steps toward the car.

Brad frowned again, and the lines in his forehead were deeper than I remembered.

"Right. Yeah. Okay. We'll figure it out."

"Where's your truck?" I asked, watching Ethan run across the lawn toward the shining, red beacon of a mid-life crisis in our driveway with Eva following at a much slower pace.

Brad looked up, but his eyes didn't quite meet mine. "I sold it."

"You sold your truck?" I asked. "To buy that?"

"I traded it in. It was a great deal, and I couldn't pass it up."

"Mom! You gotta come see this!" Ethan exclaimed as he plopped down in the passenger seat. "It's a convertible! It's awesome!"

Brad looked back at me before turning to walk toward the kids. "Here, Eva! Get in the driver's seat!"

He tossed the keys to her, and she caught them with one hand while opening the car door with the other.

"It's an Audi," he told her. "A TT Roadster."

I stood at the top of the steps with my arms still crossed and my temper threatening to explode.

His impulse shopping had been an issue when we were married, but he seemed to have gotten worse since the divorce, like he was looking for a new image and desperately purchasing anything that might fit the one he'd created in his head.

Sadly, it didn't surprise me that Brad had neglected to think about his children when purchasing a vehicle. He'd spent most of their lives not thinking about them, or anyone, when he made decisions. He thought of Brad first, and then figured out how to make it work for everyone else afterward.

"Can I drive it around the block, Daddy?" Eva asked from the driver's seat in her most pleading tone, wooed out of her sullenness by the siren call of the red convertible.

"No, Eva," I said before Brad could answer. "You still have another six months before you have your learner's permit. If Daddy still has this car then, you can drive it. Not until."

It was tough to tell who looked at me with the most disdain, Brad or Eva.

"Driving around the block won't hurt anything," he said.

"Yeah, c'mon, Mom. I won't even leave our neighborhood. Shannon's mom lets her drive all the way to the mailboxes up by the entrance without anyone in the car with her."

"No, Eva."

"But, Shannon—"

"Eva, I said no. Now get out of the car and give the keys to your dad."

Her ever-present teenage scowl slid back into place as she opened the door and climbed from the car.

"Hey, Dad, how *are* we all going to fit?" Ethan asked as he looked at the lack of space behind the seats and the small, almost non-existent trunk. "And where's the tent going to go?"

"Um, yeah. About that," Brad said, his brow furrowed in deep concentration.

"Did you really get rid of your truck?" Eva asked, standing with her arms crossed as she stared at the car.

"Yeah. I saw this baby sitting there, and it was a great price, so I went in and made a deal."

"Some deal, Dad. Your truck was an extended cab and had room for everyone. Why on earth would you give that up and buy a two-seater?"

Eva's tone echoed my thoughts, and I leaned against the porch column and watched Brad squirm.

I recognized his expression. I'd seen it plenty over the years when he'd made an impulse decision without thinking things through and then been presented with reality. He was irritated with us for stealing his joy.

"Does this mean we're not going camping?" Ethan said, his smile gone.

"No, no, no," Brad said, waving his arms. "Not at all, buddy. Of course, we're going camping! I said we were, didn't I?"

Eva rolled her eyes, and I knew I should correct her for the disrespect in the gesture, but his statement was so ludicrous that I couldn't bring myself to do it. The list of his broken promises had grown too long to count.

Our divorce agreement granted Brad visitation every other weekend, but he'd never maintained that frequency. In the beginning, when he was still with Tatiana—the paralegal he'd left us for—he took them more often, but once that relationship had fizzled and the kids' schedules became too much for him to manage, he'd started canceling more often.

I don't know which was worse—the weekends he would show up on Friday and take them away, leaving me to lay in bed with the covers pulled over my head in a gloomy depression until they returned, or the number of weekends he neglected to pick them up, leaving me to dry their tears and soothe their disappointments.

It should have come as no surprise that he offered as little engagement as possible in their schedules, their activities, and their lives. He hadn't been involved while we were married; why would he change once he was free?

But with each broken promise, I grew angrier, and so did Eva. Ethan still clung to hope and tried to see the best in his dad, but Eva had grown cold to the disappointment. She expected Brad to screw up, and only on rare occasions did he surprise her by not doing so.

"Okay, so what do we do now? We obviously can't fit in that car," Eva said with a sigh, pulling her hair up into a ponytail and wrapping it with the band around her wrist.

"We're still gonna go. Right, Dad?" Ethan asked. "We're going camping, aren't we, Dad?"

"Yeah. We are," Brad said, his eyes darting from the kids to the car and back as we all watched the mad scramble to find a solution play out on his face. Suddenly, his eyes widened, and he snapped his fingers. "I know! Here's what we'll do." He turned and pointed to me. "Mom will take the Roadster for the weekend, and we can go camping in Mom's Tahoe. Boom! Problem solved." He clapped his hands together and then held them up for the children to give him high-fives. Ethan obliged the request, but Eva turned toward me.

"Mom? Are you gonna take the Roadster?" Eva asked.

I didn't want to. Partly, because I didn't want to bail him out for the millionth time, and partly because I didn't want to drive around in his stupid car for the weekend. But it was hard to say no when I knew how much the weekend meant to Ethan.

"C'mon, Caroline," Brad pleaded. "It's not like you need the SUV if the kids aren't around. Hell, it's not like you ever have plans if the kids aren't around." He chuckled, but I didn't. The statement was too true to be funny. "But hey, you don't need plans! With a convertible, you can just drive around with the wind in your hair."

"I don't like the wind in my hair," I said.

"So then close the top. Here, it's easy. Just the push of a button." He motioned for me to come over to the car as he opened the driver's door.

"Yeah, c'mon, Mom!" Ethan shouted as he ran to take my hand and pull me toward the car. "You should leave it down and let the wind blow your hair all around. It'll be fun!"

While I saw nothing fun in the proposed plan, I ended up agreeing to it, of course. As much as I wanted Brad to squirm in the mess of his own making, I didn't want to be the reason the kids couldn't spend time with their dad.

I helped them pack the Tahoe, and then I stood on the porch and waved goodbye as they drove away in what had been the family car for years. I stared at the red Audi goading me from the driveway, determined that I would not so much as even sit in that car for the entire weekend.

But that was before the phone rang.

CHAPTER 2

I'd just finished a dinner of leftover meatloaf and mashed potatoes when the call came. If the kids had been home, I would have let it go to voicemail since I didn't recognize the number, but with them away, I had to answer.

"Hello," I said, hoping it wasn't bad news.

"Oh, hi. I'm so happy you answered. I was worried I might get a machine."

I grimaced, preparing to give my standard telemarketer speech about not being interested and wanting to be removed from their list.

"My name is Patsy Lannister," she said, "and I'm trying to reach a woman by the name of Caroline Miller. Her maiden name was Klinefelter, and I'm hoping this is the right number."

"I'm sorry. *Who* is this?" I said, still apprehensive. "Why are you calling?"

"Well," she said after a pause, "I'm not sure how to say this, so I'll just get straight to the point. If you're Caroline Miller, you registered on a website recently saying you'd be interested in information about your birth mother."

My heart skipped a beat, and my grip tightened on the phone.

"Yes, I did. This is Caroline."

"Well, I know where your mother is, and she would very much like to connect with you."

My knees went weak, and I sank into the chair behind me and braced my elbows on the table, reminding myself to stay wary and stay calm.

I'd been skeptical of entering my personal information online, knowing that scammers like to prey on those who are desperate and seeking answers. But the need to find my mother, which had always been there lurking at the back of my mind, had grown insatiable since my divorce.

I think part of it was being without my own children when they left to go stay with Brad. I don't know that a mother ever gets accustomed to saying goodbye like that. I certainly haven't, even after all this time.

In the beginning, it was all-consuming. Every time they left, it was like a wound was reopened and reinjured.

My dread of them going away on Friday would begin around bedtime the Sunday night before. It built throughout the week, and when they drove away smiling with their father and his beautiful girlfriend, it was as though a chunk of my heart was ripped away, leaving a gaping hole that rendered me unable to function.

The grief and despair those first few months threatened my sanity and my physical health.

I rarely left my bed when they were gone.

I couldn't muster the energy to shower. To get dressed. To be bothered with eating or conversing with other humans. Phone calls from well-meaning friends went unanswered, and their never-ending flow of invitations for social interaction went ignored.

It was during those dark nights that I began obsessing about finding my birth mother.

Brad had always discouraged me from searching for her when we were together.

"You never know what you're gonna find," he'd say. "She gave you up for a reason. She's probably a drug addict. She may have a criminal history. You need to think about our children. You can't bring someone into their lives without knowing anything about her. You already have a mom. Why do you need another one?"

He was right. I didn't know anything about her. I didn't know what I might find. And I did have an adoptive mother who loved me, had sacrificed for me, and would always be there for me.

But I wanted to know who gave birth to me. In order to know who I was, I needed to know who she was. No matter what I found.

So, one Saturday night as I was missing my children, I couldn't help wondering if somewhere out there, she was missing me. After a couple of glasses of wine for courage, I began my search on the laptop. I found several sites and databases for finding birth parents, and after reading reviews and doing as much research as I could, I chose some and registered.

I checked my email every few minutes the rest of that weekend, and almost hourly for the weeks to come. But when a month had passed with no word, I began to lose hope. Then soccer season started back up for Ethan, Eva's competition season started in ballet, and Brad began leaving them with me on his weekends so I could manage their busy schedules.

My obsession with finding the woman who carried and delivered me faded into the background.

But here she was, back at the forefront of my mind with a simple phone call.

"Where is she? Can I talk to her?"

"She's staying with my husband and me right now. Recently, she shared with me about your birth. I've left no stone unturned in trying to find you for her. She very much wants to meet you before it's too late."

Any euphoria I felt at the thought of finding my mother was short-lived as I considered the woman's words.

"Too late? What do you mean? Is she ill?"

"I'm afraid so. She's been in and out of the hospital battling pneumonia for the past few months. Every time she seems to be on the mend, it hits her again. It's been scary, but she's a fighter, and she's pulled through so far."

All skepticism and wariness were forgotten as my thoughts turned to panic with the possibility of her dying before we met.

"Where is she? Can I talk to her? Can I come and meet her?"

I rushed to the desk to search for a piece of paper and a pen, silently berating my children for never putting anything back where it belongs.

"I think she would like that very much."

"When? When can I come? Where are you?"

"In Cedar Creek, west of Orlando. You live near Gainesville, right?"

"Yes, but I could come tonight." I glanced at the clock on the oven. It was twenty past six. It would be eight-thirty before I could reach the small town of Cedar Creek, and that was if Friday night traffic wasn't heavy through the city.

"Oh, I don't think tonight would be good. That would put you on the roads late, and you wouldn't have much time to visit as Caterina tends to go to bed early these days."

Caterina. My birth mother finally had a name. I had come up with several for her over the years, but none seemed right. Caterina. How pretty! I wondered what ethnic background she had. Which then meant what ethnic background *I* had.

"Could you come tomorrow? Maybe around eleven or so?" Patsy said. "I could fix us some lunch."

I'd waited thirty-five years, and part of me wanted to refuse to wait any longer. To insist that I needed to meet my birth mother right away. Patsy was right, though. It would be four hours of driving round-trip, and when I considered the health issues Patsy had mentioned, I reluctantly agreed to wait until the next day.

Patsy gave me the street address, and I thanked her for calling me, but a bit of skepticism lingered.

"Can I ask why you're calling instead of Caterina?"

"She gets winded easily. Her voice isn't very strong, especially for the phone. She's prone to coughing fits. You'll see tomorrow."

We exchanged our goodbyes, and I went through the rest of the evening in a blur, my thoughts consumed with Caterina.

When I'd fantasized about meeting her as I was growing up, I imagined the connection between us being immediate. In nearly every scenario I conjured, we knew the moment we looked into each other's eyes that whatever had been missing was found.

We'd laugh and hug, the tears would flow, and she'd remark how much I looked like her.

That was one of my biggest pet peeves as a child about being adopted. I looked like no one. Not my cousins, not my grandparents who tried so hard to treat me equally to the others, not my absentee father who disappeared two years after he adopted me, and not my well-meaning mother, Lorna, who never intended to raise me alone but did the best she could.

So, the birth mother of my dreams was my mirror image, only older. She, too, had gone through middle school with freckled skin and hair red enough to draw taunts and teasing.

I was certain it was her grey-blue eyes I saw in my reflection, and I just knew she had to share my tall, thin frame—unlike Lorna, who was curvaceous in my teenage years when I was built like a boy and who seemed to grow more plump every year while I struggled to keep on weight.

None of my musings about my birth mother had considered that she might be ill, and my mind struggled to add that fact to the mental image I'd constructed over the years.

I'd changed into my pajamas and had just finished brushing my teeth when Lorna rang with her nightly check-in.

"Hi, Mom."

"Hey, sweetheart. What time did the kids leave?"

"Around six."

"I know Ethan is probably over the moon to be camping. I hope Eva has a good time as well. I picked up a journal for her today. It has a mermaid on it. Does she still like mermaids? I know she's getting to that age."

I listened to her ramble on about her shopping adventures, but my mind was preoccupied with thoughts of meeting Caterina.

I'd debated all evening on whether to share with my mom that I was going to meet her predecessor the next day. Part of me reasoned that it would be best to know if this was a legitimate lead before telling Lorna, but another part of me knew she'd be hurt if I didn't tell her beforehand.

"I got a call tonight," I said, blurting it out before I changed my mind again. "Evidently, someone saw my information on one of the websites. She says she knows my birth mother. She's invited me to lunch tomorrow. To meet her. To meet my birth mother."

The words were stilted and hard to say out loud.

Lorna was silent, and the ticking of the grandfather clock down the hall grew louder and all other sounds fell away as I waited for her response.

"You there?" I asked, when the pause continued.

"Yes, I'm here. Are you sure it's her?"

"No. But how would I be? It wasn't like I could ask for proof on the phone. I know nothing about her."

Another extended pause.

"Seems like they should be able to give you something," she said, her voice quiet.

"Mom, we don't even know what city I was born in. You said

when the adoption lawyer contacted you and Dad, the records were all sealed. No matter what proof they offered me, I wouldn't know if it was true or not."

"What are you going to do?"

"I'm going to go to lunch. I'll meet her. See what she has to say." She paused again.

"Where is she?" she asked, her voice barely above a whisper.

"Cedar Creek."

Lorna cleared her throat, but when she spoke, the emotion in her voice was still thick. "Do you want me to go with you?"

I considered it for a moment, and though I would have loved to have someone by my side for the journey, I knew it was too much to ask of her.

She'd always been supportive of my questions, and she knew I'd actively searched, but on some level, I sensed she felt insecure about me finding this other woman of importance in my life.

I didn't want to make either of them uncomfortable, and I didn't want my first reaction to my birth mother to be tempered by concern over my mom's feelings about the matter.

Best to confront the past on my own, and then I could figure out how to merge it with my present.

"No, that's okay. You have water aerobics in the morning, and I'll need to leave early to get there before lunch. The GPS says it's about two hours. I'll take a ride down there and see what it brings. I'll call you when I'm done."

"Okay, love," she said, and I wondered if I was imagining the relief in her voice. "If you change your mind for any reason, just call. I'll be happy to go if you need me to."

I already knew she would, and that was enough. It made me love her even more.

Perhaps it was selfish of me to look for my birth mother when I already had a mom who was everything a daughter could want and then some. She'd given me unconditional love and support from the day she'd brought me home, and she'd been my rock and my inspiration through all life had flung my way.

But I still wanted to know where I came from. Who I was, and who'd created me.

Sleep eluded me most of the night, and whenever I did drift away for short stints, I'd find myself in endless dream loops of meeting women who claimed to be my mother, never knowing who was honest and who was there to deceive me. I'd wake in a panic, my breath rapid and shallow as I fought to discern between reality and what was my mind's fear at play.

When the sun's rays began to filter through the window blinds, I went ahead and got out of bed, turning off the alarm that wasn't scheduled to sound for another two hours. I made a pot of coffee and scrambled an egg, which I ate along with a piece of toast and some jam. When I'd eaten, washed the breakfast dishes, and put them away, I took a nice, long bath.

None of it calmed my nerves much, but it helped pass the time.

It took five wardrobe changes to find an outfit I was comfortable with; I worried about the impression I would make on this total stranger who'd given me life. I opted for a pair of jeans so I didn't come across too fussy but paired them with a peach-colored long-sleeved rayon shirt that kept it from being too casual. I knew the peach complimented my hair and skin tone, and I finished the look off with a pair of high-heeled sandals that accentuated my height.

I stared at my reflection in the hall mirror at the foot of the stairs, wondering what the day would bring. When I returned home, would I know more about my identity? Would the puzzle of my life have another piece filled in?

I grabbed my purse from the counter in the kitchen, dreading the drive alone and wishing I'd asked a friend to take the ride with me.

In all the chaos of the phone call and the mental drama that ensued, I'd completely forgotten about the convertible until I saw its keychain hanging on the hook by the kitchen door.

I didn't even have the comfort of my own car for the trip.

CHAPTER 3

Traffic was lighter than expected for a Saturday morning in Gainesville, and my GPS showed my estimated arrival to be fifteen minutes earlier than expected.

Once I'd left the city and the four-lane highway behind, I found myself on a winding road lined on either side by dense forest. The skies were blue above me, and the sunlight flashed through the tree tops like a strobe light.

The Roadster sat much lower to the ground than my Tahoe, and though it was a smoother ride than I'd expected, I still couldn't get used to the claustrophobic feel of the car.

Perhaps it would have been better to keep the top down, but then my hair would have been a rat's nest. Not a great first impression.

I was only about twenty minutes away from Patsy's when an explosive bang filled the air, and the whole car shook. The steering wheel jerked hard to the left beneath my hands, and the telltale roar of a blown tire drowned out Tom Petty on the stereo as I veered across the line into the other lane, thankful there was no other traffic on the road.

The incline of the hill slowed the car somewhat, and I fought to maintain control and get back on the right side. The road had no shoulder to speak of, but I managed to get the car all the way off the pavement, though not by much.

My hands were shaking as I climbed from the car, and as I stood, I realized my legs were shaking, too.

The back left tire had blown, and while I was thankful that I hadn't fully lost control of the car or crashed, I was frustrated to be stranded in the middle of nowhere in a car I shouldn't have been driving.

The fact that the trunk held no sign of a spare or a jack only served to fuel my anger at Brad for putting me in the situation.

He and the kids were far north of me in the Ocala National Forest, and even if I had been willing to disrupt their trip by calling him to come help, it would have taken forever for him to reach me.

A quick search on my phone revealed an auto repair shop about fifteen miles away, just outside Cedar Creek.

The mechanic said he could send a tow truck, but it would be a half hour minimum before he arrived. I called Patsy to let her know I'd be running late but got her voicemail on the first ring. I left a message and then walked over to lean against a tree, too nervous to sit in the car with it so close to the road.

By the time the truck arrived forty minutes later, I was hot, sweaty, and beyond irritable. I had tried Patsy's number again while I waited, but it went straight to voice mail again, even though it was past time for us to meet. I wondered if perhaps it had all been some sort of scam. Was there even going to be anyone at the address when I arrived there? Had she contacted me without Caterina's permission, or had my birth mother perhaps changed her mind about the meeting? I'd had too much time to think, and I went back and forth between seriously doubting whether the meeting was a good idea to almost being in tears at the senseless delay keeping me from meeting my birth mother.

My irritation escalated when we arrived at the repair shop and they told me the tire couldn't be repaired and had to be replaced.

"I strongly suggest you buy two tires. It's not a good idea to put on one new one," said the girl behind the counter as she smacked her bubble gum from cheek to cheek. "And you need to put the new ones on the front and move the old ones to the back."

I didn't want to spend a dime on the stupid car, much less the cost of two tires, so I told her one would be fine. Brad could deal with any other replacements.

"How long will this take?" I asked. "I was supposed to be in Cedar Creek like an hour ago, and I really need to get back on the road."

"Oh, not long," she said as she swiped my credit card in the outdated machine. "Probably like an hour."

My mouth dropped open and my eyes widened. "An hour? You've got to be kidding me. You're putting on *one* tire, not a whole set."

"We've got people in line ahead of you, though."

I looked around the empty lobby and gazed out the window at the empty parking lot. "Where? Are they invisible?"

She laughed. "No, everybody usually waits at the diner. You should wait there, too. You could get some lunch. They do a great burger."

"I'm supposed to have lunch in Cedar Creek." With a very important person.

"Oh, well, they've got air conditioning at the diner. We don't."

I cursed under my breath as I put my credit card back in my wallet and headed to sit in the air conditioning.

There wasn't a table available, so I sat at the counter and ordered a glass of unsweet tea.

I tried Patsy once more, flinging the phone to the counter when her voicemail picked up.

The whole situation was infuriating, from Brad's thoughtlessness to the car breaking down to my birth mother being almost within reach but me not being able to reach her.

I ordered a salad to pass the time but had no appetite when it came, so I paid the tab with the plate untouched and headed back to the repair shop. I knew they wouldn't be done with the car yet, but I figured they might move a little faster if I was standing there watching them.

Which might have worked, if the car had been where I left it.

CHAPTER 4

"What do you mean the car isn't here?"

The tall, thin man removed his cap and scratched his forehead with mechanic's fingers blackened by grease and labor. "It's, um, well, it's a funny story, to be sure," he said.

"Really? Because I'm not laughing." I crossed my arms and tilted my head to one side, taking in deep breaths and trying to hear him stammer over the blood pumping in my ears.

"If you could, uh, give me a minute, I have someone who can explain," he said, his eyes darting to the open bay at the front of the shop. "He should be here any time now. He said he'd be right back."

"Who? Who said he'd be right back? The man who took my car?"

He squeezed the brim of the cap in his hand before settling it back on his head. "Something like that."

I dug in my purse for my phone, anger rolling off my skin in hot waves. "I'm calling the police. This is ridiculous."

"You're not calling anyone," came a voice from behind me laced with a combination of sarcasm and humor. "I told you payback was coming, and here it is. You might as well grin and bear it. You earned it."

I turned to face the man who was entering the shop and speaking to me with such familiarity. I'd never seen him before in my life.

He was of average height, but muscular in build. The denim jeans he wore fit snugly, and the short sleeves of the black shirt revealed thick, rounded biceps. His brown hair was cut close, and the brown eyes dancing beneath the brim of his cap sparkled with a teasing mirth that matched the huge grin on his face.

That grin promptly faded as he stopped short and stared at me.

"You're not Piper."

"No, I'm not. Who the hell are you?"

19

He looked from me to the mechanic. "Mike, you said it was Piper's car."

"I thought it was. She looks a lot like Piper. Or she did. When she first came in, anyway." Mike shrugged. "I don't know. It's been a long time since I saw Piper Ward."

"You said you were certain it was Piper!"

"Excuse me!" I yelled, stepping between the two of them. "I don't know who Piper is or what she has to do with any of this, but as I am obviously *not* Piper, I'm going to call the cops if someone doesn't return the vehicle I brought in. Immediately." I waved my phone at both of them.

"I'm so sorry, ma'am," the man in black said, holding his hands out in front of him like a shield. "This is all just a misunderstanding. Mistaken identity. Mike here thought you were a close friend of mine, and I took the car thinking it was hers."

"Do you regularly steal cars from your close friends, Mr.—?"

"Parker. Levi Parker," he said, extending his hand to shake mine. I refused, crossing my arms instead. "It was a prank. She and I play these jokes on each other, and she recently had my truck taken and deposited out in the middle of the woods. I'd been promising her payback, and when Mike said you came in with a red Audi TT—"

"Sounds like a lovely relationship the two of you have," I interrupted, and then I turned to Mike the mechanic with a glare that I hoped would convey my sincere distaste for his involvement. "And how professional of you to take a client's car, a client who had been stranded and in distress, and offer it up for a joke. Without even confirming the identity of the owner. If either of you had taken even a moment to look at the paperwork your receptionist had me fill out, you would have known I wasn't this Piper person."

Mike swallowed hard, his eyes on the ground. "Yes, ma'am, I see now that I was wrong."

"Ma'am —" Levi started, but I cut him off.

"Would you both please stop calling me ma'am? My name is Caroline. Your attempts at polite titles don't even begin to make this situation better. Now, if you'll return my car, I'll be on my way to my destination. I believe I've been delayed long enough, and in light of your error in judgment," I said to Mike, "I would hope that I'll be receiving some compensation off the cost of your services."

"My boss would have to approve that, and he's not—"

"It's okay, Mike. I'll pay her bill. It's the least I can do," Levi said.

"Thank you." I turned and gave him a quick nod and slid my phone back in my purse, eager to be done with the entire ordeal and on my way. "Now if someone could give me the keys and pull my car around, I will be happy to let this go."

The two men exchanged a glance that conveyed my bad day had not yet ended.

"Where is my car?" I looked at Mike, and he looked at Levi. I looked at Levi, and he looked at Mike. "Gentlemen? My car?"

"Um," Levi said, removing his cap and twisting it in his hands. "If it's not already there, it is in the process of being placed on the roof of a barn."

"What? Are you kidding me?" I grabbed my phone from the purse and dialed 911.

"Wait, please," Levi said, stepping toward me. "We'll get it back here."

"Step aside, Mr. Parker. I think you've done quite enough." I walked past him and back to the diner, attempting to keep my voice calm and level as I explained to the operator what my emergency was. In what may have been my only stroke of luck for the day, a sheriff's deputy was in the area about ten minutes away, so I settled onto the same stool I'd vacated only moments before and watched for him to arrive.

He barely had time to exit the car before I approached him.

"Are you Mrs. Miller?" he asked.

"I am, sir. Thank you for coming so quickly."

"No problem, ma'am. Now, you say your car was stolen? From the mechanic?"

"Hey, Tristan," Levi said as he joined us. "Look, man. This is all a big misunderstanding."

"Oh, great. You two know each other. Deputy—" I paused to look at his name badge "—Rogers, this man took my car and when I asked him to return it to me, he says it is on top of a barn."

The deputy's eyebrows raised, and I couldn't help but notice a hint of a grin playing at the corners of his mouth.

"On top of a barn?" he asked Levi.

"Yeah. I was paying my check, and Mike called and said Piper had just come in the shop with a flat."

"I am not Piper," I said.

"Obviously," the men said in unison.

"I ran out the back and over to the shop while she was up front. The car was still up on the tow truck—a red Audi TT Roadster just like Piper's—and I threw Ramsey a twenty and asked him to drive it over to Toby Bullock's barn once she'd gone to the diner. Then I called Toby and had him waiting there with his crane, and neither of them are answering their phone right now, so I have to assume they are in the process of putting the car up on the barn."

Deputy Rogers put his hand up in a poor attempt to hide the grin spreading across his face.

"I fail to see what's funny in the situation, Deputy."

His mouth returned to a grim line, but his eyes still held their humor. "Of course, ma'am."

"Why does everyone keep calling me ma'am? I have a name. It's Caroline."

The deputy nodded. "Yes, ma'— sorry. Caroline. You're right. I can see where this situation holds no humor at all for you, and it's quite unfortunate that you've gotten caught up in my friend's ongoing war with his employer's daughter."

"Unfortunate? He stole my car. I'm basically trapped here at this godforsaken cafe in the middle of nowhere for God only knows how long. My trip was already delayed by the flat, then I was stranded and waiting on the side of the road for the truck to come. When I got here Susie Bubble Gum told me they were backed up, even though I only saw one car inside the shop. She said it would take an hour to put on one tire. Now I think she was lying about how long it would take to cover for her friend stealing the car."

"No, she didn't know anything about it. Look, we weren't stealing the car," Levi said, more to Deputy Rogers than to me. "I thought it was Piper's."

"You took my car without my permission. No matter whose car you thought it was, you have admitted you didn't have permission to take it."

"True, but it was supposed to be a joke."

"Auto theft is no joke, Mr. Parker," I said, turning my back on him to face the deputy. "So how soon can I get my car back?"

"You said they're not answering their phones?" Deputy Rogers asked Levi, who shook his head.

"I've been trying them since we realized the mistake."

"Well, I guess there's nothing we can do until you get in touch with them. Have Ramsey bring the car right back if he hasn't already left there."

My mouth dropped open. "That's it? *There's nothing we can do?*"

"Ma'am—uh, Caroline, the quickest way to get the car back to you is to have the tow truck bring it. So, until we can reach him…"

"This is ridiculous! I was supposed to meet someone in Cedar Creek almost two hours ago. Now you expect me to sit around and wait for the man who stole my car to get in touch with the driver he paid twenty dollars to help him steal it? No. I'm calling my lawyer."

"I can take you to your meeting," Levi offered.

"Are you *kidding*? Like I would go anywhere with you. You'd probably steal my purse and dump me out on the side on the road."

"No, I'm not like that. I'm not a thief. I swear, this is all a misunderstanding. It was meant in fun. A prank, nothing more. Tristan, tell her. You know me."

The deputy sighed and looked across the parking lot where several people stood under the eave of the diner staring at us.

"I've known Levi since the third grade, and he doesn't always have good sense, but he's not a thief. Despite how it may seem from his warped sparring with Piper Ward, he's actually a good guy, and I have no qualms vouching for him."

"Thanks," Levi said.

"That being said, you certainly don't have to go anywhere with him."

A voice came across the deputy's radio, and he sat in the car to answer it.

The crowd had grown, and I could see several faces pressed to the window inside the cafe as though we were providing the entertainment highlight of the week.

The only spectator not enjoying the drama was Mike the mechanic, who stood in the doorway of the auto shop's open bay, wiping his hands with a rag as he watched us with eyes wide with apprehension.

Tristan explained to the voice on the other end that he would need a moment to respond, and then he stood and turned his attention back to me.

"As much as I hate that you got caught up in this, it appears to have been a misunderstanding, nothing more. Now, of course, if you want to fill out a report, I'm happy to oblige you, but I'm not sure what it would accomplish or how it would help you get on your way sooner. Might be best if I go ahead and take you where you need to go, and then we can have the car brought to wherever you are."

"Please, let me take you," Levi said. "It's the least I can do. I feel awful about this whole mess, and I know me saying I'm sorry doesn't make up for your loss of time or the stress involved, but I *am* sorry. I want to do what I can to make it right. I'll drive you wherever you want. I'll be your personal chauffeur until your car is back in your possession." He sort of bowed with a smile, and on any other day under different circumstances, I might have found him charming. Handsome, even.

"Up to you," Deputy Rogers said to me. "How would you like to proceed?"

I closed my eyes for a moment, rubbing my temples to ward off the stress headache I could already feel stabbing me around the edges.

The issues I'd left at home and the issues I was on my way to confront were too big to walk away from, but I could remove myself from the current situation, as least for a short time.

"Fine," I groaned. "You can drive me, Mr. Parker, but Deputy, I'd like you to stay on top of this situation, and I'd like for you to personally communicate with me regarding the progress with my vehicle."

"Yes, of course. Let's make sure dispatch took down your number correctly."

When the deputy had finished verifying my contact information, I climbed into a truck with a total stranger I knew nothing about other than he steals cars from his friends.

If only I hadn't been driving that stupid red Audi.

CHAPTER 5

"So, where are we headed?" Levi asked as he put on his seat belt and adjusted the radio's volume.

I read him the address from the piece of paper in my purse, and then held up my phone. "I have it plugged in on my GPS if you want to use that."

"Nah. I know where it is, generally. We can use that thing once we get close if we need to."

He pulled onto the highway, and I hugged my purse to me and looked out the window.

"You visiting family?" he asked.

"Something like that," I mumbled.

"You ever been to Cedar Creek before?"

"No."

"We lived in Cedar Creek when I was born, but we moved to Jensen when I was in the third grade," he said, apparently oblivious to my desire for silence. "I still know some people in Cedar Creek, but it seems like a lot of new people have moved to town since I lived here."

I didn't respond, so after a brief pause he continued.

"Yeah. It's grown quite a bit actually. I think all the Orlando suburbs are full, so people are moving farther out. They like the lakefront houses and the small-town feel."

"You live in Jensen now?" I asked, even though I didn't care. He seemed determined to talk, and maybe the ride would be less awkward if we exchanged pleasant conversation.

"No, I'm back in Cedar Creek. Well, north of town a ways. I work for Ward Farms."

"Yeah, I know. It says so on your shirt."

He glanced down at the logo embroidered on the shirt pocket and chuckled.

"I guess it does. What about you? Where do you work?"

I exhaled loudly and shifted in my seat, still frustrated with the situation and not caring to reveal my life to a stranger.

"You drive all that way to get a burger?" I asked.

"Oh, the diner? Yeah. They do make a good burger, but I'm usually gone before lunch. My dad and I meet there every Saturday morning for breakfast, but today I lingered, talking with some of the old folks."

"Lucky me. Your family still lives in Jensen, then?"

"No. Mom and Dad live in Orlando, but the diner is a good place to meet up. My sister lives between Jensen and Cedar Creek. A little closer to Cedar Creek. Dad goes by her place after we finish."

My phone vibrated in my purse, and I tore the bag open to search for it. It was Lorna calling, and I pressed *decline* to let it go to voicemail, having no desire to explain the day's events to my mom in front of Levi.

I dialed Patsy's number once more, my heart sinking when it went straight to voicemail again.

"Hi. It's Caroline. I'm on the road again, but I'm not sure if you're getting these messages. Please call and let me know if we're still on for lunch or for meeting."

I shoved the phone back in my purse and ignored Levi's gaze.

"I'm sorry I made you miss your meeting," he said, his voice quiet.

"Me too," I growled. "It was a very important meeting. Like a once-in-a-lifetime kind of meeting. Something I'd waited my whole life for." Tears stung at the back of my eyes, and I blinked them away, determined not to cry in front of the stranger.

"Wow," he said. "Now I really feel bad."

"You should," I said. "I don't even know if anyone will be home when we get there. Or where the hell I'll go if they're not."

"Um, well, I can take you wherever you need to go. Is there another number you could call to try and reach them?"

I shook my head. "I don't even know these people. For all I know, it's a scam, and I'm about to get the biggest letdown of my life."

"Are you sure you want to go there?" Levi asked.

A lump of emotion had lodged itself in my throat, and I swallowed hard, but it wouldn't move.

"I don't know. I do, and I don't."

"Okay," he said. "Well, tell me if you decide you want to turn around."

"What's your mom like?" I asked, and his eyes widened a bit in surprise.

"My mom? She's cool, I guess. Why?"

"Do you look like her?"

He cocked his head to one side and shrugged. "Some folks say I do. I don't know. We have some similarities, I guess, but she looks like her, and, well, I look like me. My sister looks more like her, I think."

"How many siblings do you have?" I asked.

"Just the one sister. Rachel. She's two years younger. What about you? Do you have any brothers or sisters?"

My immediate response was no, but when I opened my mouth to speak, the word faltered.

"Uh, to tell the truth, I have no idea. I was raised as an only child, but I was adopted. So maybe I have a whole slew of brothers and sisters I know nothing about."

"Oh, okay."

"I was supposed to find out today, but now I guess that's up in the air."

I had no idea why I was confiding my life story to a total stranger, especially one who had caused me so much stress, but before I knew what was happening, I'd explained the whole thing to him. The phone call the night before, the fact that my birth mother didn't call me herself, the health problems Patsy described, and the bizarre lack of communication even though I was alarmingly late for lunch.

"Maybe something came up. Something unexpected. You know, with her health," Levi offered.

"But why wouldn't Patsy have called to tell me? Why wouldn't she have answered my call?"

"I don't know."

I turned in my seat to face him. "Do you know them? The people at this address? The Lannisters?"

He shook his head. "The only Lannisters I know are on *Game of*

Thrones, and I wouldn't want to drop you off with them."

His attempt at humor didn't make me laugh. My apprehension and anxiety were building the closer we got to the address. If I'd had my own vehicle, I might have turned around and gone back home. But as things were, my best option seemed to be forging ahead.

There was a silver Cadillac in the driveway when we arrived. The sprawling one-story was well-kept, situated on a sloping hill overlooking Cedar Lake. Large picture windows spanned the front of the house from one end to the other, and the screen of a pool enclosure in the backyard was visible from the drive. The manicured landscaping gave way to an expansive green lawn that extended to the other side of the road where the house had a parcel of grass for lakefront access. A boathouse matching the main house sat over the water with a dock jutting out past it.

I sat and stared at the house as Levi turned the truck off, the popping and clicking of the cooling engine loud in the absence of the radio.

"Do you think there's anyone here?" Levi said.

He was looking at me, and I knew it was time for me to get out of the truck and go to the door, but I felt glued to my seat.

So many emotions were coursing through me that I found it hard to process them all. The fear was paralyzing. Fear of the unknown. Fear of rejection. Fear of disappointment. Fear of being lied to or tricked.

This was a moment I'd imagined a thousand times over throughout my life, and though I'd never been certain how it would go, it didn't seem to be going according to any of my dreams so far.

"You want me to go with you?" Levi asked, his voice soft and filled with kindness. "To the front door?"

I turned to look at him, and the concern in the deep brown eyes caught me off guard.

None of the scenarios I'd imagined for meeting my mother the first time included a handsome stranger who'd stolen my car, but in that moment, he was the only person available to walk by my side, and I nodded, suddenly thankful that I wasn't alone.

CHAPTER 6

We hadn't even reached the front steps when a woman approached us from the house on the right.

"Excuse me! Hello? Are you Caroline?"

I turned, and as I did, my foot kicked something on the edge of the sidewalk. I looked down and saw a small flip phone just beneath the low hedge. I bent to pick it up, surprised at how hot it was in my hand. It had obviously been sitting in the sun for quite some time.

"Yes, I'm Caroline," I said, handing the phone to Levi as I walked toward the neighbor.

"Oh, thank goodness. Patsy's been worried sick that I wouldn't catch you. She said to watch for you. She lost her phone in the chaos, and—oh, is that her phone?"

Levi stepped forward and handed it to the woman, who recoiled at the heat of it and handed it right back.

"It's hot!" she said. "Must have been sitting in the sun. I hope it's not ruined. Where'd you find it?"

I pointed to the bushes lining the sidewalk. "Over there. Where is Patsy?"

"Oh, they rushed Caterina to the hospital this morning, and Patsy rode in the ambulance with her. They're still there."

My mouth dropped open with a gasp, and my hand flew up to cover it. "Oh my gosh! Is she okay? Caterina? Where? What hospital?"

"Why, Jensen Memorial. The only hospital there is nearby."

I had already turned to go before I remembered I was with Levi in his truck, but no sooner had the thought occurred to me than he was already walking beside me. "C'mon," he said. "It's not far."

"You don't have to—"

"Don't be ridiculous. Let's go."

"Thank you," I called to the neighbor over my shoulder.

Levi pulled the truck out of the drive and sped toward the stop sign.

"What if she's not okay?" I whispered, afraid if I said it too loud, it would make it more real. "What if I get this close and don't get to meet her?"

"You can't think like that. She's gonna be okay, and you're gonna meet her. The hospital's not far. It won't take us long to get there."

"They took her by ambulance. That can't be good." I bit down on my lip and held onto the dash as he rushed through the curves and turns of the road.

"It might be a precaution," Levi said. "If she's been ill, you know? Didn't this Patsy woman say she'd been in and out of the hospital? Maybe it was just to be safe."

I shook my head. "I can't believe this. I can't believe after all this time, I get a call that my birth mother wants to meet me, and now when I'm within a few miles of her, she might ..." I couldn't bear to say the words.

"I'm so sorry, Caroline. I'm so sorry I delayed you, and that you couldn't be here on time. But I'm gonna get you there as soon as possible. It's gonna be fine. She's gonna be fine."

He brought us to a screeching halt under the hospital's entryway, and then he jumped from the truck and walked in beside me.

"You can't park there," the receptionist said as we came through the front door. "You have to park in the garage."

"I'm looking for a patient who was brought in this morning. Caterina—" I turned to Levi with wide eyes. "I don't know her last name. Patsy never told me her last name. How could I have not have asked her last name?"

"Sir, you have to move that truck," the girl said.

"I will," he replied. "First, I want to make sure she gets where she's going. Can you search for a patient by first name?"

"No, I'm sorry. I have to have the last name, and I'm going to need you to move the truck now. It's a safety hazard."

Levi removed his cap and grimaced. "I'll move the truck, but you have to help us find someone. Her name is Caterina, and she was brought in by ambulance earlier today."

"Again, like I told you, I need the last name," the receptionist said, repeating each word succinctly. "Now, please move the truck or I'm gonna have to call security."

"Okay," Levi said, leaning over the desk. "Call security. Maybe they can help us find her without a last name."

"What about Patsy Lannister? She rode in the ambulance with Caterina. Do you know if someone named Patsy Lannister is here?" I asked.

The receptionist had picked up the phone receiver and was poised to dial security, but she hesitated and put the receiver back in its cradle. "Is that a patient? Is that the patient's name?"

Levi walked away, and I assumed he was going to move his truck.

"No. She's a friend of Caterina's, I think. She rode in the ambulance with her. Caterina is staying at Patsy's house."

The girl chewed on her bottom lip and stared up at me. "I'm sorry. I'd have to have the patient's last name."

"Well, how many people came in an ambulance today? The town's not that big. Can't you just look at the ambulance records and see if there's someone named Caterina?"

"Caroline!" Levi yelled from the doorway, where he stood holding his phone to his ear motioning for me to join him. "My buddy Zack works in the ER," he said when I reached him. "He's going to see what he can find out. What time were you supposed to be at Patsy's?"

"Eleven."

"And if she wasn't answering her phone then, they must have already left in the ambulance," he said to me before speaking back into the phone. "Yeah, man, must have been this morning. Some time before eleven. Okay. Good. We'll be in the lobby."

He shoved the phone in his pocket. "He's going to check the admissions this morning and see what he can find."

"Thanks. Do you need to go move your truck?"

"Not until I know you're where you're supposed to be."

"Thank you, Levi." I managed a smile, but he shook his head.

"Don't thank me. It's my fault you weren't already here."

"True, but if they left in the ambulance before eleven, I wouldn't have been there before she was gone anyway. I appreciate you sticking around."

It was oddly comforting to have someone with me, even if it was someone I didn't know.

Security arrived the same time as Patsy Lannister, both from different directions.

She was short and plump, with hair white as snow and blue eyes that seemed to glow against her fair skin. I wondered for a moment if perhaps we were related to have such fair coloring in common.

"Caroline? Oh, bless you, child, I'm so happy you found your way here. When we got her settled in, I went to call you, but my phone was nowhere to be found. It must have come out of my pocket somehow in getting Caterina in the ambulance."

Levi pulled the phone from his pocket and handed it to her.

"Oh, heavens. There it is! Where on earth did you find it?"

"It was on the sidewalk in front of your house. Under the bushes along the edge," I said. "How's Caterina?"

"We're going to need you to move the truck, sir," the security guard said.

"I'll be right back," Levi said to me.

I nodded and turned back to Patsy. "Caterina? How is she?"

The blue eyes clouded with tears, and the frown lines on her forehead deepened.

"They've put her on a ventilator, so she's heavily sedated, almost like a coma. They say that's best for her body while it fights off the pneumonia."

I drew in a sharp breath and held it. All I heard was coma. Her condition *was* serious. Grave even.

"Can I see her?"

A large, lonely tear rolled down Patsy's cheek, and she swiped it away and sniffled.

"I know she wouldn't want this to be your first impression of her. She's always been so vibrant. So full of life. To see her lying there, with those tubes, it just breaks my heart. This is not what she would have wanted for the two of you."

A slight panic rose in me at the thought that I might not be able to see her.

"I don't mind the tubes," I said. "I've come all this way to see her."

"I know," Patsy said, patting my hand in hers. "I didn't have your number with me without my phone. I wish I could have reached you."

"I want to see her," I said, my voice breaking with emotion.

She paused for a moment and then nodded. "Of course, you do."

She took my hand and led me past the receptionist, who had turned her attention back to the magazine on her desk. We meandered through a series of hallways and up an elevator to the second floor, where Patsy stopped at a nurse's station.

"She needs to see Caterina."

"Is she immediate family?" the nurse asked.

Patsy glanced at me and then back to the nurse. "Yes. Yes, she is. She's Caterina's daughter."

A protest formed on my lips, but it died away as I considered that it might be the truth, and it might be the only way I could see Caterina.

"ID, please."

I pulled my driver's license from my purse and handed it to her, wondering what proof of relation they might ask for, but none was needed. She wrote my name on the clipboard by her side and gave me instructions about the time limit for visitation.

"Only one visitor at a time, ladies."

Patsy walked me to the door of the room and patted my shoulder. "I wish this could have all played out differently," she said. "I suppose it is what it is."

She stepped back, and I looked up to see the nameplate on the door frame. *Caterina Russo.*

Italian. Was I of Italian descent? Perhaps it was her married name. But if so, where was her husband?

With another glance over my shoulder at Patsy, I pushed the door open with a deep breath and stepped inside my birth mother's room.

CHAPTER 7

I wanted to see her eyes. The eyes are the windows to the soul, they say. Revealing so much about mood, inclination, reaction and thoughts. The eyes give away emotions. They speak truth.

For an onlooker, the eyes are the life of the body, much more so than the heart, pumping away safely hidden in the deep entombment of the chest.

Caterina's eyes were closed.

She lay motionless beneath the white sheets of the hospital bed, giving no indication she even knew I was in the room.

Her cheekbones were high, her nose straight, and her eyebrows sharply arched. I couldn't see her lips behind the breathing tube inserted in her mouth, but the rest of her features were strong, and so I imagined her lips to be full.

The long lashes that lay against her skin were as black as the hair upon her head, though it was streaked with gray and a few brilliant swipes of white as though sections had been painted.

Her hair was pulled back and fastened at the nape of her neck, leaving a ponytail to lay across her shoulder.

No freckles marred the beautiful olive skin, and very few wrinkles were evident other than a gathering of fine lines at the corners of her eyes, indicating a life with much laughter.

The stranger lying in front of me looked nothing like the mother I had imagined.

Our coloring could not be more different. The voluptuous curves and petite frame outlined beneath the sheet was a far cry from my flat chest and tall, straight body.

Was I truly flesh of her flesh, and bone of her bone? Did we share DNA, this beautiful sleeping creature and me?

I wished for an emotional connection. An immediate draw that would tell me I was hers and she was mine.

But as I stared at her comatose form, nothing came.

I picked up her hand and laid it flat in my palm. Her fingers were long and slender like mine, the nails flawlessly shaped and painted a vivid shade of violet. I held my other hand alongside hers for comparison, searching for any similarity to confirm this was the woman my heart had longed for.

Like mine, her hands were smooth on the back, without any hair except a small rectangular patch just beneath the bottom joint of the pinkie finger.

It was a small trait, and one that I probably could have matched with any number of people on the planet, but I so wanted some indicator of our connection that I was willing to take it as some measure of confirmation and reassurance.

Maybe she *was* my mother. Perhaps she had carried me in that very vessel that lay there betraying her, and perhaps she had talked to me and sung to me just as I had with Ethan and Eva in the womb.

I folded her hand and clasped it between my own, leaning over to whisper, even though there was no one else in the room to hear me.

"Hello, Caterina. My name is Caroline. I think we might be...related. I don't know. I wish you could talk. I wish you could open your eyes and tell me who you are, and who you were. I have so many questions. But I know you need your rest right now. I don't want to interfere with your healing. We have a lot to discuss, but there's plenty of time. You just get better, okay? Let your body do what it needs to do, and then when you're ready, I'll be here."

I had to believe that somehow she could hear me, and no matter who she was and whether she was connected to me or not, it was important for her to know someone was there. Someone was waiting for her to open her eyes.

The remainder of my visitation window passed in silence as I stood and stared at the stranger, her hand in mine, wondering if it was possible that we were mother and daughter. Wouldn't I feel something? Wouldn't there be some cosmic spark that passed between us? Shouldn't I be in tears? Shouldn't I feel more distraught if she was truly my mother, lying there in such grave danger?

I didn't know. It wasn't like I'd been given a guidebook on how to feel in such circumstances.

My emotions were scattered. I was sad for the lost opportunity to talk to her. Frightened that she may die without me ever knowing the truth. Excited to be in the presence of someone who might be the one.

But I didn't know her as a person. We had no history, no memories. I couldn't weep for her the same as I would if Lorna had been the one in the coma.

Lorna! I'd never called my mom back. She would be sick with worry about how this meeting went, having no idea of the tire trouble, the mistaken identity mix-up, or Caterina's comatose state.

I needed to get to a phone.

It didn't seem right to just walk out even though Caterina had given no sign that she knew I was there.

"I'm gonna step out, but I'll be back, okay?" I whispered, laying her hand back on the sheet. "Just focus on getting better."

The nurse told me when I exited the room that Patsy had gone to the family waiting room, and she gave me directions to get there.

"Is there a place I can make a call? Privately?" I asked, and then I went to the small alcove she'd indicated.

Lorna answered on the first ring. "Hey. How did it go? Is she the one you were looking for?"

"Hey, Mom. It's been a little crazy. I had a blow-out on the way here."

"Caroline!" she gasped. "Oh, no! Are you okay? You didn't wreck, did you?"

"No, no. Nothing like that, thank goodness."

"I thought those tires were relatively new. Didn't you just get tires?"

I settled into the chair in the alcove and rested my head against the wall. "I wasn't driving my car. Brad got a new car, well, new to him anyway, and it only has two seats."

"Two seats? What on earth? How does he expect to drive his children around in that?"

I sighed. "I don't know, but long story short, he took the Tahoe, and I got stuck with his car for the weekend."

"I declare, Caroline, why you let that man talk you into things, even now, I will never understand! He has always railroaded you into doing whatever he wanted you to do, and you just go along with it. I understood it better when you were married to him, but now that you're divorced, you need to stand up to him. Stop letting him dictate your decisions."

My head had begun to throb, and I closed my eyes against the pain.

"Mom, can we not get into that for the millionth time? I do what I have to for my kids. You know that."

"Yes, and I know you are teaching those kids lessons when they see you cave in to whatever Brad demands over and over again. Not good lessons, mind you."

"Mom, not now, please?"

My stomach growled and roiled, and I realized I hadn't eaten since that morning. What I would've given to have that untouched salad from the diner in front of me!

"What happened?" she said. "Did you get the tire fixed? Where are you?"

Another deep sigh escaped me as my stomach growled again.

"I'm at the hospital."

"What! Where? Are you okay?"

"Yes, I'm fine. It's Caterina. My...the woman I was supposed to meet. She has pneumonia, and she's in a medically-induced coma."

"Caroline! No! Oh, I'm so sorry. Where are you? I'll come."

"No, no. There's no need. I don't even know how long I'll stay. It's just been quite a day."

"Oh, sugar. Do you want to meet for dinner? What can I do?"

"I don't know, Mom. Nothing, I guess," I stood and stretched. "Let me go find Patsy, the woman who called me. I'll ring you when I'm on the road again."

CHAPTER 8

I left the sanctuary of the alcove and made my way to the family waiting area, which was bustling with conversation and waiting families.

Patsy made eye contact with me right away and rose to meet me.

"Hello, dear. How is she?"

"Okay, I guess? I don't know. She's just lying there."

We sat next to each other, and she smiled.

"She would be so excited to know you're here. I'm sure she knows on some level, though. Oh, your husband said he'd be right back. He had something to take care of."

I turned to her in shock. "My husband?" My thoughts had immediately gone to Brad and trying to figure out how he knew where I was and where my children were if Brad was here.

"Seems like a nice young man. How long have the two of you been together?"

It was then I realized she meant Levi.

"Oh, no. That's not my husband. We're not together. We don't even know each other," I blurted out, the words rushing together in a panic to set her straight.

"Oh," she said, her face scrunched in confusion. "But he's been waiting here for you."

"He has my car. Well, not *my* car. It's a long story."

My stomach growled loudly, and I put my hand over it in an attempt to silence it.

"Sounds like you need something to eat," Patsy said.

"Oh, I'm fine. I'll get something in a bit."

She nodded and reached up to pat her hair, tucking a stray strand back in place. She was much older than I had noticed before. She looked tired. Haggard.

"Do you need something to eat?" I asked. "They have a cafeteria downstairs, I believe."

"Yes, they do. I got a sandwich down there earlier, before you arrived." She looked across the waiting room to the large window and frowned. "I was in the middle of fixing a nice lunch for the three of us when she collapsed. Scared the dickens out of me. I thought the ambulance would never get there, and George was off fishing with our son, so I couldn't get her in the car to bring her myself." The blue eyes clouded again, and her hands trembled as she unfolded and refolded the tissue she carried.

"She's lucky you were there," I said, wanting to offer her reassurance.

Patsy flashed me a weak smile. "That's why she's staying with us. I thought I was going to have to tie her up and drag her across the lawn to get her to come to our house. Cat's fiercely independent. But after this last hospital stay, I wasn't taking no for an answer."

"How did the two of you meet?" I asked.

"She bought the house next door to George and me soon after she started her foundation. We became fast friends, and it wasn't long before she had me working for her. Her enthusiasm for the work is quite contagious, and I wanted to be part of it. We help place children in the foster system with adoptive parents and help prospective parents navigate all the red tape and financial hardships of the system. She has a heart for those involved with adoption, that's for sure. I suppose it all began with you." Her smile widened, and she reached over to pat my hand.

"Is she married? Does she have other children?" I asked, curious as to why no one else was at the hospital on Caterina's behalf.

"No, she never married, and she never had any other children. Well, other than her foster children. She's had many of those!"

So, I was still an only child.

"I so wish the two of you could have met today and talked," Patsy said. "I feel like I'm sharing things about her that she may rather say herself."

I looked up to see Levi walking toward us. He took the empty seat next to me.

"Hey. How's she doing?" he asked, leaning forward to rest his elbows on his knees so he could see both Patsy and me.

"She's basically in a coma," I said with a shrug. "Not any change."

"Any word from a doctor? What are they saying?"

"Her doctor should be around any time now," Patsy said, looking at her watch. "They said the doctor would make his rounds around two, and it's getting close to three."

"Do they know you're here?" Levi asked. "In the waiting room? Should I go tell them?"

Patsy smiled. "Oh, they know where I am. They know I sit in here and knit."

I studied her face, the worry lines creasing her forehead and the concern evident in her clear, blue eyes. "You said she's been in the hospital a lot lately. Do you come here with her often?"

"Oh, yes. Every time. Cat's more than an employer for me. Why, we've become family over the years. My own son lives in Daytona with his wife and kids, and well, he's quite busy. Cat's parents have both passed, and the kids she's fostered come back from time to time for a visit, but she has no other family here."

I'd wondered so often if I had another family out there and whether they knew about me. Lorna's parents had accepted me as theirs from the first moment they saw me, and I'd grown up with cousins, aunts, and uncles who all welcomed me as their own. Even Pete's parents and sister stayed in touch with Lorna and me after he left us, and I'd never lacked family, or knowing I was loved.

How sad to think that Caterina had no one.

"Oh, here's the doctor now," Patsy said as she stood to greet him. "Hello again, Doctor Davis."

"Good afternoon," he said, smiling at Patsy and then looking at me as I stood.

"This is Caterina's daughter," Patsy said. "Caroline."

His eyes registered shock for a split second before regaining his professional composure. "Oh, I wasn't aware she had a daughter."

"She lives out of town and has just arrived this afternoon," Patsy explained. "How's Cat?"

"Unfortunately, I don't have much news to bring. Her vitals are good, but the infection is still strong and she's not responding to the antibiotics as quickly as we'd hoped. We're keeping her heavily sedated while we wait for them to kick in. Best for the machine to breathe for her and let her rest. It may take a while to get the results we're hoping for."

"Is she out of immediate danger?" Patsy asked.

"Well, any time we're dealing with pneumonia, it's risky. We're doing all we can to stop it from worsening until we can figure out what will improve it. I'd say right now, let's be cautiously optimistic and hope any change we see is for the better."

Patsy asked a few more questions as I tried to absorb everything that was happening. I didn't even know for sure if Caterina *was* my mother, but fear gripped me as I considered that she may not recover, and I wouldn't be able to talk to her even once. I sat down with the weight of it all.

"You okay?" Levi asked as the doctor walked away. "You want me to get you some water? Anything?"

"She needs something to eat," Patsy said. "Why don't you take her down to the cafeteria, and I'll stay here in case they need to reach us?"

"No, no. I'm okay," I said, pressing my hand to my forehead and closing my eyes to shut out the world.

"Nonsense!" Patsy scoffed. "You need to eat. Take her downstairs. I have my phone now, so I can call if there's any change."

I sat up to look at her. "Is it working? Is your phone okay? It was in the sun a while."

"Seems to be working fine. I called George and told him what had happened. They're bringing the boat in now, and he'll be up here soon, I imagine. But you go. Eat. We were supposed to have lunch hours ago." She leaned around me and gave Levi a stern look. "Take her downstairs and make sure she eats something."

"Yes, ma'am," he replied with a smile, standing and looking down at me. "You heard the lady. Let's go."

My stomach churned in agreement with them, and I stood and followed Levi to the elevator.

"You don't have to stay, you know. You can go. I'll probably be here a while."

"Man's gotta eat," he said as we stepped inside the elevator. "I'm always up for trying a new dining establishment."

"I don't know that a hospital cafeteria qualifies as a dining establishment."

He smiled and pushed the button to carry us down. "They serve food, don't they?"

I wondered if I should protest and insist that he go on about his day, but some part of me found comfort in having him there. I felt like a fish out of water in the whole situation, and though I didn't know him any better than I knew Patsy, I somehow felt calmer with Levi there, which was odd considering the only reason I was with him was because he stole my car.

CHAPTER 9

"Oh, the car! What's happening with the car?" I asked as we stepped into the cafeteria line.

"Safe and secure in the hospital garage," he said, fishing in his pocket for the keys and handing them to me. "They replaced both front tires, and you should be good with the back ones for a while."

"Thanks," I mumbled, putting the keys into my purse. "I can pay for—"

He held up his hand in protest. "Not a thing. You're not paying for a thing. I feel awful about what happened and what the delay may have cost you. The least I can do is pay for the tires and buy you lunch."

His smile was tentative, a bit sheepish, and he met my eyes and quickly looked away.

He was handsome. His eyes were a rich chocolate brown, the lashes framing them thick and dark. He had brilliant white teeth, so straight that I was certain he must have worn braces in his youth. He had a strong jaw with a slight hint of a scruffy shadow beginning to emerge. The cap he'd worn earlier was nowhere in sight, and his dark brown hair was a bit tousled on top where he'd obviously tried to ruffle what had lain beneath the cap.

"Mike mentioned it had an oil leak, not sure if you knew that," he said, choosing items for his tray as we moved through the line. "Might want to get that checked."

"Oh, it's not my car," I said as I grabbed a chef's salad and a packet of ranch dressing. "But I'll pass that information along."

His eyebrows raised slightly. "Oh? Well, tell whoever owns it that the tires have an excellent warranty, and the oil leak needs to be checked."

"It belongs to my husband. *Ex*-husband," I corrected. "He took the kids camping, and they couldn't fit in that car."

"How many kids do you have?" Levi asked as he handed the cashier a twenty.

"No, I can pay for my lunch," I said, reaching for my wallet.

"No way." He nodded toward the cashier. "I've got hers."

"You didn't have to do that, thanks. And two. I have two kids. Ten and fourteen."

We found an empty table by the window, and Levi grabbed silverware and napkins for us both.

"Thanks."

"Fourteen, huh? That's got to be fun."

I chuckled. "Oh, yeah. Loads of fun. One minute I'm her best friend, and the next, I'm the devil. One minute she wants me to do everything for her, and the next I'm not supposed to even look her direction."

He laughed. "I remember my sister turning fourteen. My father threatened to put a bathroom in the shed and move out there until she was grown. I begged him to take me with him."

"I always wanted a sister. Or a brother. I imagined it would be cool to have someone who was there for you no matter what. Are you and your sister close?"

"Yeah. We are now. I guess we always have been, but you know, high school I was too cool to be seen with my sister. Then she went to nursing school and got married and had her own life. Unfortunately, her husband passed away a few years back. We've gotten closer since then."

"What about you? Are you married? Ever been?" I was surprised at how anxious I was to hear his answer. I don't know why it mattered so much since I'd probably never see him again, but I very much wanted to hear him say he wasn't married.

"Me? No. Not even close. Nowhere near it."

I laughed, trying to ignore the strange sense of relief that washed over me. "Sounds like you feel strongly about it. Not the marrying type, huh?"

"I wouldn't say that, but I haven't found anyone yet I thought I wanted to spend a lifetime with. I heard a comedian once who said he had never married because he hadn't met a woman he'd like to look at through a screen door when he showed up to pick up his kids. I guess that makes sense to me."

"Wow. Okay. Kind of a cynical view."

"Well, what about you? You say ex-husband, so you've been married before. Would you do it again, knowing what you know?"

I took a long swig of tea as I considered his question.

"I don't know. I'd like to think so. Just because it didn't work out with him doesn't mean it couldn't with someone else. But who knows? My parents didn't last, but my grandparents did. My mom's sister and her husband are still going strong. So, it can happen."

"Oh, I know it can. My parents have been married nearly forty years. Speaking of parents, do you think Caterina is your mother? You saw her, right?"

I put my fork down and wiped my mouth with the napkin. "I did. Hard to tell much about a person who's lying there motionless with tubes coming out of them, but I don't know. Do you think I would feel something? Do you think I would know? If she was my mother, I mean?"

"I don't know," Levi said. "Hard to say. I mean, maybe if the two of you talked. If you found out you shared a lot in common or something? But I don't think you'd know just from looking at her. Especially with her, you know, like that."

"I need to ask Patsy why she called me. Why they thought I was Caterina's daughter. What proof they have. Everything happened so fast when we got to the house and they weren't there, and now here I am, sitting around waiting for medical updates on a total stranger. Patsy told them I was her daughter, for Christ's sake. And no one even blinked. No one asked for proof. The doctor looked a little skeptical, but he still discussed her case with me. Isn't that odd?"

"Patsy obviously believes you're Caterina's daughter. I'd say she's seen something that leads her to be certain. As far as the hospital, if she's been coming with Caterina all this time, and now she's telling the hospital you're the daughter, I don't know that they would question it."

"It's just so surreal. I don't even know this woman. I don't know Patsy. Hell, I don't even know you. And yet, here I sit, eating a salad in some hospital waiting on pins and needles for Caterina Russo to come out of her sedated state. It's been a very odd day."

"There you are," Patsy said, and I looked up to see her approaching with a tall gentleman with gray hair and thick black-rimmed glasses. "George, this is Caroline and her, um, friend, Levi. This is my husband, George."

We all shook hands and exchanged pleasantries, and then George and Patsy joined us at our table.

"You live in Gainesville?" George asked. "What section of town?"

George said he had attended the University of Florida in Gainesville many years ago, and we talked for a while regarding the city and some of its finer points.

We'd been talking and sharing for perhaps a half hour when Patsy's phone rang. It was the nurses' station, requesting that we come to Caterina's room.

"Is she awake?" Patsy asked, her excitement evident, but her face soon fell back into the concerned expression she'd worn since I met her.

"She's still in the coma," Patsy said when she ended the call. "The doctors just want to update us before the evening shift comes in."

"I should probably go," Levi said.

"Aren't you gonna come and hear the update?" Patsy asked, looking back and forth between Levi and me.

It made no sense at all for him to stay. I might not have known Caterina, but I had a reason to be there. He was a stranger who knew no one in the situation. He'd already spent the better part of his day with me, though that was of his own making with his prank and his decision to stay even after the car was delivered.

Still, I was reluctant for him to go. The weird circumstances of the day had thrown us together, and it was odd to think I'd never see him again.

"You want me to come up?" he said, his eyes searching mine as though he, too, wasn't sure he was ready for us to part.

"Um, no. You don't have to. You've already, well, no."

He smiled, but I swear I saw disappointment in his eyes, and that confused me as much as the disappointment I felt.

"Okay, then. I'll head out. Here." He took a business card from his wallet and handed it to me. "Give me a call if you need anything. It was nice meeting you, Caroline. I wish it had been under different circumstances."

I took the card, shocked at the jolt I felt when our hands brushed. Our eyes met as I pulled my hand away to slide the card into my purse. "Me, too. I would say thanks for everything, but…"

"Yeah. No need to thank me. Thank you for being so cool about everything."

I looked over my shoulder at Patsy and George, who had walked away and were lingering near the elevator.

"I gotta go," I said.

He nodded. "Hope everything goes well with Caterina. I hope you find what you're searching for."

I watched him walk toward the entrance of the hospital, unsure of why I felt so sad for him to go.

"Sure seems smitten with you," Patsy said as we stepped onto the elevator.

A warm blush crept into my cheeks, and I bent my head, allowing my hair to fall forward and hide me. "Oh, no. It's not like that. We don't even know each other. Really."

Which was true. But why did I feel like I wanted it not to be?

CHAPTER 10

It was a little after six when the evening doctor came around and told us there was no change in Caterina's condition.

"I would suggest you go home and get some rest," the doctor said. "She's as comfortable as we can get her. We'll continue to monitor her progress throughout the night, and if there's any change, you'll hear from us right away."

"How long will she need to be on the ventilator?" Patsy asked.

"Hard to say. It depends on how she responds to the antibiotics. If her condition worsens, or if she shows no sign of improvement, then obviously we'll have to take her treatment to the next level."

"What would that be?" I asked.

"We have several options, but I don't want you to get alarmed about those when they may not come to pass. Let's see how she does in the night. Go home, get some sleep, and we'll talk again in the morning."

When the doctor had finished, we said our goodbyes to Caterina's sleeping form and walked in silence to the elevator, then out the front lobby doors to head toward the garage.

"I guess I'll head back home," I said, not sure what I was supposed to do.

"Oh, please don't," Patsy said. "Come stay with us. We have plenty of room. I hate to think of you driving all that way tonight. And what if she wakes up? What if the morning comes, and she's awake?"

I could see the benefit to being close by, but I didn't want to spend the night with Patsy and George, the strangers who had become my fast friends for the day. I had no extra clothes, no toothbrush, nothing to sleep in.

"I probably should just head back. I can always drive back down tomorrow if she's awake."

She took my hand in hers. "And what if it goes the other way? What if she gets worse? I sure hope that doesn't happen, but if this is all you're going to get with the woman who brought you into this earth, then don't you want to be there for it?"

I pulled my hand from hers, not sure I wanted the depth of emotion she was pushing onto me.

"Patsy," George said. "Caroline is capable of deciding what she thinks is best. It's her decision."

"I know that," Patsy said. "But I'd hate to see you have any regrets, Caroline."

The hot evening air was thick with humidity, and I could practically feel my hair frizzing from it. I pushed it back over my shoulder, wishing I had worn it up.

"I don't have any clothes with me," I said. "My kids are coming home tomorrow night, and I have some things I need to take care of before they're back."

Namely, packing up stuff for Goodwill in preparation of our move, something I knew would be much harder if the kids were protesting the value of every item I put in a box.

"Okay. I understand," Patsy said, even though her face conveyed that she didn't. "I'll call you if there's any change."

"Thank you. I appreciate that."

I sat behind the wheel of the car for quite some time before cranking it. Then after a quick search on my phone, I found a drugstore and purchased a toothbrush, some toothpaste, makeup remover, and a tube of mascara. They had a bizarre pair of Tinkerbell pajamas for adults on an end-cap, and on a whim, I added those to my purchases.

Then I drove to Patsy's, unsure of whether I might stay, but certain that I wanted more truth before leaving town.

"I wondered if I could ask you a few questions," I said when Patsy answered the door, her blue eyes twinkling at the sight of me and a smile playing at the corners of her mouth.

"Of course, yes. Come in, come in."

She ushered me past George, who was snoozing in the recliner in the living room, and into a large kitchen where the nook's bay windows overlooked the lake.

"You want a cup of coffee? I was just trying to salvage what I'd started for lunch to see if I could throw together dinner."

"No, I can't drink coffee this late, or I'll be up all night."

"I have decaf," she offered. "Iced tea. Water."

"Water's great, thanks."

I watched her move about the kitchen, throwing away any food items that had been sitting out since Caterina collapsed, and sorting through the refrigerator to put together a meal.

From the small amount I knew of her, she was a kind woman. A good friend to Caterina, for sure.

"Patsy, why do you think I'm Caterina's daughter?"

"I don't *think* you are. I know you are!" she said as she cut up a cucumber. "I don't have any doubt."

"But why? What makes you so certain?"

She wiped her hands on a kitchen towel and walked past me to what appeared to be a den on the other side of the kitchen. She came back with a folder and handed it to me.

"There. Take a look at that."

I opened the folder to find a record of my childhood. Photos of my parents accompanied a stack of stapled papers detailing their job titles, financials, and family background at the time of my birth. An envelope held baby pictures of me from birth through my toddler years. There was a handwritten note about my father leaving the family, and then there were annual reports of some sort detailing my achievements in school and my medical history. For each school year, there was a small photo attached that looked like a proof image for the school yearbook.

"Where did you get this?" I asked, my heart beating fast and my skin flushed with the vulnerability of feeling exposed.

"Cat had it. As part of the agreement with your adoptive parents, the adoption lawyer they used provided information regarding your well-being on a regular basis. Cat believes her mother maintained the file to ensure that you had what you needed as you were growing up. When her mother entered an assisted living center, Cat found the file while sorting through her papers. She only recently shared it with me."

"But I don't understand. How would they get all this information?

My immunizations? My medical records? My school grades? Aren't there privacy laws?" My mind spun with the thought that I'd been watched or followed throughout my childhood.

Patsy came and stood at the table, her hands crossed on the back of one of the chairs. "Yes, there are. This information could not have been accessed by just anyone. I can only assume that someone associated with you shared the information. Have you talked with your adoptive parents about your beginnings?"

"Yes, yes, of course. My mother has always been upfront with me. She told me about my adoption at a very young age. I was seven, I think, and my cousin had just had a baby and I had way too many questions about pregnancies and deliveries and such. My mother said the records were sealed. That she knew nothing about my birth parents or where I came from."

"She's right. It would have all been sealed. The flow of information was probably one-way, based on the terms your adoptive parents agreed to."

"I don't understand. Why would my mother not have told me that she gave information about me to the adoption lawyer? This makes no sense. She must not have known. This had to have been done without her knowledge."

Patsy bit down on her lip. "I don't see how. Perhaps I shouldn't have given you the file. I didn't see what it could hurt, now that you and Caterina both knew of each other, but I wasn't aware you didn't know the lawyer had maintained an interest in your life. It was for your benefit, as best as we can tell."

She moved forward and flipped through the papers, pointing to one receipt in particular. "See here, a donation was made toward the purchase of the home you lived in. And this one." She shuffled through to find a piece of paper at the back of the folder. It detailed a grant for my benefit made out to my college.

"What? You've got to be kidding me. No, I received that grant from an anonymous donor based on my academic achievements. The school counselor said it was a benefactor who chose several students each year."

Patsy's brow furrowed, and her lips set in a grim line. "I'm so sorry, dear. I never meant to cause you distress. I wasn't aware you didn't know any of this."

Had my mother known? Did my mother willingly send information about me all those years? Had she accepted money for our house? Did she know about the grant's origin?

I flipped over the grant letter and found nothing in the file past that date.

"Where's the rest of it? Why does it end here?"

"The agreement extended until you reached adulthood, or your eighteenth birthday. So once your college tuition was met, Cat's mother must have felt she'd met her obligations. There's no further contact with the lawyer and no further donations past that point."

She sat in the chair and twisted her hands together. "When Cat found this folder, she made the decision to let you live your life without any further interference. She saw this as an invasion of your privacy. She said she figured if the time came when you wanted to know about her, you would look. And if it was your decision and what you wanted, then she'd come forward and answer anything she could, be involved in whatever capacity you chose."

I sat back in the chair and let the details of my life fall from my hands onto the table.

Patsy leaned forward. "When Cat shared this with me, she'd somehow gotten a notification that you'd registered on a website to find her. She asked me to help her find you. To connect the two of you before it was too late. Her illness had already progressed by that point."

"So why didn't she just go through the website like I did? How did you find me?"

"It's really not that hard to find someone these days, especially when you have the pertinent details," she said, pointing to the folder. "Marriage records, divorce records. Any public records make it easy to search for someone. Social media, too. We all leave, what do they call it, a *footprint*? George has a buddy in Orlando who's a private eye, so he pointed me in the right direction. Showed me where to look."

The walls of the room suddenly seemed to be closing in.

"I need to step outside," I said, standing slowly as my head swam in circles and I struggled to catch my breath. "I need some fresh air."

Patsy stood and led me through the den and through a set of French doors into the pool enclosure. I gulped in breaths of air, my heart pounding as I tried to absorb the implications of all I'd learned.

Was there any way my mother had been honest in all this? Was there any way she hadn't lied about what she knew?

I'd been watched. I'd been monitored. Observed. Like some science experiment I'd never agreed to participate in.

Beneath all the confusion, the feelings of betrayal and violation, a truth was emerging, and it kept repeating inside my head louder and louder until I could no longer ignore it.

Caterina Russo was my mother. She had given birth to me.

I had finally found the one I'd been searching for my whole life.

She was mere miles from me, but she lay in a coma in grave danger of passing without us ever sharing a word.

This wasn't fair. It wasn't right. It wasn't supposed to turn out like this. None of my imaginings had such irreversible complications.

I needed to talk to Lorna. And I needed to go back to the hospital. To see Caterina again, now that I knew the truth.

CHAPTER 11

"Are you okay?" Patsy stood behind me on her patio and wrung her hands. "I'm so sorry. I shouldn't have, well, I just don't even know what to say. I didn't realize, that's to say I didn't mean to, oh, I'm sorry."

"It's okay, Patsy. I wanted proof. I wanted verification. You were able to give me that. But now I need some answers for a whole new set of questions. Could I have a moment? Please? I need to make a call."

"Sure, sure, honey. Take your time."

She closed the French doors behind her as she went inside, and I immediately dialed Lorna and paced back and forth as I waited for her to answer.

"Hi sweetheart," she said after the third ring. "Any updates? Are you on your way home?"

"You told me the records were sealed and you knew nothing at all about my birth parents."

"I didn't. Caroline? What are you talking about? I didn't know anything."

"But you took money from them. You sent reports about me every year. You took their money. Did you know the grant I got for college was from them? Did you know that?"

She was silent, and I stopped pacing and strained to hear her breath so I would know she was still there.

"Mom?"

"Why don't you come here? Let's talk about this in person." Her voice broke with emotion, and the realization of her guilt stabbed me so hard that I had to sit down.

"No! We talk now! Tell me what you knew."

She exhaled with a loud sigh, and I closed my eyes against hot tears.

"Your father and I had visited several agencies. We'd been through the necessary approvals, but we were short on funds. The church had given us some, and we'd saved quite a bit, but we couldn't make it over the top. One of the agencies called, and they said there was a baby available and there would be no fees. It was a wealthy family, and they wanted the child placed immediately, and we fit what they were looking for."

"Which was what?"

"I don't know. I didn't ask. I wanted a baby, and someone was offering me one. Your father was against it. He was afraid there would be strings attached. Some ulterior motive. He wanted to know when—if—we adopted a child, it would be ours, free and clear. But I begged him and begged him to do this one thing for me, so he did. They had a lawyer who drew up the agreement. He laid out the terms, and we had to agree to send your medical records and school records each year so they would know you were being cared for and needed for nothing. We also had to agree that if the time came that we couldn't care for you properly, we would contact the adoption lawyer and ask for help."

I lay back against the reclining patio chair and put my hand over my eyes.

"Go on," I said when she paused.

"Your father lost his job just after you turned two. I didn't know what we were going to do. We had very little left in savings by then, and I thought we would lose the house. I only had a part-time job. There was no way I could support the three of us. I called the lawyer in a moment of desperation, and the next day, the bank called to say the mortgage had been paid off. Later that day, I got a call out of the blue with an offer to go to work at the hospital. Full-time hours with benefits. I'd never even applied at the hospital. It saved us, Caroline. *They* saved us. But your father was furious. He couldn't accept the assistance, and he thought I'd betrayed him. That I'd gone behind his back. That I made him look weak. Like he couldn't provide."

She took a deep breath, and I could tell she was crying.

"I just wanted you safe, Caroline. I wanted to know you'd be okay. And I was willing to accept whatever terms they gave me. To give them updates or information. I figured they wouldn't want to know if they didn't care about you."

"Is that why he left?" I asked.

"I don't know. We weren't the best at being married."

All my life I'd thought that my father left because he didn't want to be a father. Because parenting was more than he'd bargained for, and he didn't want any part of it. This was all new information, and it was a lot to process.

"When I told you I wanted to search for my birth parents, why didn't you tell me any of this? Why did you tell me you knew nothing about them?"

"I didn't! I still don't. I had no idea who they were. I never had contact with them, only the lawyer. I never knew a name or anything beyond the office address and phone number I was given to send the information to."

"But why didn't you tell me any of this? You told me the lawyer's office would be no help. That the records were sealed. Obviously, he was still involved with my birth parents long after my birth. His office could have easily gotten in touch with them. Told them I wanted to be found. She's dying, Mom. Caterina is dying, and I may never even have a conversation with her. Why didn't you give me all the information you had? Why didn't you encourage me to talk to this lawyer? You told me you didn't even remember the name of the damned place."

"Because I didn't want to lose you, okay?" she shrieked into the phone. "Maybe I didn't really want you to find your birth parents. To find some other set of people you'd rather belong to. You were all I had, and I didn't want to lose you, or Ethan and Eva."

"Why would you lose us?" I said, rising to pace again. "That's ridiculous. You're my mom, and nothing will ever change that. Nothing will change how Ethan and Eva feel about their grandmother. But you knew how important this was to me. You knew I was searching, and you kept this from me."

"I didn't keep it from you! It wouldn't have mattered. That lawyer's office wouldn't have told you anything. They couldn't. You were never meant to know."

"They might not have been able to tell me, but they could tell her I was looking. But now it may be too late. I have to go. I need time to think."

"Caroline, don't go. Don't hang up. Let's talk about this. Please don't go."

"Mom, listen to me. Finding my birth mother doesn't take away the life we've lived together. It doesn't erase our memories or the relationship we have. But I have to know who I am. Where I came from. Please. I need your support. I need you to be okay with this. I thought you were."

"I want to be. I want to be okay with it. I know it's important to you, and I want you to be at peace. It's just hard."

"I know. But finding her has nothing to do with you, okay? It's not like you failed or you weren't enough or whatever crazy stuff you're thinking. It just means I want to know the rest of my story."

"I know that. I understand. Really, I do. I just didn't expect it to be so hard. I'm sorry. I do support you. I do."

"We'll talk more later. I gotta go."

CHAPTER 12

"I'm going to drive home," I told Patsy when I went back inside. "I have a lot to think about. A lot to process. I'd like the time alone on the road."

"Of course, dear," Patsy said. "Whatever you need. I feel like I've messed this up right royal."

"No, not at all. I asked you for proof, and you gave me that. I agree with you that it appears Caterina is my mother. I'll call you in the morning, and if there's no change, I'll probably stay home. If she's better, or…not, then I'll come back to the hospital."

She stepped in closer, her blue eyes wide with concern. "You sure you're going to be okay driving? You're welcome to stay here."

"I'm fine," I said, pulling my purse strap onto my shoulder with a deep breath. "I have brand-new tires, and the car was checked out by a mechanic hours ago."

Patsy smiled. "It wasn't the car I was worried about."

I returned her smile and walked toward the front door. "I'm fine. Really. I just need some time alone."

I'd barely left the city limits of Cedar Creek when the long stretch of road ahead of me made being alone a much less desirable prospect.

Overruling my mind's most logical protests, I pulled into a service station parking lot and dug Levi's card from my purse, dialing his number before my mind won the battle.

"Levi Parker," he said after the second ring, and an inexplicable sense of calm settled over me as soon as I heard his voice.

"Hi, it's Caroline."

"Hey, is everything okay? Is Caterina okay?"

I lay back against the seat and closed my eyes. "Yeah. I mean, I guess. There's been no change." I hesitated, not sure what to say next. Not even sure why I'd called him, or what his reaction might be. He'd probably think I was nuts. He'd gotten roped into a circus of a day with his little prank gone wrong. It wasn't likely he'd want more.

"You okay?" he asked. I could hear people talking in the background, the loud chatter of a restaurant or bar. It was Saturday night. He was probably out with friends. Telling them what a crazy day he'd had. Calling him was a bad idea.

"I'm fine. I'm sorry. I'm not sure why I called. I'll let you go."

"No need to let me go. I'm not doing anything. Just sat down at a table to order some dinner."

I stared out the window at the young couple coming out of the store; she was holding an Icee and a Snickers bar, and he was smacking a pack of cigarettes against the palm of his hand. They laughed at something he said, and he held the truck door open for her. She kissed him before she climbed inside.

The night seemed lonelier as they pulled away.

"Where are you?" Levi asked.

"The Chevron station just outside of Cedar Creek. I'm on my way home."

"Oh. Okay. Is the car all right?"

"Yeah. It's fine."

We were quiet for a moment before he spoke again. "There's a great seafood place fairly close to there. I could go for some oysters if you're up for it. They make a good shrimp po-boy, too. If you're not in a hurry to get back home, that is."

I sat up and checked my appearance in the rearview mirror. I looked like I'd had a hell of a day, but what did it matter? He'd spent most of that day with me, and it wasn't like I'd ever see him again.

"I don't do oysters, but I could eat a po-boy. Aren't you already at a restaurant, though?"

"Yeah, but I haven't ordered anything other than iced tea, and there's plenty of other people at the table so the waitress won't even know I'm gone. I'll tip her well for the tea."

"Oh, if you're with friends—"

"Trust me, I see plenty of these guys. Every day, in fact. I'd rather have a big ole plate of oysters, anyway. I can be there in about twenty minutes."

He gave me directions to the restaurant, and I found it easily. I went inside to use the restroom and freshen up while I waited for him to arrive. I pinched my cheeks to try and give them some color and rubbed my pinkie across the lipstick and then on my lips, hoping to give just enough tint that I looked alive without looking like I'd tried too hard.

I wet a paper towel from the dispenser and tried as best I could to erase the smudges beneath my bottom lashes, hoping the tube of mascara I'd purchased would perk up my tired eyes. The foundation and powder I'd applied that morning had worn thin, causing my freckles to peek through more than I would like. I sighed and hoped that Levi wasn't as anti-freckle as Brad had always been.

How long had it been since I cared about my appearance to see a guy? I couldn't remember. Brad and I had started dating when I was eighteen, and I married him when we got pregnant at nineteen. He'd been my only guy since then.

It had been a long time since I'd worried about my appearance for Brad. The passion was gone between us long before he left me for Tatiana. We rarely spent time with one another that didn't involve the kids, and I couldn't tell you the last time we'd participated in anything resembling romance.

But I thought that was just how marriage went after thirteen years and two kids.

It had grown boring and predictable, but at the time, I was so caught up in the hamster wheel of life that I didn't see what was missing.

Intramural sports, dance recitals, piano lessons, field trips, cultural enrichment, community volunteering, birthday parties, sleepovers—my calendar was filled with color-coordinated appointments, commitments, and reminders. Very few of which included Brad or required interaction with him.

My life revolved around Eva and Ethan.

So, it stands to reason that when my husband packed his clothes and his golf clubs to move into Tatiana's condo downtown, it was less his absence and the loss of my marriage that gutted me and more the heartache my children went through.

I hadn't really thought about the opposite sex in years. It wasn't on my radar. In fact, there was no room on my radar for it.

The woman in the mirror stared back at me, and I searched for the girl I once was in her tired eyes and pale skin.

The door of the restroom swung open and a young mother came in with two small kids. I washed and dried my hands as she admonished them not to touch anything in the stall and begged the young boy not to sit on the floor as the poor woman tried to pee.

I smiled, glad to be beyond those years of parenting. My smile faded as I caught my reflection again, and I frowned at it, telling myself that my appearance didn't matter. This wasn't a date. He wasn't a guy who was interested in me, and I certainly wasn't interested in him. I just needed companionship for an hour or so. Something to distract me from the whirlwind of chaos that had swept me into its vortex for the day.

Maybe I could pretend just for the space of one meal that none of it existed. Perhaps I could lose myself in conversation with a handsome guy and not think about Caterina, Lorna, the impending move and how it would affect my kids, Brad's irresponsibility, my failure as a wife, or the myriad of other concerns that flooded my mind.

I pulled the lipstick from my purse again and applied it directly to my lips, then I bent and ran my fingers through my hair to fluff it out, flipping my head back over and forcing the woman in the mirror to smile back at me.

CHAPTER 13

He was standing by the seating hostess podium when I came out of the restroom. He still wore the black shirt and denim jeans he'd had on earlier, and by the look of his hair, he'd put the cap back on when he left the hospital.

"Hey," I said, and he turned with a smile.

"There you are. I was worried you got lost."

The hostess led us to a table in the corner, and I took in the quaint fish nets, seashells, and lighthouses that seemed to adorn any available space on the walls.

"You come here often?" I asked.

"Not really, but they do have the best oysters around, so I make the drive from time to time."

The waitress introduced herself and asked what we'd like to drink.

"I'd love the biggest glass of Chardonnay you can bring me. Like a gallon jug if you have it," I said, and she and Levi both laughed.

"I'll just have iced tea," he told her before turning back to me.

"Not a wine drinker?" I asked.

"Not a drinker. Period. I did my share of partying when I was young, but I found the older I got, the harder it was to get up in the morning and work in the sun all day if I'd been out all hours the night before. I put it down and never looked back."

"What is it that you do on this farm where you work?"

"I'm the farm manager. I oversee the other folks working there, deal with the outside people we do business with, maintain the facility, and oversee the care of the horses. It's a glorified title that basically means someone to do whatever no one else has time for or wants to do."

"Oh. How big is the farm?"

"Thank you," he said to the waitress as she set down our drinks. "Three hundred and fifty acres."

"Wow, that's sizable. How many horses?"

"It varies. We have some that belong to the farm, that were born and raised there or bought for the farm, and then we have a rotating door of horses owned by other people. We have the largest training and rehabilitation facility in the area. One of the largest anywhere outside Kentucky, in fact."

His face beamed with pride as he said it, and I couldn't help but smile back at him.

"You enjoy what you do. It shows."

"Very lucky, I am. Fell into what I wanted to do at a young age, and I've been doing it ever since. What about you? What do you do?"

"Oh, I raise kids. Training, rehabilitation, care, you name it. Maintaining the facility. Overseeing schedules. Budgets. All that. I'm basically the farm manager for my house, I suppose."

He laughed. "Certainly a full-time job. And one that you're very good at, I'm sure."

We ordered our entrees and chatted about the area, small talk that felt like a first date but without the pressure since we both knew it would go nowhere. We lived much different lives very far apart, even if my mind did keep reminding me that I'd be closer once our family relocated to Orlando.

"Did you get a chance to talk to Patsy? To ask her why she seems certain about you and Caterina?" Levi asked as we ate.

"I did. She had a file, or I guess I should say Caterina had a file, that pretty much summarized every year of my life from birth through college. I didn't know who they were, but I guess they've known who I was all along. Evidently, Caterina's mother wanted to know I was doing okay, so she kept tabs."

"Well, that's a good thing, right? I mean, I don't know the circumstances of why Caterina couldn't raise you herself, but I think it has to be a good thing that they still cared what happened to you."

I shrugged as I took another bite of the po-boy and chewed slowly. "I guess," I said once I'd swallowed. "It just feels weird. Like someone was spying on me. My mother knew. Lorna, my adoptive mother. She was giving them information every year. It feels like everyone was in on the secret except me."

He slid an oyster onto a cracker and popped it into his mouth, and I shuddered at the thought of the slimy mass going down his throat.

"How can you eat those things?"

"They're good! Have you ever tried one?"

"No. Don't they have, like, bacteria or something? Aren't they dangerous?"

He chased it down with a swig of tea and grinned. "It's best to avoid them some years. When the water temperature stays too high. And I usually don't eat them in summer months. That whole no month without an R thing. But they're too good to pass up. And some say they're great for, well, um, energy."

I laughed. "Yeah, I think I heard that, but it wasn't energy they were supposed to enhance. But okay." I watched as the waitress refilled my wine, enjoying the warm euphoria from the first glass. It felt so nice to be unencumbered by anything or anyone. No one knew where I was. No one knew who I was with. No one needed anything from me. Not a soul in the restaurant had ever even seen me before. I felt free. Unrestricted. Uninhibited. Like I was someone I used to be, before marriage and kids and life.

"Do you dance?" I asked Levi as I watched the band play in the far corner.

"Not here," he answered as he followed my gaze. "But I've been known to two-step my way across a dance floor if the music's right. So, if Caterina knew who you were all this time, why are you just meeting her now?"

"Patsy said Caterina didn't know about the file until I'd started college. I guess her mom, which would have been my grandmother, went into an assisted living center my freshman year. Caterina found the file, but she told Patsy she felt like it was an invasion of my privacy to use it to find me. I guess she left word with the lawyer's office who had handled the adoption to get in touch with her if I ever requested she be found."

Levi sat back in his chair and folded his napkin to lay it on the table beside his plate. "So why didn't you go to this lawyer sooner? You said you'd been searching a while."

"Oh, only for the past year or so. My hus—ex-husband didn't think it was a good idea to find my birth parents, so I didn't look until several months after we divorced. Besides, my mother kind of shut down that avenue. She told me she didn't remember the lawyer's name, which I believed then, but knowing she had to contact them every year of my life for nineteen years makes me question if that's true."

"Well, you found her now. I guess that's what you have to focus on."

I dragged a French fry through the ketchup on my plate, drawing a *C* without thinking about it. "If she lives. If she wakes up. If not, then it's like I never found her at all."

"That's not exactly true," Levi said. "Even if you never get to talk to Caterina—and I'm sure you will; I'm sure she's gonna pull through—you know where you came from now. You told me this afternoon on the way to meet her that one of the most important things was to know your history. To know who you were and where you came from. Your ancestors. Your lineage. Well, now you know. You can still research Caterina's family and find out about yourself."

I dropped the fry and turned up the wine glass once more, almost draining it as I pushed from my mind any thought of Caterina not making it.

"She has to make it," I said as put the glass down. "She has to. I have so many questions for her. I want to know why. I want to know what happened. And I want to know who my father is. Maybe he's still alive. Maybe he's out there looking for me. I might have brothers or sisters with him. Who knows?"

Unexpected tears stung my eyes, and I looked up at the wrought iron light fixture above our table and blinked several times, keeping them at bay.

"Can we talk about something else, Levi? I'm tired of thinking about all this today."

"Sure, of course. You want to get out of here? Do you know how to two-step? Mickey's Saloon isn't far from here, and they've got a great band on Saturday nights."

I looked at his handsome smile and asked myself what the hell I was doing. Was I really about to go dancing with a total stranger in some backwoods saloon?

But then again, why not? He'd already been vouched for by local law enforcement, there was no one waiting for me at home, and it had been years upon years since I'd worked up a sweat on a dance floor.

The prospect enticed me, and the fact that it was so out of the norm only added to the excitement.

The rest of the wine was gone with a gulp, and the last of my hesitation went with it.

A half hour later, I was on the dance floor with Levi—underdressed for a Saturday night, out of step, and having the best time I'd had in years.

CHAPTER 14

"Oh, God! I have to sit down," I said, laughing. "I need to catch my breath."

Levi grabbed my hand and pulled me through the crowd and off the dance floor, leading me to a table near the bar.

"I might have to sit down, too," he said. "My feet are mighty bruised."

"I said I was sorry! I told you I didn't know how to do these dances."

He grinned as I held my hair up off my neck and fanned myself with the cocktail napkin from the table.

"I'm just teasing you. You did good. You're a quick learner," he said as he flagged down a waitress. "You want another drink?"

"Water, please. I probably wouldn't be stepping on your feet as much if I didn't have a wine-buzz right now."

"It's fine," he said after asking the waitress to bring two waters. "These boots are tough."

"I can't believe I'm out here dancing. My daughter would be shocked. I should have you take a picture of me so I can show her."

The thought of telling Eva I'd run off dancing with a stranger was sobering, and I frowned at the idea.

"What? You okay? What happened there?" Levi asked, tilting his head to one side as he looked at me. "You lost your smile."

"Nothing. Just thinking about Eva. She's having a hard time right now. She's gotten taller, and she's not doing as well in ballet. We're moving as soon as the kids are out of school, so she's nervous about going to a new high school. She says she wants to quit dance all together, and I don't know whether to make her continue or let her give it up. She's struggling, and I don't know how to help her. I guess

I was thinking it may not be a good idea to take a picture of me out drinking and dancing with a stranger."

"A stranger?" Levi said, his brows scrunched together in confusion. "Surely, we're not strangers anymore, are we? Hell, we spent the whole day together. The whole evening, too. I stole your car, hung out at the hospital with your mom you've never met, and let you stomp all over my feet. I would think we would have gotten past being strangers by now."

I smiled and released my hair to tumble around my shoulders. "You're right. We've had quite the adventure together so far."

He reached to move a strand of hair away from my face, but his hand lingered, cupping my cheek for the briefest moment before pushing my hair behind my ear. My skin burned where he'd touched it, and I almost leaned toward his fingers as they left me, aching for more.

How long had it been since a man had looked at me the way Levi was? How many nights had I spent alone? Or before the divorce, not alone but lonely?

A spark of longing ignited deep within me, and I had no desire to extinguish it. Quite the contrary, I wanted to fan the flames.

He watched my lips as I leaned closer to him, stopping mere inches from him as he lifted his hands to cup my face and bring our lips together. It was soft, tender even, but a fire raged inside me, and I pulled him closer, desperate to get more.

I felt rather than heard his groan as the band played on, and then his hands were in my hair, down my back, and around my waist as I melded my body to his.

Somehow, I must have bumped the small table and knocked over our cups, and the shock of the cold water hitting my back was enough to pull us apart.

"Let me get a towel," he said, moving through the crowd toward the bar as I held my silk shirt away from my skin.

"Oh, wow, you're all wet. That's too bad," said a girl who looked to be in her early twenties with long, blonde hair and a dress so short it was like she'd forgotten to put on pants.

I looked at her in confusion, wondering who she was and how long she'd been standing there.

Before I could respond to her, Levi returned with a dry bar towel.

"Here, let me dry your shirt, and then we can wipe up the table."

"Hey, Levi," she said, a coy smile playing across her lips. She thrust her chest up and put her hand on her hip as she spoke, her words ending with a slight pout of her lips.

"Hey, Mallory," he said, with barely a turn of his head.

She frowned at the dismissal and glared at me before she disappeared into the crowd.

"Friend of yours?" I asked, taking the towel to finish drying my back and mop up the water on the table just as the waitress arrived with a towel of her own.

"Not exactly," he murmured under the music as he picked up the overturned cups and put them on the waitress's tray.

"You want more water?" she asked as she took the dripping towel from me.

The band launched into a slow, soft ballad, and Levi shook his head. "Not right now. We have someplace to be."

"We do?" I asked, laughing as he took my hand and pulled me onto the dance floor and into his arms.

I slid my arms up and around his neck as he encircled my waist, our hips locked together as we swayed back and forth.

His eyes held mine as the music carried us around the perimeter of the floor. The crowd became background noise as we moved together, and the desire burning inside me became almost unbearable. A thirst I had to quench.

I didn't want the song to end, to have the moment broken, but as the last strains played out and he leaned forward to press our lips together, I wanted the band gone along with the rest of the dancing crowd.

My lips parted to receive him as his tongue darted inside, and I ran my hands up his neck and across the hair on the back of his head as I opened myself wider to his exploration.

A faster-paced song started, and Levi pulled back to look at me with a grin. "You want to get out here?"

I nodded, ready to follow him anywhere. We were almost to the door when I caught sight of Mallory standing at the bar with two other girls, all three shooting daggers at me that would have killed me if they'd been knives instead of stares.

"What did you do to Mallory?" I asked as we walked across the gravel lot hand-in-hand toward our cars.

His eyes widened in surprise, and he shrugged. "I didn't do anything to her. I mean, we went out a couple of times. We had a good time, but she wanted—oh, holy hell!"

I looked to see what had upset him, and my mouth dropped open in shock. The shiny red paint of the Audi had a jagged line keyed across the driver's door and back fender.

"Oh my God! Who did this?" I asked, kneeling beside Levi to take a closer look.

"I could take a good guess," he growled, his jaw set tight and his mouth a grim line.

"Mallory?" I asked, looking over my shoulder. There were several people walking across the parking lot and a couple of lovers making out against cars, but no sign of the beautiful blonde with the murderous eyes.

"Unless I have some other enemy I know nothing about. Or unless you do," he said, one eyebrow raised. "It's your car."

"Technically, it's not *my* car. But I don't think Brad has any enemies in Cedar Creek or Jensen or wherever we are right now."

He stood, and I stood with him.

"You want to call the cops?"

I thought about the amount of time it would take for the cops to arrive, and the hassle of doing a police report. "Not really."

Levi sighed, rubbing his hand across the stubble on his chin. "I know a detail guy, but he won't be open until Monday."

"You know what?" I said, turning to face him. "I've spent enough time on repairs for this stupid car this weekend. Brad can deal with this."

"You sure?"

"Oh, I'm positive. But I think you might want to watch your back. If this was Mallory, she seems a bit scorned."

He shook his head. "Believe me, I've tried to make peace with that situation. She won't have it. But I'm very sorry if she did this to you. Or to Brad, or whatever his name is. She's never attacked anyone that I know of."

"Is this a *recent* development?"

"Not really. We last went out about three months ago."

I smiled. "Well, I'd say the torch is still burning. Lucky you."

He turned back to the car and rubbed his thumb across the raised paint and frowned.

"Hey," I said, taking his hands in mine and pulling him closer to me. "I'm not worried about this. I'm telling you, if I hadn't had two kids watching me, I probably would have keyed the damned car myself yesterday afternoon when he pulled up in it. So, don't let this bother you on my account, okay?"

He brought my hands to his lips and then released them to wrap his arms around me, pulling me against him as we kissed once more.

But the fiery passion of the dance floor had gone, and he seemed pensive and irritated.

I stepped back and flipped my hair over my shoulder as I smoothed my shirt down.

"As much as I hate to say it, I need to get on the road," I said. "I have a long drive ahead of me, and if I'm not home by midnight, I'll turn into a pumpkin."

Levi leaned back against the car and pulled me with him. "You're going to be hard-pressed to make it to Gainesville before midnight, Cinderella. Besides, wouldn't it be the car that turned into a pumpkin?"

"This car? More likely a lemon."

"True. You know, you could stay out at the farm. It would be close to the hospital in the morning so you could check on Caterina."

I pulled back with a laugh, tempted to pursue my desires, but determined to make common sense prevail. "Yeah, okay. We may have progressed past strangers, but let's not press it. We've only known each other a day."

He rolled his eyes upward and grinned. "That's not what I meant. There's an apartment over the barn that's sitting empty. It's for visiting trainers or prospective clients to stay in. I mean, I'm more than happy for you to stay at my place, don't get me wrong. I even have an extra bedroom, so there wouldn't have to be any expectations, but the apartment is nicer. It has better amenities."

I didn't want to drive two hours. I didn't want that much time in my head alone. My house was empty, and my children were gone. I'd gotten a text from Eva earlier that afternoon saying they had no signal at the campground, so I couldn't even call them to say goodnight.

Plus, it did make sense to be closer to the hospital so I could check on her progress first thing in the morning.

So, in what seemed a rather fitting end to such a bizarre day, I found myself following Levi Parker through the gates of Ward Farms.

CHAPTER 15

Once we had entered the wrought iron gates between the massive brick lamp posts, the drive wound through rolling hills of pasture and woods. Towering oaks lined the narrow path, the Spanish moss swaying from their limbs almost ghostly in the dark of the night.

We had passed a couple of buildings on the property when Levi turned down a road to the right, and we ventured farther back into the woods. Soon the road opened into a large circular drive with an enormous, brightly lit fountain in the center that featured four horses on their hind legs facing in different directions. Behind the fountain was a stately home lit with spotlights that glittered across the expanse of windows and white columns. I wanted to stop and stare at the beauty of it, but Levi had gone around the roundabout and was leaving me behind.

We stopped behind a two-story building near the house, and Levi indicated I should park in the gravel area next to his truck. I gathered my purchases from the drugstore before joining him by the building's door.

His expression turned quizzical when he saw the bags.

"I had stopped and picked up a toothbrush and some pajamas to stay at Patsy's."

"The apartment is pretty well-stocked with spare toothbrushes, soap, lotion, shampoo, and stuff like that. But no pajamas."

"I come prepared. Whose house is that over there?"

"William's," he said as he opened the door and flipped on the lights. "We call that the big house. This was originally a barn, but now it's the office for the farm. Plus a few meeting rooms, a media room, and the apartment."

We entered a large central room with hallways venturing off to the left and right. Pictures of horses filled the walls, and a large case displayed ribbons and trophies. An open door on the left revealed a spacious office with three desks and several file cabinets. Another room on the right held vending machines and a couple of tables.

Levi continued to the staircase on the other side of the room, and I followed him up to the second-floor landing, where there were three doors along a narrow hallway. He stopped in front of the third door and pulled a large key ring from his pocket, fishing through the jumble of keys to find the one he was searching for.

"Are you sure it's okay if I stay here?" I asked.

"Yeah. It's not a problem at all. No one's using it until next week."

"Do you live close by?"

He opened the apartment door and turned on the lights. "We passed my house on the way in. The second one on the left."

"Oh, so you literally live *on* the farm?"

"Yeah. Horses don't really take a day off. It's sort of a twenty-four hours a day, seven-days-a-week kind of job. So best to be as close as possible when needed. The housing is a perk and a necessity."

What he had called an apartment in a re-purposed barn looked much more like a luxury condo. The immaculate and sumptuous decor featured dark woods with rich navy and burgundy accents, and as to be expected, there were horses here and there in statues, paintings, lamp bases, and carved into the back of the dining chairs. It was elegant but not overdone, and much nicer than I had expected.

Levi opened the fridge in the small kitchen and bent to look at its contents.

"There's coffee and sugar in the cabinet." He pulled out a container of creamer and sniffed it. "Yeah. It's fresh. There's some sodas, waters, sparkling waters, juice. Pretty much whatever you want."

He closed the refrigerator and opened the pantry door "Snacks in here." He turned and pointed to the bar on the other side of the dining table. "And a fully-stocked bar over there. There's cable and pretty much every movie channel in existence on the TV."

"Wow," I said with an appreciative nod. "I might just stay here until you kick me out."

"Yeah, like I said, much better amenities than my place. I might have coffee, and I think there's about a half a pint of ice cream in my freezer. But no snacks and no bar. I've got cable, though."

"I'm only gonna be here a few hours, and I plan to be sleeping pretty much the whole time, but it's great. Thanks for offering it up."

"No problem. I'm glad I could help."

The easy banter and charged sexual tension of earlier had subsided, replaced with an awkward silence and uncomfortable uncertainty. The night had come to an end, and so had my reckless abandonment of my normal self.

"I should probably get some sleep," I said, hugging my arms around my waist. "It's been a long day."

"Yeah. Definitely. I'll head out then. If you need anything, just call. I'm literally like a hop, skip, and jump away."

"Thanks, Levi. Thanks for dinner…and dancing…and helping me kind of get out of my head for a while."

He nodded. "I enjoyed it. I had a good time. Hey, you mentioned your daughter was upset about moving. Where are y'all moving to?"

"Oh, um, Orlando. My ex-husband's firm has offices there, and he's been transferred. The kids and I are going to move as soon as school's out. You know, so they can be close to their dad."

"Orlando's nice. Do you know which area yet?"

I shook my head. "Still doing research on schools and neighborhoods. I've been procrastinating the whole process because I hate packing. And unpacking. Moving. The whole thing, pretty much."

"Yeah. Moving's no fun."

We stared at each other in a deafening silence neither of us seemed willing to break.

"I should go," he finally said, but he didn't move.

"I should sleep." I didn't move either.

The silence returned, and then he grinned. "Okay. I'm going."

I dropped my arms to my sides, wanting him to come and kiss me. To hold me. To take me back to the exhilaration and heat I'd felt before. But also wanting him to walk on by. To leave without me making decisions I'd regret or taking me places I might wish I hadn't gone.

He walked toward me, his eyes dark and intense, and a tremor of anticipation rippled through me.

God, it had been so long. My body longed to be touched. My loins ached. My skin tingled.

He stopped in front of me, so close that I could feel the heat from his body and the air of his breath on my skin. His gaze lingered on my lips, then back to my eyes, and then on my lips once more.

I held my breath as he tucked his finger under my chin, moving to press his mouth to mine with a touch so gentle that I nearly cried out, begging him for more.

He brushed his fingers against my cheek as he moved them into my hair, softly caressing the back of my neck as he pulled me closer. His lips took mine again, more demanding this time, and I flicked my tongue across his in an invitation I hoped he wouldn't ignore.

The kiss deepened, and as his grip on my neck tightened and his other hand moved to the small of my back, I leaned into him, abandoning any thought of denying myself the pleasure he could offer.

I wrapped my arms around his neck, pressing my body to his as our tongues danced and the world swayed. I moaned as his lips left mine, his mouth wet and hot on my neck, leaving a trail of fire as he pulled my hair back and took my ear lobe between his teeth.

As he continued his heavenly assault with his lips, I moved my hands across the muscular ridge of his shoulders and spanned my fingers across his back, exploring each sculpted curve and groove as I pictured him shirtless in my mind. The image only served to make my pulse race faster, and I slid my hands beneath the hem of his shirt and up his back to access the rock-hard muscles without the hindrance of fabric between us.

His mouth found its way back to mine, his tongue claiming my own as he walked us toward the wall, slamming my upper back against it as I raised my knee along his outer thigh and tucked my heel behind his calf, pulling him even closer. His hands were on my hips, lifting me against him, his desire evident between us.

There was no question in my mind where we were headed, and there was no doubt of where I wanted to go. I was no longer a soccer mom, or an ex-wife who had lost her husband, or a daughter who had been betrayed. I was a woman, hot-blooded and passionate, feeling beautiful and highly aroused, yearning to experience sensations long neglected but not forgotten.

But then he pulled back, his lips swollen and wet, his eyes darting back and forth as they searched mine. The desire in his eyes was as undeniable as the bulge in his pants. His gaze was dark and enticing, but there was also uncertainty, and a tenderness that caught me off guard.

He took a step back, and I almost fell forward onto him without the support of his body holding me against the wall.

"God, I don't want to go," he whispered, his hands cupping my cheeks as I struggled to understand what he was saying.

"So, don't." I stepped forward as he released my face and took a step toward the door.

"Good night, Caroline."

Then he was out the door, and I was left in a state of aroused shock, practically panting as my heart raced and my nerves buzzed with unsatiated need.

CHAPTER 16

I woke a little before seven, and it took me a few minutes to figure out where I was. I'd tossed and turned most of the night, unable to get comfortable in the unfamiliar surroundings; my mind in a state of confusion and my body in a state of dire need.

I'd taken a cold shower after Levi left, but it did little to diminish the fire he'd started. It was like the sensual side of me had awakened after being dormant for years, and it was just my luck I'd picked a gentleman to be aroused by.

At least, I hoped that was the reason. My mind had churned over the possibilities every waking moment of the night, and I didn't like any other option when it came to explaining his rejection.

He would have to be blind and deaf not to know I was his for the taking, and the way he looked at me and the passion with which he kissed me ruled out him not being interested. Not to mention the obvious physical evidence of his arousal.

I considered there being another woman involved, which would explain why he brought me to the apartment instead of his own house, but I couldn't imagine him taking me out dancing in public and then bringing me to his place of work where I might be seen if he was in a committed relationship.

The only theory that made his leaving sting less was to think it was because he was a gentleman who didn't want to take advantage of my emotional state. Even if I'd wanted to be taken advantage of at the time.

I'd made coffee before showering, and having no wardrobe option other than the clothes I'd worn the day before and no make-up to apply other than the mascara, I was dressed and ready to leave in record time. Unfortunately, I had nowhere to be.

I had no idea if the hospital had set visiting hours, but I wasn't too keen on going there to sit without Patsy. She had planned to arrive around nine if she hadn't heard from the doctors in the night, and since my phone had no messages from her, I assumed there'd been no change in Caterina's condition.

Neither Cedar Creek or Jensen seemed big enough to have a selection of clothing stores, and even if there was a random shop available, they likely weren't open until ten or later, if they were even open on a Sunday at all.

The pantry's selection was limited to pretzels, popcorn, nuts, cookies, and chips, so if I was going to have a decent breakfast, I'd need to venture out and find a restaurant.

I pondered calling Levi and inviting him out for eggs or a waffle, but I decided against it. I didn't understand all that had transpired between us or why he had left so abruptly, and without knowing if he was an early riser, I didn't want to risk waking him. He hadn't mentioned getting together again when he left last night, so perhaps I'd taken up enough of his weekend already.

I left a note for him on the dining table thanking him for his hospitality, and I gathered my drugstore bags and opened the door to head downstairs.

The sound of men's voices startled me, and I stepped back inside the apartment even though there was no way they could see me from the room below.

"I never saw her at Mickey's before, but she was dancing all close with him, and they were swapping spit like there's no tomorrow. He didn't even acknowledge us. Like, he didn't even look our direction," a gruff voice said.

"How does he do it, man?" said a deeper voice. "How does he find a different girl every weekend, and none of them can keep their hands off him? If I had half of whatever he's got, I'd be happy."

The words stung as I realized they were talking about me, and I quietly stepped forward to listen more closely.

"He's always been that way," said a higher-pitched male voice. "The boy's just got it."

"But where does he find 'em?" asked the first man. "I see the same damned women everywhere I go, and none of them want to give me the time of day. But if there's a beautiful woman anywhere in the tri-county area, somehow that boy finds 'em."

"I suggest you fellows keep it down," said a new voice from elsewhere in the building. "There's a car parked out back, and he left instructions for me to be quiet this morning because someone's sleeping upstairs. I'm pretty sure I heard someone moving around up there before y'all came in babbling on so loud."

"Who? We don't have anyone scheduled in until next week. Where's the schedule?" said the high-pitched man.

"Ain't on the schedule. I checked. And there wasn't nobody here when I left at ten last night, so whoever it is got here after that."

"You think it's the redhead?" said the first man.

"I have no idea. I didn't see who it was, I told you," the deep voice growled.

"Why would she be upstairs? Why wouldn't she be in his bed?" asked the high-pitched man.

"Maybe he ain't quite as skilled as you think he is," the gruff one said.

The high-pitched voice laughed. "Look, I've known that boy since he was still wet behind the ears, and I'm telling you. There ain't never been a girl what could keep her eyes off him. Hands either. It don't take much more than a smile, and he's got them on a hook for the taking."

"Why don't y'all find something else to do and somewhere else to do it?" A female voice joined the discussion. "Have you ever thought that maybe it's not something Levi has, but something you guys don't have?"

"Yeah, yeah, yeah," said the deep-voiced man. "C'mon, fellows. Piper's in a mood."

My ears perked at the name, and curiosity filled me. I wanted to get a good look at Piper, the woman whose resemblance to me had been enough to get the Audi stolen.

The entry door opened and closed, and the men's voices faded as they walked away from the building. I tiptoed toward the stairs, looking down just as she started up.

"Oh, hi. You're awake!" she said.

She was younger than me by several years, but we were roughly the same height and the same lean build, though her arms showed more muscle definition than mine. Her hair was a couple of inches longer than mine, but it was the same red, perhaps a touch more golden as though she spent a lot of time in the sun. Her eyes were brown, but even from the top of the stairs I could see a brilliant blue fleck in each iris. The effect was striking, and though I felt complimented to be mistaken for such an attractive lady, I could see why Levi and Tristan hadn't thought the resemblance so strong.

She wore tight denim jeans stuffed into well-worn, brown cowboy boots, and a sleeveless, buttoned-up, collared shirt in a pink and white plaid.

"I'm Piper," she said, taking a few more steps up toward me. "Levi asked me to bring you some clothes. He said you'd sort of gotten stranded away from home for the night."

I looked at the stack of clothing she carried, relieved at the idea of a clean outfit, but at the same time put off by wearing a stranger's clothes.

"Oh, that's okay," I said. "I'm fine."

"I wasn't sure what you'd want, so I brought a couple of things," she said, ignoring my feeble protest. "He said you were visiting the hospital, so I brought a light sweater, too, in case it's cold in there. He was right; we look to be about the same size."

She'd reached the top of the stairs and handed me the stack.

"Um, thanks, but I can just wear what I've got on."

Even as I said it, I knew my clothes carried the faint smell of smoke, sweat, and the general funk of dancing at the saloon the night before, and I took what she offered and thanked her for it.

"No problem. Here, let me get the door." She opened the door to the apartment as I stood with my hands filled with clothes, shopping bags, and my purse. I followed her inside and laid everything on the dining table, scooping up the note I'd written for Levi.

"Mike must not have seen you up close," Piper said as she leaned against the bar. "I can see where we look alike with our height and our coloring, but I don't think there's any resemblance past that, do you?"

I studied her face for a moment and shook my head, wondering what else Levi had shared with her.

"I'm Caroline, by the way," I said, though it seemed obvious and a bit late for the introduction. I'd been rendered somewhat speechless first by the men's words and then with her appearance.

"Breakfast is almost ready at the big house, if you're hungry," she said, looking over her shoulder toward the apartment's kitchen. "I can smell that you found the coffee, but there's not much to eat here other than snacks, right?"

I nodded.

It was odd in a way I couldn't put my finger on. There was something about her that seemed familiar, but she was right. Other than height and coloring, we didn't look much alike at all. Our eyes were different. Her lips were much fuller than mine. But the hint of resemblance was there, and I could understand better how the mechanic had gotten us mixed, even though it didn't excuse what he'd done.

The silent pause grew awkward, and I cleared my throat and picked up the stack of clothes. "I'll just step in the bedroom and get changed, thanks."

"No problem. I can walk you over to the house for breakfast. Take your time."

I took the stack of clothes and moved past her into the bedroom, closing the door behind me. My desire for clean clothes had outweighed my discomfort for wearing someone else's garments, but I wasn't sure I wanted to go and have breakfast with a group of strangers.

Would Levi be there? Had he sent her to fetch me? When had they talked and what all had he told her? He was obviously awake already. Why hadn't he come himself?

I still hadn't been able to process what I'd heard from the men downstairs and what that meant in relation to me being there. If Levi was the charming player they'd made him out to be instead of the gentleman I'd hoped, why had he left me to sleep alone? Why hadn't I been invited back to his place if that seemed his norm? And why did I even care if he was actually the scoundrel they'd described?

The jeans she'd brought fit me like a glove, more snug than my normal taste, but not too tight to wear.

I chose a short-sleeved shirt from the selection she'd brought, and then I refolded the other items and opened the bedroom door to grab one of the plastic bags from the drugstore to stuff my dirties in.

Piper was standing at the window looking out across the trees, and she turned immediately as I came out.

"Okay, good. They fit."

"I can wash them and get them back to you." I realized as I said it I had no idea if I would ever see her again.

She fanned her hand in a dismissive gesture. "Don't even worry about it. I have too many clothes to wear them all, as I'm sure my father would tell you. Take them."

"Oh, no. I'll return them. I just have to figure out how."

"Levi can get them back to me," she said, scooping up the stack I hadn't worn.

"Oh, I don't know if..." I stopped, not sure what I wanted to say and how much to reveal. She already seemed to know much more about the situation than perhaps even I did. I wondered again how much she knew.

"You hungry?"

I shrugged. "I don't want to intrude."

"Nonsense. Gaynelle cooks for twenty every morning, even though we usually only have around ten on Sundays, so there's plenty. She hates the sight of leftovers, so you'd be doing us a favor by joining us."

It seemed rude to refuse her after I'd stayed in their guest apartment and put on her clothes, but it seemed awkward to join in as well.

"Sure," I said when I realized she was waiting for a response, opting for relieving my hunger the easy way over going out in search of food.

She opened the door and led the way downstairs as I followed behind, looking for any sign of Levi or the men who'd disparaged him.

CHAPTER 17

L evi opened the entry door just as we reached the bottom of the stairs.

"Good morning," he called out, his face lighting up with a smile when he saw me. "I see Piper found you some clothes, and you two met. Good deal."

"Did you check on that horse?" Piper asked. "Seem okay to you?"

He stood in the doorway as we reached him, and his smile faded as he talked to Piper. "No. Something's definitely up. I called the vet. He'll be out within the hour."

"Should we move her?"

Levi shook his head. "I don't think so. No need to upset her before he gets here. I'll ride back out there once I get something to eat." He looked at me, and his smile returned. "Sleep okay?"

"Yeah," I lied, wishing that Piper wasn't standing between us. I would have liked a private moment with him. The men's words lingered in my mind, and I wanted something from Levi, though I wasn't sure what. Reassurance, I suppose, as silly as that sounds. Perhaps an explanation as to why he ran out on me without finishing what we'd started.

"Hungry?" he asked. "There's a breakfast buffet at the big house. You're welcome to join us."

"I've already invited her," Piper said before I could answer. "Let's get a move on, so we don't keep Gaynelle waiting."

The three of us walked toward the main house, stopping by the Audi so I could put my clothes and bags inside.

"You like the car? I love mine," Piper said.

"Oh, it's not mine. It's my ex-husband's. He had to borrow mine for the weekend."

"Levi mentioned that. How's the ex going to feel about the key stroke down the side?" She knelt to inspect the scratch in the paint, which looked much worse in the light of day.

"I'm sure he's not going to be very happy," I said, trying not to look too closely to the damage or give much thought to Brad.

"I bet. Oh, there's Malcolm. Let me catch him and tell him the vet's coming," she said, throwing her hand up to wave at a trio of men coming across the grass. "Malcolm, a word?"

Levi bumped my fingers with his when she'd left us.

"Sorry I didn't get over here to say good morning and warn you about Piper. She came by early to get me to check on a horse, and I asked her to get you some clothes. Hope that was okay."

"Yeah, thanks," I mumbled. My thoughts and emotions were a jumble. I wanted to know what had prompted his departure the night before, what was up with what those men had said, and why he'd needed to share every detail of our day together with Piper. How close were they anyway? I tried to remember the initial conversations of the day before when it was first discovered that the car didn't belong to her. He'd said they were friends, but was there anything else?

At the same time all those thoughts were racing through my head, I also wanted desperately not to care. This wasn't my life. I'd never see these people again, and part of me wanted to get in Brad's damaged car and drive straight home to crawl back in my cocoon where none of this would matter.

"Any word on Caterina?" Levi asked.

I shook my head. "Nothing yet. I figured I'd head to the hospital after I got something to eat. Are you sure it's okay if I eat here? I feel kind of funny tagging along for breakfast without knowing anyone."

"It's fine, trust me. Gaynelle, William's cook, never knows how many people she'll be feeding on any given day, so she just makes a ton of food and somehow it always gets eaten. I do have to warn you, though; it can be a little loud and boisterous."

Boisterous was an understatement. As soon as we entered the front door of the house, we could hear the conversations and laughter coming from the rear, rising in volume as we walked through a wide foyer lined with a staircase on either side, photos filling nearly every available inch of wall space.

The house itself was even more beautifully done than the apartment, and every room we passed was filled with light from too many windows to count. The large dining room spanned almost the entire width of the house, and Piper hadn't been exaggerating when she'd mentioned feeding twenty. The massive wooden table had at least that many chairs around it, and a long counter of buffet chafing dishes sat steaming along the wall next to the kitchen.

I'd never seen such a large dining room in a residence before, and I'm sure the shock registered on my face.

"Pretty impressive, isn't it?" Levi said with a wink. "William's wife, Revae, wanted the family to eat dinner together every night, and as they kept hiring more full-time staff and more people to live on the farm, the more people she considered family. So, she had William knock out a wall and build a room big enough for everyone to eat together. We have a smaller crowd on Sunday mornings, but most nights this place is filled with people for dinner. Just the way Revae liked it."

I stared at the 'smaller crowd' of at least ten men already seated around the table, not a woman in sight except for Piper.

"Are there no females on your staff?" I asked.

"Revae wasn't much for hiring women," Levi said quietly, though I'm sure we wouldn't have been heard over the din of conversation. "There's a few wives that live over in the housing circle, but they usually have meals with their own families over there. Only the single folk tend to congregate here for breakfast."

I wanted to ask him why he spoke of Revae in the past tense, but we'd been noticed, and the room quieted as every head turned and every eye stared.

"Everybody, this is Caroline. Please make her feel welcome," Levi said.

Hellos and welcomes bombarded me, and I smiled and said hi as Levi pulled out one of the heavy chairs and waited for me to be seated before pulling out his own to sit next to me.

"Breakfast will be served as soon as Daddy gets off the phone," Piper said to me with an eye roll. "If my mama was alive, she'd have skinned him for being on the phone when it was time for breakfast."

A loud chorus of agreement erupted around the table, and I leaned toward Levi to whisper, "So is Revae—?"

"She passed away a few years back."

Someone across the table asked him a question, and he looked up to answer him before I could get more information about Revae.

"Vet's on his way. Should be here within the hour."

"Good. I'm not sure what's causing it, but he'll know. Oh, and Juan said there's a section of fence down, so I may take a ride over there this afternoon."

Their chatter resumed to the level it had been before we entered, and the way they took my presence in stride made me wonder if it was routine for Levi to bring someone to Sunday breakfast.

"Okay, my apologies, but that was a call I had to take."

I looked up to see William Ward enter. I knew immediately who he was not only because of his reference to the call his daughter had already mentioned, but because she looked so much like him. He was tall and lean, with her red hair and pale skin, but he had a deep red beard and many more freckles. His eyes weren't her burnt orange brown, but rather the clear sky blue of her flecks.

"Who do we have here?" he asked, his voice soft and his smile easy as he looked at me.

"This is Caroline," Piper said just as Levi and I both opened our mouths to speak. "She got stranded with a family situation, so Levi offered her the apartment last night."

"Well, I'm glad we were able to assist, and I'm glad Levi offered our assistance. Welcome to our home."

"Thank you. I appreciate your hospitality," I said, flushed with embarrassment as the men's attention turned to me once more, their gazes lingering as William called to Gaynelle that breakfast could be served.

Gaynelle was tall and thin, nothing like the stereotypical image of a chef who enjoyed sampling her own wares. She wore a long white apron over her jeans and plaid shirt, and her greying hair was pulled up into a bun.

"Listen up, y'all. Let the ladies go first," she said as she opened each buffet dish and leaned back to avoid the rush of steam.

"Ladies? Are you counting Piper as a lady?" one man asked, and I recognized his voice as the high-pitched one I'd heard earlier. He was older than I'd imagined, probably late sixties. He had a thick moustache and a thick head of hair, and he laughed when Piper punched him in the arm.

"I'm a lady!" she protested, thumping another one on the head as he laughed. "Y'all shut up!"

Levi stood to pull my chair out, and I reluctantly followed Piper through the buffet line as the eyes of the hungry men bore into our backs.

"If y'all are lucky, we'll leave ya some," she taunted them as she piled sausage and eggs on her plate and covered them with two biscuits.

I couldn't believe the amount of food that was laid out. It was like a feast, and if they did this every Sunday, I didn't know how on earth the whole bunch wasn't waddling around in the throes of obesity.

"All right, mind your manners," Gaynelle demanded of the men as I made my way back to my seat, steering clear of the chairs being shoved back as the men formed a hasty line.

William took his place at the end of the line, gazing out the window with a melancholy half-smile, half-frown. He carried himself in such a non-assuming, humble way that it was hard to imagine him being the leader of such a rowdy crew, much less the father of such an outspoken daughter.

He must have felt my eyes upon him, because he turned and looked at me. He smiled, and I smiled back before looking down at my plate, embarrassed to have been caught staring.

CHAPTER 18

The meal continued with various conversations taking place around and across the table, and rarely did any length of time go by without a burst of laughter erupting.

"You okay?" Levi asked in a low voice directed only to me. "You seem awful quiet."

"It's a lot to take in," I said. "Hard to keep up."

He chuckled. "Yeah, I guess so. You get used to it. I've been having meals with this group since I was about twenty years old, so I guess I forget it's not a normal family breakfast."

Gaynelle cleared the plates as we each finished, and I wondered if I should offer to help her in the kitchen. I hated doing the dishes for my own small family, so I couldn't imagine cleaning up after all these people. But before I could extend a hand, Levi had stood.

"C'mon, I want to show you a little of the farm before you head over to the hospital."

He led me back through the house and into the foyer, and I paused to look at the photos, curious as to what Revae looked like and still fascinated by my resemblance with Piper.

While a few horses appeared in the pictures here and there, these were predominantly family photos, some of them so old they'd faded and had wrinkles and tears.

There were a few of Piper as she'd grown up, all of them portraying a tomboy who appeared happiest when barefoot and on horseback or somewhere outdoors. A senior portrait of her polished and preened looked almost out of place, or out of character, I suppose.

Piper had certainly taken after her father. She looked nothing like the raven-haired beauty beside William in so many of the photos.

Revae had been much shorter in stature than either her daughter or her husband, but the dancing eyes and exuberant smile in every photo of her conveyed a love of life and a fire much like I could see in her daughter.

I'd always been fascinated by mothers and daughters, but it was the photos of Piper and William that my eyes were drawn to more than the ones with Revae.

"These on this side are William's family," Levi said, pointing to the photos on the right. "Those are Revae's."

I glanced up at the photos of Revae's childhood and her family ancestors, but my attention quickly turned back to the other side.

None of the houses in the background of William's upbringing had the opulence or luxury of his current accommodations. He appeared to have several brothers and sisters, and based on what I could tell, he was probably the youngest.

The light from the window above the front entry door glared off some of the glass in the frames, and I moved forward and took a step closer to see them better.

Suddenly, I saw Ethan staring back at me from a sepia-tinted photo of a young boy, maybe five or six years at most. I gasped and looked closer, my hand to my chest as I stared at the image so much like my own son.

"What's wrong?" Levi asked, following my gaze.

"Who's that?" I pointed to the picture.

"I think it's William. It might be his brother Henry. They resemble the most, but I think that's William."

It was hard to tell the hair and eye color in the sepia tint, but it looked to be the same red and blue combination of my son. The deep freckles that dotted the face and the shy grin with snaggled teeth made it almost identical to Ethan's first grade school picture.

I pushed onto my tiptoes and strained to see the photo closer.

"What is it?" Levi asked his voice more concerned than before. "Is something wrong?"

"That picture," I whispered. "It looks like my son. Ethan." I moved to the side to see it from a different angle, but no matter how I looked at it, I could clearly see Ethan's grin in the face staring back at me. "That's so weird."

"Yeah, that is weird," Levi said. "Want me to find out for sure who's in the picture?"

"Which one?" William said as he walked into the foyer behind us.

I jumped at the sound of his voice and stepped back from the photo.

He stopped beside us and peered at the wall, pointing to the picture I'd been staring at. "That one? That's yours truly back in, oh, nineteen-something. I was probably six in that photo? There's another one somewhere—" he scanned the wall and pointed up to it when he saw it— "there. That one was taken the same day. That's me and my brother, Henry; my brother, James; and my sisters, Patricia and Helen."

I looked at the group of children, searching only for William to see if the creepy resemblance to Ethan was there. It wasn't as pronounced as in the picture of William alone. The group photo had all the kids lined up, and William was turned looking up at his sister, but had glanced back at the camera for the shot.

"They're wonderful photos," I said. "I love how you have the old and new intermingled here."

"Well, that was Revae. She believed family history was a vital part of who we are, and that we couldn't look forward without looking back. There's no telling how much she spent restoring old family photos and getting them framed. They're all over the house."

"It's a beautiful home," I said.

"Thank you. That was Revae, as well. I can't take credit for it."

He spoke of her with such fondness that the love they shared seemed undiminished by her absence.

I wasn't sure what words were appropriate, or if any were even needed, but it felt wrong not to acknowledge a loss he so clearly still felt. "I'm sorry to hear of your loss."

His tender blue eyes met mine, and the pain there pricked at my heart.

"Thank you. Cancer is a cruel demon, and no matter how much land you own and how successful you seem to be, it can still rob you of what matters most." He turned and clapped his hand on Levi's shoulder. "Are you gonna give Caroline the nickel tour? Show her around the farm?"

"I'd be happy to if she's interested," Levi said, and they both looked me at with smiles of expectation.

The strong resemblance in the photograph had set the wheels turning in my mind, and while I didn't necessarily want to ride around and look at barns, I did want to learn more about William Ward and his family.

"I'd love a tour. I just need to make a quick call to Patsy and make sure everything's okay at the hospital." I smiled at Levi as he held the front door open for William and me to walk through it. "Hey, William, you wouldn't happen to know someone by the name of Caterina Russo, would you?"

William squinted his eyes against the bright sunlight and scratched his head. "Russo? I don't believe I do."

"Are you sure? What about Caterina? Do you know someone named Caterina? Or did you know someone named Caterina? Like, a really long time ago?"

William shook his head. "Can't recall a Caterina. Why?"

"Oh, no reason. She's from this area, so I thought perhaps you might know her."

"No, I'm sorry. The name doesn't ring a bell."

Disappointment settled over me, though I don't know what I had expected. It wasn't like William was going to immediately recall a tryst from over three decades ago and confide it to a total stranger.

"Okay. It was a long shot."

"So where are you from?" William asked as we walked down the front steps.

"I live in Gainesville now. I grew up in Jacksonville."

"Ah. East Coast. Well, it was nice meeting you, and if you need to stay another night, our door is always open."

"Thank you. I'll be heading back home this afternoon, though. My kids will be back from their camping trip."

"Oh, how many kids do you have?" William asked.

"Two. Eva is fourteen and Ethan is ten. He'd love this place. All these trees to climb. The horses. He'd be running wild."

"Well, feel free to bring him anytime. We do formal tours of the farms on Tuesdays, but any time you'd like to come, a friend of Levi's is always welcome here. I'm sure he wouldn't mind giving them a tour as well. You should invite them to Farm Day."

We said goodbye to William and continued walking toward the parking area.

"What was that all about?" Levi asked once his boss was out of earshot. "Why did you think William would know Caterina?"

"I don't know," I said. "I just couldn't get over how much that picture looked like Ethan. It's probably just my imagination, what with finding Caterina and all. I guess I'm seeing family members everywhere I look."

"You think William is related to you? To Caterina?"

I shrugged as I opened the Audi's door and dug my phone out of my purse.

"No. I mean, I don't know. He could be. They're both from this area, right?"

"I think William's family is from up around Ocala. He moved to Cedar Creek when he and Revae got married, and they built this farm together."

I flipped through the photos on my phone and found an older picture of Ethan, turning it around to show Levi.

"This is Ethan about two years ago. But if you saw a picture of him when he was six, I'm telling you, it's uncanny."

"Oh, wow. Yeah. I can see where you thought there was a resemblance. But if he didn't know Caterina, and he's not from this area, I don't know. Maybe someone else in his family is connected to you?"

"At this point, so much is unknown that anyone could be related to me. Hell, you could be related to me for all we know."

He chuckled as I dialed Patsy's number.

"Hello, dear," she said. "Did you make it home okay?"

"Actually, I ended up staying in Cedar Creek. How's Caterina? Any change?"

"No. I got here about a half hour ago, and the doctor hasn't been by yet. Are you coming to the hospital?"

"Yeah, but I had something I wanted to do first, if you think it's not urgent that I come right away."

"I can't see that it would be. Nothing has changed, and like I said, they haven't even gotten to her yet."

Levi had walked around to the driver's side of his truck, but I turned my back to him and stepped farther away in case he could still hear me.

"Patsy, did Caterina ever tell you anything about my father? Do you know who he is?"

"No, honey. She didn't want to talk about that, and it seemed an emotional issue for her, so I didn't press the matter."

"Okay. I'll be there soon. Call me if you get any news from the doctors or if there's any change, okay?"

"Sure."

"Everything okay with Caterina?" Levi asked when I'd finished my call with Patsy.

I had looked up several times to see him watching me, and I knew he was probably curious as to why I'd walked away and spoken so quietly.

"No change. So, what's this about a tour?" I said as I walked to the truck and climbed in the passenger seat.

We set off with Levi explaining the history of the farm and how William and Revae had started with two acres and two horses. They'd built the little block house near the entrance of the farm, and the business had grown under their passionate dedication and hard work. William's focus was on training and rehabilitation, and Revae's had been on breeding and racing. Together, they'd been a powerhouse couple in the world of thoroughbreds.

The rolling green hills and regal oaks made for a picturesque backdrop to Levi's history lesson about the farm, but my thoughts kept returning to my own history and the unknown.

Was I somehow connected to William Ward? That would explain my passing resemblance to Piper, his picture's resemblance to Ethan, and my strange sense of recognizing him. But he'd said he didn't know Caterina. Perhaps it was a brother of his who filled in the missing piece of my puzzle?

"Okay, what's going on in that pretty head of yours?" Levi asked.

"What? What do you mean?"

"I just told you that stable was for the dancing pink elephants, and you nodded and didn't seem the least bit surprised. You've been half-listening since we got in the truck, and it might be nothing more than a statement about my tour guide skills, but I'm guessing it has something to do with the picture on the wall."

I turned in my seat to face him as he slowed the truck to a crawl. "I can't stop thinking about it. I don't know how to explain it, but I have this feeling I'm somehow connected to William Ward."

"But you asked if he knew Caterina, and he didn't."

"Maybe he just doesn't remember her? I mean, it was thirty-five years ago."

"Which would have made William, what? Seventeen? I can't speak for every teenage boy, but knowing William Ward like I do, I'd be willing to bet his experience with girls at that age was somewhat limited. I'm not thinking he'd forget something like that."

"Maybe one of his brothers, then? They're older, right? So maybe they visited this area and met Caterina?"

Levi gazed out across the pasture and sighed. "Maybe. I don't know Henry and James as well as I do William, so I'm not sure where they were at that time."

"But you could find out, couldn't you?"

He looked at me and grinned. "You want me to ask Henry Ward or James Ward if they slept with someone named Caterina thirty-five years ago?"

"Technically, thirty-six or maybe even thirty-seven given my age and allotting time for pregnancy. And you don't have to ask if they slept with her. Who does that? Just maybe bring up her name the next time you see them."

He lifted his cap and rubbed his forehead before pulling the cap back on. "I think it's a better bet to ask Caterina who your dad is when she wakes up."

"*If* she wakes up." A tremor danced over my skin as I said the words, but I had to be realistic. "Levi, I don't know if Caterina is going to pull through this, and I don't know what she'll tell me if she does. Patsy said Caterina didn't want to talk about my father."

"She might not have told Patsy, but I'm sure she would tell you. I mean, it's your father. Surely, she wouldn't keep something like that from you."

"I don't know. I've found out quite a bit people were keeping from me the last couple of days. Why would she be any different? I may have to find my father on my own."

It was strange to realize that I'd never fixated much on who my father was. I think it may have been because my own father left me at such a young age. Not having a father made the concept of having one somewhat blurry and out of focus. I knew what it was like to have a mother, so I obsessed with what my birth mother might be like. But I'd never given my birth father much thought.

Now that the idea of finding him had taken root, I knew it was something I had to do. It wasn't enough to know who one of my parents had been. If I was going to understand who I was and where I'd come from, I needed both sides of the story.

CHAPTER 19

L evi's phone rang, and I could tell by the look on his face as he listened that it wasn't good news.

"Afraid I'm going to have to cut our tour short. The mare's in trouble, and it looks like the foal is gonna get here much earlier than we'd planned."

He turned the truck around, barely missing the fence that lined the winding drive, and then he sped through the curves and the roundabout to take me back to my car.

William was standing in the gravel lot talking to one of the men I'd seen at breakfast, and Levi called to him as we got out of his truck.

"She's foaling."

William frowned and gave a little shake of his head in either disbelief or disappointment. "You headed up there?"

"Yeah, I wanted to see Caroline off first. You coming?"

"I gotta get on the road to Ocala," William said. "Keep me posted."

Levi came around the front of his truck as I opened the door to the Audi and waited for him to finish with William.

The events of the morning since I came downstairs had been so chaotic and fast-paced that I hadn't had much time to consider what had transpired between Levi and me and what it meant, if anything. It was hard to believe we'd only known each other less than twenty-four hours. There was a comfort and ease between us that seemed much closer and more familiar than it should.

We'd spent the morning discussing William and the farm, and we still hadn't talked about our encounter the night before. Levi had been the perfect gentleman all morning, not even coming close to touching me, despite my nerves buzzing with awareness of him being near.

Now it had come time to say goodbye, and we had an audience.

"Sorry I have to rush off," he said, stuffing his hands in his pockets and squashing any hope I'd had for a passionate parting.

"No problem. I need to get to the hospital anyway." I hoped my voice didn't convey my disappointment.

"I wish I could, well, I wish we could…" His voice trailed off, and he shifted his weight back and forth on his feet. I knew he was antsy to go.

"It's okay, Levi. I know you need to get to the horse. I understand. Thanks for showing me around. For last night. The apartment, I mean. The place to sleep." I blushed as my words tumbled out on top of each other.

"I'm glad I could help," he said, and the handsome grin appeared, nearly undoing me.

It was all I could do not to throw my arms around him and lay one on him.

He stepped a bit closer, and his eyes lingered on my lips before coming back up to meet my gaze.

I wanted to scream, *"Kiss me already!"* but instead I said, "Okay, maybe I'll see you around."

He reached and took my hand, the contact like a lightning bolt shooting a burst of energy through me.

"Can I call you? Later?" he asked.

I nodded, and our eyes locked as we stood there silent, my hand still in his.

"Okay, well, goodbye, Caroline."

"Goodbye."

He planted a soft kiss on my lips, not nearly as passionate as I would have liked, and then he was gone. He was in his truck and pulling away as I stood there wondering how my life had grown so complicated in so short a period of time.

I realized William and the other man were still standing in the same spot, watching me with bemused expressions on their faces.

"Um, nice meeting you all," I said with a smile as my face burned red. "I hope the horse will be okay."

"They'll save her. I have no doubt," William said. "I have the best team she could hope for. She's in great hands."

He said goodbye to the other man and walked toward me.

"I hear you've got someone in the hospital over in Jensen."

I jumped at the opportunity to talk to him further. I knew it was a long shot that anyone in his family might be related to me, but I had nothing to lose in pursuing the theory.

"Yes, my birth mother. Caterina."

"Nothing too serious, I hope."

"Pneumonia, unfortunately. She's sort of in a coma. Like, not a real coma, but one they put her in. They sedated her. The whole thing's strange because I've never met her, actually. We were supposed to meet yesterday, but she was rushed to the hospital before I got the chance."

"Levi told me about the mix-up with the car and you getting delayed. I'm sorry you got caught up in their foolishness. My daughter has had a bit of an unconventional upbringing. I was probably a little too loose on those reins. Especially after her mom passed. Piper's a mouthy one, and she dishes out quite a bit with the boys on the farm. Some of them don't hesitate to give it right back to her. As they should."

The melancholy smile I'd seen earlier was back. It was like half his mouth was smiling, and the other half wasn't.

"I have a teenage daughter," I said. "Fourteen. So, I understand the mouthy part. I don't think I've held the reins very well, either. Not since her father and I split, anyway. I think before, I was the disciplinarian and the one who enforced the rules, which was hard. I still am, but after the divorce, it's seemed like more of an uphill battle, and I've probably let them get away with a lot I shouldn't have because I feel guilty for their pain."

"I suppose we do the best we can with managing their pain along with our own pain, too. Some days we do better than others. Parenting is much tougher than raising horses, that's for sure." He sighed and rubbed his knuckles across his beard. "But again, I'm sorry you got caught in the cross fire with Piper and Levi. He came to work here when she was ten, and the two of them have always been like brother and sister, teasing each other mercilessly."

He glanced at his watch, and I could feel the seconds ticking by faster as my time with him was coming to an end. I hadn't yet gotten the answers I needed, and my mind raced as I tried to figure out how to find out more without coming right out and asking him if it was possible one of his brothers had known Caterina Russo around the time I was conceived.

"My kids tease each other, too," I blurted out, trying to prolong the conversation. "I feel like I should wear black and white stripes and carry a referee whistle most days."

He chuckled, and I looked down at the phone and keys in my hand, desperate to come up with any way to find out if our histories were connected.

"Wanna see a picture of them?" I asked, flipping through the photos to find the one I'd shown Levi. "This is Ethan, my ten-year-old. He has red hair, too."

"So, he does," William said, smiling as he took the phone for a closer look. "He's a right handsome fellow."

"Yes, he is. He sort of reminds me of that picture of you in the hallway. You guys have similar coloring. And the freckles, of course."

William studied the picture as I watched his face for any sign of recognition or consideration of it.

He smiled as he handed the phone back. "Florida sun is a curse for those of us with freckles. Teach him to use sunscreen now. You said you have a daughter as well?"

I found a picture of Eva and showed it to him, and he proclaimed her a beauty. "Like her mother," he said with a wink. "Well, I'd best get on the road, and I guess you have some place to be as well. I hope your mother is better soon, and that your meeting with her goes well once you get to talk."

"Thanks again for your hospitality, William."

"No problem," he said with a nod. "Glad we were able to help."

The melancholy half-smile reappeared as he turned to go, and I hoped it wouldn't be the last time I'd have a chance to talk with him.

CHAPTER 20

My phone rang as I was parking in the hospital garage. I grimaced when I saw it was Lorna. I'd meant to call her once I left the farm, but the events of the morning and the night before had consumed my thoughts.

It was almost like I'd been whisked away to an alternate universe where my real life didn't exist.

"Hey, Mom," I said, not sure I was ready to confront my life again.

"Where are you? I went to your house this morning after yoga to bring you a bagel and make sure we're okay. I was so upset when we hung up last night, but I tried to respect your wishes and give you space. I thought surely you'd call first thing this morning, but when I didn't hear from you, well, are you okay? Where are you?"

I took a deep breath and pondered lying to my mother about my whereabouts for the first time since I was in high school.

"I'm fine. I ended up staying in Cedar Creek last night, and I'm heading into the hospital now to check on Caterina."

"Oh," she said, her voice quiet and her disappointment clear. "You're still there?"

"Yes."

"Oh."

"I'll be home this afternoon," I said, gathering my purse and getting out of the car.

"But aren't the kids coming home this afternoon?"

"Brad said they'd be home by five, so I have plenty of time." I locked the door and headed toward the entrance of the hospital.

"Well, don't cut it too close. You never know what he's going to do."

"True. He might bring them back before noon if the weekend was too much for him. I'll text Eva and ask her to let me know when they're on their way."

"Have you heard from them? Are they enjoying themselves?"

I dropped the keys and bent to pick them up, spilling the contents of my purse in the process.

"Crap. I just spilled my purse everywhere. Eva texted yesterday evening to say it was going okay, but I haven't heard anything from them today." I squatted to pick up the lipstick, sunglasses, half-eaten roll of mints, and random receipts.

"Really? And you're okay with that? I'd think you'd be a nervous wreck by now if you hadn't heard from them."

"Eva would text me if anything was wrong. I gotta go, Mom. I'm getting in an elevator."

I thought about her words as I put the phone back in my purse and straightened Piper's shirt. If I'd been home alone, I would have been climbing the walls wondering what time they'd come home. While I looked forward to seeing them and hearing about their trip, it felt nice to have something else occupy my thoughts for a change and keep me from obsessing. It had been liberating, in a way.

Patsy was seated in the family waiting room, and she jumped up to meet me as soon as I entered.

"You're here! Let me tell the nurse. She just came by saying the doctor wanted to speak with us, and I asked if she could give you a few minutes to get here."

"You didn't have to do that," I said as she rushed out of the room, beckoning me to follow. "You could have talked to them and told me what they said."

"I figured it was better to have you here so you could ask any questions you might have. Nurse? If you could, please let the doctor know we're ready. Caterina's daughter is here."

I flinched at the title, still uncomfortable with carrying it, even if it was true. Caterina and I didn't know each other, and my inclusion in her medical discussions seemed an invasion of her privacy.

The nurse led us to a small meeting room with posters on the wall bearing inspirational quotes and photos of doves and sunset tides.

"Are you okay?" Patsy asked.

I nodded, unsure of how to answer the question. I felt different.

Like the past twenty-four hours had changed me. My world had splintered, and suddenly there was light coming in from all these new directions.

"I'm fine. Just tired. I didn't sleep well."

That much was true, though it wasn't entirely the reason behind what I'm sure was a dazed expression. It was all a little much to comprehend.

The door opened, and the doctor entered, wearing the stereotypical white coat and stethoscope.

"Good morning," she said with a bright smile. "My name is Dr. Agustin. Unfortunately, I don't have much news to share. We've gotten Ms. Russo's blood pressure and heart rate stable, but the pneumonia has not responded as we'd hoped with the first round of antibiotics."

"That's bad, isn't it?" asked Patsy.

"Not necessarily. We certainly would have preferred to have this cleared up on the first try, but it's common for there to be some effort in finding the right antibiotic for the job. We still have several options in our arsenal, and we'll continue until we find the one that knocks this out and gets her up and breathing on her own."

"How long will that take?" Patsy said. "Isn't there a limit to how long she can be on the ventilator?"

"Yes, but we've got time. For right now, she's comfortable. The ventilator makes it much less work for her to breathe, and the sedation also allows her brain to rest and not exert as much energy. We want to maintain that while we search for the best antibiotic."

The doctor answered a few more of Patsy's questions and then asked if I had any of my own, but I shook my head. Even if I'd had questions, I don't know that I would have asked them. I felt too much like an intruder, listening in on Caterina's medical prognosis and pretending to be a family member when I was, in fact, a stranger.

When she was finished, Dr. Agustin escorted us back to the family waiting room and assured us they were doing all they could and would update us if there was any change.

I sank into a chair and rubbed my eyes after the doctor left, overwhelmed by everything I needed to process from the last couple of days.

"Let's go get you a cup of coffee," Patsy said. "You look beat. I'm sure this is a lot to take in."

"I don't think there's a cup of coffee strong enough to help take all this in, Patsy." But I stood and went down to the cafeteria with her anyway.

Once we were seated, I texted Eva asking her to let me know when they left the campground.

"On our way home now. Be there in about half an hour" was her reply.

I nearly spewed coffee all over the table and Patsy.

"Oh my God! I have to go!"

"Why? What's wrong? What's happened?" Patsy cried.

"I have to call my mom."

I dialed Lorna's number and prayed she didn't have the phone silenced for a movie, her favorite Sunday pastime.

"Hi, sweetheart. Is everything okay? You on your way back so soon?"

"No, but Brad's on his way to the house with the kids. They'll be there in half an hour."

Patsy's eyes widened as she heard my words.

"What?" Lorna said, her disapproval clear. "But he said he wasn't going to be home until five!"

"Well, he obviously left the campground early. I need you to go to my house and be there when they get there."

"I knew he'd do something like this. I'm sure they'll be fine until you get there, though. They've been home alone before. Eva's fifteen, and you'd been staying home alone for years when you were fifteen."

"It's not that, Mom," I said, walking away from Patsy. "I don't want Brad to drop them off and no one be there. Please, Mom? Can you just drive over there? Like, now? If you leave right now, you can probably be there around the same time they arrive. Maybe even beat them there."

"But the girls are here, and we've made margaritas and we're gonna watch a movie."

"Mom, please!"

"Oh, fine. I declare, you get yourself in such a tizzy over Brad Miller not being happy about something. When was the last time *he* cared what *you* thought and whether or not you were happy?"

"Please don't start."

Her sigh was so heavy I could practically feel it through the phone.

"Do you need me to stay until you get home, or can I head back here once Brad leaves? Is he going to be okay keeping your car?"

I'd completely forgotten we switched cars. "Oh, crap! Damn. I have his car. Okay, when you get there, just tell him I had to run some errands, and I'll bring the car to his apartment when I'm done."

"You want me to lie to him?"

"It's Brad, Mom. He's been lying to us for years. It'll be okay. Just tell him I'll bring him the car, please? I don't want to get into it with him about where I'm at and why I'm here."

"And what should I tell the kids?"

I closed my eyes and took a deep breath, trying to think of the best scenario to give them that would be honest and factual but limit the number of questions I had to answer.

"Tell them I had a friend who was ill and needed me to visit her in the hospital. Tell them I'll be home soon. I'm leaving now."

I texted Eva that I was out and Grandma would be waiting for them at the house, and then I walked back to Patsy's table and gathered up my coffee cup, stirrer, and empty cream container. "I've got to go. My kids are coming home early."

Patsy stood and helped me wipe the table with a napkin. "It sounded like that was unexpected news. Do drive carefully, and I hope the car doesn't give you any problems."

"You'll call me if anything changes with Caterina?"

"Of course, yes! Go. Take care of your kids, and I'll handle things here. Don't you worry at all."

I was torn between wanting to go upstairs to say goodbye to Caterina and wanting to get on the road and minimize the amount of time I was away from my kids. Caterina didn't even know I'd been there, so she'd hardly notice me being gone. But I couldn't shake the fear that something would happen to her, and I would live the rest of my life knowing I didn't take the chance when I had it.

"I'm gonna go up and see if they'll let me see Caterina again before I leave."

Patsy smiled. "That would be lovely. If you're sure you have time."

"I'll make time."

We took the elevator together, then Patsy went to the family waiting room while I asked the nurse if I could visit Caterina.

She looked exactly the same as she had the day before. The breathing tube and ventilator kept a steady rhythm as the heart monitor beeped in time, and Tim McGraw sang softly in the background on the CD player Patsy had brought in.

I took her hand once more, admiring the slender fingers and pretty violet nails.

"Hi, Caterina. It's Caroline. I'm back, but I have to head out. My kids are coming home, and I need to be there for them. Patsy's going to keep me updated, though, and I'll come back to visit as soon as I can. We have so much to talk about, and I can't wait to meet you. Awake, I mean."

I stared at her long, thick lashes, wishing she'd open her eyes and say hello.

Unlike the first time I'd seen her, this time I knew for sure that she was my mother, and it tugged at my emotions to have to leave her.

"I wish I could stay longer," I whispered, leaning closer to her, hoping somehow she could hear me in her state. "I'm so happy to finally find you. I'm sorry I have to go. You take care."

When I left her room, I went back to the family waiting room to say goodbye to Patsy, surprised to see her in conversation with Levi, who was seated next to her.

My heart leapt at the sight of him all showered and fresh with a powder-blue collared shirt and a pair of snug jeans.

"Hey, what are you doing here?" I asked, my somber mood transformed.

He stood and greeted me with a huge smile. "I felt bad that we didn't get a proper goodbye, so I thought I'd drive over. Patsy says I nearly missed you."

"Yeah, I have to head back home. The kids are coming in early."

I couldn't believe how happy I was to see him. It was a bit ridiculous, actually. I didn't even really know the man, and yet, you would have thought he hung the moon the way my heart was racing and my insides were tingling.

"What about the mare?" I asked. "How's she doing?"

"She's up. She's good. A little weak, but I think she'll be fine."

"Did she have her baby?"

"Yeah," he said, his smile widening even more. "He's a bit small, but he's already nursing, so that's a good sign."

"Good, good."

"Can I walk you to your car?" he asked.

"Yeah, just let me say goodbye to Patsy."

I bent to hug her, and she half-raised from her seat, her knitting supplies spilling from her lap. Levi scrambled to catch the yarn before it unraveled, and then he picked up the rest of her things and put them in the basket by her feet as she stood.

"Thank you so much for everything, Patsy. For calling me. For giving me the proof. Thank you most of all for being such a good friend to Caterina. She's so lucky to have you."

We hugged tightly, and she grabbed me by both arms and squeezed. "Cat is going to pull through this, and the two of you are going to have years of catching up together. I can feel it."

"I hope so. Call me if there's any change."

She smiled and hugged me once more. "You know I will. And this one here?" she whispered against my ear. "He's a keeper. Don't let him go."

We told her goodbye and headed down to the garage, both of us silent the whole way.

"Well," I said when we'd reached the Audi, "I guess this is goodbye. Again." I opened the door and tossed my purse into the passenger seat, then turned back to face Levi, who stood on the other side of the door.

I wondered if he was thinking the same thing I was, and if he was as disappointed as me to think it would likely be the last time we saw each other.

"So, will you be coming back down soon to visit Caterina?"

"I hope so. Our schedule during the week is insane, but I'm keeping in touch with Patsy, and she'll let me know if there's any change. I guess I'll figure something out when the time comes."

"Let me know if you're in town. Maybe we could get together. I'd like to see you again."

"I'd like that, too." I smiled, enjoying the small ray of happiness shining in the midst of the stress cloud surrounding me.

He grinned as he leaned over the window, the door swinging

toward me with his weight.

"I had a good time last night, Caroline, and I wish this morning hadn't been so crazy. That we could have had more time."

He leaned closer still, and I moved forward to meet him, cursing the door between us as he stroked his fingers along my cheek and softly pressed his lips to mine. The lingering sensations he'd stirred the night before came roaring back to life as the kiss deepened. Levi threaded his fingers into my hair and tilted my head back as his tongue sought mine. I opened up to him without hesitation, savoring what might be the last kiss I would get for a long while.

We pulled apart breathless, and I could see the hunger I felt reflected back in the dark desire of his eyes.

"Damn. I gotta go," I said, not ready to say goodbye but unable to shut off the nagging thought of Eva and Ethan arriving at the house with me gone.

"I know. Just one more for the road."

He smiled and stepped around the car door, taking me in his arms as he gently pushed my body back against the car, his mouth claiming mine as a moan escaped me.

When I'd been kissed thoroughly and passionately, he pulled back, tracing his thumb over my bottom lip as he whispered, "Drive carefully. Don't have any blowouts or need any tow trucks."

"I'll certainly try not to. I'd hate to get the car stolen again."

He chuckled and shook his head, looking across the garage and then back to me. "Can I call you later?"

I nodded, and he tucked his knuckle under my chin and planted one more quick kiss on my lips before turning to walk away.

I sank into the driver's seat in a daze, flushed with the heat of the fire raging inside me.

God! That man could fire me up so quickly. Just one touch and I was blazing, ready to go.

Somewhere in the whirlwind of finding my birth mother and sparking an interest in who my actual father might be, Levi had awakened something in me. Something invigorating and intoxicating, and I wanted to feel more of it.

After years of a ho-hum existence, I felt alive again. Like a woman again, instead of just a mother, a daughter, or an ex-wife.

I told myself it must be the length of time my body had been dormant. Or maybe it was just the heightened drama of the weekend and the circumstances that had thrown us together in so many intense encounters. Whatever it was, I didn't remember ever experiencing such a strong physical reaction to anyone before.

The words of the men from earlier in the morning came back to me, and I shook my head to push away their remarks on Levi's charm and his skills with the opposite sex.

Perhaps they were right about him and I'd already become his latest victim, but in that moment, it felt too good to care.

CHAPTER 21

"Where are you?" Brad said in the call I'd been expecting since leaving Cedar Creek.

"I'm driving home now, and I can be at your apartment in about an hour and a half."

"An hour and a half?" he yelled. "Where the hell did you go in my car?"

"A friend fell ill and was admitted to the hospital, so I went down to visit her. You have the Tahoe if you need to go somewhere."

He groaned. "I have plans tonight, and I was looking forward to driving my convertible. I bought the damned car on Thursday and had to hand it over to you on Friday. I haven't even broken it in yet. And what friend do you have that far away? Who's in the hospital?"

"It's a new friend. Not anyone you've met."

He scoffed. "Where'd you meet a new friend that lives hours away?"

My initial reaction was stress as I considered explaining to him about Caterina. I could already hear him admonishing me for wanting to meet my birth mother and chiding me for making the trip.

But then I reminded myself of what my therapist had been drilling into me—that Brad was no longer entitled to knowing every detail of my life, and I wasn't obligated to share anything with him that didn't directly affect the kids.

"What time are your plans?" I asked. "Would it work better for me to meet you somewhere else or is the apartment okay?"

"You didn't answer my question."

"And I'm not going to. Do you want to meet me at the apartment or elsewhere?"

A rush of adrenaline surged through me. Throughout our

relationship, any defiance was met with swift retribution, sometimes verbal and sometimes in passive ways that I often didn't realize until afterward, so I'd learned to just go along with whatever he wanted to keep the peace in our lives.

I'd gained a measure of independence over the weekend, though. I'd had experiences that weren't connected to either Brad or my children for the first time in seventeen years. The taste of freedom had been empowering, and it felt good to tell him no.

"The apartment, I guess. Not like I have a choice since you're holding my car hostage."

"I didn't ask to borrow your car, Brad. You needed me to take your car so you could borrow mine. I'll see you in an hour and a half."

Lorna called as soon as he had left the house. "Whew, he's mad. I haven't seen him that angry since Ethan broke the front window with the Frisbee. He wasn't happy when he got here and you weren't home, but when he got off the phone with you, he was furious. What did you say to set him off?"

"I simply told him that I was bringing the car to his apartment. He acts like I asked to borrow it or something. If he'd brought them home at five like he said he was gonna, I would have been home, and none of this would have happened."

Well, he still would have exploded once he saw the key damage on the driver's side, but I refused to let him make me feel guilty for driving the car when he left it with me for the weekend.

"Okay, well, the girls are waiting for me at my house, and the margaritas are melting, so can I head back home? The kids should be okay until you get here, right?"

"Yeah, that's fine. Put Eva on the phone, please?"

"Hey, Mom," Eva said. "Where are you? Dad was really mad you weren't here."

"I'm on my way home. I'll be there in a couple of hours."

"A couple of hours? Geez. Where'd you go?"

"I had to visit a friend in the hospital, and now I have to return the car to Dad's. I'll be home after that."

"He's really angry, Mom."

I took a deep breath and let it out slowly, forcing myself not to say anything negative about her father. "How was your weekend?"

"Horrible," Eva sighed. "The mosquitoes nearly ate us alive. Dad couldn't get a fire started so we had to drive into town and get something to eat. Ethan has some kind of rash all over the right side of his body. It's itching him something terrible. And Dad was mad the whole weekend about not having a cell signal. He kept pacing the campsite holding his phone up to the sky and cursing."

"Sounds like a great weekend! I'm sorry it didn't go well, sweetheart. Has Ethan put anything on the rash?"

"Nope. He's playing video games in the den. I told him he's not allowed to do video on Sunday, but he said Grandma told him it was okay."

"We'll make an exception to the no screen time rule for today. I imagine you guys have gone without screen time all weekend, right? Have Grandma look at the rash and tell her there's some Benadryl in the medicine cabinet upstairs. Better yet, will you go find it and bring it down to her? I don't want her rummaging through the cabinet and questioning everything in there."

"Sure. Do you want to talk to her again?"

"No, that's okay. She's gonna head home, but make sure she gets some cream on Ethan first."

"Will do. And Mom? Thanks for the screen time."

I smiled as the call ended, surprised to hear gratitude from my daughter.

I hoped Lorna knew how thankful I was for her. For the mother she'd been. For the support she'd always given me. For dropping everything and leaving a group of elderly women partying alone in her house with margaritas so she could deal with my ex-husband and take care of my kids.

My thoughts turned to Caterina and the fact that she had no one other than Patsy. I wondered if she was lonely. I wondered if she had thought about me over the years and if she'd ever regretted the choices she'd made.

Had my father known about me? Had they decided together it would be best to have another family raise me? Had they continued dating after that? Or had that been what split them up?

I wondered if she'd stayed in contact with him, and if he knew any of the information in my file about my whereabouts and my upbringing.

I had to get back to Cedar Creek. I had so many questions, and my only chance of finding the answers lay in the tiny town nestled among the hills of Central Florida.

The miles flew by with my mind so preoccupied, and I pulled into the parking lot of Brad's building with five minutes to spare.

His voice was gruff when I called to tell him I was there. He came storming down the stairs with a frown plastered on his face, and whereas it would have set me trembling in the past to see him so angry, the knowledge that I could get in my Tahoe and drive away without suffering the consequences of his ire kept me from reacting.

"Where the hell have you been?" he asked as I stepped out of the car, and then the open door caught his eye. He came around the front fender and spread his arms wide. "What is this? What the hell? What did you do to my car?"

"Someone keyed it."

He knelt and ran his fingers across the jagged line before jerking his hand back and standing to glare at me.

"I can see that, Caroline! Who keyed it? Did you do this?"

My mouth dropped open in shock. "Excuse me? You think I would key your car? C'mon, Brad. Give me a little credit here."

"I don't know what you'd do, Caroline. You take my car traipsing all over the state God-knows-where and bring it back with the paint ruined. You refuse to tell where you were or who you were with. What the hell is the matter with you?"

He stopped and cocked his head to one side, his hand on his hip.

"You seem different. You look different. Did you do something with your hair? And what are you wearing? Those jeans are too damned tight. You look like a sausage squeezed into a casing that's too small for it. Have you gained weight?"

I took a step back as his words slapped my pride.

"No, I haven't. If you'll just give me my keys, I'll be on my way so you can proceed with your plans."

"Not now I can't," he yelled. "You ruined my car. How am I supposed to pick someone up with any measure of pride and bring them out to see this?" He gestured toward the car and then shock registered on his face. "Wait a minute. Is that a new tire?" He bent to look at the front tire, and then stepped back to look at the back one. "You put a new tire on my car?"

"Two, actually. The back tire blew out on me and nearly got me killed. The mechanic said it was best to buy the tires in pairs, and that it would do better with the new ones on the front, so he moved the old ones to the back."

He moved around the front of the car to see the other side and then looked back at me.

"You can't make those decisions without me. What if I don't like these tires? What if that's not how I wanted things handled?"

"Then you should have taken care of the tire before suggesting I drive the car for the weekend. If you don't like these, you can go buy another set. I don't care. Just give me my keys. It's been a long weekend, and I'm ready to go home."

"You still didn't tell me how this happened." He walked back to the driver's side of the car and pointed at the line through the paint.

"Well, I didn't *see* it happen, so I can't say for sure, but it looks like someone dragged a key down the side of the car."

"Obviously. Where?"

"In a parking lot."

He stepped toward me and crossed his arms.

"I assumed it was in a parking lot, smart ass. What did the police say?"

I shrugged and shifted my weight to one side, bracing for the escalation of his anger.

"I didn't call the cops."

"What?" He leaned forward to tower over me, using his height for intimidation. I tried not to shrink back, knowing he would never hit me. At least, he never had before.

"They wouldn't have been able to find out who did it. These things happen in parking lots all the time."

"Really? Do they? Because I've been in many parking lots, Caroline, and I've never had someone vandalize my vehicle. Why won't you tell me where you were? Maybe they had security cameras."

"They didn't."

"Where were you?" He leaned closer, and I took a step back despite my best resolve not to.

"I was at a bar, okay? What does it matter where I was? It happened. I'll pay for the repairs."

"With what? Money that I give you every month? Money that's supposed to go to taking care of my kids, by the way. Not for you to be out whoring in a bar. What bar? Where were you? Who were you with?"

He stepped forward again as he spat out the questions rapid-fire, and I stepped back, my hip landing against the side of the car.

"None of your business. I don't ask you what you do on the weekends when I have the kids. I expect the same courtesy from you."

"Because you're not supporting me!" he roared. "As long as I pay your damned bills, I have some say-so in how you spend your money. I don't think it's appropriate for my children's mother to be wearing tight-ass jeans and hanging out in bars where vagrants vandalize the parking lot. What kind of mother does that?"

My anger snapped, and I met him toe-to-toe. "Don't you dare even insinuate I'm not a good mother. I am a damned good mother, and it has nothing to do with the size of my jeans or how I choose to spend my time on the weekends. You gave up the right to tell me where I could go and what I could do when you chose to end our marriage to pursue your affair."

"Well, maybe I wouldn't have needed to look elsewhere if you had put out a little more often."

"Um, excuse me," said a woman pushing a stroller on the sidewalk, the young boy at her side staring at us wide-eyed and open-mouthed. "There are children playing in this area. Could the two of you take this discussion inside?"

"I'm sorry," I said to her, and then to her son. "I'm leaving, actually. There's nothing more to discuss."

I dangled the keys to the car in front of Brad, pulling them back when he reached for them. "My keys?" I asked, holding my palm open.

He dug in his pocket and tossed them to me, and I handed him back his keys.

"This conversation is *not* finished," he said. "Not by a long shot."

I turned to go, my entire body trembling with anger, frustration, and a smidgeon of fear.

CHAPTER 22

It wasn't like I didn't shoulder any blame for the failure of our marriage. I realized I'd been too preoccupied with the kids. I knew I'd been oblivious to the growing distance between Brad and me until it was too late.

Life was like a treadmill on a high-speed incline, and it was all I could do to keep up without crashing. The chaos of parenting seemed never-ending, so there was no time or energy left over at the end of the day for *us*. I wasn't focused on Brad's needs.

When Brad first announced that he was leaving our life behind, I was blindsided. Devastated. Embarrassed and ashamed.

How could I not have known what was going on right under my nose?

In hindsight, the signs were all there. The late-night meetings, the overnight trips and weekend conferences, the obsession with having his phone on him at all times. His new affinity for slim-cut suits and those fancy button-down shirts with the patterned fabric on the cuffs.

So, I took the blame whenever he dished it out, certain that it had been all my fault.

It took months of therapy to see that while part of it may have been on me, I didn't get us there alone.

I reminded myself of that as I drove away from Brad's apartment feeling deflated and guilty. I told myself there was nothing for me to feel guilty for. I didn't vandalize his car. I might have been in a bar, but I hadn't acted inappropriately. Okay, so maybe I was making out a bit with a guy I'd only met hours before, but it wasn't like I'd slept with him. Well, okay, so maybe I would have if he had stuck around that night, but he didn't, so we didn't.

Nothing I'd done had in any way made me a bad mother. Not even Piper's jeans, which admittedly were more snug than any I owned, but they weren't nearly as tight as Brad made them out to be.

I struggled not to give in to the old patterns we'd constructed over the years, choosing instead to allow my therapist's warnings to echo in my mind about not falling victim to Brad's controlling tendencies and his constant berating and put-downs.

After all, it wasn't only his needs that weren't met in the marriage, and if there was anything I'd learned over my whirlwind weekend, it was that my own needs were very much alive and well, and there was more to my life than soccer practice and ballet recitals. It was high time I reclaimed a little piece of me.

"How did it go with Brad?" Lorna asked on her nightly call.

"About as good as could be expected," I said, easing my bedroom door closed to keep the kids from hearing me. "I've been thinking that I want to get a job when we move."

"What kind of job?"

"I don't know, but it's time I went back to work. I need something in my life that's *for* me, separate from what the kids need *from* me. Besides, I'm tired of Brad scrutinizing every penny I spend. Eva's in high school now. She'll be driving soon, so she can get herself places and maybe even help with Ethan's schedule. They're able to be home alone for short periods. It's not like I'd never be there. I'd work while they were in school."

"You already know how I feel about you relying on Brad. I told you years ago when he first pushed you to stop working that it was so he could control you, and I can't believe you still let him do it after all this time. He's going to give you fits about this, though. He'll stop the alimony, I guarantee it."

"So? I don't care if he does. I never asked him to pay alimony. He forced that issue, not me. It takes everything he makes and then some for him to pay me to stay home. There's no way he could afford it if his parents weren't helping him, so you'd think he'd be happy for me to go back to work."

"Hmph," Lorna scoffed. "Maybe they need to help him buy a decent car for his children to ride in so they aren't in something used with only two seats and bald tires."

"They're not bald anymore. He's got two brand-new tires now."

I turned on the faucet and sprinkled bath crystals across the water's surface. I only sprinkled a little out of habit, a behavior I'd picked up after years of Brad complaining about the flowery smell lingering in the bathroom. I frowned at the memory and dumped enough of the crystals in to turn the water bright blue.

"Could you afford the bills without his money?" Lorna asked. "Because as you well know, I don't have the bottomless checking account Brad's parents have."

"Well, we're already moving, so I'll look for a place I can afford on my own. We'll downsize. The kids and I don't need all this space."

"Are you sure you want to go through with this move?"

I groaned as I tossed Piper's clothes in my hamper and twisted my hair up into a messy bun.

"Not this again."

"I know you're tired of me saying this, Caroline, but it makes no sense for you to take off after him to Orlando. Your life is here. The kids' lives are here. Their friends. Their hobbies. Their schools."

I grabbed a towel from the linen closet and placed it on the marble counter by the tub.

"Then they'll make new friends at a new school in Orlando, where their dad will be. Being promoted to partner is a big deal for him, and he can't turn it down. The four of us agreed as a family that we'd go with him rather than have him not be able to be involved in the kids' lives."

"But he's not involved in their lives now! How many soccer matches has he made? How many dance recitals? How many weekends does he call off coming to get them? Orlando's only a few hours away. He could drive from there to see them if he wanted to. I bet he probably wouldn't see them any less than he does now."

I eased into the warm water and sighed as its silkiness glided over my body.

"Look, Mom, I know you don't want us to move and be farther away from you—"

"It has nothing to do with me. I've already told you that. I'm concerned about those kids. It's going to be harder than you think. New schools, new friends. Especially with Eva in high school and Ethan having been on his soccer team so long. I think they'd be better off having the life they know and being a few hours from their father than being completely uprooted when he probably won't be around anyway."

I clenched my eyes shut and wished I could disappear into that alternate universe I'd found over the weekend. I'd run the water too warm, and her words were ramping up my stress level much faster than the bath could take it away.

"I hear what you're saying, okay? I do. And you're right. He's not involved, and he sucks at showing up for our kids. But don't you see? If we live farther away, it makes it that much easier for him to check out. I grew up without a dad, and I don't want that for Eva and Ethan. So, if I need to follow him to Orlando to make sure they get whatever time with him they can, I'll do it."

"And what about you? What about what you need? You don't know a soul in Orlando. You're going to be on your own, because you know he won't help you."

"Which is yet another reason for me to get a job. I'll meet people. Maybe I'll find a hobby. I need to start taking time for me anyway. Making my own life a priority. I think this move is a clean slate. A chance to start something new."

My phone beeped, and I looked at the screen, sitting up and splashing water everywhere when I recognized Levi's number.

"Mom, I gotta go! I have another call coming in."

I rushed her through goodbye and good night and clicked over to his call, hoping it hadn't already gone to voicemail.

"Hello?"

"Hey there."

I could hear the smile in his voice, and I smiled back immediately.

"Did you make it home okay?" he asked. "I didn't get any calls about red convertibles being towed."

I sank back down in the water, allowing it to flow over my shoulders as I leaned back against the tub and closed my eyes, picturing Levi's face.

"No blowouts this time."

"That's good to hear. How's Caterina?"

"I talked to Patsy just before she headed home from the hospital, and the evening doctors had been around to say there was no change. They want to give her the new antibiotic a full twenty-four hours. How's the mare?"

"She's good. Up and at 'em."

"And the colt?"

Levi chuckled. "He's good, too. Clumsy, but good. Malcolm and I just left the stable, and I'm gonna take a shower and then we'll head into town to get some dinner. I thought it might be too late to call when we got back, so I figured I'd try you now."

"Mom!" Ethan yelled from outside my bedroom door. "Eva won't let me have the pink part of the ice cream. She said that's hers, and I can only have the white and the brown."

"Levi, can you hold on?" I sat up and leaned over the edge of the tub. "Ethan, I'm on the phone. You and Eva need to work this out."

"But she isn't even eating the pink part. She just won't let me have it in case she wants to eat it another night."

"Tell her I said to let you have it." I lay back in the water, but I couldn't find the comfortable position I'd had before. "Still there?" I asked Levi. "Sorry about that."

He chuckled. "No worries. My mother used to get so frustrated with my sister and me fighting that she'd send us both outside and make us sit on the porch until we came to an agreement."

"That's not a bad idea. Maybe I should try that." I shifted my weight, searching for a position where the tub didn't grind against the bony parts of my spine.

"Mom! He's eaten almost that whole container by himself. I only like the strawberry, and I don't eat it as fast as he does. Why can't he just eat the chocolate and vanilla and save the strawberry for me?"

"Eva Marie, I will buy you more strawberry ice cream. For the love of God, can you please just let me take a bath in peace? If you're not eating it, then let your brother have it."

"Fine!" She stomped back down the hall, and any progress I'd made with her earlier gratitude withered away.

"Sorry, Levi."

"Don't be. You're a mom. That's what moms do. They moderate."

Though I hated to admit it, I'd overdone the amount of crystals, and the aroma was stinging my eyes. The relaxing bath I'd envisioned wasn't coming to fruition, so I stood and reached for the towel.

"Well, evidently, I need work on my moderating skills because those two are at each other's throats nonstop. Did you get a chance to talk to William?"

"About?"

I wrapped the towel around me and struggled to tuck the end in while balancing the phone between my ear and my shoulder.

"Whether or not one of his brothers may know Caterina? Or if they remember knocking anyone up around, say, thirty-five, thirty-six years ago?"

"Um, no. Somehow that didn't come up in conversation. He did ask about you, though. He asked if I'd be seeing you again."

"And what did you tell him?" I stared in the mirror at my dripping reflection and smiled as I waited for his answer.

"I told him I sure hope so. No idea yet when you're heading back this way?"

"No. There's really nothing I can do until Caterina wakes up, you know?"

"Mom! Eva just ate all the pink. She didn't even want ice cream until I asked for it, and she just stood there and stuffed her face with it so I couldn't have any."

I pressed the phone to my chest to muffle my yell. "Ethan! Go back to the kitchen. I'll be downstairs soon, buddy."

"But what do I do about the ice cream?"

"Eat the white and the brown. I'll talk to Eva."

Levi was laughing when I put the phone back to my ear.

"Ice cream wars, huh? Maybe you should get them each their own container."

"They'd still find a reason to argue. I guess I should go moderate, as you put it."

"Go get 'em, tiger. I need to get in the shower anyway. Malcolm will be here soon. Can I call you later in the week?"

I turned away from the grinning reflection in the mirror and leaned back against the counter.

"Sure. I'd like that."

"Well, then I'll talk to you later. Have a good night and a good week."

"You, too."

I hung up smiling, and I kept smiling while I put on my pajamas and rubbed lotion on my arms, hands, and feet. Then I headed downstairs to keep the peace between my children, excited for the first time in a long while about what the future might bring.

CHAPTER 23

As soon as the kids left for school Monday morning, I started scouring the internet for any mention of Caterina Russo. It turned out she'd led quite the public life.

She'd worked with a high-profile private adoption organization in New Jersey before leaving that behind to start her non-profit foundation in Cedar Creek. Over the years, she'd been instrumental in lobbying to refine and create better laws to protect adopted children and adoptive parents, and there were several photos of Caterina in DC meeting with congressmen and senators to further her cause.

She seemed beloved by the adoption community, and she'd been granted numerous awards and accolades for her efforts in the industry.

It was hard not to be impressed by all she'd accomplished, and harder still not to feel somewhat emotional about me possibly being the driving force behind her passion. Was all that she had done for other children and their parents a direct result of her decision to give me up all those years ago?

The pictures of Caterina gave me much more to go on than her comatose body in the hospital bed and her sleeping face with tubes protruding from it. The gray streaks in her hair seemed to have been a recent development, because in most of the older photos of her, thick, dark waves framed her beautiful face. It was hard to tell the color of her eyes from the online photos, but they were dark, maybe brown or green.

I liked to think I could see some resemblance to Eva in Caterina's appearance, but maybe I was engaging in wishful thinking again.

There was a video of her accepting an award at a banquet a little over five years ago, and I watched it over and over, even bringing the laptop to the living room with me as I folded laundry. I was fascinated by the nuances of her voice, the deep timbre of her laughter, and the light in her eyes as she talked and smiled.

It was hard not to get choked up when I considered that these online snippets may be all I would ever have of her.

This was my mother. This was the woman who conceived me and carried me. Who handed me over to others to raise for reasons I didn't yet understand.

I wanted to know her. I wanted to hear her laughter in person and see that light in her eyes as we talked.

I'd seen her age listed in one of the articles, and if it was accurate, she would have been seventeen when I was born.

Wow. Only three years older than Eva. Granted, I'd not been much older when I got pregnant, but it seemed so young to me now that I had a daughter approaching that age.

My mind drifted back to the question of my father, and the same unanswered queries replayed in my thoughts. Had theirs been a serious relationship? Did they make the decision to give me up together? Had her family kept him updated on my whereabouts as well? Not likely, if Cat herself didn't know her mother was keeping tabs. Was it possible he didn't even know he had a child?

Up until the foundation began, there was no mention of Caterina Russo ever being in Cedar Creek.

I wondered why she'd chosen the tiny town to host her foundation, which appeared to have a national appeal. Surely, a larger city in New Jersey or New York would have better suited her needs, or even DC where she could have interacted more easily with lawmakers.

As much as I hated to admit it, my findings pretty much destroyed my theories about William Ward's family connection. If Caterina was from New Jersey, then there was very little chance that one of William's brothers could be my birth father.

Evidently, the strong resemblance in the photograph was a coincidence. Perhaps I'd seen William's gentle manner, his success, and his love for his own daughter and felt a pang of envy. Maybe I'd wanted something like that for my own story so much that I'd concocted the possibilities in my mind without any evidence to back them up.

So, if my father wasn't one of the Ward brothers, who was he? His identity reverted back to a needle in the haystack of the world, and without talking to Caterina, I'd likely never find him.

My obsessive thoughts were interrupted by the phone, and I frowned to see Brad's name on the caller ID. His calls were rarely, if ever, good news.

"My insurance company wants more information about this key incident. Where were you, and why didn't you file a police report?"

I sighed and tucked the cordless phone between my ear and shoulder so I could take the folded towels to the bathroom.

"I told you I'd pay for the damages. Why are you even going through insurance for that? The deductible will probably be much higher than it will cost to fix it."

"Why can't you just tell me where you were?"

"Why do you need to know?"

"The receipt for the tires was in the glove compartment. It's from a mechanic in Cedar Creek. What the hell were you doing in Cedar Creek? There's no hospital there. I looked."

I slammed the cabinet door shut and scowled at the mirror.

"The hospital is in Jensen. Last time I checked, where I go and what I do on my own time was none of your concern."

"When you're driving my car, it is! I loan you the car for the weekend, and you bring it back scratched up with two cheap-ass tires on the front."

"You and I both know those tires aren't cheap, but if you want different tires, by all means, go buy them. You would have had to replace the bald ones anyway, and these didn't cost you a thing."

I picked up the stack of Eva's clothes from the folded laundry piles and headed up the stairs to her room.

"Evidently, they didn't cost you, either. Who's Levi Parker?"

My steps faltered, and Eva's pajamas toppled from the stack onto the stairs. I bent to pick them up, but with my shoulder against my head for the phone, I couldn't reach them without risking the whole folded stack tumbling down the stairs. I stepped over the pajamas with a sigh and continued toward Eva's room.

"Well? I'm waiting," Brad snarled. "Who's Levi Parker, Caroline? And why is he buying tires for my car?"

"It's a long story. If you don't like the tires, go buy different ones."

I swung open Eva's bedroom door and nearly tripped over her dance bag in the middle of the floor. She'd told me she was going to ride to the studio with Shannon after school since Ethan had soccer at the same time Eva had dance.

The sight of the bag made me groan. It meant I'd need to take her bag to the high school and drop it off before picking up Ethan. I'd already promised Lorna I would take her to the eye doctor and drive her home since her eyes would be dilated. An extra stop at the high school didn't fit in my timeline.

"Who is Levi Parker?" Brad roared, and I almost dropped the phone as his volume shocked my eardrum.

"What does it matter?" I said, rubbing the outside of my ear as I switched the phone to the other side.

"Why did he pay for these tires? Who is he?"

I threw the ballet bag over my shoulder and started back down the stairs, sighing when I saw the pajamas. "Again, it's a long story, Brad, and the outcome is simply that you have tires on the front of your car." I didn't care to explain the whole saga to him, and I was sure he wouldn't be amused by his car being stolen and hefted onto a barn. I hadn't been. Why would he be?

"Are you sleeping with him?"

"What? No!" I dropped the ballet bag and scooped up the pajamas, heading back up the stairs to Eva's room and trying not to think about how close I came to sleeping with Levi Parker. If only he hadn't walked away.

My skin flushed hot with the memory of Levi's mouth on mine and his body pressed against me.

Brad's voice brought me back to reality. "Why else would some guy pay for your tires?"

"You think I slept with some guy to get tires for *your* car? Really? This conversation is over."

I ended the call and refused to answer when he called back.

Whatever feelings I had for Levi had no bearing on my real life. There was no need to bring Brad into that mix. Besides, even if I had slept with Levi or was planning to sleep with him—which, I wasn't— it would be none of Brad's business. He had certainly dated his share of women since our divorce, and prior to it, evidently. I wasn't about to feel bad about one night of dancing and a taste of passion.

CHAPTER 24

I took the bag downstairs and texted Eva.

"You left your dance bag here. I guess now I have to drive to the high school and drop it off. Not very responsible."

I put away Ethan's clothes and transferred the jeans from the washer to the dryer before checking for her reply.

"No need to drop it off. Not going to dance."

Thinking perhaps I'd missed a schedule change, I consulted the calendar hanging over the desk, but it clearly said she had a dance lesson after school.

"Did it get canceled? What's up?" I texted back.

Three dots danced in the lower left corner of the screen indicating she was typing.

I packed Ethan's after-school snacks and a thermos of Gatorade for soccer practice while I waited.

When her text came through, it was only three words.

"I quit dance."

I stared at the phone as shock and anger washed over me. She'd been telling me she wanted to quit. That she was no longer passionate about it. She'd reasoned that we were moving and she wouldn't know anyone at a new studio anyway, but I'd thought it was just jitters about a new place.

Eva had been obsessed with dance since she was three years old. Her life—and by extension, *our* lives—had revolved around dance recitals and dance rehearsals, auditions and workshops, blistered feet and tight hair buns.

I couldn't believe she'd just quit after we'd talked about sticking it out until we got to a new studio.

"What? When? Were you going to tell me this? I thought we agreed you'd

stay with it until we got to Orlando and found a new group. See what you thought then."

The three dots were maddening as I waited for her reply.

"I talked to Dad about it this weekend while we were camping. He said I could quit, so I emailed Ms. Showers last night and told her."

The anger that had been simmering reached a boiling point almost immediately.

"Were you going to tell me this? So where were you planning to be after school today if not at dance with Shannon? I can tell you where you'll be now. With me on the soccer sidelines. You're grounded."

I dialed Brad's number before she had a chance to reply.

"I shouldn't even answer your call after you hung up on me," he said. "Do you know how childish that is? Ask your therapist. See if she thinks it's okay for you to hang up on me."

"You told Eva she could quit dance?"

"She hates it. She's done with it."

"Didn't you think maybe that was something we should discuss? I called you when she first said she wanted to quit. I told you I thought it was angst over moving, and she should stick it out until we got to the new place and found a studio for her. We agreed."

"I wouldn't say we agreed," Brad said. "You told me what you thought, and I didn't argue with you. This weekend, she told me what she thought, and I didn't argue with her. We had a good weekend. I didn't want to upset her."

My mouth dropped open as I resisted the urge to scream. "You let her quit because you didn't want her to be mad at you? Guess what? Teenagers get mad at their parents. It's a fact of life. But you have to think about what's best for them, Brad, not what's best for you."

"How is it what's best for her if she doesn't want to do it?"

His entire philosophy of parenting summed up in one question. It applied to every decision he made regarding the kids. Eating vegetables. Observing bedtimes. Finishing homework before going outside. Honoring a commitment.

I inhaled deeply and let it out slow, reminding myself that staying calm and reasonable was much more likely to get results than yelling and screaming.

"She agreed to finish out the school year. She made a commitment to the studio and to the other members of her troupe.

She's already been rehearsing for the spring recital. It's in less than a month. She can't just drop out of that. There needs to be some responsibility and some follow-through on her part."

"Whatever. She's been doing this for years. If she's done, she's done. I'm sure they'll have someone to take her place in the recital. Those damned things are God-awful boring anyway. No one's going to notice if one dancer is missing."

"That's not the point. Well, it is part of the point. But what does it teach her if you just let her quit? She needs to follow through. She needs to work through her fears about moving and meeting new dancers. Quitting lets her avoid the challenge."

"I'm sure she'll find something new to do once we move. You should be happy she quit dance. Now you'll have more time on your hands to look for a house in Orlando and get everything packed up for the move. I'd say I helped you out. Now Eva will have free time to help you, too."

I squeezed my eyes shut against the mad tears that burned the backs of my eyelids. How could I have ever thought this was the man I wanted to spend the rest of my life with? How could I have thought he was the one to father my children?

The answer was simple, of course. I wasn't thinking about all that back then. When we met in our freshman year of college, I was awestruck by Brad Miller. He was handsome and popular. He was outgoing. The life of the party. Everyone wanted to be around him. To be in his group. To be invited to the massive parties he threw at his parents' estate.

When he picked me, I felt like the luckiest girl in the world. I was suddenly at all the right places with all the right people. My social calendar got propelled into a different stratosphere. We had front row seats to every concert, and there wasn't a party in town we weren't invited to. We stayed in his parents' beach house with our friends for spring break, and we traveled with them to Colorado to ski for the winter break.

It was a fairytale life compared to what I knew growing up with a single mom in a working-class neighborhood.

I wasn't thinking about his qualities as a father or how irresponsible he was with money.

I was thinking Prince Charming had come calling in a BMW and wanted me to be his princess.

It wasn't until much later that I realized the charm and charisma he oozed had a dark side, and there wasn't much substance beneath it all.

"You still didn't tell me who Levi Parker was."

"He's no one, okay? There was a misunderstanding at the mechanic's, and he paid for the tires to make up for it. I gotta go."

"I don't know what's gotten into you, Caroline, but I don't like it, not one bit."

He hung up, but then he called again within seconds.

"Eva just texted me that you grounded her. You can't ground her for something I gave her permission to do."

"She didn't even tell me, Brad! Neither of you did. She told me she was going to the studio with Shannon after school today. She lied to me. She emailed Alicia Showers last night to quit and never even mentioned it. I'm grounding her for lying."

"Well, she was probably too scared to tell you. She probably thought you'd freak out about it, and she was right!"

"Then you should have told me."

"Maybe I would have if you'd been home when I dropped them off. But no. You were in Cedar Creek for some unknown reason having my car vandalized and getting some stranger to pay for tires. Or maybe he's not a stranger. More likely."

"I have to go. I'm picking up Lorna for the eye doctor."

"Of course. God forbid Lorna do anything without your help. I'll be so damned happy when you're not in the same town with her, and she's not able to have you jump at her beck and call."

I knew it would do no good to explain that she was my mother. That she'd do the same for me, and had done for me anything I asked of her for years. It would fall on deaf ears, as it always had.

CHAPTER 25

"This is so stupid," Eva said as she climbed in the back seat behind Lorna after school. "I can't believe I'm grounded for doing something Dad said I could do."

"You're grounded for lying to me and doing something behind my back without telling me."

"Don't you want to be in the spring recital, dear?" Mom asked.

"No. I don't. It's stupid. They put Elena right up front just because her mom complains that she can't see her in the back since she's short. She's ahead of the music the whole time, and then it throws everyone else off. It's ridiculous. Besides, I think I might be able to get a bigger part in the play if I don't have dance rehearsal every flipping night of the week."

"But you already got a part the play," I said as I navigated the mine field of teenage drivers, teenage stragglers, and teenage lovers to make my way out of the high school parking lot.

"Yeah, but Starry Peters might have to drop out because her parents are taking her to Europe for a month, so she'd miss rehearsals altogether. Mr. Llewellyn said he'd consider me for her part if I don't have dance rehearsals."

"But you're such a lovely dancer, Eva," Mom said, and I cut her a look to lay off it.

The more pressured Eva felt, the harder she'd dig in her heels and refuse to back down. Better to wait and discuss it with her one on one with no other influences around. If she had her mind set on quitting dance and Brad to back her up, there wasn't much I could do about it, but I wanted to make sure she understood the consequences of her choices for her and the other members of her troupe.

She sulked through Ethan's soccer practice, and she sulked

131

through dinner, asking to be excused early to go upstairs to her room.

Between Eva's mood and mine, even Ethan's upbeat persona was dampened, and we all had retreated to our own space before nine o'clock rolled around.

I was going through my closet, determining which of the ridiculous number of sneakers I owned could be tossed in the box for giving away, when the phone rang. I almost ignored it, but on the slight chance it could be Patsy with news about Caterina, I crawled out of the closet and reached for the phone on my nightstand.

"Hey," Levi said, and my whole demeanor changed in an instant.

"Hey! What are you doing?"

"Just finished dinner, and I'm heading back to the house. I know I said I'd call you later in the week and it's only been one day, but I wanted to hear your voice."

The giddiness inside me spread throughout my limbs, bursting across my face in a huge smile.

"How was your day?" I asked, not sure how to respond to his comment.

"Good, I guess. Bills. Accounting. Office work. Which I hate, but it's necessary."

I sat cross-legged on the bedroom floor and leaned back against the bed.

"I can't picture Levi Parker sitting behind a desk doing office work. I see you in a barn. Covered in horse sweat and hay."

"That's a pretty accurate picture, but unfortunately, some days involve a desk in between stints with horses and hay. Usually Mondays end up being office time. How was your day?"

"Not stellar. I always thought when people warned me about the teenage years that they were exaggerating. Or that they didn't know my little angels. Boy, was I wrong. I don't know if I'll survive until they're both grown."

"My mom says every gray hair on her head came from me and Rachel."

"I would believe it. If I'm gray the next time you see me, you'll know why."

"So when will that be?" he asked.

"I don't know. There's been no change with Caterina."

"Well, I wanted to let you know we're having a festival of sorts at the farm this weekend. Kind of an open house thing where kids from the community can come out and learn about farm life. They can tour the stables. Tour the rehab facility. One of our guys worked on a cattle ranch before coming here, so he teaches kids basic roping. There's a petting zoo. Stuff like that. We do this event like twice a year. You're welcome to bring your kids. It's free, and everyone's invited. It's usually a good time."

For about a half a second, I considered how awesome it would be to take Eva and Ethan to the farm. I could picture Ethan's face lighting up with all that open space to run and all those trees to climb, and while Eva wasn't too much on outdoor activities, I knew she'd be wowed by the horses and the gorgeous big house.

But then reality set in. The kids didn't even know about Caterina yet, and I didn't intend to tell them until she was awake and I knew more about the situation.

I certainly had no intentions of introducing my children to Levi Parker. Whatever physical attraction was going on between the two of us had no bearing on my kids, and there was no way I was going to add that layer of complexity to what was nothing more than a harmless crush.

"You still there?" he asked.

"Yeah. That sounds like fun, but Ethan has soccer Saturday morning, and Eva's in a bit of situation right now, and, um, the kids don't know about Caterina. They don't even know I'm adopted. Their dad thought it would confuse them and make them see my mom differently, so he didn't want them told. Obviously, I have to figure out a way to tell them now that I've found Caterina, but until she's awake and I know what the situation is—I don't know. I'm just taking one day at a time."

"Of course, yeah. Still no change, huh? What are the doctors saying?"

"They're trying another antibiotic, so hopefully that will work. Maybe I could drive down during the day later in the week. Get someone to pick up the kids after school and just come down to the hospital in the morning and drive back that afternoon."

"If you do, let me know, because that hospital cafeteria had some good chicken noodle soup. I was thinking I might head back over there and get some more. I could meet you for a bowl if you'd like to try it."

I laughed and stood up, stretching my legs as I watched my reflection in the mirror above my dresser.

"Who knew the hospital cafeteria was the best kept secret in Cedar Creek?" I asked. "What did you call it? A *dining establishment?*"

"Yeah. Truth be told, if you were going to be there, I'd come even if they weren't serving soup that day. I can't stop thinking about you."

I closed my eyes and touched my fingers to my lips, remembering how it felt to have his mouth on mine. My body reacted immediately, and I shuddered at the tingling in my deeper regions. But then the words I'd overheard about Levi echoed in my head again, a warning to stay wary of a player's smooth talking.

It didn't matter, of course. I wasn't planning on being involved with him. It was fun to look forward to the phone call, and if I was in Cedar Creek, I'd definitely meet up with him if the timing worked. There was no denying I'd love to explore what I felt when he held me in his arms, but again, it was a crush. A dalliance as I reclaimed my womanhood, nothing more.

"I need to go," I said, my voice sharper than I'd intended. "It's getting late, and I need to make sure the kids have their lights out."

"Did I say something wrong?" Levi asked.

I sighed, pressing my forehead to the cool wood of the door frame. "No. Not at all." On the contrary, he'd said everything right.

"Can I call you later in the week?"

"Sure," I said, though my voice didn't sound certain.

"Okay. Good night, Caroline."

"Good night, Levi."

I went through the motions of getting the kids settled for the night and doing my nightly bedtime routine, then I lay awake staring at the ceiling, thinking of all the reasons I needed to stop talking to Levi Parker, but *feeling* all the reasons I didn't want to.

CHAPTER 26

The doctors tried all week to bring Caterina back to a point where she could be taken off the ventilator to breathe on her own, but she didn't respond.

I discussed coming down again with Patsy, but until there was a change in Cat's condition, it didn't make much sense for me to drive an almost five-hour round-trip just to sit when she didn't even know I was there.

Or know me, period.

When we talked Friday night, Patsy had left the hospital early to take care of some things at the foundation's office, which had been in limbo with Cat hospitalized and Patsy remaining by her side. She said unless there was any change, she'd wait until Saturday night to call with an update since I'd be with the kids all day.

Levi had called every night, and each night we'd ended up on the phone longer than the one before. I'd get the kids to bed and retreat to my room, and we'd spend hours just talking. It was amazing how many different subjects we covered, and no matter how tired I was the next day, I couldn't wait to talk to him again that night.

It was somewhere around three-thirty when we finally said goodbye Saturday morning, so when the alarm went off at six to get up and get out of the house for an eight o'clock soccer match, I was dragging.

Eva couldn't believe I woke her and made her go to the game with us, and she sulked as we sat side-by-side on the sidelines of the soccer field, sweating and wishing the clock would run down faster.

We were up by four goals, and there was nothing to indicate the other team would rally for a comeback, so I was ready to pack up and get inside the air conditioning when my phone rang.

I stood and walked away from Eva and the other parents to take Patsy's call.

"I just got to the hospital," she said, "and the news this morning isn't good. Cat's developed some kind of bloodstream infection and they're saying it's caused sepsis. Her blood pressure has dropped again. It's not looking good," Patsy said. "Can you come?"

The sideline erupted behind me, and I turned to see that Ethan's team had scored yet another goal.

"I'm sorry. I can't," I said, watching the team give each other high-fives. "I'm at Ethan's soccer match. My mom's out of town. I have the kids."

"Okay," Patsy said. "I just thought maybe, well, I understand. I'll call you if there's any change."

When we hung up, I dialed Brad. "Hey, is there any way you could take the kids this afternoon? Maybe overnight?"

"It's your weekend."

Eva tapped me on the shoulder. "Mom, can I go get a drink? Please? It's so hot out here."

I dug a five-dollar bill from my pocket and handed it to her, waiting until she walked away to respond.

"I realize it's my weekend, Brad, and if you want to count how many of your weekends I've had the kids, I think we could fairly say it would be okay for you to take one of mine."

"This isn't about keeping score, Caroline. I have plans."

"Okay, I realize it's short notice, but something's come up, and I need to take care of it."

I watched as Eva stopped just before the concession stand. She was joined by a boy, and the two of them got in line for water together. I didn't recognize him, but their easy laughter and close stance as they talked made it obvious they knew each other pretty well.

"Does this emergency of yours have anything to do with Levi Parker?" Brad asked.

"No. Why would it?"

"Oh, I don't know. You won't even tell me who the guy is. Or why he paid for my tires."

The boy bent his head to say something to Eva, and she tossed her hair and laughed, and then playfully swatted his arm. She'd never shown much interest in boys, and I marveled at the flirtatious side of my daughter I'd never seen before.

"Brad, I told you he paid because of a misunderstanding. Look, I've never asked you to take them not even once since the divorce. I'm asking you now. I need to be somewhere. Can you please take the kids? I need your help. Please?"

I hated having to grovel and beg him to spend time with his own children.

"Look, I'm in Orlando," he said. "So even if I wanted to help you out, there's nothing I can do. Can't your mom take them?"

"She's out of town with her girlfriends. Some kind of purple hat thing in Savannah."

"Have them call a friend."

The buzzer sounded, and the entire sideline erupted in cheers for our victory. Eva had gotten her water and was still talking to the boy, but at the buzzer, she looked out across the field and then met my eyes before saying goodbye to the boy to head back toward me.

"Eva's still grounded, and I don't know if I'll be back tonight, so I don't want to ask someone else to keep them without knowing."

"What do you mean, you don't know if you'll be back tonight? Where are you going?"

I bit down on my lip, not wanting to tell Brad more than I had to, but I'd been too distracted by Eva to think about how much I was saying.

"My friend in the hospital has taken a turn for the worse. I need to go be with her."

"Who is this friend? What hospital? Are you making this up so you can go shack up with some guy? I think it's pathetic if you're pawning your kids off on me so you can spend the night with this Levi guy."

I gritted my teeth and swore under my breath as a veil of anger colored my world red. "Are you kidding me? *My* kids? Last time I checked, they were *our* kids, Brad. And I'm not *pawning* them off on you. Most fathers want to spend time with their children, you selfish jerk. You've got some nerve. No, this has nothing to do with a guy, but even if it did, wouldn't you be the pot calling the kettle black as many times as you've canceled on them to be with some woman?"

Eva came walking up with the brightest smile I'd seen on her since I couldn't remember when.

"Thanks for nothing. I gotta go." I shoved the phone in my back pocket and forced a smile for my daughter.

"Who was that?" I asked, and she giggled as she turned up the water bottle and took a drink.

"No one," she said, wiping a dribble of water from her chin with the back of her hand. "Just someone in the play."

"Ah. A fellow cast member. What's his name?"

"Greg."

"Greg who?"

Her smile was contagious, and I found myself smiling back at her, wanting to freeze time and hold onto the sheer look of bliss on her face that had been missing for so long.

"Greg Lewis. He's new. He moved here from Houston."

"Oh, nice."

Ethan came running up, his freckled face red and dripping with sweat.

"Did you see me? Did you see me? I made the last goal! I kicked it past him! Did you see, Mom? Did you see?"

It must have been the goal that was scored while I was on the phone with Patsy. I felt horrible. I'd been faithfully sitting on the sidelines for years with my eyes glued to the field, even back in the beginning when he was four and the entire team would get distracted by a butterfly and run the opposite direction of the goal.

How unfair that my baby boy had finally scored, and I missed it.

"Oh, honey! That's awesome!" I kept my comment generic because there was no way I could lie to him and no way I could tell him the truth.

"Way to go, champ!" Eva said, giving him a fist bump.

I stared at the cordial contact between the two of them with a bit of shock. Who was this cheerful impostor, and what had she done with my moody daughter?

But underlying the celebrations was a shrill alarm going off in my head, telling me I needed to get to Caterina before it was too late. I may not ever get to say hello, but I wanted to make sure I said goodbye.

"Coach says he's taking the team for ice cream. Can I ride with Billy?" Ethan's snaggle-tooth grin filled his face as he looked up at me.

"Let's go talk to Billy's mom," I said.

"She already said it's okay!"

"I need to ask her something else. Eva, get our chairs packed up and meet me over by Melinda, please?"

Her smile faded somewhat, but the scowl replacing it was less bitter than usual, and she set to work folding the chairs without any complaint as Ethan and I made our way through the throng of parents and players to reach Melinda and Billy.

"How about Ethan getting it in there?" Melinda asked, grinning at the boys as they tore open the straw wrappers on the juice boxes she gave them. "Were you going nuts when he kicked it in? My voice is hoarse from screaming."

"Yes! I'm so proud of him!" I exclaimed, hoping Melinda wouldn't want to discuss the specifics of the goal I'd missed. "Can I talk to you for a second?"

"Sure, what's up?"

"I've had a bit of an emergency pop up, and I was wondering if Ethan could come hang out with Billy this afternoon. I might be a while."

"Oh, I'm sorry. You know we love having Ethan over, but we're leaving right after lunch to go to Tom's mother's. It's her birthday, so we're all going over to celebrate and then take her out to dinner later tonight."

"Okay. No problem, thanks."

I approached a couple of the other parents, but one had a gymnastics meet for their daughter that afternoon, and the other had tickets to a theater matinee.

"What's up?" Eva asked as we walked toward the car. "I heard you tell Ms. Donnelly that you had an emergency."

"Oh, um, my friend who's in the hospital isn't doing well, and I need to go and see her."

"Well, I can keep Ethan."

"No. I don't know how long I'll be gone, and Daddy and Grandma are both out of town. Besides, you're grounded."

She rolled her eyes and tossed her hair over her shoulder. "Right. Which means I have to stay home. Which is exactly what I'm asking to do."

"No, Eva. I don't feel comfortable leaving the two of you home alone when there's no one in town for you to call."

"There's plenty of people I could call."

The lack of sleep combined with the stress of the situation and the anxiety of the unknown had my nerves on edge, and I snapped. "I said no, Eva. Drop it."

"Geez," she muttered as she put the chairs in the back of the Tahoe.

"Without the attitude, please. Just drop it without saying anything."

I turned the key in the ignition and cranked the air conditioner as high as it would go, cursing the oppressive Florida heat.

"I didn't say anything," she mumbled.

"Eva, please."

I couldn't deny Ethan a celebratory ice cream for the first goal he'd ever made, but I sat with my foot tapping the entire time the team celebrated, my mind distracted by a barrage of feelings.

I felt guilty for even considering dragging the kids with me not knowing what the day would bring, but at the same time I knew I'd feel guilty for not going if it ended up being the last time I could see Caterina.

I also felt resentful that Brad could take off and do whatever he needed to without even considering the kids or what their needs were, and I felt angry that the universe had seen fit to bring me back together with my birth mother but then not allow us even one conversation before threatening to take her forever.

By the time we pulled into the driveway at home, I had made up my mind that I was going to see Cat. I'd spent years putting everyone else first. This was something I needed to do for me, and for once, the kids were going to have to come second.

"Ethan, hop in the shower and be quick about it. Eva, I need you to pack some snacks for us because it might be a long day. I don't want you staring at screens all day, so both of you need to gather something to read or something you can do quietly to occupy yourself."

"Why?" Ethan asked. "Where are we going?"

"To a hospital," Eva sneered. "Mom doesn't trust us to stay home alone so we have to go sit in a hospital with some sick person we don't even know."

"Eva! Enough! It's not that I don't trust you, but I would have better peace of mind if you were with me. Can you please not fight me about every single thing?"

"I'm not fighting you. I just don't understand why we have to spend our Saturday in a hospital. That's so boring."

"I don't want to go to a *hospital*," Ethan moaned, and I motioned for him to go upstairs before turning to face Eva.

"Grab your toothbrush and an outfit to wear tomorrow. Oh, and something to sleep in just in case."

"We're spending the night? At the hospital?"

"No, not at the hospital, but I may need us to stay somewhere overnight."

"Why? We don't even know this person. How do *you* know this person? What's her name?

"Her name is Caterina, and I need you to do what I asked so we can get on the road. Now."

"Fine," she said, walking toward the kitchen with her arms crossed. "I've never once heard you mention anyone named Caterina. How close of a friend can she be if your own daughter doesn't even know her?"

I wanted to scream at her that *I* didn't even know Caterina, but I swallowed the words and picked up my phone to dial Patsy instead.

"Hey. Any change?"

"No."

"Okay. I'll be there as soon as I can."

"Oh, thank the Lord. The nurses have asked where you are and if you're coming. What will you do about your kids?"

"I'll just have to bring them with me." I glanced over my shoulder toward the kitchen and walked farther away from Eva's earshot. "They don't know about, well, about Caterina, or about me. Being adopted, you know. So, unless I figure out a way to tell them on the ride there, this is going to be tricky."

"You do what you think is best, dear. I'll go along with your wishes."

"Thank you. I think you're the only person willing to do that today."

CHAPTER 27

The long ride to the hospital was silent, due in part to both kids wearing headphones, but also because both were mad at me and didn't want to talk. While I didn't welcome their anger, I needed the time to think about how I was going to tell them such a bombshell piece of information.

I think in my mental imaginings of this reunion, I'd always met my birth mother first, and after we'd hit it off fabulously, it had been a seamless transition to explain to my children that I had been adopted and then introduce them to their new additional grandmother. They'd be in awe of her, of course, and everyone would live happily ever after.

But a silent Caterina in danger of dying didn't play into that scenario very well.

"Why don't you guys wait here?" I said as we entered the lobby, wanting a chance to touch base with Patsy and see how crowded the family waiting room was without the two of them groaning in the background.

The sullen faces didn't even bother to respond before throwing their backpacks in chairs and returning to their screens.

I took the elevator up and found Patsy knitting in the waiting room, exactly where I expected her to be.

"Hi. How's she doing?"

"She's not any worse, which is good news, I suppose. Sepsis is serious. Not something to take lightly. As if pneumonia wasn't already enough for her to contend with."

Patsy's white hair, which had been perfectly coiffed each time I'd seen her, was rumpled and flat on one side like she'd been lying on it. The dark circles under her eyes only served to magnify the pallor of her skin, and I wondered if I wasn't the only one who hadn't had much sleep this week.

"Are you okay? Have you eaten? Can I get you something?" I asked as she tucked her project back in her bag.

"No, no. I'm fine. Just tired. I stayed up too late last night trying to figure out the books. Cat's always handled the finances of the foundation. I know nothing about any of that. But with her out for a week now, I was worried we might be missing payments or deadlines. I tried to go through the accounting last night, but she uses a lot of shorthand and symbols I don't understand. I searched through her files and found a couple of things that need to be paid by week's end, but I'm not authorized to sign a check, so I'll need to contact those people on Monday to see what can be done if, well, depending on how she's doing, of course."

She exhaled deeply, and I wanted to put my arm around her, to console her. I'd grown fond of Patsy in the short time we'd known each other, and it pained me to see the toll Cat's illness was taking on her.

"Maybe I could help," I offered. "I'm not an accountant, but I had planned to be. I had a couple of years toward a degree when Eva came along, and though I'm sure much has changed since then, numbers are numbers. I'd be happy to take a look."

Patsy patted my arm as she smiled. "That would be wonderful. I'd really appreciate it. I've never been a numbers person. I would hope Cat would be fine with me asking someone to help if it means keeping the foundation on track."

"I'm sure she would."

"Maybe we could go look when you leave here."

"Sure." I wondered when that would be, and under what circumstances. I'd felt such a sense of panic to get to the hospital when Patsy first called that I hadn't thought much beyond anything other than seeing Caterina. "I guess if I'm going to make this visitation window, I'd better get in there."

"Yes, of course."

I checked in at the ICU nurses' station and made my way to Cat's room, taking a deep breath before I entered, unsure of what I'd see.

She looked the same, and whatever battles were raging within her body, her outward appearance was calm and serene.

Flashbacks of the video I'd watched of her replayed in my head, and I imagined her sitting her up and talking, smiling and laughing as though she was happy to see me.

I stood beside her bed and hugged my arms around me, willing her to open her eyes.

"I want so badly to meet you," I whispered. "To talk to you and find out more about who you are. I've seen pictures of you. Videos. I've read about your accomplishments, your determination, your passion. I admire you already, and I don't even know you. I have so many questions. So much I want to know."

I moved closer to her and took her hand in mine.

"It's not fair that I've found you and might lose you so soon. I wish I'd searched sooner, that I hadn't let Brad talk me out of looking for you. I wish I could have stood by your side while you fought for adoptive rights. I never had the courage to speak out about my beginnings and do something with it like you have. I basically tried to hide being adopted my whole life. Like it was something to be ashamed of. I look at all the good you've done, and I know I could have been doing more."

A nurse came in and checked the machine beeping Cat's lifeline before switching out her IV bag.

"Hi, I'm Cindy. How are you today? You're Caterina's daughter, right?"

I nodded. "Caroline. Nice to meet you. How is she? Any better?"

"She's still fighting it. Unfortunately, sepsis is a risk with pneumonia, and it's serious, but we've added additional antibiotics based on the results of her blood work. It should be a matter of time until those kick in, but she's stable for now. She doesn't have a fever, and her blood pressure is good. Those are good signs. Do you have any questions for me?"

"I don't think so. Thank you. Thanks for all you're doing for her."

"Oh, you're welcome. We love Cat here. She's so sweet to all of us, and we're rooting for her."

"That's right; I'd forgotten she's been here before. So, you've all met her when she was awake." I felt a pang of envy that they knew my mother, and I didn't. I was the only one visiting her bedside who had never seen her not in this condition.

"Yes, everyone knows Cat. She's one of those people that you feel like you've known forever the moment you meet her. She makes everyone feel at ease. But, of course, you know that! She's your mom! I'm glad you were able to be here with her. Mrs. Lannister says you live out of town, and it's hard for you to get here."

"Yeah," I mumbled, wishing I had something more to say. Some experience with Cat that validated my presence and made me feel like less of an impostor every time someone called me her daughter.

"Well, I'm sure she's going to be up and around, cracking jokes, and making everyone smile again before you know it," Cindy said. "I noticed y'all brought in some CDs for her. Feel free to bring in her favorite lotions and rub them into her arms and hands. Maybe turn on the TV with her favorite programs. Anything to let her know you're here and give her something she enjoys. Something familiar."

She left the room, and I stared down at the Cat everyone knew but me.

I had no idea what her favorite scents were or whether she even watched TV. Based on Patsy's CD selection, I assumed Cat liked country music, but beyond that, I wouldn't have a clue what she would enjoy. My presence certainly wasn't a familiar one.

CHAPTER 28

"I'm gonna go down and check on the kids. Do you need anything?" I asked Patsy when I returned from visiting Caterina.

"You go ahead. I'm going to finish knitting this row, and then I'll head down and get some coffee in the cafeteria. I'd love to meet them if that's all right."

"Sure, yes," I said, wondering how I'd introduce her. "We'll see you downstairs."

They were both sitting where I'd left them—Eva texting furiously on her phone and Ethan absorbed in a video game on his tablet.

"Hi, guys."

"How long do we have to stay here?" Ethan asked. "Can I get some ice cream?"

"You've already had ice cream today, buddy. Eva has snacks for you in her bag."

"But how long do we have to stay?"

"A little while longer. I'm waiting for my friend to get better."

"How long will it take her to get better? And what if she doesn't get better? How long will that take?"

"That's rude," Eva said.

"What? What did I do?" he asked.

Eva rolled her eyes and shook her head, her thumbs still flying on the keyboard.

I sat beside Ethan and smoothed his hair back off his forehead, frowning at the pink in his skin despite a generous lathering of sunscreen before the soccer match.

"I need you to be patient, okay? I know this isn't much fun, but I need to be here, and I don't know how long it's going to take."

"But this is so boring!" he moaned.

"If you were at home, what would you be doing?" Eva asked.

"Something better than this!"

"Okay, look," I said, standing. "What if we go to the cafeteria and play cards? Eva, you packed the deck of cards like I asked, right?"

"Yes," she said, looking up from her phone. "Do I have to go? I'm fine sitting here."

Of course you are, I wanted to say. *Anything to be on the opposite side of what I need you to do.*

"I'd like us to go to the cafeteria together," I said instead.

You would have thought I'd asked her to mop the hospital floors with her toothbrush. "God, Mom. Why? I'm not complaining like he is. I'm perfectly happy sitting here texting my friend. Why do I have to go to some dumb cafeteria to play cards? I don't even like playing cards. And cafeterias smell weird."

"I don't know of much you do like these days, Eva. Grab the bag and let's go."

"I like texting. I like being at home in my own room. I like being left alone and not being asked to play something stupid like cards."

"How long do you think it will be?" Ethan asked. "Like thirty minutes? Or longer?"

"Longer. Let's go."

I started walking toward the cafeteria, ignoring the groans behind me.

Prior to our divorce, I'd played the role of the strict parent, enforcing the rules and keeping the attitudes in check while Brad pretty much allowed them to do anything they wanted.

Since he'd left, I'd been more lax than I should have. Partly from mental and emotional exhaustion, and partly from not wanting to rock the boat any more than I had to while we all adjusted to the new norms. But with Eva's hormonal Jekyll and Hyde syndrome, and Ethan getting closer to pre-teen, I realized I needed to step up my game or soon they would both be walking all over me.

I couldn't count on Brad to help in that regard. If anything, he modeled behavior that encouraged them.

"Let's get a table away from the windows," I said, dropping my purse on a chair. "That sunlight coming in is brutal."

"Do I have to play?" Eva said.

"Eva, you've been on that phone for the entire two-hour drive, and I'm sure you've been on it since I left to go upstairs. Why don't you put it down for a bit? Give your eyes a rest, and let's play a game."

"But Greg has a swim meet later, and I won't be able to text him then."

"You've been texting Greg this whole time?" I asked, surprised that it had never occurred to me. I had assumed she was corresponding with her friends.

"Yeah. He has to leave in like thirty minutes. Can't I please wait until he leaves, and then I'll play whatever stupid game you want?"

The attraction to this Greg kid was a bigger deal than I had realized, and I was caught off guard, not ready to deal with this aspect of parenting on top of everything else.

"Um, okay. Thirty more minutes, and then that's it."

Her face lit up with a smile and the sour, bitter person who'd been glaring at me moments before was gone.

I dug through the bag for the playing cards, tossing a plastic bag of carrot sticks to Ethan. "Here's some carrots if you're hungry."

"Carrots? Why can't I have ice cream?"

"You already had ice cream. Carrots are good for your eyes. You need good eyesight if you want to keep scoring those goals!"

"Well, hello," Patsy said behind me.

The kids both looked up, and I turned and smiled, wanting to hug her for rescuing me from my own children.

"Hi! Ethan, Eva, this is my friend, Patsy!"

"Hello."

"Hi."

"I've heard so much about you," Patsy said. "It's lovely to finally meet you both. I was going to get myself a cup of coffee. Would anyone like anything?"

"Ice cream?" Ethan asked, but then looked down when he saw my frown.

"I thought I heard your mom say you'd already had ice cream when I came walking up. I see you have some carrots there. How about I get us one of those little cups of ranch dressing to dip them in?"

"Okay," Ethan shrugged.

"Anything for you?" she asked Eva, who had already turned back to her phone.

"Eva?" I prodded.

She looked up like she had forgotten we were there. "Oh, I'm sorry. No. Thank you anyway." And she was lost in her conversation again.

"My granddaughter hasn't looked up from her phone in a year or more," Patsy whispered. "I worry their skulls are gonna fall off their necks bent over like that all the time." She laughed, and I smiled. "You want anything, Caroline?"

"I'll come with you and get some coffee. Ethan, why don't you shuffle the cards?"

"He can't shuffle," Eva said without even looking up. "He spills the cards everywhere."

"Do not!" Ethan grabbed the cards from the center of the table.

"Well, Eva, he can't learn if he doesn't try. Shuffle carefully, buddy."

Patsy and I walked to the coffee station and poured ourselves each a cup.

"They've been through a lot with the divorce and everything. I fear I've been too lenient with them, Ethan especially. Brad says I baby him too much. I just hate to see them unhappy. They're certainly unhappy today," I frowned as I stirred the creamer into my coffee. "I feel like I need to be here with Caterina, but I don't know what to do with them. I know they don't want to sit here all afternoon."

"I could ask George to come get them and take them to the house. They could swim."

"Thanks, but they don't have suits with them, and I wouldn't want to ask that of George. Levi said they're having a family day out at the farm, but I wouldn't feel comfortable being that far away from the hospital, just in case. I feel like I need to be right *here*, you know?"

"Oh, that's right! Farm Day! I saw that in the paper. That sounds like fun. I could have George drive them over there."

"I don't know. I don't feel right having them go without me. They don't know anyone."

"What's Farm Day?" Ethan said, and I turned to see him standing behind us. "I wanna go!"

"What's up, buddy? I asked you to stay at the table and shuffle the cards."

"I wanted to know if I could get honey mustard dressing instead of ranch."

"Honey mustard with carrots?" Patsy asked, wrinkling her nose in disgust.

"Honey mustard tastes good on anything," Ethan said. "If you use enough of it, you can't even taste the carrots."

Patsy grinned. "I'll have to try that. C'mon, let's you and I see if we can find some honey mustard."

I paid for my coffee and walked back toward the table, watching Eva's smile as she typed. She looked older somehow, and I longed for the days when I knew all her friends and what was going on in her life.

The hurt still stung from her subterfuge earlier in the week. I couldn't believe she'd quit dance behind my back and then lied to me about going with Shannon after school. Where had she planned to go? She'd obviously planned something for after school; I just didn't know what.

Was this Greg person the reason that the play was suddenly more important than dance?

I needed to find out more about him. Who were his parents? What else should I know? Was I supposed to meet him? I wasn't ready for this phase.

Patsy and Ethan soon returned with Ethan carrying a container of chocolate pudding like it was a prize he'd won. He was grinning from ear to ear.

"That doesn't look like honey mustard," I said.

"He assured me he's allowed to have pudding," Patsy said. "We made a deal. If you don't want him to have the pudding, I'll eat it. But if you say he can have the pudding, he has to eat the carrots first."

Ethan's eyes were pleading as he watched for my answer. I worried about his non-stop appetite. It had appeared since the divorce, and I didn't know how much of it was growing boy and how much was feeding his feelings.

"If you eat the carrots first, then you can have the pudding," I said.

"Thanks, Mom." He tore open the wrapper on the plastic spoon and struggled to get the lid off the pudding.

"Carrots first! And thank Mrs. Patsy. She's the one who got you pudding."

"He thanked me when we got it," Patsy said, smiling at me over Ethan's red hair as she mouthed the words, "Sorry. Hope that's okay."

I nodded and waved her concerns away with my hand. "It's fine."

"What are we playing?" she asked, pulling out a chair.

"What's Farm Day?" Ethan said with a mouthful of carrots.

"Don't talk with your mouth full."

"Farm Day is like a fair, from what I can tell," Patsy explained. "They have games, food, face painting, and some other activities, but I don't know specifically what they are since I've never been. Oh, and you get to meet the horses and maybe even ride them."

"I want to do Farm Day!" Ethan exclaimed.

"You get to ride horses?" Eva asked, suddenly engaged in the conversation. "Where?"

"At a horse farm not far from here," Patsy said. "Over near Cedar Creek, where I live."

"Can we, Mom?" Ethan asked.

"Yeah, Mom, can we?" Eva chimed in.

"I don't know, guys. I came down to be at the hospital for Caterina. I kind of need to stay close by."

"But she said George could drive us there," Ethan said, pointing to Patsy. "Who's George?"

"George is my husband."

"Why can't you take us, Mom?" Eva asked. "She said it's close to here. You could drop us off and come back to the hospital. I could call you when we're done."

"No, you can't go without me, and I need to be here."

"But George could drive us!" Ethan said.

"Mr. George," I corrected. "And no. I'm not asking someone else to take you. We didn't come here to do Farm Day. We came because I need to be at the hospital."

"But *we* don't need to be," Eva said. "Why can't we go there, and you stay here?"

"I certainly don't want to interfere," Patsy said. "You do what you feel is best, of course. But Cat's condition seems to have improved a bit based on what the nurses were saying. Maybe you could drive them over there and let them have a bit of fun. If there's any change here, I could call you, and you could come right back. It is fairly close."

I wavered, torn between what I felt was the right thing to do for Cat and wanting to make my kids happy. I tried not to let the possibility of seeing Levi even be a factor in the decision, but I couldn't deny that it had crossed my mind.

"I don't know, Patsy. You yourself said when you called that I should be here, and that's why we came."

"Let's go upstairs and talk to her nurses," Patsy said. "See how she's responding to the medication. They'll tell us if it's dire enough that you shouldn't leave."

Ethan and Eva both looked to me with anticipation of my answer, and I caved in and nodded. "Okay. Mrs. Patsy and I will go get an update. The two of you stay here."

For once, neither of them argued, groaned, or protested.

CHAPTER 29

The nurse said that Cat seemed to be responding well, and though she wasn't out of the woods by any means, her condition had stabilized again.

I'm sure they all thought I was the worst daughter ever. First for not showing up any of the previous times she'd been hospitalized, then being gone an entire week as she lay in intensive care, and now I'd been here a little more than an hour and was already heading out the door.

I wanted to explain the situation—to tell them that I didn't even know Cat and she didn't know me—but I knew doing so would only complicate things, so I kept silent.

The kids were playing cards together when I got back to the cafeteria.

"Okay, so we'll go to Farm Day for like, an hour, tops. Then we come back here and neither of you complain about sitting here so I can be with my friend, right?"

"Right," Ethan said without even considering what he was agreeing to.

"Sure," Eva said with a bit more resignation, hesitant to commit but eager to get a reprieve.

They were much more excited walking to the car than they had been coming into the hospital.

"Have you ever ridden a horse, Mom?" Eva asked.

"No, and I don't know that we're going to be riding any horses, okay? Let's just go check out the farm and be happy about that."

"But Mrs. Patsy said we could ride the horses. And who is she, anyway? How'd you suddenly get all these friends in Cedar Creek and in, where is the hospital? Jensen? I didn't even know these places

153

existed. How did you meet these people?"

"Actually, Patsy said *maybe* ride horses, but I'm saying probably not."

"Why?" Eva asked.

"I don't want to ride horses," Ethan said as he climbed into the back seat. "I hope they have corn dogs."

"Why are you always hungry?" Eva turned in her seat to glare at Ethan as she put on her seat belt.

I wished I'd taken a moment to step away and at least call or text Levi to let him know we were coming. Everything had happened so quickly once Patsy called that I hadn't had a chance to tell him we were in town, and now I was showing up at the farm unannounced. He'd said Farm Day was open to everyone, but it didn't feel right not to give him a heads-up.

Part of my concern was to caution him not to let on that we were anything other than friends. Not that we were in a relationship or anything, but the last thing I needed was for him to see me and greet me with some passionate kiss while Eva and Ethan stood and watched.

I didn't need that complication, and I certainly didn't need anything getting back to Brad when there was no need to involve him. Whatever was happening with Levi wasn't serious enough to merit meeting my children or dealing with their father.

Perhaps it was best that I hadn't called him. Maybe we could make it through an hour of Farm Day without him ever knowing we were there or seeing the kids.

The radio blared out Sheryl Crow as we drove to the farm, and Eva surprised me by singing along with me. It had been a regular occurrence before she hit her teens and got too cool for car concerts with Mom, and I missed those moments of connection. I didn't want the song to end.

Balloons danced from the fence line as we neared the entrance to the drive, and the wrought-iron archway that spanned over the gate held a colorful banner that proclaimed it was Farm Day at Ward Farms.

We hadn't traveled too far onto the property before we came to vehicles parked on both sides of the drive ahead.

"Wow. This must be a really popular event," Eva said.

An oversized golf cart was parked across the drive, and a gentleman I recognized from breakfast was sitting behind the wheel. He stood and walked toward my window as we approached.

"Y'all need a ride up to the festivities?"

I nodded, hoping he wouldn't recognize me and say something in front of the kids.

He motioned for us to pull off the pavement behind another SUV, and I maneuvered the Tahoe into the space. I caught a glimpse of myself in the mirror and grimaced. Wild wisps had escaped my soccer-mom ponytail and were flying loose all around my face.

I pulled the elastic band out and ran my fingers through my hair, smoothing it as best I could before pulling it back up and twisting the band back in place.

"What's taking you so long?" Eva asked as I pinched my cheeks and pulled my lipstick from my purse. "What are you doing?"

"I look tired. I thought I'd give myself some color. Tell Ethan to come here so I can put sunscreen on him."

"How are you?" the farm hand said once we'd finally gotten on the cart. "Caroline, right?"

I nodded and said hello, ignoring Eva's stares as Ethan pointed at the huge oaks lining the drive.

"Wow. Can I climb those, Mom? Are we allowed to climb 'em?"

"You should ask Piper. She knows the best trees for climbing," the man said.

"Who's Piper?" Ethan asked.

"She lives here. This is her farm. She'll be around up here somewhere. Probably under the volunteer tent. Your mom can introduce you."

"You know the people who own this farm?" Eva asked, her eyebrows scrunched together.

"Yes," I said. "Ethan, get your arm in. What if he has to get close to a car and you've got your arm hanging out?"

"How do you know them?" Eva asked as the cart came to a stop. "Holy cow, there's a lot of people here."

It was being held at one of the barns, and though I knew we'd passed it on Levi's tour, I couldn't remember which one he said it was. I thought maybe it was where they kept the colts.

Tents were set up all around the perimeter of the barnyard, and flags and balloons waved against the passing clouds.

"There's food trucks!" Ethan yelled, pointing to a large barbecue smoker set up on the back of a flatbed truck. Smoke billowed from its chimneys, and the savory aroma filled the air.

"That's not a food truck, silly. It's a barbecue grill," Eva admonished.

"It's food, and it's on a truck," Ethan replied.

"He's got you there," I said with a smile.

We thanked our driver and made our way into the crowded barnyard. Try as I might to convince myself I wasn't there to see him, my eyes remained unconvinced, searching the crowd for any sign of the brown-haired, brown-eyed cowboy who quickened my pulse and made my limbs tremble.

He found me first.

"Caroline! You came!" Levi shouted from my left, making his way through the throng with a huge smile on his face. I smiled back without hesitation, but then I remembered Ethan and Eva were with me, and I tried to warn him with my face.

It didn't work.

He wrapped me in a huge bear hug as soon as he reached me, picking me up and spinning me around once before setting me back down.

"I'm so happy to see you. I thought you said last night—"

"Hey," I interrupted, pushing against his chest and stepping back to gesture toward the kids. "I'd like to introduce you to Ethan and Eva."

Ethan's eyes were on the barbecue pit, so I wasn't even sure what he'd seen, but Eva's face was frozen in shock, her eyes wide and her mouth gaping.

"Oh, snap. Hi," Levi said, extending his hand to shake Eva's.

She stared a moment longer and then blinked a couple of times before taking his hand. "Hi. Who are you?"

"This is my friend, Levi," I said, cringing inside. Not at all how I would have preferred the situation to go down.

"Wow, Mom. You have a *lot* of friends in Cedar Creek." Her eyes held a mixture of shock, disbelief, and mirth, and I chose to look away, placing my hand on Ethan's shoulder and bringing him back to attention.

"Ethan, say hello," I said, nudging him as Levi extended his hand for Ethan to shake.

"Hi," Ethan mumbled, clumsily shaking Levi's hand. "Is barbecue all they have?"

"Best barbecue in Florida," Levi said. "They have the ribbons to prove it. There's a man over there that makes a mean pot of chili." He smiled at Ethan, and then looked at me. "That's William's brother-in-law, Dax. He owns a cattle ranch east of Orlando, but he dabbles in chili cooking as a hobby."

I nodded, and he clapped his hands together and rubbed them back and forth. "Okay, so are you guys ready for some fun? We've got a roping activity over there by the barrels and a petting zoo behind the barn. There's face painting where you see that umbrella, and then there's going to be an exhibition race at five down at the loop. We'll have a bus start taking people there around four-fifteen."

"Oh, we can't stay long. I have to get back to the hospital. I just brought the kids to give them some entertainment and a break from the waiting room."

"How's Caterina?"

"Wait," Eva said. "*You* know Caterina? How does everyone know Caterina but me? Does Daddy know Caterina?"

"No!" I said with a little more volume and vehemence than was necessary.

Eva and Levi both looked startled, and I smiled to cover my tension.

"No, Daddy doesn't know Caterina. Daddy doesn't know anyone in Cedar Creek."

I glanced to my left to see Ethan heading through the crowd toward the barbecue pit.

"Ethan!" I called out, walking after him as I heard Eva ask Levi behind me if she could ride a horse.

Somehow, the tailspin of my life had continued to spiral, and now my alternate universe was blending with my real life. It seemed the whole thing was on the verge of spinning out of control.

CHAPTER 30

The line at the barbecue pit was long, so Ethan decided he'd rather visit the petting zoo instead.

"I'll take him," Eva said. "You know, give you two some time *alone.*" She stressed the last word with a sly grin, and I knew I had some explaining to do.

"Be sure you don't touch your face while you're in there. And wash your hands as soon as you come out of there, okay?" I called after them.

"Got it!" Eva shouted back as they went through the gate.

"There's a sanitizing station on the other side where they exit," Levi said.

"Good." I turned to face his handsome grin, and though I hated to admit it, I was excited to see him, too. I'd enjoyed our late-night phone conversations, but nothing beat seeing him in person and being able to look into his eyes.

"Sorry about that. Back there," he said, nodding toward where we'd first seen each other. "I just caught a glimpse of that red hair, and I was so excited to see you I didn't really pay attention to who you were with."

"No, it's my fault. I should have told you we were coming. I just, well, they don't know, I mean, I've never really, I guess what I'm trying to say is they've never seen me with anyone other than their father. I mean, not that we're *with* each other. I wasn't saying we're together or anything."

Levi laughed. "Caroline, relax. I get it. No worries. As far as those kids will know, I'm just a friend from Cedar Creek who wants to show them a good time at Ward Farms."

"Thanks, I appreciate that."

He leaned in a little closer, and his voice dropped to a whisper almost too low to hear above the crowd around us. "As long as *you* know that it made my day to see you, and I'd love nothing more than to take you in my arms right now. But I won't. I'll be on my best behavior."

A tremor of desire rippled through me at the thought of being in his arms, and as I smiled, a warm rush of blood heated my cheeks.

"Maybe I could get a rain check on that," I said, and the look in his eyes when he smiled left me with no doubt that I could.

I looked away to find Eva and Ethan in the petting zoo enclosure, relieved to see they were both smiling and laughing together. It was a welcome sight, and I was glad I'd let Patsy talk me into bringing them.

When they'd exited the petting zoo and visited the sanitation station, they came running back to us animated and excited to move on to the next thing. We continued making our way around the various tents and activities, and although Eva gave Levi the occasional bit of curious side-eye, neither she nor Ethan seemed bothered by his presence. He and I never so much as bumped into each other, but I stayed on high alert, constantly aware of his proximity.

Nothing he said or did would have led anyone to believe we were anything more than casual acquaintances, but when our eyes occasionally met, the spark was undeniable.

It was easy to smile and enjoy our meandering with Levi by my side and both kids happy, but Caterina was never far from my thoughts. I kept my phone in my hand and checked it often to ensure I didn't miss a call from Patsy.

"Any word on your friend, Mom? Is she any better?" Eva asked as we waited in line to get Ethan's face painted. Levi had gone to check on the arrangements for the race later in the day.

I looked at the phone again, even though I'd checked it only seconds before. "No. We should probably be heading back soon. We've been here an hour, and I don't want to stay away too long."

"Thanks for bringing us, Mom," Ethan said. "This is awesome."

I smiled and ruffled his red hair, damp with sweat. He had already been pink from the morning's soccer, and I couldn't tell if the increased redness I was seeing came from heat and exertion or the sun. I'd squeezed the last remnants of sunscreen out of the tiny emergency tube in my purse, and I decided I would ask Levi if he could get his hands on more when he returned.

"Well, hello there."

I turned to see William smiling at my children. "Everyone having a good time?"

"I think so," I said. "William, this is my daughter, Eva, and my son, Ethan. Guys, this is William, and he lives here."

"Wow, you live in a barn?" Ethan said. "Cool!"

William tossed his head back laughing and then clapped Ethan on the shoulder. "I probably spend more time in the barn than I do my house, kid, but no. I live in a boring old house, just like you."

"I wouldn't call your house boring by any means," I said.

"You know him too?" Eva asked, but then she seemed to remember her manners as she smiled and offered her hand to William. "Nice to meet you."

"Nice to meet you, too. Your mom spoke very highly of the two of you when we met."

Eva smiled, and Ethan stepped forward to take his turn in the makeup chair for his face painting.

"Hey, William, would you happen to have any sunscreen I could use? I had a small tube in my purse, but I've used that, and Ethan's very sensitive to the sun."

"I feel his pain," William said. "I thought I was too cool for sunscreen for years, and that's how I ended up pretty much covered in these freckles and suffering from the consequences of sun damage. I commend your efforts to keep him covered."

He turned and pointed to a tent on the far edge of the enclosure. "That's the volunteer tent. Piper's in there, and she should either have some or know where to find some."

I'd much rather have gotten the sunscreen from William or Levi rather than Piper, but I couldn't very well refuse after having asked for it.

"Eva, stay here and watch Ethan. I'll be right back."

Eva nodded and moved to stand closer to her brother, who was having his right cheek transformed into a spider.

I smiled up at William as we walked toward the volunteer tent.

"What a fun event! Thanks for hosting it."

"Oh, you're most welcome. We enjoy having it. There's Piper," William said, pointing her out as we neared the tent. "The two of you are easy to spot in a crowd with that red hair."

I wondered if he'd seen the resemblance.

"What about you?" I asked. "You're a redhead too."

"I don't look for myself in a crowd," he said with a chuckle. "If anything, I try to keep myself out of crowds as much as possible. In fact, I'm about to remove myself from this one for a while. Tell Piper if she needs me, I went to check on the hay bales at the race loop. I've got my phone."

I stepped into the shade of the tent, grateful that the sun had stayed behind the clouds for most of the time we'd been outside. It was still stifling hot and quite humid, but the lack of glaring sun was a help.

Piper was talking to three people on the other side of the tent, so I walked near them and stood waiting for her to finish.

"Welcome," she said when her conversation had ended. "Having a good time, I hope?"

"Yeah. It's a great event. Good turnout. Your dad said you may have some sunscreen? My son is rather fair-skinned, and I used up what I had with me."

"Sure! I have some over here somewhere." She led me to a stack of boxes behind a table and began to look through them. "So, you brought your kids?"

"Yeah, they're having a blast."

"Awesome! That's what we love to hear. Does Levi know you're here?"

"Yeah. We saw him earlier, but he had to go take care of something."

She raised her eyebrows and cocked her head to the side. "Wow. Levi met your kids? This must be getting serious."

"No," I said, taken aback. "Not at all. We're just friends."

She handed me a tube of sunscreen and shoved the box back under the table, then stood to face me with her arms crossed. She was no longer smiling.

"You know, I probably shouldn't tell you this, but—"

"Don't worry, Piper. The guys have already warned me in a roundabout way."

This time she looked taken aback. "What guys? Warned you about what?"

I glanced around to see if anyone was listening to us, but no one seemed to care what we were saying in the beehive of activity beneath the tent.

"I overheard some men talking downstairs the morning you brought me the clothes. Which I still need to get back to you, by the way. They were talking about how much of a player Levi is. How he has a different woman every week. But you don't have to worry about me. I'm not expecting anything from him. It's not serious. We're just enjoying each other's company."

"Oh. Well, I wasn't worried about you. I was worried about him." She flashed a half-smile and held up her hand. "Don't get me wrong—there's some truth in what they said. I wouldn't go so far as to say there's someone different every week, but Levi's always been a charmer, and he's never had any shortage of girls wanting to be with him."

She pulled back the tape on the box sitting on the corner of the table and began removing protein bars from it to place in a basket.

"But I'll tell you this," she said as she worked, "Levi takes his job very seriously. In the fifteen years he's lived on this ranch, I can probably count on two hands the number of weekends he's asked for time off. I know he took off when his sister got married, and then again the weekend her husband died. And I think there may have been a time his mom was ill or something, and his dad was out of town."

She flattened the empty box before tossing it under the table.

"I'm sure there were a few others, but still. It doesn't add up to many times over fifteen years, and it was usually something to do with his family. But then last weekend, he called my Dad out of the blue and said he needed the rest of the day off. Then he blew off his buddies and left them at a restaurant that night and failed to acknowledge their presence when he saw them later at Mickey's. Then he took the afternoon off on Sunday after nearly losing a mare that morning and not knowing for sure if she was out of danger."

She smiled as she crossed her arms, but the smile didn't carry to her eyes, where the ice blue flecks seemed to glow against the russet background.

"What's your point?" I asked.

"My point is that's not like him, Caroline. Not at all. Levi doesn't just blow off work because he met somebody. So, I'm not sure what kind of spell you've got him under, but if you're telling me you have no intention of pursuing it, you need to make sure he knows that. Because I've never seen him act this way with anyone before."

She turned and walked away, leaving me feeling chastised and dressed down. I couldn't believe she was somehow looking down on me. How dare she insinuate I was going to hurt Levi. Wasn't he the one with the reputation for being a player? Granted, he'd been nothing but a gentleman with me, so I'd never seen that side of him, but still. She was worried about *him?*

Her words kept replaying in my head as I walked back toward Eva and Ethan.

The heat of the day had become more suffocating, and I was ready to leave and put distance between me and Piper Ward.

I cared more for Levi than I was willing to admit, and on some level, it felt good to hear that he cared for me, too. But I couldn't be involved in anything serious. I couldn't take a chance on bringing someone into my life.

I had my kids to think of. I had an impending move that would demand my time and attention. I needed to find a job and stand on my own two feet.

There was no room for romance in my life.

I had to end whatever it was with Levi before it got out of hand.

CHAPTER 31

L evi was standing with Eva and Ethan near the face painting umbrella when I returned, and my heart hurt at the sight of the three of them laughing together.

Why couldn't I have that?

Why couldn't I be allowed some little measure of happiness?

I'd tried to do all the right things. I'd been faithful in my marriage. I'd put my kids first. I'd done all I could to encourage their relationship with their father even though he did all he could to destroy it.

I didn't go out. I didn't hire babysitters. I didn't date. My life revolved around the kids and what they needed from me.

Why couldn't I have this one little thing that was bringing me joy?

I loved talking to Levi. Our conversations went in a million directions, yet no matter how late it got or how long we'd been on the phone, I still wanted to listen to him longer.

The mere thought of his touch sent my heart racing, and my body had never reacted to anyone the way it did with him.

And all we'd done was kiss! I couldn't imagine how explosive it would be to go further, but God, how I wanted to find out.

He was a great dancer. A great kisser. He was kind and compassionate. Handsome and smart. A hard worker. Devoted to his family. He loved animals. And Piper was right; he was quite charming.

Who in their right mind would walk away from someone like that?

"Mom!" Ethan yelled when he saw me, running to greet me and show off the massive spider that appeared to be crawling up the side of his face.

"Wow! Scary! That's pretty realistic-looking, buddy. Do you like it? Did they show you a mirror?"

"Yeah. It's cool," he said. "Can we go do the roping thing now? Levi said he would show me how."

"Mom," Eva said, her face lit up with excitement. "Levi said I could ride if you say it's okay. Please say it's okay."

I never should have brought them to the farm. I never should have let them meet Levi.

My two worlds were colliding, and I had lost all control of the situation.

I couldn't let my kids get attached to him. I was having a hard enough time managing my own feelings. I didn't want them falling for him, too.

When Brad started taking them to Tatiana's place right away, I'd tried to be the voice of reason in telling him it was too much to expect them to accept her on the heels of our separation.

Then when they broke up, it was me who got to explain to the kids that they wouldn't be seeing Tatiana anymore.

They'd met a procession of girlfriends since then. They never knew who would be there on the weekends they went to stay with Brad.

I couldn't do that to them. I didn't want to drag them through more drama.

No matter how much I wanted to spend more time with Levi, I had to think of what would be best for Eva and Ethan.

"I think we should get back to the hospital, guys."

"Mom, c'mon. I've never ridden a horse. This may be my only chance," Eva pleaded.

"And I've never roped," Ethan said. "I don't even know what that is, but if we leave, I won't ever find out."

Levi's eyes met mine, and he tilted his head as his brow furrowed. "Everything okay?"

I looked away, determined not to let those brown eyes sway me.

"I said we'd stay an hour. It's time to go."

"Can't *we* stay?" Eva said. "You could come back and get us."

"Yeah, Mom. Can't we stay?"

"Guys, if your mom says you need to go, then you need to go," Levi said. "Maybe you could come back another day, and we'll rope and ride then."

"But—" Ethan started, and I cut him off.

"No buts. Let's go."

My phone buzzed in my pocket, and I pulled it out as I ushered the kids toward where we'd gotten off the cart.

"How do we get back to our car?" I asked Levi as I slid my finger across the screen to answer Patsy's call.

"Caroline?" she said, her voice breaking. "You better get back up here. She's taken a turn for the worse. A-R-something. A-R-D-S? Maybe? They say it's common in people with pneumonia and sepsis, but I don't know how much more her body can take. Her blood pressure has dropped again, and the nurses are running in and out of her room. How far away are you?"

"Oh no! Oh God! I'm at the farm," I said, walking faster even though I wasn't sure where to go. "I'm on my way. I'll be there as fast as I can."

"This way," Levi said, leading us behind one of the tents to where a cart was parked. "Hop on."

My hands were shaking as I cradled the phone in my lap, trying to hold my emotions in check so I didn't freak out the kids.

I never should have left the hospital. I never should have come to the farm. I shouldn't have brought the kids with me to Cedar Creek, and I never should have let them meet Levi Parker. I should have stayed close to Cat's side.

As my mind ruminated over the colossal errors in judgment I'd made, my heart repeated the same plea over and over.

Hold on, Cat. Hold on. Please pull through. Please make it.

The cars on either side of the drive were a blur as Levi sped us back to the Tahoe.

"What happened, Mom?" Ethan asked. "Did your friend not get better?"

I opened my mouth to answer him, but the words wouldn't come.

"Ssh," Eva said. "Don't bother her right now."

"I'm not trying to bother her. I want to know if she's okay."

"I'm okay, buddy. I'm okay."

Levi pulled the cart beside the Tahoe, and the kids both got off as I clicked the key fob to unlock it.

"Thanks, Levi. I appreciate you getting us back so quickly."

I couldn't look at him. I worried my emotional state might make me cry.

His hand moved like he was going to take mine, but then he hesitated and placed it on the wheel instead, sighing as he twisted to face me. "Let me talk to William, and I'll be up there as soon as I can."

"No," I said, finally meeting his eyes. "I don't want you to do that. I want you to stay here and do your job."

"Part of my job is delegating. I want to be there for you. Let me be there for you."

"No." I looked at the kids waiting in the car and stepped off the cart. "I don't want them to see us together again. It's not a good idea."

"Caroline," he started, but I shook my head.

"I have to go. Please don't make it harder."

"Can I call you later?"

I couldn't bear to tell him no, so I just turned and walked away.

He sat silent on the cart, and for as long as I could see him in the rearview mirror, he didn't move.

CHAPTER 32

Patsy and George were standing in the lobby when we arrived at the hospital, and after a brief introduction, he offered to go with Ethan and Eva to the cafeteria while I went upstairs with Patsy.

I'd tried to explain to the kids on the drive from the farm that Caterina's condition had taken a bad turn, but I didn't have much information myself, so I couldn't tell them a lot.

"I'll be back down in a few minutes, after I check on things upstairs," I said

"Okay, Mom. We'll be fine," Eva said, her green eyes sad as she watched me. "Don't worry about us."

"I hope your friend's okay," Ethan said, and I bent to hug him.

"Thanks, buddy. I hope so, too."

Patsy's eyes filled with tears as soon as we were on the elevator.

"This is bad, Caroline. She could die. I looked it up on my phone, and it's bad. I don't know if they can save her."

"Okay, well the first thing we need to do is *not* look up anything on your phone. That's never a good idea when it comes to medical stuff. C'mon."

I grabbed her hand and moved past her as soon as the elevator doors opened, pulling her with me to the nurses' station.

"Hi, I'm Caterina Russo's daughter," I said for the first time ever. "I need to talk to someone about my mother's condition."

"Of course, let me page her nurse for you. There's a briefing room right over there if you'd like to wait inside."

Patsy and I walked to the room with the sunset posters and inspirational quotes, but neither of us could sit. We paced the room together in opposite directions as she explained what had happened.

"I went in to sit with Cat for my visitation slot. At first, she looked the same to me, but then I noticed her lips seemed to be purple. I thought maybe it was from having that tube in her mouth for so long now, but then I realized her breathing was odd. Not slow and steady like it had been all week with the machine's rhythm. Then the machine started beeping and alarms started going off, and oh Lord, Caroline, I thought she was going to die right there in front of my eyes."

Tears streamed down Patsy's face as she relived the drama replaying in her mind. "I ran to the door to call for a nurse, but before I could get there, they were already running in. A whole team of people rushed in, and they asked me to leave, and I had no idea what was happening."

I put my arms around her and hugged her to me, trying to console her and make up for not being there. "I'm so sorry, Patsy. I should have been here."

She pulled back from my hug and grabbed a tissue from the box on the end table. "You couldn't have done anything if you were here. It would have been just as traumatic, so don't you feel bad about that. You were where you needed to be."

Christy, a nurse I'd met before, came in, her smile quick but her face tense.

"Hi, Caroline. I'm not sure how much Mrs. Lannister may have brought you up to speed, but I'd be happy to answer any questions for you."

"Can you tell me what's going on with my mother?"

"Let's sit down," she said, motioning toward the chairs, and I obliged her request though I was much too antsy to sit still.

"One of the biggest complications we see in patients with pneumonia that progresses into sepsis is a condition called Acute Respiratory Distress Syndrome, or ARDS, for short. Basically, what happens is the air sacs in the lungs fill with fluid, which prevents the lungs from filling with enough air to supply the organs of the body. In severe cases, this lack of oxygen can damage organs or even shut them down."

"How severe is her case?" I asked, thankful I was sitting down.

Christy's gaze was steady but stern. "Pretty severe. Her body is in a weakened state from her prolonged battle with pneumonia, and then the toxic attack from sepsis. Which means she's already compromised."

I sank back against the chair's cushions and exhaled. "Okay, so what do we do? What are you doing? How do we fix it?"

"There's not a quick fix. We're already giving her a combination of antibiotics to fight the infection and inflammation in her lungs. We already have her on a ventilator that can breathe for her, so her body doesn't have to do the work."

"But can't the ventilator just give her more oxygen?" Patsy asked.

"Well, we are giving her high doses of oxygen, but the challenge is that her lungs aren't able to expand fully when they're compromised by the fluid. While the ventilator is certainly helping to deliver oxygen, it can't solve the problem."

"What can?" I asked, silently pleading for any shred of hope.

"Time," Christy said with a timid smile. "Time for the medications to work. Time for her lungs to recover. We're monitoring her condition and adjusting as needed. We're watching closely for any sign of organ failure or damage due to lack of oxygen."

"What about her brain?" I asked as my mind connected the dots of what Christy was saying. "Your brain can't survive without the right amount of oxygen."

Her expression grew somber once more. "There is a possibility of brain damage if the supply of oxygen is depleted enough or cut off for an extended period. In some cases, patients experience memory loss. But again, we're monitoring her very closely. We're on top of it. We caught it at the beginning stages, and we're doing everything within our power to provide the support and care her body needs to fight this."

We thanked Christy and sat in stunned silence for a few minutes after she'd left the room.

I rubbed my eyes and pressed my fingers against my temples. "You know, Patsy, when you told me she had pneumonia and was on a ventilator, I thought that was bad. Like, really bad. Like, worst case scenario kind of bad. Then when you called and told me about the sepsis, I thought, oh wow. That's even worse. Worse than worst case. You hear about sepsis, and how it's basically the body becoming toxic to itself, and that's bad." I inhaled a deep breath and let it go quickly. "But damn. It's like we're in a downhill slide that won't stop sliding. Because from what's Christy's saying, it sounds like this ARDS stuff is even worse than pneumonia *or* sepsis. How much worse can it get?"

"Don't ask that. The answer is obvious," Patsy whispered.

"I'm beginning to think Caterina *really* doesn't want to meet me."

Patsy looked up with startled, wide eyes, but I smiled to let her know I was joking, and she relaxed.

"She's always had a flair for the dramatic, but this is ridiculous," Patsy said.

I laid my head back against the chair and closed my eyes. "I can't believe I went from not even knowing who she was, to being on pins and needles about meeting her, to sitting here feeling gob smacked that she may be about to—"

"Don't say it! Don't utter those words."

She put her hand over her eyes, and I noticed it was trembling.

I knew how stressed and scared I felt, and I didn't know Caterina on any level. I couldn't imagine how much more the situation must be affecting Patsy, who was close enough to consider Cat family even though there was no blood relation.

I sat up and slapped my hands against my knees, looking back at Patsy as she dropped her hand and stared at me in shock.

"Okay. That's it," I said firmly. "We're not going to let Caterina go. We're just not. You need your friend. I need to meet my mother. I need to find out who my father is. So, she can't leave us yet. We're not done with her. Let's stop moping around and acting like this is the end. It's not. It can't be."

Patsy attempted a smile and reached to take my hand, giving it a firm squeeze.

"You're right. She hasn't given up, and neither should we. Our Cat is a fighter. She's a determined, driven, hard-headed lady who does not stop when she has her mind set on something. She knew you were coming. She knew she was going to finally meet her daughter. And I have absolutely no doubt she is doing everything she can to make that happen. So, yes. Let's stop moping and start cheering her on."

CHAPTER 33

Three hours later, we were still waiting for any good news they could give us, but the best we got was that her condition hadn't worsened.

Eva and Ethan had been troopers, keeping themselves occupied during the long wait, and not complaining about the cafeteria's limited selection for dinner. I think they realized from my demeanor and Patsy's how grave the situation was, and I made sure they knew I was grateful for their compassion and understanding.

"Are you ever going to tell me how you know this Caterina person and all these other people in Cedar Creek?" Eva asked as we sat outside on the bench in the courtyard and watched Ethan run his hands under the fountain. "When did you meet them? How did you meet them? How come Ethan and I never met them?"

I sighed and stretched my legs out in front of me, wishing again that the whole situation could have played out differently. Wishing I'd told her the truth long ago so it would be easier to explain now.

"It's a long story, sweetie. I don't even know where to begin."

"At the beginning?" she said. "You could say, oh, I don't know, maybe, *here's how I met these people and how they became my friends*? I thought maybe it was like a friend from college or something that you just hadn't seen in a while and maybe that's why I didn't know her. But then we go to that farm, and you know all these other people. Speaking of which, who is Levi and what's up with that?"

Heat crept into my cheeks, and I was thankful for the dim lighting and the dark of night. Levi had been a constant in my thoughts throughout the evening, and I wanted so badly to call him and tell him what was happening.

To hear his soothing voice and feel like I wasn't alone.

But I couldn't. I knew he was busy with the activities at the farm, and I knew if I told him how serious it was with Caterina, he would have already come, even though I'd lied and said I didn't want him to. I couldn't be the reason he ditched work. I didn't want to be the person who made him shirk his responsibilities and act out of character.

That wasn't the only reason I couldn't call him, of course. The reality was we had no future. We had no chance. It was foolish to keep leading him on and engaging with him when I knew it couldn't go anywhere.

I had two kids who needed my focus, and he had a full-time job that required his undivided attention. We lived in separate worlds in different cities, and even though we'd be closer when the kids and I moved to Orlando, it would still be inconvenient for us to see each other on a regular basis with our respective hectic schedules.

No, it was better to nip it in the bud before it went any farther. Now. While it was still new and superficial, and there weren't *real* feelings involved yet.

"I told you. He's just a friend." It was a lie, but I needed it to be true.

"Mom. C'mon. I've never seen one of your friends pick you up off the ground and spin you around. I'm not stupid, you know. I saw the way you guys looked at each other. All googly-eyed and sappy."

"No, it's not like that," I said, standing to avoid the conversation. "Let's head back inside and find Mrs. Patsy."

"Where are we staying tonight, Mom?" Ethan said. "Are we driving home, or are we getting a hotel or something?"

The question had been plaguing me since I'd realized how serious Cat's situation was. I certainly didn't want to drive back to Gainesville and be too far away to get to the hospital quickly if I needed to. But I hadn't had the forethought to pack clothes or toiletries for any of us, despite being in the same situation the weekend before.

"I'm working on that plan, Ethan. I'll let you know as soon as I figure it out."

"I think we should head home," Eva said. "You could get up early in the morning and come back here. I can stay with Ethan at home. Grandma will be back tomorrow, so if we needed anything, we could call her."

The idea was enticing, but I couldn't bring myself to leave Cat hanging by a thread for the night.

My phone rang, and my heart leapt at seeing Levi's name on the screen.

"Why don't you guys go inside and see if Mrs. Patsy and Mr. George are still in the cafeteria? I need to take this call."

I watched the two of them go through the double glass doors and then slid my finger across the screen, anxious to hear his voice despite all my mental objections.

"Hey."

"Hey. Is everything okay?" he asked.

"No."

"What's wrong? What happened? I texted you a couple of times asking about Cat, but you didn't answer me."

"I couldn't." That was true. I couldn't bring myself to reply and keep him on the hook, but my resolve had worn down by the time he called, and I had to answer. "Caterina has developed a condition called ARDS. From the way I understand it, her lungs have filled up with fluid, like worse than the pneumonia or sepsis, and it's possible she could die, like, quickly and at any minute, or she could live and have brain damage."

"Oh, man. That's not good."

The rumble of his voice vibrated against my ear, and I wished he was with me. I wished he was holding me, and I was feeling the vibration of his voice with my ear to his chest instead.

"No. It's not good," I whispered as I closed my eyes and imagined him standing in front of me.

"Can I come and see you?"

I squeezed my eyes closed tighter but I couldn't stop the tear from escaping. Every logical part of me knew I should say no for so many reasons, but every fiber of my being wanted him there with me.

"I don't know," I finally managed to say. It wasn't no, and it wasn't yes.

"I don't have to come inside," he said. "The kids don't even have to know I'm there. I can meet you in the garage. By your car. I just want to see you. I want to hold you. I want to kiss you."

My resolve melted, and none of it mattered anymore.

"Yes. Come. Text me when you get here, and I'll come out to meet you."

CHAPTER 34

Eva and Ethan were in the cafeteria with Patsy and George when I went back inside, and it was all I could do to carry on normal conversation as I waited for Levi's text.

My nerves were buzzing with anticipation of his touch, and I couldn't sit still and pretend I wasn't wired and giddy.

"You okay?" Eva asked. "You're acting weird."

"I'm fine. Why?"

"You're pacing. You keep checking your phone, and you keep looking toward the door. What's up?"

I silently cursed her sleuthing skills and wished we'd thought to bring her phone charger so she would still be texting and ignoring me.

"It's probably anxiety," Patsy said. "Different people handle stress in different ways. It's been a long day, and we're sort of in a limbo pattern while we're waiting to hear an update."

"I didn't sleep much last night," I told Eva, though, of course, I didn't mention it was because I'd been on the phone with Levi. "We were up early today for soccer, and then the drive down here, the trip to the farm, and like Patsy said, anxiety. I'm just keyed up, that's all."

"You're keyed up, and I'm ready to go to sleep," Eva said with a yawn. "This is some kind of role reversal or age reversal or something."

"Y'all are going to spend the night with us, right?" Patsy said. "You're not thinking of driving home this late, are you?"

Her own exhaustion was evident in her droopy eyes and her haggard appearance, so I was hesitant to say yes. I didn't want to add more to her plate with a house full of people.

"We have plenty of room," George said, almost as though he could read my thoughts. "It's no trouble at all, and we'd love to have you."

"Can we, Mom? Please? I don't want to have to drive home tonight!" Ethan pleaded.

I looked at Eva, and she shrugged, too tired to put up much of an argument even though I knew she'd rather be at home.

My phone buzzed in my pocket, and I jumped, startled and excited.

I ignored it, not wanting to draw Eva's investigative eye. Instead, I yawned and told the group that I was going to get some aspirin from the car. I asked Eva to watch Ethan and told her to stay with Patsy and George until I returned.

I managed to walk at a normal pace out of the cafeteria and to the front doors of the lobby, but once the double doors closed behind me, I sprinted toward the garage, unable to wait a minute longer to be in his arms.

He was standing beside the Tahoe, looking at his phone, and my stomach fluttered at the sight of him, the flame immediately rekindled.

He looked up as I approached, and a slow grin spread as I walked straight into his arms and threw my hands around his neck. Our mouths met and melded, tongues dancing as the tension in my body ebbed away and passion took its place.

His hands were in my hair, releasing my ponytail, and then trailing down my back to cup my rear end and pull me against him as I pushed my hips forward to meet his. His body responded immediately to the contact, leaving no doubt he was every bit as turned on as I was.

I dug my fingers into his shoulders, kneading the corded muscles as he thrust his tongue deeper inside my mouth to explore.

Someone nearby in the garage began to whistle a show tune, probably as a courtesy announcement that we weren't alone.

I pulled back, but his arms around my waist held my hips firmly against his as he smiled at me.

"Well, hello there. You make me think you might have missed me."

I pressed my lips softly to his in answer, and he chuckled against my kiss.

"I missed you, too," he said softly. "I'm sorry I couldn't be here earlier."

The conversation with Piper flooded my thoughts, and I shook my head against it and pulled at a button on his shirt.

"It's fine. I knew you were busy. There was nothing you could do here anyway."

"This." He flexed his arms to tighten them around me.

"Well, you're here now, doing this." I smiled, happy to be looking into his eyes and feeling that joy again.

"I was worried about you earlier," he said. "What happened? Your whole mood changed."

I shook my head again, not wanting to think about it much less discuss it. I'd have to face the issues eventually, but it didn't have to be right now. I could allow myself a few minutes of contentment.

He tucked his thumb under my chin and lifted my face so my eyes met his.

"You sure you don't want to talk about it?"

"I'm sure."

"Okay. If you say so. I'm not sure I believe that everything's okay, but I'll assume you'll tell me when you're ready."

I nodded, not trusting my voice to be steady if I spoke.

The stress of the day, the rollercoaster of emotions, and the lack of sleep were all wreaking havoc on me.

"I can't stay out here long," I whispered. "No one knows you're here."

He nodded and touched his nose to mine.

"Okay. Thanks for meeting me out here. I understand why you want to be cautious with the kids, and I respect that. I really do. I'll follow your lead. However you want to handle things."

I dropped my head back and looked up toward the ceiling, cursing the universe for its horrible sense of humor.

First, it gave me my birth mother but didn't allow me to talk to her or get to know her before wrenching my heart over her.

Then, it sent me the most wonderful man, but put him out of my reach, both logistically and emotionally as long as I had to put the kids first.

"I've been doing a lot of thinking since you left the farm," he said. "I've wavered back and forth on whether I should say anything, but I think I'll regret it if I don't."

I dropped my gaze to meet his, uncertain of where he was going and whether I wanted to hear it.

I almost told him not to say anything, but curiosity got the best of me. I wanted to know what had him looking so nervous.

Levi took a deep breath and cleared his throat, and I got the impression that whatever he was about to say was taking a great effort on his part.

"I'm thirty-four years old, Caroline, and I've been a committed bachelor my whole life. I had seen other people who had love in their lives, but I was skeptical of it. Cynical about it. I thought it could never happen to me."

I drew in a sharp intake of air as my mind predicted what was coming. Was he about to profess love for me? Did I want that? Was I ready for that?

"I never thought I'd meet anyone who could turn my world upside-down," he continued. "Who could make me think of her first when I woke, and have her be the last thing on my mind before I slept. Someone who could occupy my thoughts all through the day, and make me smile for no reason at all. Someone I'd be willing to drop everything for and not even care about the consequences."

He cleared his throat again, and I realized I'd been holding my breath, but I didn't dare let it out yet. Not until I knew what else he was going to say.

"I know this is crazy. I know we just met. I know we live in different cities, and we both have lives that are hectic and jam-packed with responsibility. But I don't care. I want you in my life. Whatever that looks like, however we have to work it out to make it possible. It doesn't matter. I don't want to go back to the life I had without you."

I threw my arms around his neck and hoped my kiss would answer what I couldn't yet say in words.

When we finally tore ourselves from each other and I bid him goodbye, I walked back toward the hospital entrance with a mind racing with doubts but a heart filled with hope.

I didn't know how we would make it work or if we could. But I knew I didn't want to say goodbye to Levi Parker yet. Whatever our connection was had only just begun, and I wasn't ready for it to end.

CHAPTER 35

I was looking at the ground in front of me as I walked, so I didn't see Eva sitting on the bench by the entrance until I was almost upon her.

"Hey," I said, startled. "What are you doing out here?"

"How long have you been dating Levi?" she asked, her jaw set and her mouth a tight, grim line.

My heart pounded with the guilt of being caught red-handed, and I knew she'd seen us.

"Eva," I started, but she stood.

"Who are you? What's going on with you? I feel like I don't even know you, Mom. You won't tell me how you know all these people, or why we're camped out at the hospital for someone Ethan and I have never even met, and now I see you making out with some guy from the farm. It's like you're living a double life or something. When do you have the time?"

Embarrassment washed over me, leaving my skin hot and my stomach roiling in nausea.

"I'm sorry, Eva. I never meant for you to see that."

"Obviously!" she scoffed. "But you couldn't have been more obvious if you'd tried. Taking your secret call and then freaking out watching your phone and the door and almost breaking your neck to get outside when your phone vibrated."

I felt like we'd had a total role reversal, and I was the teen about to get grounded and Eva was the angry and disappointed parent.

"Look, Eva, —"

"Would you please for the love of God just tell me what's going on? Why are we here? Who are these people? Are you in love with him?"

I sank onto the bench, clutching my hand to my stomach to hold the waves of nausea at bay.

"I'll tell you everything, but does Patsy know you're out here? Where's Ethan?"

"I told Mrs. Patsy I left something in the Tahoe. I figured I'd follow you and see what you were up to. Which, I did," she said with an eye roll. "Ethan is playing cards with Mr. George."

"I'm gonna text Patsy and let her know you and I are talking so she doesn't worry, okay?"

Eva stood staring at me while I texted Patsy, and I could feel her eyes boring into me like lasers.

"You wanna sit?" I asked her once I'd put the phone back in my pocket.

"I'm fine standing," Eva said, leaning back against a pole with her arms crossed and looking more like Brad than I'd ever seen her.

"Okay, well. Where do I begin?" My mouth was dry, and my thoughts jumbled, like I couldn't find the words to say. "I guess at the beginning is the best place. My beginning. There are very few people in my life who know this, and it's something I've often struggled with. Something I was embarrassed about, I suppose, and I didn't want people to know. But it's something you should know, and I'm sorry I haven't told you before now." I took a deep breath and rushed the next words out on the wind of the exhale. "I was adopted."

"What?" Eva's eyes widened, and her eyebrows rose. "For real?"

I nodded. "Yeah."

"Does Grandma know? Oh, God, what am I saying? Of course, Grandma knows. When? How old were you?"

"I was two days old."

"Wow. That's wild. Why would you be embarrassed by that?"

I shrugged and looked away from her. "I don't know. I found out when I was seven, and it sort of warped my sense of who I was. I suddenly felt like I didn't belong to my family. Like I was the outcast. The other cousins were blood relatives, but not me. It messed with my head. Like, my mom wasn't my mom. My dad wasn't my dad."

Eva came and sat on the bench next to me, her anger replaced by curiosity. "But your dad was already gone by then, right?"

"Yes. He left when I was two. But when I found out I wasn't

really his, I wondered if maybe that was why he left. It made me feel, I don't know, like I was somehow less than what I'd been before. I guess maybe that's why I didn't want people to know. I was ashamed."

"But being adopted is nothing to be ashamed of," Eva said. "It wasn't like you did something wrong."

"I know that now, but I'm trying to tell you how I felt then and why I always kept it to myself."

She sat back against the bench and crossed her arms. "I can't believe you never told me this. It's like my whole life is a lie."

"No, it's not! Don't say that!" I sat up and tried to take her hand, but she pulled it away. "Eva, I didn't tell anyone. I can think of maybe three friends I ever told. It just wasn't something I liked to discuss."

"Does Daddy know?"

"Yes. And we talked about telling you and Ethan, but we didn't want you to feel differently about Grandma or anyone else in the family. I didn't want you to feel what I did. That you didn't belong."

Her eyes were filled with hurt when she looked up at me. "But don't you see? By not telling me, you just made me feel that way. The person I've always thought was my grandmother is not my grandmother. My aunts and uncles and cousins are not related to me."

"Grandma is still your grandmother, and she always will be. She's my mom. She's always been my mom, and nothing changes that. Those are still your aunts and uncles and cousins. They're your family. This doesn't change that."

She looked away from me, and the pain in her face wrenched my heart. "I don't know who I am."

It gutted me to think that she was now struggling with the same thought I'd battled since I found out.

"You're Eva Marie Miller. You know who you are. You know who your parents are. You know who your family is. This just adds another layer to your identity. It doesn't take anything away."

I hoped my words would be more convincing to her than they ever had been for me.

She stood and paced back and forth in front of the bench, and her anguish was like a knife twisting in my gut. I hated that this aspect of my life was causing Eva pain. I didn't want her to experience the doubts and fears that I had.

She stopped and turned to face me, her eyes blazing with anger.

"You're my mom. I'm supposed to be able to trust you. I'm supposed to be part of the inner circle of people you trust. We *are* family. We *are* blood. Why didn't you tell me? What else have you kept from me? What else don't I know?"

I wanted to say there was nothing else. I wanted to assure her that she could trust me. That she could feel secure in our relationship. But I knew I was still holding another card yet to be revealed.

CHAPTER 36

I rubbed the backs of my arms and hugged myself, gathering the strength to tell all.

"Last Friday when you and Ethan left to go camping with Daddy, I got a call from Mrs. Patsy. I'd never met her and had no idea who she was, but she told me she had information about my birth mother. That my birth mother wanted to meet me."

She walked closer as I talked, the curiosity eclipsing her anger once more.

"We set up a meeting at her house in Cedar Creek for that Saturday, but before I could get there, my birth mother was taken by ambulance to the hospital. To *this* hospital."

Eva's mouth flew open, and her eyes widened. "Caterina is your birth mother? Like, she's my grandmother?"

I nodded.

"Does she know you're here? Did you get to talk to her?"

"No. She's sedated, so we don't know what she's aware of, but she hasn't been awake since I got here."

"So that's your mom up there? Like, your real mom?"

I stood and walked to her. "Lorna is my mom. My *real* mom. Caterina may have given birth to me, and I hope I have a chance to get to know her and have a relationship with her, but nothing changes that Lorna is my mom. Or your Grandma."

"I still can't believe you didn't tell me," Eva said, her voice quiet and her expression a mixture of anger, hurt, and disbelief. "Not only that you didn't tell me you were adopted, but that you didn't tell me why we were here. Who she was. Or how you knew all these people in Cedar Creek."

I reached to smooth her hair back, and she didn't pull away. "Eva, it all happened so fast. It's been a whirlwind. Finding out my birth mother wanted to contact me, then finding out she may be dying. Seeing her but not being able to talk with her. Then there's this whole other layer of trying to figure out who my dad is."

Her eyes met mine, and shock registered on her face again. "Who is your dad?"

"I don't know," I said with a shrug. "I'm hoping Caterina can tell me."

"Is she gonna die?"

Panic gripped my heart at the thought of the very real possibility.

"I hope not."

"What's the deal with this Levi guy? How does he tie into all this?"

Somehow that question seemed harder to answer than explaining my adoption.

"I met Levi when I came to Cedar Creek to meet Caterina."

"And now you guys are dating?"

The line of questioning made me squirm, and I retreated to the bench, tucking my feet beneath me as I sat.

"I don't know that we're *dating*, but I enjoy his company."

"Obviously, from the way you were kissing him."

The heat of embarrassment flooded over me again, and I shifted my position and looked at the ground.

"Why have you never dated anyone?" Eva asked, leaning her shoulder against the pole.

"What?" I looked up at her, once again seeing Brad in her inquisitive stare.

"Daddy has had God only knows how many girlfriends since the divorce, but you haven't had even one boyfriend. Why not?"

"Well, partly because I haven't met anyone I was interested in."

That was true, but it was only a small part of the equation. I couldn't tell her I didn't want to date anyone because she and her brother needed to be my top priority. I didn't want her to feel responsible for my choices, and I didn't want to infer that they weren't a priority for their Dad. Even though they weren't, really.

"And now you're interested in this Levi guy?"

I hesitated, not wanting to admit it. Not wanting to put it out there and make a thing of it. But also not wanting to lie to my daughter in the midst of coming clean to her.

"Yes."

She looked away for a moment, her face pensive as she mulled over whatever thought was at the forefront of her mind.

"I like him," she said, looking back at me. All traces of anger were gone from her face, and her voice seemed to have relaxed. "He seems like a nice guy."

It felt like we were back to role reversal, and she was giving me her stamp of approval.

"I think he is," I said.

She sat down next to me and pulled a section of her hair between her fingers, plaiting it into a tiny braid as she stared at the ground.

I wanted to reach for her. I wanted to take her in my arms and make everything okay the way I could when she was younger. But Eva was growing up. She was becoming a young lady, and mommy kisses couldn't fix her hurts anymore. Especially when mommy had done the hurting.

"I truly am sorry, Eva. I didn't mean to hurt you. I wasn't trying to hide things from you. I was trying to protect you. To protect myself as well, I suppose."

She didn't say anything as she continued to unbraid and rebraid her hair.

"I tell you what," I said, leaning forward to better see her face. "Let's you and I make a pact. No secrets between us. From this day forward, you and I will be open and honest with each other, no matter what. We won't hide things. We won't do things behind each other's back. We won't lie to each other. What do you say?"

She shot me a sideways look and then sat back against the bench, staring into the night.

"I know, I know," I said, taking her silence as condemnation. "That should be a given already, but since we've both kind of screwed that up lately, how 'bout we just decide from here on out to reaffirm that as our policy and do things differently?"

She had glared at the reference to her own recent dishonesty and omission, but then she ran her fingers along her temples and scrunched her fists into her hair, groaning in frustration.

"Okay, you're right. If we're gonna be honest with each other, I have a confession to make."

She didn't look at me as she spoke, and the roles switched back so quickly that my head swam as I went into concerned mama mode, wondering what she was about to reveal.

"I've been skipping dance to hang out at play rehearsals with Greg. Ms. Showers gave me a verbal reprimand, and she was going to call you, so I went ahead and quit dance. I didn't want to do it anymore, and we're moving anyway. And about that—"

"Whoa, wait a minute. What do you mean you've been skipping dance? I've been dropping you off at dance or picking you up there when you ride from school with Shannon's mom."

Eva dropped her hands to her lap and sighed, all the anger gone as her expression turned sheepish. "Yeah. I'd stand outside or go in the lobby and wait when you dropped me off, and then once you left, I'd get in the car with Greg and go to play rehearsal. Then he'd bring me back before it was time for you to pick me up."

I was floored. Stunned. Here I was, yet again, clueless about what a member of my family was doing.

"You've got to be kidding me! How long has this been going on?"

"Only like a month. And I didn't skip every rehearsal. I only skipped on days Greg could get his mom's car."

"You've been riding around with some boy without my permission?" I stood, unable to contain my anger and hurt in a seated position. "You know how I feel about teenage drivers! You know you aren't supposed to ride with anyone!"

"He's a senior, Mom. He's been driving for a long time. He's a very safe driver. Nothing happened. We didn't wreck or anything."

"He's a senior? You're fourteen, Eva Marie. Fourteen! You're barely a freshman. You have no business riding around with a senior."

"See, this is why I didn't tell you. I knew you were going to be like this."

She got up and walked toward the hospital doors.

"Stop! Do not take another step, young lady!" I went and stood in front of her, struggling to remain calm. "Yes, I'm upset. Why wouldn't I be? You've been sneaking around behind my back. You've been lying to me. And you've been making choices that could have put you in danger against what you know my wishes were."

"And you've been sneaking around behind my back and lying to me. What's the difference?"

I sighed and crossed my arms. "The difference is I'm an adult, and sometimes I have to do what I think is best for you and make decisions without involving you. You, on the other hand, are not an adult. You are a teenager. You're *my* teenager. And you aren't to the point yet in life where you can decide what's best for you and make those decisions without involving me or getting my input."

Her face was an angry mask again. "That's not fair."

"Yeah, well, life's not fair. It's not ever going to be."

We stood silent, staring at each other in mirrored stances of crossed arms and stiff backs.

My phone buzzed in my pocket with an incoming call, and I ignored it, unwilling to break away from Eva at such an important moment.

"Look, I love you. I may not always do the right things or say the right things or make the right decisions, but you are always first and foremost in my mind and in my heart. I want what's best for you. And sometimes that means making you do things you may not want to do or keeping you from doing things that aren't in your best interest. Sometimes it means making you have consequences for your choices."

"What are your consequences for your choices?" she asked, arching one eyebrow.

"Life. Missing out on a career. Losing my own identity. Raising my children as a single mother. Having no financial independence. Depriving myself of passion and male companionship. The list goes on and on. No matter how old we are, our choices have consequences. It's my job to help guide the choices you make so that hopefully, you'll have more positive consequences than negative."

Patsy, George, and Ethan came through the double doors of the hospital entrance, and Ethan ran to me.

"There you are! Where have you guys been? Mrs. Patsy tried to call, and you didn't answer."

"Eva and I were having a little discussion, so I wasn't able to answer the phone. Everything okay?" I looked to Patsy, and she smiled, her eyes darting to Eva, who stood still as a statue staring straight ahead.

"Yes, but visiting hours are over, so George and I were going to head home. Are you coming to the house?"

"Can we, Mom? Please?" Ethan asked, dancing around me with the hyped-up energy of a ten-year-old without a care in the world.

My body felt drained of all energy. My limbs were heavy, and my neck and back ached with the tension I'd been holding in. I didn't want to make any more decisions. I didn't want to confront any more issues. I didn't want to decide what was best for anyone. Not me or my kids or George and Patsy.

So, I nodded and took the easiest way out.

"Okay, we'll stay. If you're sure it's no trouble."

"No trouble at all," George said. "I'll even make us some waffles in the morning."

"Ethan, honey, why don't you ride with Mr. George and me?" Patsy said, looking at Eva again and then at me. "I think your mom and Eva may need a bit more time to finish their discussion. If that's okay with your mom, of course."

I nodded, and the three of them led the way to the garage with Eva following behind us in silence.

The sight of the Tahoe took me back to my encounter with Levi, and a little flicker of joy sparked inside me, but then the weight of everything else in my life snuffed it out.

CHAPTER 37

"What is it about Greg that makes him so special?" I asked as Eva and I drove behind Patsy, George, and Ethan on the way to their house.

No response.

Eva hadn't spoken since before the others had come outside, and I wanted to find some way to break down the defensive wall she'd erected.

"What part does he have in the play?"

No response.

"C'mon, Eva. I'm trying. I'm trying to understand. I'm trying to stay calm and get a better understanding of your feelings instead of just freaking out. But I need you to try, too."

No response.

"What's your favorite thing about him?"

She shifted in her seat with a small sigh, and I waited to see if she would answer me.

No response.

"Eva, please."

"He's funny," she mumbled, barely loud enough for me to hear her.

"Funny? Well, a good sense of humor is important. What else?"

She shrugged. "He's smart. He makes good grades."

"Also important. What else?"

Her head turned away from me, and I could barely hear her when she spoke.

"He's a good kisser."

I nearly drove off the road. I wanted to slam on brakes. I wanted to yell and scream that I was not ready for this yet. That she wasn't

189

old enough yet. That time was moving too quickly, and I wasn't prepared to lose my little girl yet.

Luckily, I kept it under control to avoid shutting down the conversation all together. Above all, I needed to keep an open dialogue with her.

"Okay. Well. Is this why you've been so interested in theater all the sudden?"

I could see her nod in my peripheral vision.

"Is this the reason you gave up dance?"

Another shrug. "Partly. I mean, I am kind of bored with it. Plus, I don't want to have to start at some new studio where I don't know anyone, and they don't know me. Do we have to move? I know I said I wanted to when you and Daddy first brought it up, but that was before, well, before I started enjoying high school."

Before she found out Greg the senior was a good kisser.

"Does Daddy know about Greg?" I held my breath for her answer, selfishly hoping she'd only confided in me.

"What? No! Are you kidding? I'm not going to talk to Daddy about Greg! Gross."

A part of me rejoiced.

"You know you can talk to me about anything right? I mean, me and Daddy; you can talk to us both. But you know you can tell me anything, right?"

No response.

"Eva?"

"I don't know. I never know when you're gonna freak out. Like before."

"Well, that was a lot to take in before. I was hurt. I was upset."

"I'm sorry I didn't tell you," she said, looking at me until I looked in her direction, and then she turned away again.

"And I'm sorry I didn't tell you about being adopted. And Caterina."

"And Levi?"

It was my turn not to respond.

"So, we're making the pact, right?" I asked, turning to look at her while we were stopped at a traffic light. "Eva? No more secrets? No more lies?"

"Yeah. I guess."

"You guess? What kind of answer is that?"

"Am I allowed to keep seeing Greg?"

The traffic started moving, and I gripped the steering wheel tight as I tried to maintain a calm voice.

"I don't think that's a good idea."

"What? Why?"

"Eva, you're fourteen. He's too old for you. Besides, he's been sneaking around behind my back, too. He's been part of your deception. That says a lot to me about who he is and how much respect he has for you and for me."

"This is so stupid. He's only three years older than me. Three years. That's like, nothing. What if I had told you? What if I'd been upfront with you in the beginning? Then could I have dated him?"

"Probably not. But then you wouldn't be grounded for lying. Which is now going to be longer by the way. And you must tell your dad. It's only fair that he knows what's going on."

"Can't you tell him? Please? I can't talk to Daddy about boys, Mom. I can't!"

If the situation was reversed, I would definitely want Brad to insist that Eva tell me what was going on. I felt I owed him the same courtesy.

"I tell you what. We'll talk to him together, okay?"

She was quiet until we turned into Patsy's driveway.

"So where are we going to sleep? I don't have to sleep with Ethan, do I?"

"I'm sure you won't, but it's one night, Eva. We only have to make it through one night."

"Can I see her? Caterina?"

"Sure, but I think it might be best if you wait until she's awake."

"Did you want to wait until she was awake?"

"No." I opened the truck door and grabbed my purse, the exhaustion making my limbs feel heavy.

Patsy offered me their guest room, put Eva in their son's old room, and Ethan on the foldout couch in the den.

I went in to say goodnight to Eva after getting Ethan settled.

"I can't believe we're staying at a total stranger's house. This is so bizarre."

Strange that Patsy didn't feel like a stranger to me anymore.

"It's only one night, Eva."

She groaned and fluffed the pillow, reaching for her phone.

"There's something else I wanted to tell you," I said, sitting cross-legged on the foot of the bed. "I'm thinking about getting a job when we move."

"Why?"

"Because it's time that I went back to work. I've been home with you guys all this time, but you're in high school. Ethan's in middle school. You don't really need me at home during the day, so I'd like to do something with my time."

"Like what?"

"I don't know. I don't know what I want to do with my life now that I'm all grown up. I wanted to be an accountant when I first started college. When I met your dad."

"An accountant? That's boring."

I chuckled. "I enjoy numbers. I like working with things that are black and white. That follow a set of rules that doesn't change."

"Do we really have to move?"

Her eyes were so sad that it twisted my insides.

"Oh, sweetheart. I wish I knew of an option that would make everyone happy. Daddy has worked very hard for this promotion. It means a lot to make partner in a large firm like his. We agreed it would be best for us to go to Orlando with him so he can still see you guys and be a part of your lives."

"But he never sees us, anyway. He's only a part of our lives when it's convenient for him. Couldn't he just drive to Gainesville?"

I no longer knew for sure what the right answer was. Was I wrong to try and make it easier for them to see their dad? Should I just let him go live his life in Orlando and the kids and I stay in Gainesville? Why should I keep trying so hard if he seemed not to care and it didn't matter to Eva? Would Ethan be upset either way?

"It's been a really long day, Eva. I'm tired, and I can't think straight. I can't solve all our issues right now. Can we get some sleep and talk about this another time?"

She nodded, and I bent to kiss her forehead, wishing our problems were still as simple as they were when she was younger.

"Hey, Mom?" she asked as I turned out the light and opened the door to leave.

"Yeah?"

"Could Greg come over for a few hours and you actually get to know him before you say no?"

The need for sleep was eclipsing everything else in my mind, and I had no energy left to put others first.

"We'll talk about this tomorrow, okay? Goodnight. Love you."

When I'd finished brushing my teeth and removing the tired remnants of my makeup, I slid between the cool, crisp sheets of Patsy's guest bed and yawned as I checked my phone one last time, smiling when I saw the text on the screen.

"Hope Caterina is better. Miss you already. Call me when you can."

He answered on the first ring, and the tension in my body released at the sound of his voice.

"Caterina is still the same," I told him. "We decided to stay at Patsy's tonight."

"Good. I was worried about you driving back so late."

We chatted for a few minutes about the day, and then we said goodnight, ending the call early for a change. I went to sleep with a smile on my face, and I dreamed of the brown-haired, brown-eyed cowboy who had stolen my heart.

CHAPTER 38

I awoke early to the smell of bacon and the sound of Ethan laughing. It took me a few minutes to figure out where I was and if I was dreaming.

When I got my bearings and recognized Patsy's pale green guest room, I rose and went to the kitchen to watch my child delight in making waffles with George. The two had become fast buds, and it warmed my heart to see Ethan so happy.

The kids had never had a grandfather on my side, and Brad's father was generous with gifts but stingy with his time.

"Oh, you're up!" Patsy said as she came in from the screened porch with a watering can. "I was wondering if you'd like to go next door to Cat's and look at the accounts. See if you can make heads or tails of what she's got."

I jumped at the chance to visit Cat's house and learn more about her, but once we were there, the feeling of being an intruder came over me again.

Her home was spacious and clean. No clutter in sight. The bright tangerine-colored walls of the living room were adorned with paintings and prints that Patsy said were from Cat's travels, which appeared to have been extensive. The few framed photos sitting around were of Cat with children whom Patsy identified as her fosters. The sofa was sleek and contemporary, with white cushions and a dark wood frame. A round Papasan chair sat in one corner with a plush suede cushion and a couple of throw pillows. Another chair in the opposite corner looked to be some type of modern design recliner with a dark wood frame and multi-colored cushions.

We passed through a hallway of doors that were each painted a different jewel-tone color, and then into a bedroom that had been converted into an office. The walls were white, and the back wall of the room featured a sliding glass door looking out onto a screened pool enclosure filled with luscious greenery and inviting hammocks and loungers.

Everything about the home was inviting. Colorful. Cheerful. Playful. Warm.

It spoke volumes about the woman who lived there, and my heart ached to meet her. To know her.

It didn't take long at all to realize the books were a mess. Cat's shorthand accounting symbols weren't too hard to decipher, but it was clear that she wasn't too diligent or meticulous when it came to record-keeping. Receipts were paper-clipped to pages or stuffed haphazardly between them. There were handwritten notes on scraps of paper or on Post-its, and some entries had lines scratched through them with numbers written above the previous entry. If the numbers were correct, the foundation was fiscally healthy, but I wondered how accurate it was when the methods used to track it were madness.

"Why doesn't she use an online system or at least an Excel spreadsheet to do this? She has a computer sitting here, so why is she still doing everything by hand?"

Patsy smiled. "Cat hates dealing with the computer. She does email from necessity, and she'll use it for research, but I swear to you, something about her energy level crashes technology. You think I'm joking, but she literally has some kind of high energy field that messes with everything she touches. That's why those are there."

She pointed to a collection of stones and crystals sitting on the desk near the computer.

"Someone told her those would help."

"And did they?"

Patsy shrugged. "Maybe they do, and maybe they don't. Some days it all crashes, and some days it doesn't. She can't keep a phone working for more than a couple of months."

She picked up a file of folders and loose statements and paperwork from Cat's desk.

"I tried to go through these and put them in date order. Make some sense of them. I've got some things here on top that look like they need to be paid. I know there are adoptions pending that are waiting on financing from us. And of course, there are recurring bills as well. Do you think you can do anything with this?"

"I think I have a handle on what she's got and what's she doing, and I can certainly go through to see what's due. But are you sure she'd be okay with me doing all this? I feel like I'm overstepping my bounds."

Patsy sighed and sat in the chair of the other desk.

"I'll be honest. I don't know if she'll be okay with it or not. But I know she won't be okay with adoptions being delayed or the foundation being delinquent on its responsibilities. She didn't intend to be away for this past week, so she didn't prepare anything before she went. If you could help me keep things going until she returns, I'll be glad to own it if Cat's not happy with it."

We gathered what Patsy thought I most needed and went back to her house.

Eva was still sleeping, but I woke her to join us for breakfast. She was less grouchy than normal for a morning, and I was floored but pleased when she offered to help Patsy clean up after we ate.

We arrived at the hospital soon after visiting hours began, and the nurses greeted us with smiles. Caterina's condition had improved.

When the doctor made her rounds to update us, she said they would keep Cat on the current antibiotics since she seemed to be responding well, and if her progress continued, they could eventually start to wean her off the ventilator.

Patsy and I hugged each other in relief.

"Let's go get a celebratory cup of coffee," she said, her face alight with joy.

"Yes! Finally, some good news."

We were almost to the elevator when I put my hand on her arm. "Patsy, can I talk to you about something? Before we go down to the kids?"

"Sure, honey. Anything. What is it?"

"Eva knows about Caterina. I told her last night. She wants to see her."

Patsy nodded. "I wondered if that was what that was all about."

"That was only part of it," I said with a frown, hugging my arms around me. "She saw me and Levi together."

Patsy lifted one eyebrow with a questioning gaze, and I sighed.

"Yes, okay. You were right. There *is* something there. I didn't want the kids to see him here, so he met me in the garage to, um, say hello. Eva saw us and was pretty upset that she didn't know what was going on. With any of it. Why we were in Cedar Creek. Who Caterina was. Or even that I was adopted."

"How is she now that she knows?"

I shrugged. "Okay, I guess? I don't know. It was a lot to dump on her at one time."

"Kids are very resilient," Patsy said. "They're also more understanding than we give them credit for when we take the time to explain things to them. We just have to remember they have feelings about the situation, too."

I frowned and bit down on my lip, unable to stop the whirlwind of worries that had been occupying my thoughts.

"So you think I should let her see Cat?"

"I don't see where it could hurt if it's important to her. You need to prepare her for what she'll see. The tubes, the machine breathing for Cat. The bluish tint to her skin."

"I don't know. I feel like I'm screwing up left and right with her lately."

We stepped out of the way of a family getting off the elevator, and Patsy patted my arm.

"That's motherhood, Caroline. We all feel like we're screwing up from day to day, especially in the teenage years. Those are the hardest, I think."

"We're supposed to move to Orlando soon," I said, leaning my shoulder against the wall and lowering my voice. "And I'm doubting if it's the right choice. Their dad got a big promotion, and it seemed to make sense that we would go where he was. I don't work outside the home, so there was nothing keeping me in Gainesville other than the kids' interests. We talked to Eva and Ethan, and they both said they'd rather be near their dad. But now Eva's in high school, and she's got a boyfriend, evidently, which I need to nip in the bud."

Patsy raised both eyebrows and gave a scoffing laugh. "Good luck with that! To my experience, the harder you try to keep two teenagers apart, the more certain they are they belong together."

"He's a senior. She's a freshman. They've been sneaking around behind my back."

"And you think she'll stop because you tell her she's not supposed to? Don't you remember what it was like at that age?"

"No. I mean, I remember, but I wasn't that into boys. I didn't date much at all until my senior year, and even then, nothing serious. Brad was the first relationship I had, and I ended up married to him. What am I supposed to do? I can't just let her keep seeing him. Can I?"

"I can't tell you what to do, of course, but I would suggest that you don't cut it off completely. Nothing is more desirable than the forbidden. Maybe set up some boundaries. She can only see him in your home with your supervision. Or whatever you see fit." She shifted her knitting bag on her arm and offered a weak smile. "Generally, these things play themselves out rather quickly without our interference. Keep her where you can see her and protect her from making decisions that she can't come back from, but allow her the space for the decision to be hers and she'll learn more from it."

I mulled over her words as we rode the elevator down and met the kids and George in the cafeteria. It seemed surreal how much my life had changed in such a short period of time. It hadn't been too long ago that my daily stresses were how to get a nutritious dinner in on nights with late soccer games and how to be two places at once when they both had commitments to attend.

The stakes were much higher in so many directions lately.

But amid the chaos, there was the hope of Caterina getting better. Of me finally being able to talk to her.

And there was Levi.

CHAPTER 39

I excused myself from the mini-celebration in the cafeteria to go the restroom, dialing Levi once I was out of earshot.

"Hey!" I said when he answered. "Caterina's getting better! They said her blood gases are improving, whatever those are, and she's oxygenating better, whatever that means. Evidently, both are good because they're saying if she continues to improve, they can start to wean her off the ventilator."

"That's awesome," he said, and the smile in his voice was evident. "She should be awake soon. You'll get to talk to her."

"Finally!"

"How are things with Eva this morning?"

"Okay, I guess. We haven't really had any time alone, so we haven't discussed much."

"I'm sorry. I know you told me last night to quit apologizing, but—"

"But nothing. You offered to come see me, and I said yes. I could have said no. It was my decision. You have nothing to apologize for. It's okay. She and I needed to talk."

He was quiet for a moment, and I stared at my reflection in the bathroom mirror, wondering where on the farm he was and what he was doing.

"I would never want to cause any problems between you and your kids, Caroline."

I turned away from my reflection and gazed at the ceiling, resting my hips against the bathroom counter.

"You didn't."

"Well, given the circumstances, I know this is probably a no-go, but Malcolm still has his roping stuff set up from yesterday, so if you wanted to bring them out before you head back to Gainesville, he could run Ethan through some lessons. William's about the best person on the planet to teach someone to ride, and he said he'd be happy to work with Eva."

"I'm sure they would love that, but let me see how it goes here. Eva wants to see Caterina, so I'm not sure what's going to happen with that. I still have to figure out how to tell Ethan what's happening. So, I don't know."

"I understand. You do what you need to do," he said. "We'll be here if you decide to come."

When I got back to the cafeteria, I asked Eva to take a walk outside with me.

"I'll take you to see Caterina if you're sure that's what you want. But she isn't herself right now. I wish I hadn't met her like this. I wish I had met her awake, laughing, smiling. The way others have seen her. I wish I knew her with this incredible energy everyone else speaks of instead of the shell of a woman lying there with tubes coming out of her and a machine taking her breaths for her."

We stopped walking and faced each other.

"They say she's getting better," I said. "That soon she'll be weaned off the ventilator, and then she'll be awake. You could wait. You could meet her then instead."

Eva stared past me at the fountain where we'd watched Ethan play the night before.

"How long do you think it will be before she wakes up?"

I shook my head. "I don't know. Hopefully a few days? Maybe a week? Once they start weaning her, there's a process they must go through before she's fully awake, so I can't say really."

"Okay. I guess I'll wait. Are we going back home or are we going to wait here for her to wake up?"

"We'll go back. Now that I know that she's getting better, I feel comfortable leaving. Mrs. Patsy will keep me updated, and as soon as I know she's awake, I'll come back."

"*We'll* come back."

I cocked my head to the side and smiled. "Let's see when that is and what's going on. But you *will* get to meet her, okay?"

"When are you going to tell Ethan?" she asked as we walked back toward the entry doors.

My cheeks puffed out as I blew out my frustration with a sigh. "I don't know. Soon. Maybe when we get home?"

"Sooner rather than later would be best."

I nodded, knowing she was right but not ready to deal with it.

"By the end of the day, okay?" I pulled the door open, but then let it close while I held it. "Hey, what would you think about driving back out to the farm for a little while before we head back?"

"Why? So you can see *Levi?*"

"Nooo. So you can ride a horse, and Ethan can rope something."

Her eyes brightened, and a smile broke across her face. "You mean it? Really?"

"Yeah, I don't see why not. The offer was made, and we don't have to be back at any certain time."

"Yes! Awesome!"

I smiled at her enthusiasm and followed her into the cafeteria where she shared the news with Ethan, who was thrilled even though he still had no clue what roping entailed.

Once we'd said our goodbyes to Patsy and George, I texted Levi that we were on our way. He said to come to the office barn, and he and William would meet us there.

Ethan was so excited on the ride over that he could barely contain himself, asking rapid-fire questions about farms that I had no idea how to answer.

Even Eva was in a great mood. She didn't snap at Ethan even once, and she didn't complain about my choice of stations on the radio.

"Wow. This is really nice," she said as we entered the roundabout in front of the house.

"I'd rather live in the barn," Ethan chimed in.

William and Levi were talking to a couple of other men by the entrance to the farm office, and I bristled when I saw Piper in their group.

"Welcome back," William said to the kids as we exited the Tahoe. "Y'all ready for some roping and riding?"

"Let me see your right arm," Malcolm said to Ethan as he held his own arm up and flexed it.

Ethan mirrored the action, and Malcolm did a light squeeze of Ethan's bicep and nodded, giving a thumbs up.

"Strong arm. You'll be able to swing a rope with no problem."

"You've never ridden a horse?" William asked Eva.

"No, sir."

"Ever been around a horse?"

"No, sir."

"Well, Piper's gonna saddle up one of the work mares for you, and we'll get you acquainted. You got any other shoes with you?"

Eva looked down at her flip flops and shook her head.

"What size are you?" Piper asked, and when Eva answered, Piper nodded. "I've got something for you. Come with me."

The two of them headed toward the big house, and I was torn between wanting to accompany Eva but needing to stay with Ethan.

Malcolm pulled one of the extended carts around and stopped in front of us.

"Let's go. You've got work to do, cowboy."

Ethan grinned and climbed onto the back of the cart.

"Go ahead," William said, noticing my glances back toward the house. "I'll let Eva know you went, and I'll come get you before she's in the saddle."

"Thank you," I said, taking a seat next to Ethan as I looked at Levi. "You coming?"

Uncertainty passed over his face, his smile tentative as he asked, "You want me to?"

"Sure. Unless you have something you need to do."

"I can tag along," he said, smiling as he climbed into the front seat next to Malcolm.

CHAPTER 40

Malcolm talked to Ethan as he drove, explaining why roping is necessary on a cattle ranch like the one he worked on before coming to Ward Farms.

We arrived at the site of the festivities the day before, where a crew of farmhands were taking down the tents and cleaning up the area.

Malcolm led us into a fenced enclosure where there were bales of hay with makeshift steer heads featuring metal pipes for horns. There were also a couple of metal frames that looked like stick figure cows leaning forward, with swinging metal pipes on a hinge for the back legs.

Levi and I stood next to each other leaning on the fence as we watched Malcolm teach Ethan the proper way to hold the rope.

We weren't standing close enough to touch, but his proximity was enough to make my body respond. Every nerve felt like it was buzzing, and I was hyperaware of each movement he made by my side.

"Thanks for coming out," Levi whispered, leaning toward me. "I was hoping I'd get to see you again before you left."

"Thanks for inviting us." I smiled as I watched Ethan twist the rope like Malcolm showed him, allowing my arm to drift just enough to the left that my elbow rested against Levi's.

He sucked in a sudden breath, and I chuckled, pleased to know I wasn't the only one affected.

Malcolm took Ethan through the basics of holding the rope, and then he began showing him how to toss the loop so it would go first over one horn and land over the other.

As we watched them, Levi and I teased each other with casual brushes, accidental bumps that were in no way accidental, and sideways glances that smoldered. My body was so worked up that I would have gladly grabbed him by the hand and dragged him in the barn to find an empty stall and a pile of hay if my son hadn't been standing a few feet from us.

It had been ages since I'd flirted, and it felt good. To desire and be desired was intoxicating, and I was drinking it in like I'd been starved of it for years. Which, I had.

We both turned as a truck pulled into the barnyard behind us, and I took a step away from Levi, self-conscious as William got out of the truck and walked toward us.

"How's he doing?" he asked, nodding toward Ethan, who had progressed to swinging the rope over his head and still being able to snag both horns on most tosses.

"He's doing great," Levi said. "He takes direction well."

"Yeah, I wish he listened as well at home as he does here," I said, and both men chuckled. "How's Eva doing? Is she okay?"

"Eva's doing well," William said. "She's very intuitive. Hard to believe she hasn't been around animals."

"No, her dad has this thing about animals being dirty, so we've never had any pets. They've begged for one. Maybe it's something I should look into when we move."

"You're moving?" William said, surprise registering on his face. "Where to?"

"Orlando."

"What part?"

"I don't know yet. Still doing the research on the area. Schools and what not."

"Hmm," William said, lifting his hat up to scratch his temple. "Excellent schools in Cedar Creek from what I understand. Fairly close to Orlando when you need to get there, but none of the hustle and bustle. All that traffic and congestion. They can keep it."

"Think we've got us a new cowhand, William," Malcolm said as he came to stand on the other side of the fence across from us. "The boy's got a good arm. He's a little impatient, but he's determined."

Ethan's face was a mask of concentration, his tongue between his teeth as he stared at the horns and lifted the rope to swing it over his head. He tossed and landed it over both horns the way Malcolm had shown him, and his face lit up with pride as he looked to us for approval.

"You ready to take a ride over to where Eva is?" William asked me, and I called Ethan over to the fence.

"Let's go watch Eva ride."

"But I still have to learn that one," he said, pointing toward the standing frame.

"Maybe another time, okay? I want to go see your sister."

"Can't I just stay here with Malcolm and Levi?"

"I'm sure Malcolm has work he needs to do. Could you please thank him for teaching you, and then let's get in the truck?"

He carried the rope back to Malcolm and thanked him, frowning as he left the enclosure and followed me to William's truck.

"I didn't get to learn everything."

"You could spend years on a farm and not learn everything there is to know," William said as he held the truck door open. "You'll just have to come back another time and learn something else."

I glanced over my shoulder at Levi, wondering how we were all going to fit in William's truck. He had hung back a bit, and I realized with disappointment that he didn't intend to go with us.

"You're not coming?"

"I want to help Malcolm get these loaded up and put away. I'll join you in a few."

His eyes were soft as he smiled at me, and I tried to hide my disappointment behind a forced smile as I got into the truck next to Ethan.

Ethan asked William question after question as we rode through the farm, and William answered with patience and thoughtfulness, seeming to take a genuine interest in Ethan's curiosity. William smiled as he talked, the same melancholy smile I'd seen him wear when I met him at breakfast, where half his mouth curled up while the other half looked grim.

"It's so pretty here," I said as I gazed out across the rolling hills and majestic oaks. "The dark wood fence against the bright green grass. The trees in the background. It's like a postcard."

William chuckled. "I guess so. The dark wood is so the horses can see it. If a horse gets spooked and bolts, he's looking far ahead to where he intends to go, so you have to make sure he sees the fence before he crashes into it. It's got to be sturdy enough to hold him without hurting him, high enough that he can't jump over it, and the gaps narrow enough that he can't get his head stuck in between them."

"Who builds all these fences?" Ethan asked.

"Levi has a crew that manages that now, but I have to say, I miss the days when I'd head out with the boys to spend hours putting posts in the ground or repairing fence line. There's nothing like the steady labor of building fences to give you time to think. Clear your head. I spent many a year building fences in my youth. Fences keep things you don't want out, and they keep what we value most in. They also remind us to pay attention to what's right in front of us rather than spending all our time gazing off into the horizon for what might be. Or what might have been."

His voice had grown quiet, and his eyes had gotten distant, as though his thoughts had gone elsewhere. He looked back at me suddenly, like he'd forgotten we were there, and then he picked up the coffee mug in the drink holder and took a long swig.

"Is Russo her married name?"

I was startled by the change in subject, and it took me a second to catch up and answer. "No. She was never married."

I tried to think of a way to signal William that Ethan didn't know about Caterina being my birth mother, but in the cramped quarters of the truck, it was impossible.

"And you said she was from New Jersey. What brought her to Cedar Creek?"

"She's always been active with adoption issues, and she started a foundation to help others and based it in here in Cedar Creek. Why she chose this town, I don't really know. I hope to find out when I get to talk to her. The nurses told us today she's improving, so hopefully that will be soon."

"That's good to hear."

"What brought you to Cedar Creek?" I asked, hoping that changing the subject would keep him from revealing what I hadn't yet told Ethan. "Levi said you grew up near Ocala?"

"I liked its simplicity. The small-town feel. I guess mostly I liked that it was close enough to the business I wanted to be in without being right in the center of it. I thought I had a lot to prove back then, and in my mind, I needed to get away from those who were firmly entrenched in the business in order to do it my way."

We pulled up to a barn I hadn't yet seen, and Ethan and I followed William as he got out and led us through a gate and around to the back. Eva was standing with Piper next to a horse, and the two of them were laughing together as Piper handed Eva the reins and bent to look at something on the horse's leg.

A pang of jealousy pinched me, and I wasn't sure if it was because of my confrontation with Piper or how Eva and I didn't seem to laugh together as much lately. Perhaps it was both.

"Hey, Mom!" Her eyes were bright, and her smile was full, and it made my heart soar to see her joy.

"How's it going?"

"Awesome. This is Athena," she said, rubbing her hand down the horse's dark neck. "She's not one of the thoroughbreds. She's just a farm horse, but isn't she beautiful?"

"She is."

Eva was wearing a pair of Piper's pink cowboy boots with her denim shorts and red T-shirt, and I couldn't help being surprised at how much at ease she appeared. She would never have dreamed of wearing such a thing in front of her friends back home.

William left Ethan and I on the other side of the fence and joined the two of them, taking the reins from Eva to walk her and Athena out toward the middle of the ring.

Piper came to stand with Ethan and me, her own smile much bigger than I'd seen before.

"How'd you do roping?" she asked Ethan.

"I didn't get him every time, but I was getting better by the end."

"It takes a lot of practice to get him every time. And then once you get the hay bale cow every time, you have to try on one that's moving." She glanced at me, and her smile faltered for a split second before she pasted it back in place. "Caroline, how are you today?"

"Fine," I said, forcing a grin with a polite nod. "Thank you for helping Eva and for the boots."

"Oh, no problem. She's got a way with animals. Athena responded really well to her. I'll be interested to see how she rides."

William was speaking to Eva in low, hushed tones, and I couldn't hear his words, but Eva was listening intently, her focus on his movements conveying her respect.

"Daddy is like the horse whisperer," Piper said. "No one can get horses to do what Daddy can. It's what he's known for. He's the best to teach anyone to ride, because he exudes this calm authority that the beast and the rider give in to."

I saw the truth in her words as he helped Eva onto Athena's back, giving her instruction as to how to get settled in the saddle as Athena stood patiently, swishing her black tail to deter the occasional fly that came too close.

Eva never liked attempting new things. She was self-conscious about failing, and her fear of it often manifested in an attitude of not wanting to try or wanting to pass it off like she didn't care if she succeeded.

But with William guiding her, she remained calm and focused. She never once looked over at us to see if we were watching. There were no eye rolls, no exasperated sighs, and no tossing of the hair. Her expression was serious, intense even, but I'd never seen her look so confident in attempting something new.

She took to riding like a fish to water, and even Piper commented how natural Eva looked on horseback.

Ethan began to get bored after watching Eva go around in circles several dozen times, and Piper offered to get him on a horse of his own.

I was more nervous about Ethan on horseback than Eva, but he spoke up before I had the chance to protest.

"Um, no, that's okay. I don't think I like riding horses."

"Have you ever done it?" Piper asked.

"No, but they're awfully big. I think I might like it better when I'm taller."

I smiled, surprised to hear my wild child be timid, but thankful that my anxiety was spared.

"Athena's gonna be thirsty when Eva's done. Why don't you go get that hose over there and bring it to this watering trough?" Piper suggested. She watched him go and turned back to me, clearing her throat before she spoke. "I wanted to apologize if I overstepped yesterday. You and Levi are both adults, and what you choose to do is none of my business. He's like a brother to me, and I'd just hate to see him get hurt. That's all."

"I have no intention of hurting Levi, Piper. Nor do I want to get hurt myself, or to see them get hurt." I nodded toward Eva and looked back at Ethan, who was carrying the hose over his shoulder.

"Levi's a great guy," she said. "He's got a heart like you wouldn't believe. I've always said the woman who lassoed it would be a lucky gal."

I wasn't sure what to say to that, so I remained silent and watched Eva glide around the ring effortlessly as though she and the horse were one.

Piper helped Ethan get the hose through the fence and into the trough, and then she sent him back to turn the water on.

"Levi seems happier since he met you, that's for sure," she said when Ethan was gone.

"That's a good thing, right?"

She smiled as she tilted her head a bit and stared at me, and then the smile widened, reaching her eyes.

"It's a very good thing. And if you're happy and he's happy, then I'm happy for you."

"Thank you."

Ethan ran back to watch the trough fill and then back over to turn the water off.

"Want to come with me and feed the other farm horses some hay?" Piper asked him.

"Yeah, sure. But do I have to get close to them?"

"You don't have to, but if you're gonna learn to rope, you have to get close to the animals. C'mon. Let's go meet the horses, and you can decide how close you wanna get."

The two of them left me to watch Eva, but I wasn't alone for long.

CHAPTER 41

I turned as soon as I heard the truck coming down the drive, and my insides got all giddy when I saw that it was Levi.

"How's she doing?" he asked when he joined me at the fence.

"Good, I guess. Piper and William both seem to think she's doing well."

"They would be the ones to tell you. The two of them are known throughout the industry for their abilities in training. William's considered a master at it."

William had joined Eva on a horse of his own, and they had gone beyond the enclosure to a larger area that allowed them more room for the horses to run.

"She sits well, that's for sure," Levi said, grinning.

"And that's a good thing?"

"Yeah, if you want to be a rider, it is. Where's the little man?"

"Piper took him to feed some horses."

Levi's eyebrows rose, and his chin dropped. "Piper took him? Really?"

"Yes, why? Is that a problem? Should I be concerned?"

He laughed. "No, not at all. I'm just surprised. Piper doesn't do kids. Doesn't care to be anywhere near them."

"So then why does she host an event for the community kids twice a year?"

He propped his boot on the lowest rail of the fence and rested his forearms on the top rail. "Because her mother started it, and she continues it in her honor. But she hangs in the volunteer tent and coordinates the adults. You will rarely, if ever, see her deal with children. She must like yours. Or she likes you."

I shook my head and exhaled. "I don't think so. The kids maybe, but not me."

"What do you mean?" Levi asked, tilting his head to the side as he put his foot down and turned to face me.

"I don't think Piper is a fan of this," I said, pointing back and forth between us.

"Meh," he said with a dismissive gesture. "Piper's like a grizzly bear when it comes to her family. She's very protective, but if she didn't like you, I guarantee she wouldn't have been out here with Eva today, and she damned sure wouldn't have offered to go anywhere with Ethan."

"Mom!" Ethan yelled behind me as he came running out of the stables. "I fed the horses! They let me pet them."

His exuberance was contagious, and I clapped my hands together and laughed.

"I guess you did get close! Good job!"

"It took a little coaxing, but he warmed up," Piper said, pulling off work gloves as she walked toward us. "Did you invite them to eat?"

"I came up here to do that very thing but hadn't gotten around to it yet," Levi said. "Gaynelle made spaghetti today. Would you, Eva, and Ethan care to join us?"

"Does Gaynelle cook every meal? And is it always as big as that breakfast?"

Levi nodded. "She spoils us all."

Piper laid the gloves on the fence post and shoved her hands in her back pockets.

"Years ago, Daddy hired Gaynelle's husband, Pete, and they came to live in the housing circle. My mama couldn't even boil water, so when she learned Gaynelle liked to cook, she hired her to start making meals in the big house, and everyone was invited. Not too long after that, Daddy discovered Pete had a weakness for booze and a habit of being mean when he got drunk. So, he kicked Pete off the property and told Gaynelle as long as he owned this farm, she'd always have a place to live. Gaynelle told him as long as she lived here, he'd never go hungry. And they've both kept their promises. As the number of farmhands grew, so did Gaynelle's meals. I don't think she knows how to cook for less than twenty now."

She and Levi both laughed.

A movement caught my eye, and I turned to see Eva and William returning from their ride. Eva's face was flushed with excitement, and she was listening intently to William as he talked, nodding and answering his questions.

When they'd dismounted and gone through the process of putting the horses and equipment away, they joined us by the trucks.

"How'd you like that?" I asked Eva, but the smile on her face and the light in her eyes made the answer evident without her speaking.

"I loved it. I really loved it, Mom. When can we come back? Mr. William said he'd work with me if I want. When can we come back?"

I saw Levi's surprised expression as he looked from Eva to William, and I wondered what was behind it.

"She's got a real natural seat and a strong leg," William said. "If it's something she's interested in pursuing, I'd love to work with her."

"Oh, well, I don't know."

"Please, Mom? We could come on weekends, couldn't we? It's not that far."

Just the thought of adding one more layer of commitment to my already hectic schedule was rattling, and to consider all the other complexities of Cedar Creek made it even more daunting.

"Can we talk about this later?"

William spoke up, and to my surprise, Eva immediately quieted and listened to him.

"This is a conversation to have with your parents in private. I should have talked to your mother before I mentioned it to you." He turned to me and gave a slight bow. "My apologies. I meant no disrespect. It's just been a while since I've seen one with such an easy rhythm. I got ahead of myself."

"Oh, it's no problem. I just don't know how we'd, well, we'll have to discuss it, that's all."

"Of course," Williams said with his signature melancholy smile. "Did anyone invite them to eat?"

"Yes," Levi and Piper said in unison.

"And? Are you joining us?" He looked to me, and I nodded.

"I suppose we can. We don't have any other meal plans."

Eva rode back to the big house with William and Piper, and Ethan sat between Levi and me in Levi's truck.

Ethan and Levi talked nonstop about horses, but I couldn't concentrate on their conversation.

My mind was on Eva. I'd never seen her so passionate about anything other than dance. She rarely got that excited about anything, and to have two professionals gush over her abilities wasn't something to take lightly. But how on earth would I give Eva access to William Ward and his horses? There was no way to make that convenient on a regular basis.

Which, of course, turned my thoughts to Levi, and how hard it would be to pursue our newfound passion for each other on a regular basis.

Why must everything good be so complicated?

The other farmhands had already eaten by the time we all arrived at the big house, so it was only William, Piper, and Levi with me and the kids at the massive table.

The conversation was almost as boisterous with our small group as it had been with the large breakfast group I'd encountered, and William seemed thoroughly entertained by my children.

When we'd finished with the heaping piles of spaghetti, Gaynelle came in and asked if anyone in the group wanted ice cream.

Ethan was, of course, the first to answer, and I told Gaynelle she'd tapped into his Kryptonite. That kid would do anything for ice cream.

She took Eva and Ethan to the kitchen to choose what they wanted, and William settled back in his chair. He drained his glass of tea as Piper and Levi discussed an upcoming horse show.

"You mentioned your birth mother had started a foundation. Something to do with adoption, you said?"

"From what I understand, she helps with funding for families trying to adopt, and she helps children who are in the foster system to make sure their needs are being met. It seems to be a pretty far-reaching foundation from what I've turned up on-line, so I look forward to discussing it with her. It's called Turtle Crossing."

William's head snapped up, and his eyes were wide as he looked at me. "What's it called?"

"Turtle Crossing. I know, that's kind of a weird name for an adoption organization, isn't it?"

William pushed his chair back and stood. "Excuse me. I need to take care of something."

"Daddy, you okay?" Piper asked, her voice filled with concern. "You look like you've seen a ghost."

"I'm, uh, I have to go." He left the room, and the three of us stared after him.

"What was that about? What happened?" Piper asked.

"I don't know. We were talking about my birth mother's adoption foundation, and he just stood up and said he had to go."

"He probably forgot to do something. He refuses to set reminders on his phone, but he's constantly forgetting stuff and missing phone calls and appointments," Piper said, gathering her plate and standing to walk it to the kitchen. "Sorry about that. Something probably popped in his head he'd forgotten, and he ran off to take care of it."

"Oh. I hope it's nothing serious."

"Me, too! Last week he forgot to meet a guy at the airport to pick up an incoming horse. Luckily, he had his cell phone with him and the guy could reach him, but he had to wait for an hour for Daddy to get there. I would say it's old age creeping in, but Daddy's always been forgetful. Mama kept him in line much better than I'm able to."

Levi and I stared at each other as she left the room.

"I think this is the first time we've been alone all day," I said, my mind already thinking of ways to take advantage of the opportunity.

"I think you're right. Of course, anyone could walk in at any minute."

"True. Too bad there's not a cubby somewhere we could duck into. Steal a moment for a kiss."

He grinned and stood, offering his hand to pull me up, and my heart raced as our skin made contact.

He led me to the end of the room opposite the kitchen and through a door into a smaller room with three walls of shelves filled with books and a fourth wall of windows overlooking the back gardens and pool. There was an elegant oak desk in the center of the room with a large wingback chair behind it, and two curved armless chairs in front with seats and backs of lush sage green velvet.

It looked like a room that would be featured in an architectural or design magazine but didn't look like it saw much use.

"What is this room?" I asked as he pulled me inside and quietly shut the door.

"It was intended as William's office, but it wasn't practical, so he's always used the offices over in the barn."

He wrapped his left arm around my waist and pulled me into him, lifting my chin with his right hand as his lips found mine.

Goose flesh rippled across my skin, and I threw my arms around his neck and thrust my tongue against his. The pulsing ache I'd felt deep inside grew stronger, and I pressed my hips to his, instinctively seeking what I needed from him.

I heard the kids' voices on the other side of the door, and Ethan called out, "Mom! Where'd you go?"

Levi swore under his breath as our lips parted, and I placed my hands on either side of his face, forcing his eyes to meet mine.

"Promise me the next time we're alone and uninterrupted you won't walk away," I whispered.

"I won't ever walk away again," he said, taking my mouth one more time before he pulled back and stepped forward to swing the door open.

My pulse was pounding, and I could feel it strongest between my thighs, where the ache had built to an almost unbearable level. I rubbed the back of my hand across my mouth as he greeted the kids, inviting them to come and see all the books in William's office. I turned away as they entered, pretending to read the titles on the shelf nearest me, but in reality, I was struggling to get my breath under control and stop my knees from shaking.

"Whoa, that's a lot of books. Has he read all these?" Ethan asked Levi.

"I'm pretty sure he's read most of them, if not all. He's got a book in his hand pretty much any time he's indoors."

"How you doin', Mom?" Eva asked with a knowing smirk. "Feeling okay?"

I straightened my shoulders and reached for a random book on the shelf. "Feeling fine, Eva Marie. Why? How are you feeling?"

She laughed and walked to the windows to look out at the pool.

I replaced the book and moved to stand beside her. Unlike most Florida homes, there was no screened enclosure covering the pool. It was open air, surrounded by grass and a narrow border of river stones. Four white columns stood at the other end of the pool, and two white horses reared in front of them, a fountain of water gushing between their feet and into the pool below.

"Beautiful, isn't it?"

"The pool?" she asked. "Yeah. It is." She leaned over and whispered, "You guys are so obvious." She chuckled and shook her head, and I smiled at her teasing tone as embarrassment burned my cheeks.

"Do you know where Piper went?" she asked. "I need to give her boots back before we go."

"Keep them," Piper said as she entered the office. "I have more boots than I can count. Those are a little small on me, so if you like them, they're yours."

"Really?" Eva asked, looking down at her feet as she rocked back on her heels and moved her toes left and right. "Thanks!"

The bubble gum pink boots were not something I would have ever picked out for Eva in a million years. She'd never been a fan of pink, and I'd never once heard her mention cowboy boots in a positive light before, but she seemed delighted with Piper's gift.

"Thanks, Piper," I said. "I didn't know we were going to see you this weekend, so I didn't bring your clothes, but I'm sure I'll be back some time in the next week or so to see Caterina, so I'll bring them then."

"No worries," Piper said as she plopped down in the wingback chair and swung her leg over the side. I cringed at the sight of her being so lackadaisical with what was obviously an expensive chair, and the mom in me almost told her to sit up straight with her feet on the floor. But it was her house, and therefore, her chair, and nothing about Piper had indicated she was even remotely concerned with propriety.

We went back to the dining room and talked while Eva and Ethan finished their ice cream, and then the kids and I said our goodbyes and Levi walked us out to the Tahoe.

"Keep me posted on Caterina," he said as he stood an appropriate distance from my door.

"I will," I said, smiling as I bit down on my lip and imagined the goodbye kiss we were forbidden to have.

"Drive carefully." His eyes smoldered, and I knew his thoughts weren't far from my own.

"I will. You have a good week."

"You, too."

The ache was still there, and not being able to properly say goodbye did nothing to dissipate it, but I drove away with a smile, knowing I'd be seeing him again as soon as we could make it happen.

CHAPTER 42

Patsy and I talked a couple of times each day, and every update she gave brought news of further improvement with Caterina's condition.

When she called Wednesday, her voice was bubbling with excitement, and I sat down in one of my kitchen chairs to concentrate on her news.

"She's opened her eyes a couple of times this morning. Not while I was in the room with her, but the nurses said she had. They said she's 'moderately awake', but this is good. She's still tolerating them backing off the ventilator well, and they're going to extubate her and put her on something called a bipap this afternoon. Probably overnight on that and then some nasal something or other. But if all that goes well, she could be transitioned to a regular room by Friday."

"But she's awake?"

"Not, like, *awake* awake. I mean, they said she opened her eyes, but I don't think she's cognizant of what's going on. They said she might be groggy or disoriented for a few days due to being under so long. She may not even remember the days leading up to collapsing, so it's possible you're going to be a complete surprise."

I propped my elbow on the table and rested my forehead against my palm as I considered her words. Cat was going to be awake. Soon. But she may not even remember that they'd found me.

How ironic that for years she'd known about me when I had no information on her, and now the tables had turned somewhat. I'd gotten to know her in many ways while she was under sedation, and as crazy as it seemed, I felt close to her after all of it. Connected, somehow. But now she might wake up surprised to learn that I even knew her at all. The connection would be one-sided.

I told Patsy I'd do what I could to come down Thursday and plan to stay through Sunday, and then I texted Brad and asked if he could take the kids a night early for his weekend.

"This weekend isn't going to work. Still in Orlando. Won't be back in town."

I wasn't surprised in the least, but I was disappointed. It would have worked much easier for my plans if they could have been with their dad.

Instead, I called Lorna and asked if she could come and stay with them.

"Sure. Whatever you need."

"Thanks, Mom. I'm probably going to stay through the weekend, but I may have you drive them down Saturday. Eva really wants to meet Caterina, so if she's awake and alert, I'll have you bring her."

"Oh. I wasn't aware you'd told the kids."

"Eva found out in a roundabout way last weekend while we were there. I told Ethan when we got home Sunday night. I'm sorry. I meant to tell you, but my mind has been scattered this week. I've been trying to get the accounting sorted out for Caterina's foundation, and I've been creating spreadsheets and going back in her records to get everything included for the fiscal year."

"Does she know you're doing all this?"

"No, but she will when she wakes up. Patsy asked me to do it."

"I hope that doesn't start you off on a bad foot."

I stood to walk back to the dishwasher and finish putting away the dishes. "Me, too, but Patsy asked for my help, and I couldn't say no. I've enjoyed it, really. It's been a big undertaking, but it's been good for me. I was rusty in the beginning, but a lot of things are coming back. I think taking the Excel class last year to help Eva with her treasurer position for the after-school club came in handy."

"How did the kids react to the news that I'm not your mother?"

I added the clean plates to the stack in the cabinet and sighed.

"First of all, you *are* my mother, so that news was never presented to them. That's not what this means, and you know that. Please don't be this way."

"I'm not being any *way*, Caroline. I just want to know how my grandchildren took the news."

I grabbed the silverware tray and began to sort it out into the drawer organizer.

"Eva was upset at first, but we talked things out, and I think she's dealt with it well. She's curious about Cat, so she wants to meet her as soon as she's awake, and I've told her she can do that. Ethan asked if me being adopted was like his friend Theo being adopted and if that meant I was from Ethiopia like Theo. Once I told him no, it wasn't nearly as interesting, and he was off to play with his Legos."

"You sure you'd want me to bring them so soon? Don't you want to get to know her first? Make sure it's a good idea?"

"You sound like Brad. I've gotten to know plenty about her, and she's not the derelict drug addict Brad always conjured. She's an outstanding member of society, and she seems well-liked and respected by all who know her."

"I'm sure she is, but that doesn't mean your children need to be exposed to her until you get to know her personally."

I sighed and put the empty tray back in the dishwasher and began loading it with the breakfast dishes.

"Once I get down there and can evaluate the situation, I'll make a decision, okay? But can you plan to maybe come down Saturday just in case? I'd like to get Eva over to the farm for another day of riding if I can. She really enjoyed it, and she hasn't stopped talking about it all week. She's been researching horses online, and she's talking to me in all these terms that I've never even heard, like eventing."

"So now you're going to let her quit dance and ride horses instead?"

I scraped the bits of eggs from the plates into the trash and rinsed them under hot water before sliding them into the dishwasher rack.

"I didn't say that, but if she's determined not to do dance, and this is something she's passionate about, I'd like to find a way to help her pursue it."

"Hmmph. Next thing you know you'll be moving to Cedar Creek so Eva can ride horses, and you can help Caterina with her finances."

I couldn't say the thought hadn't crossed my mind. It was much closer to Orlando than Gainesville, and if we were going to move anyway, it might be nice to be near Cat and be able to spend time at the farm. For Eva and for me.

But it was too soon to consider such a prospect. I had no idea what my relationship with Cat or Levi would develop to be, and I couldn't make such important decisions based on maybes or mights.

Thankfully, Lorna knew nothing about Levi. Yet.

CHAPTER 43

Patsy had an eye doctor appointment Thursday morning, so I dropped off the kids at school and took my time driving down to the hospital. We'd agreed that it would be best for Patsy to see Cat first, in case she was awake and didn't remember the days prior to her collapse.

I was even more keyed up than I had been the first time I made the drive to meet Cat, and the miles seemed to drag and take forever to count down.

Patsy called to say she was on her way just as I was entering Jensen, so I waited in the parking lot for her.

We hugged as though we hadn't seen each other in weeks, even though it had only been since Sunday.

"I can't believe she may be awake today!" I said as we entered the hospital lobby. "Have you talked to any of her nurses?"

"Not yet, but when I left last night, they were fairly certain they'd be able to do that nasal thing today and if it goes well, they'll move her from ICU tomorrow."

The elevator seemed to take longer than normal, and I was rattling my keys against my thigh in anxious anticipation.

"You're about to jitter out of your skin," Patsy said with a chuckle.

"I'm just excited to meet her. I feel like I know her, but, of course, I don't. What if we don't get along? What if neither of us is what the other expected? What if I've spent all this time and she wakes up and decides she doesn't even want to see me? That's why I think you should go in first and test the waters."

"Would you stop?" Patsy said as we exited the elevator and headed for the ICU nurses' desk to check in. "I know Cat, and from what I've gotten to know of you, the two of you are going to be fine. I know how much it meant to her to find you, and there's no way she's going to change her mind about that. It will be fine. Stop worrying."

We reached the desk, and Cindy stood and greeted us both with a warm smile.

"She's been awake for most of the morning. Still groggy, of course, but she's aware that she's in the hospital, and we've explained to her what's happened."

"Can she talk?" I asked, and Cindy shook her head.

"The bipap is over her face, so she's not able to talk. But she has nodded and affirmed that she understands what we're saying to her. We'll be transitioning her to a nasal cannula soon, so she should be able to communicate better, but keep in mind, she's still likely to be in and out of it for the next few days. She's been under sedation for quite some time."

Cindy handed me the clipboard to sign in for a visit, and I passed it over to Patsy since we'd agreed she'd go in first. I glanced down as it passed through my hands, and there below the repetition of my name and Patsy's, a new signature had been scrawled.

It was marked as today's date, and the time was registered as an hour and a half prior to our arrival. I gasped at seeing the name "William Ward" in a tall, fancy script.

My stomach flipped, and my pulse raced.

"Oh my God! He was here." I clutched the clipboard to my chest, my voice going high-pitched in my excitement. "He was here, Patsy. Why was he here? Why would he be here?"

"Who? Who was here?"

"William." I flipped it around for her to see. "William Ward was here to see Caterina. Why would that be? He's told me he doesn't know Caterina. That he's never heard of her. Yet, he's asked me about her nearly every time I've visited the farm."

I turned to Cindy and pointed to the name. "Did you see this man? Tall, red hair, beard?"

She stepped back from my overenthusiastic approach, glancing at the other nurses before answering.

"Yes, William. He was here earlier. He went in and sat with Cat for the half-hour visitation slot, and then he left."

"Did he say why he was here?"

Cindy shook her head. "We didn't ask. I assumed they were friends? His sister is a charge nurse in the ER here, and she walked him up to the desk and got him signed in."

My heart rate was through the roof, and I was nearly breathless with excitement. I could only think of one reason William Ward would visit Caterina Russo. He had to be my father.

"Maybe he came by to visit his sister and checked in on Cat because he's grown fond of you," Patsy said, her tone one of caution.

"Patsy, c'mon. A busy man is going to sit for a half hour in a room with a woman he's never met just because some lady who's visited his farm told him about her? That makes no sense."

"Neither does your theory if the man swears he's never met her."

"Is there a problem?" Cindy asked.

"No, not at all," Patsy said. She pulled the clipboard from me and took my hand in hers. "We're gonna go and discuss a few things. We'll be back to visit Cat in just a bit."

"Wait! Was she awake? When he was with her, was she awake?" I asked Cindy.

She nodded. "Yes, he came to get me. He told me she was awake and seemed to be in pain, so I went in and adjusted her meds. She tried to talk, but I told her to rest. Her throat is likely very sore."

"I have to see her. I want to see her. She will be able to tell me the truth."

"Now, Caroline, think about this," Patsy said, taking my hand once more. "Do you want your first conversation with her, one-sided as it will be, to be you bursting in there and asking this question?"

I glanced at Cindy, who was staring at me like I'd grown three heads. I realized I was making a scene, and I apologized to Cindy and the other nurses standing there slack jawed as I turned and walked toward the elevator.

"Where are you going?" Patsy called after me. "Caroline, where are you going?"

I stepped onto the elevator and turned to face her, pushing the button repeatedly for the lobby, even as she stood with her hand in the door.

"I'm going to talk to William Ward. Cat may not be able to give me answers right now, but he can."

Patsy pulled her arm back as the doors started to close, and I walked to my Tahoe and drove toward Ward Farms determined to get answers.

CHAPTER 44

I dialed Levi's number as I drove, hoping he would know where William was.

"Hey there," Levi said. "Did you make it to town okay? How's Caterina?"

"William came to visit Caterina this morning."

"What?"

"Patsy went to sign in to visit her, and William's signature was on the clipboard. He visited her for a half hour this morning."

"Why?"

"The only reason I can think of is that he *does* know Caterina. He's been lying this whole time."

"Caroline, look. I can't tell you why William was at the hospital, but I can tell you I've known him almost half my life. He's one of the most honorable men I've ever met. I can't imagine he would have sat there and lied to you about knowing Cat."

"Why else would he have visited her?"

I accidentally ran a red light, and I cringed as I realized it, hoping no one would T-bone me.

"His sister, Patricia, works at the hospital. Maybe he was visiting her and checked on Cat for you?"

I groaned, not understanding how he or Patsy could think that was a logical explanation.

"You're telling me William Ward went to visit a total stranger he's never met and sat by her bed for thirty minutes just out of kindness for me? He doesn't even know me! Not really!"

"I don't know, Caroline. I can't say why he would have done that, but I can tell you I don't believe William lied."

"Why do you think he kept asking me about her? Every time I've seen him, he's brought her up. He must have confirmed that her last name was Russo at least four times now."

"Okay, and if he knew her, why would he need to confirm that?"

I sighed as I waited for the traffic to part so I could turn left.

"Maybe he didn't remember. You know? Like, maybe he thought he was telling the truth, but it just nagged at him so he kept asking, and then maybe suddenly he remembered. Piper said he was forgetful."

"I could buy that easier than him lying," Levi said. "But what does that mean? Are you saying you think William is your father?"

"What other explanation is there? Why else would I look like Piper and Ethan look like William? Maybe William is the reason Caterina came to Cedar Creek."

"Hold on," he said, and I could hear him talking to someone else, telling them to take a message.

"Do you need to go?"

"No, I'm at the office, and someone called for me. It can wait. It can't be anyone who knows me well, or else they'd have my cell. Now, you said Caterina was from New Jersey. But William is from here. Well, Ocala. So how do you explain that one?"

I chewed on my bottom lip as I considered it. "None of my research on her turned up anything before she was in New Jersey. Maybe she was here when she was younger. She would have had me when she was like sixteen or seventeen. She could have moved to New Jersey after that."

"Where are you now?" he asked.

"I'm on the way to the farm. I have to see William. I have to find out the truth."

"He's not here, babe."

My heart fell, despite the *babe*. "Are you sure? You're sure he's not there?"

"No. He left this morning to go to Orlando and buy some equipment. Besides, do you really want to do that? You said last night they expect Caterina to be able to talk today. Why not talk to her? Meet her. Find out what she has to say. Then you can know for sure about William before you talk to him. That could get really awkward if you approach the guy like he's your dad, and it turns out there's another explanation."

I pulled into the parking lot of a small convenience store and rested my head on the steering wheel.

"Oh, God, Levi. Why can't anything about this be easy? Why couldn't I just have found my birth parents and anything about it be remotely normal?"

"I don't know that there is a *normal* in life. For anybody. I think that's something we make up when we think our lives aren't like other people's. But as much as I hate what you're going through for you, it brought us together, and I can't be unhappy about that. Where are you now?"

"At the Kwik-Pick? I think that's what this sign says. It's hand-painted, so I'm not sure."

"What are you going to do?"

I sighed and slapped my palm against the steering wheel as I sat up and laid my head back against the seat.

"I guess I'll drive back to the hospital. There's no reason to come if William isn't there."

"Oh, gee. Thanks."

I smiled at the teasing tone in his voice. "Okay, well, obviously seeing you would be a good reason to come to the farm, but you're right. I need to talk to Cat. All the answers start with her."

"We still gonna get together later? For dinner?" he asked.

The thought was comforting, and I clung to it as something to look forward to no matter how the rest of the day went.

"Yes. Definitely. I'll call you when I know more."

"Okay," he said. "If you need me, just call. I can come up there any time. Just ask, and I'll be there."

I drove back to the hospital with my head in a funk. Even if Cat was awake and realized who I was, it was doubtful we'd get very far with conversation in her condition. I couldn't very well demand answers from her when she was recovering from her deathbed. Talk about a bad first impression.

Patsy was knitting when I got back to the hospital, and I plopped into a chair beside her and frowned.

"Did you find him?" she asked.

"Nope. Did you see Cat?"

"I did. She was sleeping, though, so I haven't been able to talk to her. They're doing that nasal calendula or cannula or candula." She stopped knitting and scrunched her nose as she tried to remember the proper term, but then she shrugged and waved a knitting needle in the air. "Whatever. I don't know what's it called. They said they'd let me know when we could go in to visit again."

I slumped in the chair.

"You really think he's your father?" Patsy asked, putting her knitting needles in her lap.

"I don't know. I think maybe I wish he was my father? But I don't know why else he'd be visiting Caterina. He said he doesn't know her. Levi's pretty certain he wouldn't lie about it, and I have to say, based on what I've seen of him, I think Levi's right. None of it makes sense, though."

"Well, there's only one person that can tell you everything you need to know. It's a waiting game now."

CHAPTER 45

When a half hour had passed with no word, I went to the nurses' station and asked if I could visit Cat. I didn't see Cindy, but another nurse told me that Cat had a coughing spell and had needed a respiratory treatment, so they were letting her rest after that.

Patsy coerced me into going down to the cafeteria to pass the time, but I found it hard to sit still and impossible to eat.

When we'd finally returned to the ICU floor, Cindy greeted me as we got off the elevator.

"I was just in there, and she's awake now."

The moment had come, and my nerves twisted and writhed as we walked to the nurses' desk.

"You okay?" Patsy asked as she picked up the clipboard.

I nodded, aware of several eyes upon me. I'm sure they were nervous after the outburst I'd had earlier, and I wished again that I could explain the whole situation to the nurses since they probably all thought I was nuts.

"You sure you don't want to go in first?" Patsy asked, offering me the pen.

I hesitated and turned to Cindy.

"Cindy, I know the rule is one visitor at a time, but is there any way Patsy and I could go in together? Just for this visit?"

Cindy frowned for a moment, and then she exchanged glances with another nurse who shrugged and nodded.

"Just this once, okay?"

We both signed in, and then I took Patsy's hand as we walked toward the door to Cat's room.

"How do I look?" I asked, pausing outside the door to catch my breath and steel myself for whatever happened.

"You look beautiful, sweetheart. Inside and out, a beauty. She's

227

gonna love you."

Patsy went in first, and I hesitated at the door for a moment before following her inside to meet the woman who was the key to my past.

Cat was awake, and my heart caught in my throat as I watched her react to seeing Patsy, the recognition immediate and the joy apparent.

"Hey, darlin'. It's about time you woke up."

Cat smiled, and tears streamed from her eyes. Patsy leaned over her and kissed her forehead as Cat reached up and squeezed Patsy's arm. She opened her mouth to say something but then winced, the pain evident as she squeezed her eyes shut and her face scrunched together.

"Don't talk, don't talk," Patsy said. "You've had all kinds of stuff shoved down your throat for the past week and a half. You don't need to talk."

Patsy sat on the edge of the bed, and Cat smiled at her and then looked past Patsy and saw me for the first time.

I took a tentative step forward as her eyes focused on me, the beautiful sculpted brows coming together in question as she tapped Patsy and pointed at me.

Patsy glanced over her shoulder and motioned for me to come to the other side of the bed.

"Do you remember us talking about your baby girl?"

Cat looked from me to Patsy, and then her eyes widened as she looked back to me.

She opened her mouth again, squeaking out a ragged sound as she lifted her hand to me.

I moved around the bed feeling like I was in a dream. The sun was streaming through the window, and the white sheets glowed like something surreal. I stood beside her bed, and she grasped my hand and squeezed it tight.

Her eyes were a gorgeous, deep green, and though they were filled with tears, they were warm and affectionate. Her smile lit up my heart, and I smiled back through tears of my own.

"Hi, Caterina. My name is Caroline."

She squeezed my hand harder and nodded.

"Do you remember Caroline was coming to have lunch with us before you collapsed?" Patsy asked.

Cat's eyes clouded with confusion, and she shook her head as she looked to Patsy with her brows together again.

"We found her, and I called and invited her to lunch. But then you got ill before she got here, and the ambulance came and took you to the hospital. They said the medications may affect your memory. It's okay."

Cat looked back at me, staring into my eyes as I could see her straining to remember.

"Caroline has been at the hospital as much as she could waiting for you to wake up," Patsy said. "She's been a rock for me. Just like you are. She's your daughter, Cat."

Cat lifted her hand to wipe her tears, and Patsy stood to grab a tissue from the table by the bed, dabbing it at each eye.

Cat's smile never faltered as she gazed as me, her fingers tracing the outline of my face before picking up a lock of my hair.

She tried to speak, and a hoarse whisper escaped. "Red."

Cat made a motion with her left hand like she was trying to write, and Patsy said, "Oh, yeah. That's a great idea. Let me find a piece of paper."

She dug into her bag as I looked in my own purse, coming up with a pen just as Patsy held up a scrap of paper. She wheeled the bed table over and put it across Cat's waist as she pressed the button to raise the head of the bed, making it easier for Cat to rest her hand on the table and write.

"You're left-handed!" I exclaimed as I watched her. "Me, too!"

Her smile widened again, and I smiled back, not even bothering to fight the tears any more.

"You had red hair the first time I saw you. I'm so happy to meet you!" she scrawled on the paper before passing it to me.

"I'm happy to meet you, too! I've wanted to meet you for almost my entire life."

She nodded and took the paper back. I watched her hand move across it, my emotions thick in my throat as I saw the words take shape.

"Has your life been happy?"

"Yes! Yes! A thousand times, yes. I have a mother who loves me, and who is so thankful to you for your sacrifice. I have two beautiful children whom I adore. I've been loved. I've had a full and happy life."

She started crying in earnest then, putting her fist to her mouth as she began to cough.

I felt helpless to console her. I wanted to hug her, but as the coughing fit intensified and a machine started sounding an alarm, Patsy and I both pulled back as a nurse we'd never met rushed into the room.

"Okay, what have we got here?"

She poured a cup of water for Caterina and then checked all her tubes and settings as Patsy and I stood against the wall.

She took in Cat's tears and her still trembling hands, and then looked up at Patsy and me, both still crying.

"I don't know what's upset y'all, but this lady needs some rest. She can't be taking on stress, you hear me? She needs rest. She needs calm. So y'all gone need to think of something to keep her happy, or you'll have to let her be."

Cat tugged at the nurse's hemline as she shook her head and pointed to me. "That's ... my ... daughter," she croaked out, her smile beaming through the physical pain and her tears still flowing.

"Well, no matter who she is, she can't be in here upsetting you," the nurse said, oblivious to the importance of Cat's statement. "This lady doesn't need to talk right now," she told Patsy and me. "Her throat is raw. It makes her cough to try and talk. The best thing for her is rest. There's only supposed to be one of y'all in here at a time anyway."

Patsy and I nodded and apologized, not even bothering to explain that we'd had permission. Once the nurse had gone, we returned to Cat's bedside, and she reached for my hand, squeezing it tight as she mouthed the words, *"Beautiful. Beautiful."*

"Thank you. You are, too."

"You get some rest now," Patsy said. "We'll be back after a while."

Cat shook her head, still gripping my hand. "Stay," she whispered. "I want to talk to you."

She coughed a couple of times and gripped at her throat.

Patsy grabbed the cup of water, holding it to Cat's lips as she lifted her head to drink.

"I'm gonna step out and leave the two of you alone," she said.

"But try not to talk, Cat. You have plenty of time to say whatever you need to when you're better. The important thing now is for you to rest and be able to get out of here."

Our visit passed quickly, with her writing questions and me answering. Occasionally, she'd try to speak, but it was hard to hear her, and more often than not, it made her cough, so we kept to the written question and verbal answer process.

When I went back to see her the next visiting hour, she had a list of questions written out for me, and I spent the entire time answering, recounting important moments of my life and discussing my current situation.

I wanted desperately to ask her about my father and to learn more about my birth, but I knew it would be better to wait until she could talk more easily, and I also didn't want to cloud the conversations with anything unpleasant for her right off the bat. I avoided any mention of William as I talked, choosing to leave him out of anything I brought up about Levi.

Patsy was gracious enough to give me each visitation slot the rest of the day, and by the time I left the hospital that evening to meet Levi for dinner, Caterina was pretty much up to date on all aspects of my life. She knew how I'd met Brad, and that the marriage hadn't turned out quite the way I'd hoped. She was aware of my fears about screwing up with Eva, and that I worried I'd been too coddling with Ethan. She knew I was ready to go back to work, but that I wanted it to be fulfilling and worth my time.

She hung on my every word, reacting with a laugh or a smile, sometimes with tears or a squeeze of my hand. She tired easily, and sometimes she would start to doze before I was even out of the room at the end of a visit, but when I arrived again, if she was awake, she was eager for more.

I found myself confiding things to her I'd never told anyone as my memories and thoughts came bubbling up and out of me.

And yet, as I explained to Levi over dinner, I still didn't know any more about Caterina than I had before she awoke. I had no new insight into my background or why she'd given me up. The information exchange had been all one-sided, and it left me yearning for answers.

231

CHAPTER 46

"It's just surreal," I told Levi as we came down the steps of the restaurant to go to the parking lot after dinner. "When I think that she's my mother, like, she gave birth to me, but I don't know her. I felt like I'd met her over the past week or so, through Patsy, and her house, and her notes on all the foundation stuff, but it's not like I know her. Now, I've pretty much poured out my entire life to her over the course of the day, and I still have no idea who she is. I'm telling you, it's bizarre."

"I can't even imagine. But maybe tomorrow, she'll be able to talk. Maybe you'll be asking the questions, and she'll be the one giving all the answers. You said she'll be in a regular room tomorrow, right? That means you won't be limited to half hour visits."

"I have to find out about my father. I have to know why William was visiting her. I hate to walk in there and demand to know who she had sex with, but basically, that's what I'm asking."

"That's strange," Levi said as we walked across the lot toward my car.

"Yeah, tell me about it." I was looking down, struggling to secure the lid on the box the waitress had given me for my leftovers.

"No, not that. That." He pointed. "That's Piper's car, but she's supposed to be in Ocala at a horse sale tonight."

I looked up, hoping the feeling of dread that came over me was for nothing.

"That's not Piper," I said, handing Levi the leftovers as I walked toward the red Audi TT Roadster parked next to my Tahoe.

Brad stepped out of the car before I reached it, and the set of his jaw and glint in his eyes told me it was going to be a rough conversation.

"What are you doing here?" I asked.

"I was just about to ask you the same question. I called to check on my kids, and Ethan said you were out of town. Strange. I don't remember being told you were going out of town."

My momentary shock at the fact that he'd called the kids faded quickly as my mind processed that somehow Brad was standing in front of me in a restaurant parking lot in Cedar Creek rather than where he was supposed to be in Orlando.

"How did you find me?"

He held up his phone, where a bright map was lit up with a red dot blinking in the center of it. "That's you," he said, pointing to the blinking light.

"Are you tracking me?"

My mind was still spinning from him being there, and the realization that he was there because he had tracked me and followed me was like a punch to the stomach that made me want to vomit.

He shoved the phone in his pocket. "Our cell phones are still on the same plan since I pay the bill, remember? So yeah. I can track any phone on the plan."

"Why would you want to track me? Why not just call and ask where I am? And what are you doing here?"

"If I'd called you, you would have just lied. Hospital, my ass. You got your mother to come watch my kids so you could be down here whoring around with this asshole." He motioned over my shoulder towards Levi, who up until that moment, I had forgotten was standing there in my mind's dazed state.

Levi stepped forward and offered his right hand to Brad as though they were meeting under the most cordial of terms and about to share a gentlemanly handshake.

"This asshole's name is Levi," he said. "And if you refer to Caroline in the same sentence with anything to do with a whore again, you're gonna find out how big of an asshole I can be."

Brad stared at Levi's hand with a sneer plastered on his face. "Would you mind giving my wife and I a bit of privacy? We have a few things to discuss."

"Ex-wife," Levi and I both said in unison.

"I think the lady can tell me if she wants me to go," Levi said. "Otherwise, I ain't movin'."

He placed the container of food on the top of the Tahoe and crossed his arms, widening his stance.

Brad was taller than Levi by a couple of inches, and he might have been as wide, but Levi was all muscle, and he was quite the formidable figure as he stood by my side.

"So, what are you? Her bodyguard?" Brad asked.

"Not at all," Levi said. "I have no doubt she can take care of herself. But she won't ever have to unless she wants to as long as I'm around."

Brad looked from Levi to me, and even in the dim light, I could see the red in his face grow darker and the veins on the side of his forehead bulging.

"Caroline, please tell your guard dog that you and I have things to discuss."

"I have nothing to discuss with you, Brad."

"Oh, so you think it's fine that my kids are home alone and you're down here in Hicktown laughing it up and having dinner?"

"*Our* kids are not home alone. They're with their grandmother. And where I choose to have dinner is no concern of yours."

He stepped forward, but when Levi matched his step by moving closer to me, Brad glanced at him and stepped back.

"You won't get away with this. I won't have it. I'll sue for full custody. I'll rake you over the coals and leave you broke and penniless, just like you were when I found you."

My hands clenched in fists at my sides, and my teeth ground together as I spat out my words. "On what grounds? You have nothing on me because I haven't done anything wrong."

"You think I don't have any friends in family law that could come up with a way to come after you? You don't think I could keep you tied up in court for years if I wanted to? You have nothing, Caroline. You are nothing without me, and without my money, you're destitute. You can't afford to fight me, baby."

Despite my brave outward appearance, his words struck fear in my heart. I knew he'd do it. He'd have no qualms about it. And he'd have his parents' bank account to finance it. It didn't matter that I'd done nothing wrong. He'd find a way. Brad was a successful corporate attorney because he was ruthless, and he was willing to use whatever measures it took to win.

"I'm here because I found my birth mother, Brad. That's who's in the hospital. That's who I've been coming to see. She's been very ill, and she only just—"

"What have I told you about bringing some stranger into my kids' life? It's bad enough that you've tracked down whoever gave you up, and God only knows what issues she has, but you've actually allowed this man"— he pointed at Levi —"to be with my children? Ethan knew his name, Caroline. That is unacceptable."

My entire body was trembling, and I dug my heels into the ground and pressed my fists against my legs in hopes that he couldn't see it.

"*Unacceptable?* How dare you! You've had a revolving door of women come in and out of Eva and Ethan's life, even before our divorce was final. You don't get to tell me who I can be friends with. You don't get to tell me anything anymore. You gave up that right when you walked out."

"You are the mother of my children, and I will always have a say-so over what you do that affects them, you bitch." He stepped toward me with his finger pointed at my face as he talked, and Levi calmly moved to stand between us, his arms still crossed.

"Okay, that's it. We're done here," Levi said. "I was gonna let you rant as long as she was all right with it, but now you've crossed a line."

"Get out of my face," Brad said, and I worried the two of them were about to have an actual fistfight in the parking lot of Oscar's Fish Camp.

How had my life gone from boring as hell to dysfunctional reality show in a matter of weeks?

Levi didn't move. He didn't flinch. He didn't say a word. He just stood there staring with a smirk on his face until Brad backed down, glaring at Levi as he walked backward toward the open driver's door of his car.

"This isn't over, Caroline. Your henchman won't be able to do shit for you in a court of law."

I hugged my arms around my waist as I stood behind Levi and watched Brad get in his car, vaguely aware of the stares from other restaurant patrons in the parking lot. Tears stung my eyes as a maelstrom of emotions raged inside me.

Brad backed his car out and let the window down, shouting to

Levi, "Thanks for the tires, asshole!"

"No problem," Levi said, his voice so calm you would have thought he was saying goodbye to a close friend. "Thanks for being dumb enough to let her go so she was available when I met her."

Brad slung gravel across the parking lot as he left, and once his taillights had disappeared, Levi turned and put his arms around me.

"Is he always such a nice guy?"

I collapsed into his arms, my body shaking uncontrollably as tears streamed down my face.

"Oh, God. What have I done? He's going to take me to court. He's going to fight me and try to take my kids away."

"Ssh," Levi whispered against my ear as he stroked my hair and rubbed my back. "No one is taking your kids away. No one is taking you to court. You've done nothing wrong, and there's nothing he can do to you but threaten."

I pulled back and looked up at him, shaking my head. "You don't know him. You don't know what he'll do. He'll break the bank if he has to. He's right. I don't have anything of my own. I let him talk me into being completely dependent on him, and now I have nothing to fight him with."

Levi pulled me back against his chest and wrapped his arms around me, holding me tight to him. "We'll fight him," he said. "We'll do whatever it takes. I promise you he's not going to take Eva and Ethan from you."

CHAPTER 47

I had argued with Levi that I should get a hotel room since Brad could track my every move. I didn't want to lead him back to Levi's house, where I'd planned to stay, and I certainly wasn't going to bring drama to Patsy and George's doorstep. I wasn't willing to turn the phone off or disable it while I was away from my kids, so I couldn't stop him from tracking me until I could get to a phone store the next day to purchase my own.

"No way in hell," said Levi in response to the hotel idea. "You're coming home with me."

"You could stay at the hotel with me," I pleaded. "I don't want him to know where you live."

"I don't care if he knows where I live. Hell, it won't be that hard for him to find me if he really wants to look. We're not running from him, okay?"

I called Lorna as soon as I got behind the wheel to drive to Levi's.

"Mom, have you talked to Brad?"

"No. He called earlier and asked to speak to the kids. Eva was in the shower, so I let him talk to Ethan. Why?"

"He followed me. Like, he had some kind of tracker hooked up to my phone and he followed me. He's threatening to take me to court. To sue for full custody."

"Bah!" she scoffed. "On what grounds? The man never takes his children as it is. Why would he want full custody?"

"He saw me with someone. I've sort of been seeing someone."

"What? Who? When?"

I groaned, wishing I hadn't been so reluctant to acknowledge my feelings for Levi and put myself in this position with Lorna.

"His name is Levi. He lives in Cedar Creek. I met him while I've been down here. I've been meaning to tell you, but it's just been crazy lately. I'm sorry, Mom. I should have told you. I didn't think it was going to be anything serious."

"And is it? Serious?"

I exhaled loudly, my eyes watching the truck in front of me and the man who was driving it.

"Yeah. Yeah, I think it is. I think I'm in love with him, and I think he loves me."

"Wow. Okay. Well, I'm not sure what I'm supposed to say. If you were a teenager, I could ground you for not telling me what the hell is going on like you've done Eva, but you're a grown woman. So, I guess all I've got is that I want you to be happy. But be sure it's what you want this time, okay? And for God's sake, use protection."

"Mom!"

"I'm not kidding, Caroline. Think how differently your life would have turned out if you and Brad had used protection."

"For your information, we did use protection. He pulled the condom off without telling me until afterward. Said it was uncomfortable."

She made a *blech* sound into the phone. "That was certainly more information than I needed to know. Look, all I'm asking is that you use your head and don't think with any other body parts, okay? When can I meet this guy? What's his name again?"

"Levi. You can meet him this weekend if you bring the kids down."

"What are you going to do about Brad?"

I turned into the gate of Ward Farms behind Levi, checking my rearview mirror once again for any sign of headlights behind us.

"I don't know. He was pretty furious."

"There's a guy here in the complex who was a family law attorney. Rex, I think his name is. Want me to ask him what you should do?"

My mind immediately conjured a mental image of what Rex the family law attorney who lived at my mother's retirement complex might look like, and I saw plaid swim trunks and black socks with sandals.

"No, that's okay. Maybe he's bluffing. Maybe he'll calm down, and I can talk some sense into him."

Mom sighed. "I knew something like this would happen if you

ever started dating. I knew he wouldn't take it well."

"Yeah, well, I'm not willing to live the rest of my life alone to keep from upsetting Brad."

"Nor should you. I never said that. But you do need to be careful. Lord knows what that man is capable of."

We said goodbye as I pulled into the driveway behind Levi's truck, still looking over my shoulder as he walked me to the door.

I couldn't shake the feeling of being watched. It was unsettling to think someone had been following me. Tracking me. Waiting for me. Even if it was Brad.

"Would you like a glass of wine?" Levi asked as I looked around. The living space was one large room with the kitchen, dining and living room all together. A stone fireplace dominated one wall, and a large flat screen TV hung on the wall adjacent to it. A brown leather sectional with multiple recliners sat in the middle of the room, and a wooden table and chairs set sat behind it in the dining area. The kitchen cabinets were a dark wood, and the granite countertops seemed a recent addition based on the age of the house.

It was a bachelor pad, no doubt, but it was clean, and it had a warm feeling to it.

"I thought you didn't drink," I said, following him to the kitchen and leaning against the bar counter that separated it from the living room.

"I don't. But I do occasionally have guests who like to have a glass of wine, so I keep it on hand."

"Hmm. Guests. Yes, I've been told your house has frequent guests."

"What's that supposed to mean?"

"I overheard some little birds discussing how you rarely make it home alone."

"Oh, please." He shook his head and popped the cork of a bottle of chardonnay, pouring a half a glass and bringing it to me. "I don't have nearly the number of conquests my peers say I do."

I sipped the wine, gazing into his eyes over the rim of the glass.

"Is that what I am?" I asked. "A conquest?"

He set the bottle on the counter and moved toward me, the air between us so charged that I was surprised it didn't crackle.

"I think if anyone has been conquered in this situation, it's me," he whispered, lifting his hand to cup my cheek as his thumb traced over my skin, sparking a trail of goose flesh that spread like wildfire.

I shivered and took a big gulp of wine.

"You cold?" he asked, his face suddenly filled with concern.

"Definitely not," I answered, sitting the glass on the counter before closing the gap between us.

He grinned as he held my face in both hands, slowly moving closer, his eyes on my mouth.

I felt like I would explode with desire if he didn't take me, and I leaned forward to meet him, but he pulled back, grinning wider. "Ah, ah, ah. We're not rushing this, Caroline. You've occupied my every thought. My every breath. My every waking moment. I've thought of nothing but you since the day I met you. I intend to enjoy every single inch of you, and take my time doing it."

I shivered again, and a tiny moan escaped me as his lips almost met mine, but then he moved to nibble on my ear instead, chuckling at the curse I swore under my breath. His tenderness was maddening, and I wanted to tear at his shirt and rip it from his body.

He moved his hand to my neck and gently bent my head to one side as his mouth forged a path down. He pushed the collar of my shirt aside, tilting my head back as he dipped his mouth to the hollow of my shoulder.

I relied on the counter to hold me up as he nibbled and nipped, his hands brushing against my skin as he released each button one by one. His tongue burned its way across my chest as he pushed the shirt over my shoulders and let it fall to the floor, and I swayed, clutching his head in both hands as he buried his mouth between my breasts.

"Oh, God, Levi, please. Now. Please."

He chuckled again, his hands twisting in my hair as he brought his head back up, his eyes dark and wild as they met mine, and then our mouths came together, the hunger and need overpowering his attempts at gentle restraint.

My lips were crushed in the onslaught of his plundering even as my tongue sought to hold its own against him.

I lifted his shirt from the waistband of his jeans, wanting to feel the muscles of his bare back beneath my hands and rake my nails across his skin. I struggled to pull it free, and he stepped back to sweep it over his head in one swift motion.

He was more sculpted than I'd realized, and I reached to trace the outline of his abs with my fingertips. He growled as he braced for my touch, and I grinned at the effect I had on him. The muscles quivered beneath my fingers as I dipped lower still, teasing the tip of my pinkie just inside the waistband of his jeans.

He grabbed my hand and moved it to his back, stepping forward to take me in his arms as I laughed.

"What's wrong? I thought turnabout was fair play," I said, sliding my hands up his back and then slowly bringing my nails down with the lightest touch I could manage.

"Oh, God, Caroline," he moaned, shuddering beneath my touch as he dropped his head back and pulled my hips to his.

My nails continued their teasing assault up his abs and across his chest as I watched the muscles flex and the nipples harden. I slid my hands around his neck and up through his hair, pulling his head back to me as my lips made their way up his neck to take the soft lobe of his ear between my teeth.

"I want you to take me," I whispered, biting down harder as I pulled on the lobe, enjoying the feeling of him shuddering against me as he spanned his hands across my lower back.

He slid his thumb beneath the lace strap of my bra, pausing when he didn't feel the clasp he was seeking.

"Front," I said, reaching my hand between us to release it and then arching to press my breasts against his chest as soon as they were freed.

He slid his hands along my ribs from the back to the front, cradling each breast as he bent to take first one in his mouth, and then the other.

I cried out as his teeth teased and taunted, begging him to end the torture but praying that he wouldn't stop.

I buried my nails into his shoulders as he slid one hand to the buckle on my jeans, and then I hooked both thumbs in the waistband to help him push them down, eager to be rid of any barriers between us. He knelt in front of me, his lips hot on my inner thighs as he pushed the lace of my panties aside.

My knees nearly gave way and buckled as his tongue explored, and by the time he paused to pull the panties all the way to the floor, I was panting and begging him for more.

He obliged my pleas, and my voice was hoarse from calling out his name by the time he was done.

His grin was smug and self-confident when he stood, and though it was well-deserved, I was still determined to bring him to task.

"You just wait," I said. "You're going to be begging for mercy before this night is over, and I'm not feeling merciful."

He laughed and took me in his arms, spinning me away from the counter and walking me backward down the hallway as I unbuckled his jeans.

The back of my knees hit the bed, and I let myself fall, bracing on my elbows to watch him rid himself of the heavy denim. He wore nothing at all beneath it, and I swore out loud at the sight of his desire, fully erect and larger than anything I'd seen in my limited experience.

Something told me I may be the one begging for mercy again as I watched him unroll the condom down the length of him, but I didn't bother admitting that as he eased himself onto the bed and between my thighs.

I had never known such fire inside me. I'd never imagined that I could be driven to such need. There was damned sure nothing in my past experiences to prepare me for what Levi Parker knew how to do with a woman's body.

He moved within me like we were two pieces carved from the same origin, separated too long but joined once again. I don't know how many times he brought me to the brink of madness and carried me beyond it before he roared a guttural moan with a final thrust and collapsed upon me, whispering my name as he buried his face in my hair.

When our breathing had slowed, and our pulses had ceased to pound, he rolled to the side, pulling me against him as he pressed his lips to my forehead.

I drew a figure eight on his chest with my finger as I deliberated whether I should ask the question.

"Penny for your thoughts?" he said, his voice barely above a whisper.

I propped my chin on his chest and looked up at him, smiling when he smiled down at me.

"Why did you walk away that night? Why didn't you stay with me in the apartment?"

He hugged me closer and threaded his fingers through mine, lifting our hands to look at them.

"Hard to say." He brought them to his lips, turning the back of my hand to press a kiss to it, and then hugging it to his chest once more. "Part of it was out of respect for the day you'd had, not wanting to take advantage of that."

"So you were being a gentleman?" I said, relieved that I'd been right.

"Yes, and no."

"No?"

He turned his head so he could look at me, and we stared into each other's eyes as I waited for his response.

"I think it was self-preservation. I've never felt about anyone the way I feel about you, Caroline. I knew that night. I knew you were the one. I didn't want to screw it up. I didn't want to rush it. I knew that once I was with you that would be it. I'd be done. I'd be yours. I needed to be sure you felt the same way."

"And now?"

He shrugged and rolled to put me beneath him, flashing that grin that could make me come undone so easily. "I think you love me."

"Oh, you do, do you?" I returned his grin. "Are you sure about that?"

"I'm sure that I love you," he said, his face suddenly serious as his eyes searched mine.

I reached to cup his face, rubbing my palm against the bristles on his jaw. "I love you, too."

"Damned good thing," he said, the grin returning. "Because I'm yours now. You're stuck with me."

And he proceeded to make me beg for mercy once more.

CHAPTER 48

Patsy called as I was on my way to the hospital the next morning and said she was going to stop by Cat's house and bring a few things to put in her room now that she wasn't in the ICU.

She gave me the room number and directions to get there, so I didn't even bother stopping by the nurses' desk on my way in.

My step was light, and my mood was good, bolstered by an incredible night of lovemaking and the hope of getting the answers I'd sought for so long.

I tapped on the door of Cat's room before entering, worried I might wake her if she was sleeping but not wanting to barge in if she was in a state of undress.

"Come in," she said, her voice hoarse but better than the whisper of the day before.

"Good morning," I said, flinging the door open and stopping in my tracks when I saw William standing on the other side of her bed.

My mouth flew open, but no words would form, and I stood there in awkward silence while they both stared.

"Could you give us a minute?" Cat asked, clearing her throat.

"Sure," I managed to squeak out before turning to go, my mind exploding with all the questions the moment raised.

Were they my parents? Was that the first time the three of us had been in the same room together? Was he going to acknowledge that he knew her? That he'd lied to me?

I paced the lobby as I waited for him to leave, and a good twenty minutes went by before I saw him approaching. He slowed as he saw me, and I was startled to see tears in his eyes, which he quickly wiped away with a handkerchief from his pocket.

I rushed forward to confront him, oblivious to the people around us.

"You told me you didn't know her. You said the name didn't ring a bell."

"It didn't."

"Then why are you visiting her? Yesterday, and again today. If you don't know her, why are you here?"

"I said I didn't know Caterina Russo. And I didn't. I still don't. I knew Catherine Johnson. And it's not my place to tell you any more than that."

"Who's Catherine Johnson?"

"Again, I'm not the one who needs to explain this to you. I'm still trying to process it all myself. But I didn't lie to you, Caroline. I didn't know."

His eyes filled with tears again, and his chin trembled.

It shook me to my core to see this man I knew as so strong and stoic on the verge of losing his grip on his emotions.

"I have to go," he said, stepping past me. "We'll talk soon. You need to talk to her first."

I stood there in shock as he left the building. I didn't understand what had transpired and what he'd meant by it all.

When I entered Caterina's room, she was quietly weeping, dabbing at her eyes with a tear-soaked tissue when she saw me.

"Caroline," she said, her voice ragged and weak. "I worried I had dreamed you. I thought I would wake this morning and find you'd never really been here at all."

"Who's Catherine Johnson?" I asked, moving to sit on the edge of her bed, no longer able to hold my questions back in consideration of her discomfort.

"You talked to William," she said, smiling as the tears flowed. "I can't believe the two of you met. I've lived here twelve years, and in all that time, I've seen him from afar once. But you come to town and meet him almost immediately. Seems like fate, don't you think?"

"Is William my father?" I asked, struggling to swallow the huge lump lodged in my throat.

She nodded and reached for another tissue. "Yes. He is. He didn't know that, though, so there's no way he could have told you. He never even knew you existed."

My stomach churned, and my head went all dizzy. "Why? Why didn't he know?"

She tilted her head back and looked at the ceiling, blinking rapidly as she struggled to stop the flow of tears.

"Because I refused to name him. I thought I could protect him. Keep him from getting hurt. Or worse. But I guess I couldn't protect anyone. All three of us got hurt in some way, didn't we?"

I reached forward and laid my hand on her arm.

"What do you mean, *name him?* What happened?"

She drew in a breath and immediately started coughing. I jumped up to pour more water in the cup, and she tried to drink it between coughs, lying back on the bed once she'd been able to stop.

She looked exhausted. Completely spent. I felt guilty pressing her to move forward, but I had to know.

"What happened, Cat? Who were you trying to protect us from? Who is Catherine Johnson?"

She lifted her long, thick hair off her shoulders and twisted it into a knot on top of her head, fanning her long, slender neck as she stared across the room. Then she squared her shoulders and turned her face to me.

"Catherine Johnson was a sixteen-year-old girl from a wealthy family who had high expectations for their daughter's life. She was an only child, and while her mother adored her, her father found her to be a disappointment from the moment she wasn't born a male."

Her lips were tight with anger as she spoke of him, and she exhaled slowly, drawing in a measured breath before she began again.

"I was a wild one back then. Rebelling against my father. My upbringing. The expectations of my station in life. I'd been in trouble for as long as I could remember, and my father had threatened more than once to send me away."

She took a sip of the water and cleared her throat again, coughing once, but then nodding when it cleared.

"When I met William Ward, he was on a crew building fences for the people who lived in the estate next to ours. Charlotte, their daughter and a close friend of mine, had caught a glimpse of a couple of boys on the crew and thought they were handsome, so we rode out there on horseback to get a closer look."

I shifted my weight and turned to see her better, not wanting to disturb her story, but needing to be able to watch her face as she talked.

"William was sitting off by himself, away from the group, reading a book in the middle of this field. They dared me to go and talk to him, and when I did, he seemed irritated that I'd interrupted him. I thought I was the cat's meow back then, and I wasn't accustomed to being ignored. So, I made a point of trying to get his attention that day, and every day after that, until finally, he'd put the book down when he saw me coming."

Her smile held a hint of sadness, and her eyes had grown unfocused as she stared into the past.

"He wasn't my type at all. He was this red-headed, tall, lanky, nerdy guy. Always talking about books. And horses," she said, her eyes growing brighter. "God, that boy loved horses. He'd watch them in the fields and talk about how he was going to own his own horses one day. When the fence job was finished, he hired on with Charlotte's dad as a stable boy. I liked to think it was because he wanted to be near me, but it was probably more the horses than anything else."

Her smile faded, and her eyes closed for a minute. I sat as still as possible, hoping she'd go on, but not wanting to wake her if she needed rest.

Only a few minutes passed before her eyelids fluttered open, and she looked disoriented at first, but then she saw me and smiled.

"I was telling you about William."

"It can wait, Caterina. I know you're tired. You need your rest."

She waved her hand at me.

"I need to tell you. It may take me a while, and I may have to stop and start to catch my breath, but I need to tell you."

I probably should have insisted that she rest, but I wanted her to keep going so badly that I let her.

"William was like no one I'd ever known. He was the kindest, sweetest, most compassionate boy I'd ever met. He changed me, Caroline," she said, looking directly at me for the first time since she'd started talking. "He calmed me. He soothed my soul and made me believe I was worthy of being loved."

She sighed and looked back toward the window.

"I wanted to spend every minute I could with him, but I knew there'd be hell to pay if we were found out. My father would have stroked to know I was in love with the hired help. How scandalous. I would have been sent away, for sure, and I dread to think what my father would have done to William. Charlotte knew, and she played my cover whenever she could, but the longer it went on, the more careless we got. Reckless. Not thinking of the consequences if we got caught."

She drew in a few deep breaths, letting them out slowly, and only coughing on the last one. She lay back against the pillow when the coughs stopped, closing her eyes for a moment as her breathing grew deeper.

"Do you want me to go?" I asked. "Do you need to sleep?"

She shook her head without opening her eyes, waving away my concerns with a slender hand. After a while, she spoke again, opening her eyes to gaze up at the ceiling.

"I'd been sneaking out the window at night for weeks, scurrying through the dark to wait by the road where William would pick me up in his brother's truck. We'd ride all night. Talking, laughing, doing what teenagers in love do. Daylight was too risky. Too much sneaking around never knowing who might be watching. But at night, we were free. We'd go sit in the park. We'd hang out by the lake. We'd even drive over to the coast and go to the beach. As long as I was back in my room by morning, no one was the wiser."

A haunted sorrow came over her eyes, and I leaned forward, wanting somehow to console her for the pain it conveyed.

"We were running late that night, and the sun was already peeking over the horizon when he dropped me off at the end of the drive. I was running, trying to beat the clock, but I stepped in a hole and twisted my ankle. It hurt like hell, and I could barely walk, much less run. My father saw me out one of the front windows as I came hobbling up the drive."

A coughing fit came over her, and I got up to refill her water, but she motioned for me to sit back down as she drank it.

"He was furious," she said with a loud sigh. "I refused to tell him where I'd been or who I'd been with, and it was the straw that broke the camel's back. He flew me to New York that weekend, and I was enrolled in a boarding school the next Monday."

"Did you get to say goodbye to William?" I asked, so captured by the story that I'd almost forgotten the key part that was missing. Me.

Cat shook her head. "No. I wrote him a letter and asked our maid to get it to Charlotte. I never saw William Ward again. Never spoke to him or had any correspondence with him. I didn't even know if he'd gotten my letter. Until today."

"And did he? Did he get it?"

She smiled as she looked at me. "Yes, but a fat lot of good it did him. We didn't have cell phones or email back then. I wrote that I would get word to him as soon as I knew the name of the school. That somehow I'd reach him, and we could be together once I got out. But then——"

"Good morning!" Patsy called out, entering the room with a burst of enthusiasm that shattered the somber cloud we'd been under. "How are you feeling this morning?"

She had shopping bags on each arm, and after a quick exchange of a kiss on the cheek with Cat and with me, she began to unload her wares.

I tried to smile as she showed us the small wind chimes she'd brought to hang in the window, the framed photos of Cat and her foster kids from home, and the small teapot and wooden box filled with Cat's favorite tea, but I wanted to hurry her from the room so I could hear the rest of Cat's story.

The rest of *my* story.

CHAPTER 49

"Thank you, love," Cat said to Patsy, her hand to her heart. "You've brightened the whole space with your presence and your thoughtfulness, and I can't thank you enough for all you do for me."

"Oh, hush. You'll make me weepy. Caroline, how are you this morning? You feeling okay?"

"Um, yeah," I said, trying to keep the irritation from my voice. It wasn't Patsy's fault she'd interrupted, but I was desperate to know how the story had ended and where my story without them began.

"How did your dinner go?"

"Good." I said, but then I reconsidered. "Well, not so good. Brad showed up after dinner and threatened to take my kids from me, but other than that, it went well."

"Oh my!" Patsy exclaimed.

"You should have said something!" Caterina said, reaching forward to grab my hand. "Here I've been rattling on about myself, and you've been sitting here needing to talk. I'm so sorry."

"No, no. I wanted to hear what you have to say. I still want to hear. I can't do anything about Brad. I'm hoping it will blow over, and he'll calm down without going through with his threat."

"Why would he say he wants to take your kids?" Patsy asked.

I shrugged. "He was upset that I was with Levi."

"How did he even know where you were?" Caterina asked.

"He had some kind of tracker thing set up so he could see where my phone was."

Both ladies reacted with shock and outrage.

"He's tracking you without your permission?" Caterina said.

"I don't think that's legal," Patsy said.

"The phones are all on his account. So evidently, he had something set up where he can see where they are. I just need to go and get my own phone. I need to not have anything be tied to him financially anymore."

"Very important," Cat said.

Patsy nodded in agreement. "What's he threatening to do? He can't take your kids because you had dinner with someone."

"No, but he's an attorney, so he's got plenty of friends who are attorneys. He said he can tie me up in court for years. He knows I don't have the money to fight him."

"That's total bullshit," Cat said. "You need to get a job. You need to get some independence from him. Quickly."

"I know, but I have no idea what to do about the move, and I can't really find a job until I know what's going on with that."

My phone rang, and I excused myself to take Lorna's call.

"Hi, Mom," I said as I made my way down the hospital hallway and to the fountain outside. "What's up? Everything okay?"

"Well, I know you said Eva was grounded. She's texting to ask me if her friend Greg can come over and watch a movie tonight. I don't mind, but I thought—"

"No. Absolutely not! This is the guy I told you about. The senior. She's been asking me all week if he can come over, and I told her not until after she's served her time."

"You're going to let her keep seeing this guy?"

"I don't know, Mom. I was trying to put the whole decision off and hope it fizzled out in the meantime. But regardless, he can't come over tonight. She's grounded. She can't go anywhere, and no one can come over."

"Okay, dear. How's it going there?"

"It's interesting." I looked around to see if anyone was listening, but I was alone outside. Not that it mattered since I'd had outbursts in front of most of the hospital already, but I figured I'd be discreet when I could. "I found out today William Ward is my father."

"The man from the farm?"

"Yes, one and the same." I sat on the bench and propped my elbows on my knees, putting my head in my hands.

"Oh, my. Have you talked to him? Does he know?"

"He does now. And he knows I know. But we haven't really

251

discussed it. It's complicated."

"You say *now*. Did he not know?"

"No. I'm not sure when he figured it out, but I guess he and Caterina talked today, and she confirmed it. To me and to him. So, there you go. I know who my birth parents are. William Ward and Caterina Russo. Well, Catherine Johnson. I guess somewhere along the road Caterina changed her name, but I haven't gotten that story yet. She's still in recovery mode, so she can't talk for long without needing to rest."

"Sugar, you sound tired. Are you getting enough rest? This is a lot to handle, and then you've got Brad pulling his crap. Have you heard from him?"

"No. Have you?"

"No, and he'd better not call again while I'm here. I'll give him a piece of my mind. You know I will."

"Don't say anything to him, Mom. I don't need him any more riled up than he already is."

I opened my eyes and squinted against the sun. Levi was standing across the courtyard from me, leaning against a column with the grin I'd come to love.

"I gotta go, Mom. Someone's here to talk to me." I stood and walked to him, and he slid his arms around my waist and gave me a silent peck on the lips.

"I'm guessing this means I'm not bringing the kids tomorrow?" Lorna asked.

"I don't know," I said, pulling Levi toward the bench with me. "Probably not. Let me get my head wrapped around it, and I'll call you later tonight."

He sat, and I sat next to him, throwing my legs over his and wrapping my arms around his neck after ending my call.

"What are you doing here?" I asked, nuzzling his face as we exchanged kisses.

"I had to bring some paperwork into the courthouse, and I thought I'd stop by and steal a kiss. Patsy was in the lobby and told me I'd find you out here."

"In the lobby? I left her in the room with Cat. I hope everything's okay."

"She said Cat was sleeping, so she went to the lobby to knit."

"Of course."

He patted my legs and hugged them closer to his chest. "How's it going? Did you get to talk to Cat? Did she tell you anything?"

"William's my father."

"Whoa." His eyes widened, and his mouth gaped open. "Really? For sure?" He leaned back against the bench and rubbed both hands over his face, shaking his head with a shocked laugh.

"He was here when I arrived this morning, and Caterina confirmed it for me."

Levi looked at me with a strange expression, like he was seeing me differently somehow. "You're William's daughter? Wow. How bizarre. I can't believe this."

"Yeah, well, I'm not sure it's really sunk in yet. I hope this doesn't screw up anything."

"Like what?"

"Like this," I said, pointing back and forth between us.

"Us? No. Hell, no. Not at all. Why would it? I told you I'm not going anywhere, and I meant it." He pulled me to him, kissing the top of my head as we hugged. "You okay?"

"I don't know. I don't know if I'm coming or going. I don't know who I am, or who I used to be, or who I'll be tomorrow."

"Just be Caroline," he said. "That's all you have to be."

CHAPTER 50

When Levi had gone, I went in to find Patsy in the lobby and caught her up on the events of the morning, and then I walked back to Cat's room to see if she was still sleeping.

She stirred when I opened the door, calling out my name as I was pulling it closed.

"Sorry, didn't mean to wake you," I said as I walked to stand by her bedside.

"I doze and wake off and on," she said, pushing to sit up. "Could you put that pillow behind my back?"

"Sure." I fluffed the pillow and placed it behind her, and she smiled and thanked me.

A single eyebrow rose as she looked up at me. "I'm assuming you want to know how you got here if I left town and never saw William Ward again?"

"The question had crossed my mind."

I sat in the chair by the bed and propped my chin in my hands as I watched her prepare herself to reveal more.

"I had been at the boarding school a little over a month when I realized something was wrong. I hadn't had a period since I'd arrived, and my breasts were so sensitive that I couldn't stand to wear a bra. I kept it to myself as long as I could, but eventually one of the headmistresses started questioning why I missed the morning classes but seemed to make the afternoon without a problem. I begged them not to call my parents, but, of course, they had to."

She pulled at the pillow behind her again, and I tried to help her situate it more comfortably.

"I refused to name William, and my father was beyond livid. He threatened me with everything he could think of, and I think he

254

would have forced me to have an abortion had I not been at a Catholic boarding school. I couldn't stay at the school, though, and I couldn't go home. Not that I wanted to!" she said, cutting her eyes to me with an eye roll that reminded me of Eva. She pulled the pillow out and handed it to me with an exasperated groan, and I wasn't sure how much of her frustration was with her position and how much was due to her memories.

"He ended up disowning me," she said as she lay back against the remaining pillows and exhaled. "Formally. Drew it up in the courts and everything. He forbade me to ever set foot in his home again and told my mother she wasn't allowed to speak to me anymore. She was never one to stand up to my father, but she arranged for me to go to her mother's house, my grandmother in New Jersey, who took me in and loved me in spite of my bad choices and wild behavior."

She grew quiet for a moment, and I looked away as she dabbed at her eyes. When she spoke again, her voice was thick with emotion.

"My grandmother, *Nonna*, loved me unconditionally. She took care of me. She even offered to keep the baby. You. To keep you. But my mother was scared of what my father would do if he found out, so she arranged a private adoption." Her voice broke, and her tears flowed. I stood and went to her, taking her hand in mine. She squeezed it and looked up at me as she continued. "The day you were born, I got to hold you for a total of twenty minutes. You had this amazing shock of red hair on the top of your head, which I loved, because it was William. It was like having a piece of him there with me that day. I loved you so much, Caroline."

She swallowed hard, and I handed her the cup of water, which she took with her left hand, still squeezing my hand with her right.

"Thank you, Caterina," I said through my own tears. "Thank you for carrying me. For giving me life. For welcoming me into the world as someone who was loved."

"Oh, how I loved you! I was so in love with you, and when they took you, I thought I would die. I wanted to die. But *Nonna* held me. She held tight to me, and she didn't let go. She gave me the strength to go on. She'd say, 'Caterina, head up, chin up, you must live.' And in that strong Italian accent of hers, you couldn't deny her, you know? I had no choice but to soldier on."

"Is she why you changed your name to Caterina?" I asked, smiling when she nodded.

"Catherine died that day. Caterina survived."

"What about the Russo? Was that your grandmother's last name?"

"No. I didn't want to be that easy to find. I chose Russo because it had Sicilian ties, which was for *Nonna*. It's also associated with red, so with it, I could carry you and William both with me. I changed my name on my eighteenth birthday and began to reclaim my life and my dignity. My sense of worth."

Words failed me, so I sat on the bed and hugged her, and we both cried.

When we'd gotten calm and wiped our snotty tears, we laughed at ourselves, and I ended up cross-legged on the foot of the bed.

"What am I going to say to William?" I asked. "When I saw him this morning, he said I needed to talk to you first. What now?"

Caterina shook her head, the smile gone from her eyes. "I don't know. As you can imagine, he's pretty upset with me. I think it was a shock to find out about you, even though I'm fairly certain he'd figured it out before we talked. The last thing I ever wanted to do was hurt him."

"But you never thought about contacting him? All these years? Did you ever look him up online? Try to find him?"

"No. I didn't even know he lived in Cedar Creek until after I'd moved here to be near my mother. I saw an article in the paper about him and his wife about a month after I bought my house. How's that for bad luck? Out of all the cities and all the towns in the central Florida area, I pick the one place I should have avoided at all costs."

"She died, you know. Revae. His wife."

"Yes," Cat said, looking down at her hands. "I sent flowers, anonymously, of course. I was heartbroken for him when I heard. What I wanted most of all was for William to be happy, and it seemed he was when she was alive."

"But you never tried to contact him? Even after she died?" I stretched one leg out beside Cat's to relieve the cramp starting in my calf.

Cat shook her head. "No. And say what? Hello? Here I am after disappearing thirty-five years ago? And oh, by the way, you have a daughter? But I have no idea where she is? No. Even if he'd been single all that time, I still wouldn't have chosen to drop this bombshell on him."

I chewed on my bottom lip, trying to decide if I should say what was in my thoughts. "But don't you think he had a right to know?"

"Of course, he did!" Cat said, her eyes flashing. "But once the wheels had been put in motion to rob him of that, there was no way I could make it right. I didn't dare try to reach him and tell him in those first few years because I knew he would try to find you. I knew he wouldn't stop searching until he did. I couldn't risk my father finding out it was William. I couldn't risk what my father might do to him. Even years later. Then, by the time my father had passed, you were an adult. I'd already cheated him out of your entire life at that point. What could I have possibly said?"

"What did you say this morning?"

"I said I was sorry. What else could I say?"

CHAPTER 51

I t was mid-afternoon when Levi texted me that William had asked for my number. I spent the next half hour on pins and needles waiting for him to call, and I nearly jumped out of my skin when the phone finally rang.

"Hi, Caroline. It's William. Levi said it was okay for me to call you on this number."

"Yeah. Sure. Any time."

"I didn't mean to cut you off this morning at the hospital. I was struggling to make sense of everything, and I needed some time to think. Would you be able to meet me for a cup of coffee?"

"Now? Um, yeah, sure. Where?"

He gave me directions to a place near the hospital, and I sat waiting for him at a table for two, much too nervous to consume caffeine.

I watched him walk from his truck to the entrance, and my stomach filled with butterflies. I'd thought before that he was my father, but seeing him and *knowing* it felt entirely different.

"How are you?" he asked, taking the seat across from me. "You're not having coffee?"

"No. I'm a little too keyed up for it right now. What about you?"

He shook his head. "Too late in the day for me. I'd be up all night."

An awkward silence followed, and I looked around the coffee shop at the wall decor while he stared at his hands.

"I have no idea what to say," he finally managed to get out, but he still hadn't looked at me.

"Me, neither," I admitted.

"If I'd known," he said, his voice cracking as he looked up to

258

meet my eyes, "I would have fought for you. I would have found you, and I would have raised you. I don't know how, but I would have."

I believed him with every fiber of my being, and I nodded, blinking back tears as I watched him wipe at his eyes with the back of his hand.

"Catherine was my first love. I waited for years for her to come back. I amassed what wealth I could so that when she returned, I could take care of her. But then time went by without a word, without a visit. No call. No letter. Nothing. I gave up. I moved on. I met Revae, and I knew a love so strong and so passionate that it healed all the cracks in my heart. It kills me to know that all that time, you were out there somewhere."

"I had a happy life," I said to William, knowing how important it was to Caterina to hear that. "I was loved. I am loved. My life is good."

He nodded, suddenly emotional again. "You should have had your family. My family. You should have had your aunts, uncles. Grandparents. You should have known your father."

I reached across the table to his clasped hands and closed my palm over them. "It's not too late for me to know my father, William. I would love to get to know you. In the short amount of time that I've known you, I've grown fond of you. I would hope we could build on that."

He opened his hands to take mine between them.

"I'd like that. I've grown fond of you, too. And the kids." His voice broke again, and he looked to the ceiling. "I can't believe I have grandchildren."

I smiled. "I don't expect anything from you, William. I know this is all a shock for you, and I know you have your own life. Your own daughter."

"Oh, Christ. Piper. I have no idea how I'm going to tell her. She left for Denver this morning. She'll be gone at least a week, seeing if she's a good fit for a job out there. I can't tell her something like this over the phone. I wanted to tell her last night, before she left, but I needed to hear it from Catherine first. To be sure."

Somehow, it had never really occurred to me that Piper and I were now half-sisters. The thought stunned me, and I sat back in the chair, pulling my hand from William's as I considered what that meant. I couldn't imagine that she was going to be too thrilled with the news.

"I want you to know," William said, his composure restored, "that if you or the kids need anything at all, anything, I'll do whatever I can to help you."

"Thank you, but we're fine. We have everything we need."

"I'd like to spend more time with them. With Eva and Ethan. Do they know?"

"No," I said, shaking my head. "I only found out myself today. I mean, I thought there were some coincidences that were hard to explain."

"Likewise," William said.

"But I guess I have to figure out how to tell them."

"Are you still bringing Eva to work with the horses tomorrow?"

"I don't know. I had planned for my mom, Lorna, to bring them down and meet Cat, but that was before, well, this."

"Bring them. It's not going to get any easier. Best to get it out of the way, and then we can all move forward with our new norm."

I noticed he'd thought that was the best plan for my kids, but he wasn't too anxious to tell Piper. Apparently, I wasn't the only one who thought it might not be good news.

Patsy and Caterina were talking when I returned to her room.

"How did it go?" Cat asked, her eyes anxious as she waited for me to speak.

"Good, I think. He wants to get to know me better. He wants to spend time with the kids."

She smiled, but as she looked away, I could see the sorrow in her eyes. It must be hard to know that I could forge a relationship with William, but hers had been irreparably damaged. It was evident she still cared for him in the way she spoke about him, and my heart hurt to think of how their lives had both been changed by the will of her father.

"So," she said, clapping her hands together and closing the door on her past for the moment, "Patsy told me last night that you've been working the books for the foundation. She said you suggested doing it online or with something on the computer."

"Yes, I think that would be your best bet. I know she said you have some, um, *challenges,* with technology, though."

She and Patsy both laughed, sharing a conspiratorial look.

"That's an understatement, if there ever was one," Cat said. "I can't do the computer thing, and as I'm sure you saw, I suck at keeping up with receipts and bank entries. It's simply not in my skill set. In fact, there are several things about running a foundation that I have discovered are not in my skill set," she said with smirk. "Let me hire you, Caroline. You need a job, and I need help. I can't keep working at the pace I have been without ending up back in this hospital. I'm behind on everything after being out so long, and you've seen how messy it was already."

I sat in stunned silence, unable to answer as I spun the possibilities in my head.

"Look," she said, holding up her hands, "I realize it may not be something you'd want to do long-term, but it would get you some income and some independence, and it would help me greatly. I'm assuming if you're doing something online it could be done from anywhere, right?"

"Um, in theory?"

"Okay, so then no matter where you choose to live, this would work. At least until you found something else, right?"

I thought of the work I'd be doing. Helping children and families. Working alongside Cat and Patsy. Getting back to numbers. It really didn't have any negatives other than the possibility of issues with us working together. And she'd already framed it as something I could do until I found something else, so the door was left open if I needed an out.

"You can think about it," Cat said. "You don't have to answer now."

"Yes," I said, smiling.

"Yes?" Cat asked.

"Yes."

"Woo hoo!" Patsy cried. "Thank you, Lord! This is cause for a celebration."

"What are you going to do?" Cat asked, her face filled with joy. "Ask the cafeteria if they have champagne?"

"I come prepared," Patsy said, going back to the shopping bags and pulling out a bottle of sparkling grape juice and three clear, plastic cups. "I had thought we might celebrate the two of you being reunited, but I think we could manage a toast for this as well."

After our toast, Patsy and I went to lunch and let Caterina get some much-needed rest, and then the three of us spent the rest of the afternoon discussing the foundation and how it would work best for me to join them.

I didn't realize how late it had gotten until Levi texted that he was done with work and ready to meet for dinner.

"Have him come here," Cat said. "I'd love to meet him."

I texted him back and smiled when he replied that he was on his way.

"You'll love him," Patsy said. "What a sweetheart! I told her from day one he was a keeper. Didn't I? Didn't I tell you that?"

"She did," I said. "She knew before I did."

Levi and I stayed at the hospital for an hour or so before heading out to dinner, opting for take-out so we could get back home and enjoy each other again.

"I accepted a job today," I told him as we lay tangled in his sheets, basking in the aftermath of ecstasy.

"A job? Where?"

"Turtle Crossing. Cat's adoption foundation."

He raised his eyebrows and gave a quick nod. "Nice. And what will you be doing there? More accounting stuff?"

"Yeah. Maybe a few more responsibilities. Fundraising. Networking. But yeah. Accounting is the gist of it."

"Awesome. Now, is this something you can do from Orlando? Or if you stay in Gainesville? How will this work?"

"I'll be using an online accounting system, so yes, I could do it remotely. But I'm thinking maybe not. I'm thinking maybe the kids and I could move to Cedar Creek."

He went still beneath me, and I rolled onto my side and raised up onto my elbow to look down at him.

"What do you think of that?"

"Move in here."

"What?"

He moved to cup my face in his hand, his eyes staring into mine. "Let's move in together. It will be tight, but I've got three bedrooms here, and the kids would love the farm."

I bent to kiss him, lying across his chest so we were nose to nose.

"No. As much as I would love to fall asleep in your arms every night and wake up next to you each morning, no. I need my own place. I need to stand on my own two feet and be responsible for me. Besides, the move is going to be a big adjustment for the kids. I can't ask them to move into someone else's house. That's not fair to them."

He nodded, his eyes never leaving mine.

"I understand. You're right. We'll have to take it slow with them. Give them the space they need."

I lay on my back and ran my fingers through my hair, untangling the knots we'd created in passion. "It's not going to be easy, you know. I'm a single mom. Brad doesn't take them often, and I don't know how much time you and I will have alone."

Levi rolled to his side, putting his arm across my stomach and pulling me closer to him.

"I've told you before, and I'll tell you again, as many times as you need to hear it. I'm not going anywhere. We'll make it work. We'll figure it out. I love you, Caroline."

"I love you, too."

We went for another round, and damned if he didn't make me beg for mercy again.

CHAPTER 52

I sat straight up in bed when the phone rang a little after three. Levi and I had only been asleep for a couple of hours, and I was in that deep dream state where I didn't know what was happening.

As the ringer blared again, I dove for the phone on the nightstand, and Levi mumbled, "Who is that? What time is it?"

"It's Eva," I said, springing from the bed and heading down the hallway as I slid my finger across the screen to answer, suddenly wide awake with fear.

"What's wrong? Are you okay? Is Ethan all right?"

She was crying, and I stood in the dark in Levi's kitchen, running a hundred scenarios of disaster through my mind.

"What happened? Eva, are you all right? Is it Grandma? Is it Ethan? Talk to me, baby."

She was sobbing hysterically, and I couldn't make out what she said.

Levi came stumbling down the hall, one eye half-open and the other closed, rubbing the side of his face as he came and stood in front of me.

"What's wrong?" he whispered, and I shook my head, turning away from him.

"Eva, I need you to calm down. I need you to take a breath and tell me what's happened."

"It's Greg, Mom. He doesn't love me anymore."

I collapsed against the counter in relief, and motioned to Levi that it was okay, mouthing Greg's name and sliding my finger across my throat in a cutting motion with a roll of my eyes.

"Oh, sweetie. What happened?"

I leaned over the counter and rested my head on my arms, trying to slow my pulse and allow my mind to catch up as the adrenaline subsided.

Levi patted my back and bent to place a kiss between my shoulder blades before heading back down the hallway to bed.

"He wanted me to go to this party over at the Wilsons'," Eva said between sobs. "I told him I couldn't go. That I was grounded. Not that I could have gone to a party like that anyway, but still."

She'd taken the words right out of my thoughts.

"I tried to talk him into coming over here instead, but then Grandma said I was grounded and that he couldn't come, which makes no sense since grounded means staying at home, and that's what we were going to do."

I grimaced. "I think grounded encompasses not doing social activities, such as having friends over, but finish telling me what happened."

"He went to the party without me, and in the beginning, he was still texting me, and everything was fine. But then he stopped responding a little before midnight, and no matter how many texts I sent him, he wouldn't write me back. Then I tried calling, and he wouldn't answer. I thought maybe he'd lost his phone, but when I went on Facebook, there's all these pictures of the party. He's with Tara Gordon, Mom!"

My tired brain searched through the indexes of names to see if I could find a Tara Gordon, but I came up empty. "Who's Tara Gordon, sweetie?"

I tried to stifle a yawn, but it escaped, and I opened the fridge to find liquid nourishment as I realized it might be a long conversation.

"She's only like the easiest girl in the whole school! The only reason a guy gets with Tara Gordon, well, let's just say there's only one reason."

"Eva, don't say that about a girl, okay? You never know what that girl's going through, and people could just be saying that about her when it's not true. You can't just repeat what others say."

"Mom, I'm looking at a picture on Facebook of her straddling my boyfriend and bending over with her butt in his face while she makes an obscene gesture with her mouth."

I raised both eyebrows as I pulled orange juice from the otherwise barren fridge.

"Okay. So, she makes some poor choices. Maybe they're just being silly for the camera. It's a party. There's probably alcohol involved, and they're hamming it up for pictures. Now, granted, that's not appropriate behavior for Greg to engage in, but—"

"Mom! He's got his tongue down her throat. There's pictures on here of her sitting on a counter and he's standing between her legs and they're kissing. I don't think they even know there's a camera, okay?"

I winced at her pain as I opened the cabinet doors searching for a glass.

"Oh, Eva. I'm so sorry."

"I thought he loved me. He said he loved me. He was going to take me to that stupid party, but I was grounded, and now he doesn't love me anymore."

I took a gulp of the orange juice and searched for the right words to say in my sleep-deprived mind.

"Sweetheart, he didn't cheat on you because you were grounded. He cheated on you because he's a jerk, and he doesn't know what it means to love someone. He doesn't love this Tara Gordon girl. He's just using her to make himself feel good. And if you had been at that party, he'd have been using you for the same reason. It's not your fault he's a jerk. It's not even Tara Gordon's fault that Greg's a jerk. It's Greg's fault."

"But if you had let him come over, this wouldn't have happened."

"Maybe not tonight, but it would have happened another night. He's not the guy for you, baby. He's got one thing on his mind, and as soon as he realized he wasn't getting that from you tonight, he moved on. That's not love."

She continued to sniffle in the background, and I moved to the couch, curling my feet beneath me as I sat so I didn't put my bare ass on Levi's leather.

"Eva. I know you thought this guy was special. I know he said things to you that made you feel good inside, and I know you wanted that to be real. There's nothing wrong with wanting to feel good. There's nothing wrong with wanting someone to love us. But it's got to be based in trust. It's got to be coming from the heart and not other parts of the body. As much as it hurts to realize it, Greg wasn't the guy you thought he was. It's better to know that now than after it goes too far."

She was quiet, and a little nagging fear spoke up in the back of my mind. "Eva? You and Greg haven't? I mean, you haven't, well, the two of you—"

"No, Mom. We haven't done it."

A huge exhale escaped my body, and I sat back against the sofa, the leather cold against my skin.

"Okay, well, that's a good thing. That's one less thing to regret."

"How am I going to go to school Monday? Everyone is going to know. Everyone already knows. There's so many comments on these pictures. Two of my friends already tagged me."

"I'm sure by Monday there will be some other scandal for everyone to talk about. And keep in mind that you have nothing to be ashamed of, okay? He's the one who acted like an ass. If people are talking Monday, they should be talking about him. Not you. Look, it's really late. Close the laptop, turn off your phone, and get some sleep. There's nothing you can do about this tonight."

"But what if he tries to call? I left him messages."

Oh, the naiveté of youth.

"Sweetie, he's not going to call you back tonight. He may call tomorrow. Or Sunday. He may try to talk to you at school Monday. And he may never call again. Greg is a jerk, Eva. I know you don't want him to be, but he is. He wouldn't have done this if he wasn't. You deserve better than him."

"But I wanted him to love me."

"I know, honey. I know. And some day, someone is going to love you, and they will do it so well that people like Greg won't even be worth remembering."

"When are you coming home?"

I closed my eyes and tried not to feel pulled apart by the various directions my heart was extending.

"I tell you what. Why don't I have Grandma bring you guys tomorrow after Ethan's soccer match? I'll take you to the farm, and you can ride the horses. I saw William today, and he asked if you were coming. Caterina's awake, and she can't wait to meet you."

Somehow, a phone conversation at three in the morning didn't seem to be the right time to tell her that William was her grandfather.

"Can I stay with you the rest of the weekend? Do I have to come back here?"

I looked down the hallway to where Levi was sleeping, flung across the bed on his stomach, the sheet across his hips, and his back bare above it. We'd had two nights together. Who knew when we'd get another?

"Yes, you can stay in Cedar Creek with me."

"Thanks, Mom. I'm sorry for waking you, but I didn't know what to do, and I just needed to hear your voice."

My heart soared, and I would have given up any amount of sleep to hear those words.

"You can call me any time, Eva. It never matters what time it is. I love you."

"Love you, too, Mom."

I put away the orange juice and ran water in the bottom of the glass before setting it in the sink.

I stood beside the bed for a moment, watching Levi sleep, and then I crawled in beside him, pressing my body to his warmth as he lifted his arm and rolled to his side, pulling my back against him to cradle me in the night.

CHAPTER 53

I don't know who was more nervous about Caterina and Lorna meeting, the two of them or me.

Lorna was especially chatty, a behavior I recognized as her being uncomfortable.

We'd decided it might be too much for Cat to have a room full of people at once. Her condition had continued to improve, and there was talk of her going home once she'd finished the final round of antibiotics, but she was still extremely weak, and she tired easily. Too much excitement might have set her recovery back.

I took Eva in first, and as I had expected, she and Cat hit it off right away. I could see small similarities between the two, and even though Eva had definitely taken after Brad's side of the family in looks, I liked to think her slender grace and ease of movement came from Caterina.

Ethan was a bit more shy, intimidated by the hospital bed and by the stranger who wanted to get to know him. It was rare to see him quiet, but I was thankful he was more subdued than normal since we wanted to keep Cat calm.

I held Lorna's hand as we entered, but she surprised me by asking for a moment alone with Cat once the introductions were made. I joined Patsy and the kids in the cafeteria as I waited for her to return, curious as to what the women had discussed.

Lorna was much more at ease when she joined us, and Cat spoke highly of my mom when I went in to tell her we'd be leaving.

"She's lovely, Caroline. They all are. You have beautiful children, and a mother who adores you. My heart is full having met them all."

"I'm going to take Eva to the farm," I said. "Mom is going to drive Ethan back to Gainesville because he has a soccer tournament tomorrow. But I'm going to stay, and hopefully, they'll spring you from this joint, and I can help get you settled at home."

"You don't have to stay if you need to be with Ethan."

"I've been to every game and every tournament so far until today. I think he knows at this point that I love him and I support him, but this weekend, I have somewhere I need to be."

"Have you told the kids? About William, I mean?"

I shook my head. "I have to tell Eva today. I think I'll hold off for a bit with Ethan. Wait until I'm back home to discuss it. He doesn't have to know right now, and I think Eva needs some time alone with me. She's had her first break-up. She's discovered boys are jerks."

"Oh, God bless her, are they ever!"

She sat cross-legged on the bed, which shifted the sheet and left her foot exposed, revealing a beautiful sea turtle tattoo.

"I like your turtle," I said, pointing to it.

She touched it with her fingertips, caressing it lightly as she smiled. "William and I had a turtle connection," she said. "They were always special to us, and I got this to remember him with."

We hugged our goodbyes as the respiratory staff came in to give her another breathing treatment, and I assured her I'd be back first thing the next morning.

Eva and I told Lorna and Ethan goodbye in the parking lot, and once Patsy had gone back inside to be with Cat, I drove to the coffee shop where William and I had talked.

"Let's get a coffee," I said. "Feel like coffee?"

"Sure," Eva said, her eyes tired and her heart heavy on her sleeve.

"Rough night, huh? How are you doing?" I asked as we waited in line.

"Okay, I guess. He hasn't called."

"He may not. And that's okay. You don't need him. He doesn't deserve your tears." I knew even as I spoke the words that they fixed nothing. No one's heartbreak had ever mended faster by being told it shouldn't have been broken.

"Caterina is probably going home tomorrow. I thought we'd get her settled in at her house, and then maybe you and I can hit some outlets on the way back. What do you say?"

"Won't Daddy complain if we go shopping, and it's not my birthday?"

"Well, he may, but I got a job. So soon Daddy won't be able to say anything about how I spend my money."

"You got a job? Where?"

"With Caterina. She has an organization where she helps kids who are waiting to be adopted, and she helps families who are trying to adopt. She needs someone to do her accounting for her and help with fundraising."

"Does she do that because you were adopted?" Eva asked as I paid the cashier.

"Yeah. I think she does, which is pretty cool, and I'm looking forward to being involved in that."

"Does that mean we're going to move to Cedar Creek now?"

We took our seats at the same table I'd sat at with William, and I was surprised to find I was nervous to tell her my plans. I'd decided what I wanted, and for the first time in I didn't know how long, I was excited for me. I didn't want anything or anyone to take it from me.

"What would you think about that? About us moving to Cedar Creek?"

Eva shrugged. "If we have to move anywhere, I guess it's as good a place as any. That way we could see Caterina at least. Daddy wouldn't be too far, right? Orlando's closer to here than Gainesville, isn't it?"

I nodded.

"If we moved here, could I work with the horses?" she asked. "I mean, like on a regular basis? Could I do that instead of dance? Or drama?"

"Yeah, I don't see why not. We'll have to get a smaller house here, since I'll be paying the bills. And I'd have to talk to William about the costs, of course. But if we're not paying for dance, then that frees up a lot for you to do something else."

"I like William. He knows a lot about horses, and he's very patient with me. When he talks, I understand him."

I swallowed a gulp of the hot coffee, delaying the inevitable now that the time was right.

"About William," I said. "Funny thing. It turns out that he and Caterina knew each other when they were teenagers. In fact, they actually dated."

"Hmm," Eva said, mildly interested but not getting the point.

"What I'm saying is, William and Caterina dated a little over thirty-five years ago."

"That's weird," she said, sipping her coffee.

"Eva, William is my father."

Her eyes flew open, and she nearly spilled her coffee.

"No way! Get out! William is your dad? Oh my God! Does that mean William is my grandfather?"

"That's generally how that works."

"Does he know this?"

I nodded. "Yes. He and I just found out yesterday, so it's all kind of new."

"Wow!" Her entire face lit up, and she was grinning from ear to ear. "This is so cool. So, Piper's my aunt?"

"Yeah," I said with a shrug, wondering if William had figured out how to broach that news yet.

"I'm thinking if he's my granddad, undoubtedly he'll let us use his horses."

I put the coffee down and shook my head. "No, it doesn't work like that. We don't become an instant drain on his finances just because we're related. We will ask what his going rate will be for training you, and if there's any charge involved for any of the rest of it, then we'll pay what's needed. We're not asking him for anything or making demands."

"He told me the other day he'd work with me for free, and that was before he knew we were related. I can't imagine he's going to charge us that much now that he knows."

"The point is, we're not going to ask for anything for free. Just because we found out we're related to him doesn't mean William owes us anything. I'm happy that he wants to get to know us, and I'm thrilled if he can work with you and this is something you want to do, but I won't do anything that even seems like we're taking advantage of him, okay?"

"All right. I think he has plenty of money, though. I don't think he's going to care about whatever it costs for lessons. You've seen the inside of their house. You should have seen Piper's closet. It's insane. It's like the size of mine and your bedrooms combined back home. I think their house might be nicer than Grandfather and Mitzi's."

I flinched at the thought of Brad's parents, immediately hearing his mother's voice in my head as she explained to me that she was much too young to be made a grandmother, and Eva would need to call her by her first name.

Eva had no shortage of grandmothers now, and she had two who were thrilled to have grandchildren.

Something told me William Ward was going to be a major influence in her life as well.

CHAPTER 54

I f I had thought it would be awkward for Eva and William to meet again, I had underestimated both.

"You came back for more?" he asked her as we got out of the Tahoe in the parking area by the farm office.

"Yes, sir. I'm ready to ride."

"All right. That's what I like to hear. Let's get to it. Caroline, Levi's on a call, but I'm sure he wouldn't want to miss saying hello. Why don't you wait for him in the office, and I'll take Eva up to the barn? You can join us when he's done."

I blinked at my dismissal, looking to Eva to make sure she felt comfortable, but she'd already opened the door to climb in his truck. I'm not sure what dramatic reunion I was expecting, but in hindsight, it fit William's calm manner for him to carry on with business as usual.

The farm office was bustling with people, and I scanned the room but didn't see Levi.

"You looking for Levi?" asked a guy whom I thought I recognized from breakfast or Farm Day. Maybe both.

I nodded, and he pointed down the hallway. "Third door on the right."

The door was ajar, so I pushed it open to find Levi kicked back in his desk chair, feet propped on his desk and a phone tucked between his shoulder and his ear. His eyes lit up when he saw me, and a huge grin spread across his face.

I closed the door behind me and locked it as the seed of revenge firmly planted itself in my mind.

I walked slowly toward him, shedding my clothes on the way, and his eyes grew wide as he began to stammer on the phone.

His feet hit the floor, and I nudged his legs apart with my knee, wedging myself firmly between them before kneeling.

"I'm gonna have to call you back," he said. "Something's come up. Something real important."

I chuckled as I undid the buckle on his jeans, smiling up at him as he tried unsuccessfully to end the call.

"Oh, you're right," I whispered as his zipper came down. "Something has come up. Would you look at that?"

He apologized to whoever Tommy was on the other end of the line, and then he slammed the receiver down as I slid my mouth over him.

"Holy hell. Oh my God. What are you doing? There's people all over the place. Anyone could, oh, mother of God. Oh, damn."

He shifted his hips lower on the chair and pushed the jeans down to give me easier access, and I struggled not to laugh as he tried to keep his voice down.

A knock on the door made him stiffen beneath me as both hands went to my shoulders, but I kept my eye on the prize so to speak, refusing to break rhythm.

"Yeah, man, I'll be right out. I'll be right there. Give me a minute."

His voice was high-pitched, and it warbled at the end. His hands gripped my shoulders tighter, and he let out a stream of whispered curse words that would make a sailor proud.

"Say it," I said, ignoring that my mouth was full. "Say it."

"Okay, okay, okay. Mercy. Mercy. Mercy. A-yi-ah, Mercy!"

Whatever he said after that was unintelligible, but I got the point. The score wasn't even by any means, but I'd proven I could make him beg.

"You minx!" he growled as he pulled me up and into his lap. "What if people heard me?"

"Well, it should serve to enhance your reputation," I said, wiping my mouth on the tail of his shirt.

"Oh, God, I love you!" he said with a laugh, and I stood so he could tuck himself back in and prepare to walk out of the office.

"I'm assuming Eva's with William?" he asked as he bent to pick up papers he'd knocked off the desk in the moment.

"No. She's sitting right outside the door."

His head popped up, and he looked horrified before I laughed. "No, of course she's with William. I wanted to ask you, by the way, why you looked so surprised last weekend when he said he'd work with her. Why did you react that way?"

"He hasn't taken on any training like that in years. He stopped getting in the ring one-on-one a long time ago. He's very excited about her talent, Caroline. He's not one to be effusive with compliments, and he's very complimentary of her. He told me she's as good as Piper in a saddle, but Eva can take instruction. Piper never would."

"Eva doesn't take instruction from me. Let's hope she will for him."

"Did you tell her? Does she know?"

I nodded. "Yeah. She acted like it was the most normal thing ever. She was thrilled, if anything."

"I wondered if I should say something to him when I saw him this morning, but nothing seemed to be the right thing, so I avoided it."

"What? You didn't say, so hey, William, I understand I'm sleeping with your daughter."

He shook his head with a smirk. "No. I didn't. All right, I guess there's no other way out of this office, so I'm just going to walk out there, and grin and bear it."

"You weren't that loud," I offered. "They may not have even heard you. They may not even know."

Judging from the fact that absolutely no one in the room made eye contact with us as we made our way to the door, I'd say it's a safe bet someone knew.

Levi had blushed varying shades of red by the time we'd reached his truck, and I started to feel sorry for him.

"I guess maybe I should apologize?" I said as he got in the driver's seat and started the engine.

"Caroline, there are certain things a woman never has to apologize for. And you going down on me spontaneously and joyfully is one of them. I'm a happy man. A blushing man. A man who's going to catch hell from everyone in that office, but that's okay. They're probably just jealous anyway."

We rode to the barnyard where William and Eva were riding, but they were way out past the fenced enclosure, so it was hard to be interested in what they were doing.

Levi took three phone calls within the first ten minutes of us standing by the fence.

"You seem to be a little extra busy today," I said. "You don't have to hang out here. I'm fine if you need to go."

"I'm sorry. We have a horse coming in from Kentucky this afternoon, and all the paperwork wasn't done correctly on their end, so the state of Florida is giving me hell. Let me go back to the office, I'll figure out what they need and try to get it taken care of, and then I'll meet you back here. Okay?"

"Yeah. Sure. Whatever you need to do. I don't expect you to drop everything every time I'm here, Levi. I know you have work to do."

He looked past me across the field to Eva and William, and then he leaned in and kissed me, grinning when he pulled back.

"No one was looking. I checked."

CHAPTER 55

I watched him pull away in the truck, the now-familiar ache pulsating in my most sensitive areas.

I replayed the events of the past couple of nights in my head, foolishly getting myself worked up with the memories of his touch.

When my phone rang, I didn't even bother to look at the screen. I was so caught up in thoughts of Levi, I assumed it would be him.

"Yes? How can I help you?" I said in my most seductive tone.

"Caroline? Is that you?" Brad said. "Why do you sound weird?"

I bristled, and my stomach churned at the sound of his voice.

"Yes, it's me. What do you need, Brad?"

"I don't *need* anything. I'm calling to tell you there's been a change of plans. They're moving up my transfer date and sending me to Miami instead. I told them I don't think Orlando was going to work well for my family."

"Miami? Why?"

"Why do you think? I'm not going to have you move to Orlando and be even closer to this hick you're seeing. I need to get my kids as far as possible from that influence. Miami is the best I can do and still hold onto this promotion."

"I'm not moving to Miami, Brad."

"Yes. You are. You don't have a choice in the matter, remember? I called the realtor today, and they're putting the house on the market. If it sells before the end of the school year, the kids can just transfer. People do it all the time. You guys may need to move in with me for a month or two until we find a place down there. Real estate market is a beast from what I understand, but I've secured a three-bedroom condo, so I'm set."

"Again. I'm not moving to Miami. My kids are not moving to

Miami."

"Are you gonna be a bitch about this? Look, I know you're upset about that whole tracker thing, and yeah, I can see where maybe I crossed a line. But this job is your bread and butter, Caroline. You go where I go as long as I'm paying your bills."

I paced back and forth in front of the barn as he talked, furious with him and furious with myself for letting it get to this point. I'd had enough.

"You're not paying my bills any more. I'm going on Monday to open my own checking account."

"Really? And what do you propose to put in it? If you take one cent from our joint account, I'm going to come after you, you realize that?"

"You know what, Brad? If you're going to come after me, just do it. I'm tired of being threatened. I'm tired of living in fear. If you want to take me to court, go ahead. I'll take my chances with a judge. The kids and I are moving to Cedar Creek."

"Over my dead body. I will not have my kids living with some other man. It won't happen."

I kicked at a bucket in frustration, spilling the water inside it and watching the liquid creep across the ground.

"They're not going to be living with some other man. They're going to be living with their mother, the same as they do now."

"And how the hell are you going to afford a place to live? You haven't held a job in over fourteen years. Who's going to hire you?"

"Actually, I already have a job. But you know what? You're bound by a court agreement to pay child support and alimony. That was a court agreement that you drew up and had me sign. Nowhere in that agreement does it say I can't work. So, I should be fine financially. Thanks."

"I won't pay it."

I shrugged, even though he couldn't see me.

"I don't care. It doesn't matter if you pay it, it doesn't matter if you don't. I'm moving with my kids to Cedar Creek. Whether you're in Gainesville, or Orlando, or Miami, I don't care. This is where we'll be, and I will make sure you are able to see them whenever possible."

"You can't do this!" he roared. "You can't move them anywhere without my permission."

"Again, take me to court. I would love to explain to a judge that you put their house on the market without knowing where they will go when it sells. That you couldn't wait the five weeks until school is out to do that. That you purposely changed your transfer location to make it farther from my parents and therefore, harder for the kids to see them. Not to mention your parents, too. As crappy as they are as grandparents, they still deserve to be in the kids' lives."

"What do you mean, your parents? You don't have parents. You have Lorna, and she can just move wherever you do so the two of you can be up each other's asses forever."

"I'm done with this conversation, Brad. If you're going to take me to court, take me. If it leaves me broke and destitute, so be it. But I will no longer let you dictate how I live my life."

I ended the call and turned to see Eva's shocked face and William's concerned one in the enclosed area.

"Daddy's taking you to court?" Eva asked. "Why?"

"Oh, God, Eva. I didn't intend for you to hear that."

"But why's he taking you to court?" she asked as the horse shifted under her.

"I don't know that he will. He's threatening to."

"Is this because you want us to move to Cedar Creek?" she asked, and William's head turned to look at Eva and then at me.

"You're moving to Cedar Creek?" he asked.

"Yeah. I plan to. When the kids are out of school."

"Is that why?" Eva asked again.

I groaned in frustration, unable to avoid the mess I'd walked into. "That's part of it, Eva. He wants us to move to Miami with him."

"Miami? No way! I don't want to move to Miami!"

"You don't have to. We're moving to Cedar Creek, so don't get yourself all worked up about that."

"I thought he was moving to Orlando," William said, adjusting the reins as his horse swung its head to the left.

"He changed his plans."

"Why?" Eva said. "Was it because of Levi?"

I stepped closer to the fence. "Why would you say that?"

Eva shrugged. "He's been asking all sorts of questions. About Levi. About Cedar Creek. How often we've come here. How long you stay here. Where you sleep when you're here. He's been texting me for the last couple of days. It's actually, I think, the first time he's ever texted me."

"I'm sorry. I didn't mean for you to get caught in the middle of this."

I was aware of William's eyes upon me, and I couldn't bring myself to look at him. How disappointing it must be to find you have a daughter and then learn her life is in shambles.

"Mom, you need to do what you think is best. Daddy doesn't think about anyone but himself. You can't keep trying to make him happy. If he wasn't happy when y'all were together, he's not going to be happy now. At least if you're happy, one of you will be."

"I agree with Eva," William said. "We were coming to let you know we're going out in the open field. I'm sorry if we caught you at an inopportune time."

"Oh, it's okay. Wait, you're what? Oh, going in the field. Yeah, if you're with her, and you think it's safe, I guess it's fine."

William nodded, and Eva thanked me, turning her horse to head back out into the larger area. William hung back, and he nudged the horse to walk over to the fence by me.

"I told you yesterday if you need anything at all, just ask. My legal team might not be well-versed in family law, but I guarantee they know someone who is. You don't have to fight your battles alone any more, Caroline. You're part of this family, and we stand together in a fight."

He rode to catch up with Eva, and my heart swelled as I embraced my new life.

CHAPTER 56

When Patsy and I arrived at the hospital the next morning, William was seated by Caterina's bedside. They were both laughing when we knocked, and he was slow to stand and leave, bending when he did so to kiss her forehead and squeeze her hand goodbye.

I was dying to ask why he'd been there, but Caterina acted shy about it all, immediately changing the subject when he was gone, so I granted her privacy.

They discharged her around eleven, and she didn't even argue when Patsy insisted that she stay with her and George. I'd left Eva sleeping at Patsy's, but she was awake by the time we brought Cat in, and she'd made a makeshift sign that said, *"Welcome Home, Cat!"*

Levi arrived shortly after we did, and George commandeered him to help grill the chicken while Patsy and Eva made the salad and sides. I'd sat with Cat in the den until she dozed, and then I called Lorna to check Ethan's progress in the soccer tournament.

"They've advanced to the next round, but it doesn't start for an hour, so the coach is springing for lunch."

"Give him a hug for me, will ya? I think Eva and I are going to hit the outlets on the way back, but we should be home by seven or so," I said as I read the titles on the bookshelf behind the desk.

"I can barely hear you with the boys being so rowdy here."

"Sorry. Cat's asleep, so I'm trying to talk quietly."

"The realtor came by and put out signs this morning," Lorna said, her voice conveying her distaste. "I started to go pull them out of the ground, but I left them."

I groaned and looked to the ceiling, dreading all I had to deal with once I got back home.

"They'll start showing it soon, so I guess I need to clean up. And I suppose I have to get more serious about packing. I've been slacking on that since I wasn't too keen on Orlando, but I think now with us moving to Cedar Creek, I'll be a bit more motivated."

"Well, keep in mind you have a job now, too, so that's going to take up your time," Lorna said.

I sat in the chair behind the desk and spun it to look out Patsy's front window at the vivid blue of the lake.

"Come with us, Mom. We'll get a four-bedroom house. Or maybe we could find something with a mother-in-law apartment. Something attached so we could be close."

She sighed, and I laid my head back against the chair and closed my eyes, knowing she was going to refuse me.

"Caroline, I appreciate that you would offer, but my life is here. You have exciting things happening in Cedar Creek, and you'd be a fool not to pursue them. You and the kids will be happy there. Much happier than you would have been in Orlando, I think. But for me, I love my house. I love my girls and our weekend trips. I love my water aerobics and my dance classes and my bingo. And I've grown rather fond of Rex, the former attorney."

"What?" I said, my eyes flying open as I sat straight up. "You haven't told me this. What's going on between you and Rex?"

I'd forgotten I was trying to be quiet, and I spun the chair back around to see if my excitement had woken Cat, but she was still sound asleep.

"We've been hanging out," Lorna said in a coy voice. "Nothing serious. Yet. But it has potential to be. Look, Cedar Creek is two hours away. Two and a half tops. That's nothing. I could come every weekend if I wanted to. I mean, you know, if I didn't already have plans, of course. A little bit of distance isn't going to tear us apart. I'll still be your mom, and I'll still be there for you and the kids. Whatever you need."

"Yeah, yeah, yeah. That's all great. Go back to the part where you're dating Rex, and you didn't tell me."

She laughed. "I think I need to go check on Ethan."

"I'm not dropping this," I said. "I want details."

"Let's see where it goes first. No need to share details if they're not worth sharing. I think they're ready to head to the restaurant, so let me go round up Ethan."

"Okay, give him my love. Tell him I'll be home before bedtime. And that I'm sorry I missed his games."

"He's fine, you know. He knows you love him, and he knows you'd be here if you could." She paused for a moment, and then added, "I'm proud of you, Caroline. You're a good mama. You're a good person. A good daughter. This move is a new chapter for you, and I hope it brings a happily ever after ending. You deserve to be happy, darling."

"Thanks, Mom," I said, caught off guard by her unexpected sentimentality and the lump it lodged in my throat.

As we said goodbye, the file detailing my life caught my eye. It was sitting on the desk where I'd left it the night Patsy showed it to me.

I reached to grab it and pulled it open, flipping through my life and my memories.

While it still held a creep factor of being watched, I felt a new appreciation for the effort Cat's mother had undergone on my behalf. She hadn't had the courage to stand up to her husband and insist that Catherine or me be allowed to be part of his family, but she'd defied him enough to ensure that Cat and I both were safe and well cared for.

I picked up the last photo of me, my senior portrait.

I'd hated the way my hair looked with the stupid cap on, and I'd sworn before they ever clicked the first shot that I would never buy those pictures. Lorna had insisted on getting a few for family, but I hadn't seen one for years until I came across the one in the file.

I stared at the girl in the picture. She was young. Bright-eyed. About to head off to college to get her degree and take on the world. She had no idea where her life would take her, or who she would become.

She struggled with insecurities about her identity, who she was and where she came from.

I wished that I could hug that girl. That I could tell her she was going to be fine. To stand up for herself. To look out for her own best interests. To stay true to her dreams.

But I couldn't regret where she'd been. She had two amazing kids. She was surrounded by family from all directions. She had a bright future ahead of her, even after all these years. And she had a good man who loved her.

"Babe," Levi said, leaning through the door frame as he braced his hands on either side of it. "Lunch is ready. Patsy wants to eat outside if you guys are up for it." He turned to look at Cat, curled on her side in the overstuffed recliner. "Oh, she's still sleeping, huh?"

I nodded. "She said to wake her when it was time to eat, so I'll get her up, and we'll be right out."

"Okay," he said, his grin lingering as he stared at me.

"What?" I asked, amazed at how a simple grin from him could turn me on so easily.

"Nothing. Just looking at you. And liking what I see."

He turned and left as I laughed, and then I stood, placing the photo back in the file.

I smiled at the girl, and in the photo, she smiled back. A familiar melancholy smile where half her mouth was a grin, and the other half was a frown.

And I knew I'd never again have to wonder who I was.

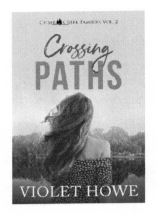

Want to know more about William and Caterina's turtle connection? Curious about what happens next now that Cat is awake and out of the hospital?

CEDAR CREEK FAMILIES, VOLUME 2 is NOW AVAILABLE!

CROSSING PATHS

CHAPTER 1
Catherine - 1982

"Look! Do you see it?" William's voice was low, and I couldn't understand why he'd suddenly chosen to whisper when we were all alone on the beach.

"See what?"

"Shh!" He put his finger over his lips as his eyes grew wide. "We have to be very quiet. You can't let her hear you."

"Who?" I whispered, scanning the surf and the sand.

He leaned in closer to me and pointed toward the waves, and I squinted as I searched the dark, inky water; the frothy white caps gleaming beneath the full moon.

"There!" he whispered, and at last, I saw her.

She looked like a log at first, rolling onto the shore as the waves crashed over her, but as she emerged from the surf, the moonlight reflected off her huge shell.

"Oh, wow! A turtle," I whispered, barely able to contain my excitement. "Can we go down there? Do you think she's okay?"

He motioned for me to talk quieter, though I swear I was being as quiet as possible under the circumstances.

"I think she's fine. She's probably coming on shore to lay eggs."

"Should we help her?"

He smiled and shook his head.

"No. She definitely won't want our help. But if we're quiet enough and still enough, we might be able to see her dig her nest. Do you think you could be quiet long enough for that?" William's grin told me that he doubted it, and we both knew it was unlikely, but I was willing to try. Moving to a crouching position, he motioned for me to step off the blanket. Then he tucked it under his elbow and took my hand before leading me behind the dunes.

"Where are we going?"

"Shh." He turned and made his way to the top of a dune, peeking over its ridge before laying the blanket on a bare patch of sand amid the sea grass. He pulled me down with him to lie on our bellies as we peered over the dune at the turtle, who was now almost directly in front of us.

"She's headed this way," I whispered against his ear.

He nodded and motioned for me to be silent.

Her journey across the packed, wet sand was slow, but it was nothing compared to her laborious pace as she made her way into the looser drifts. I thought I would self-combust with excitement and the effort to remain quiet by the time she reached the base of the dune. But once she found her ideal spot and began to scoop out a nest with her massive fins, the wonder of it all so enthralled me that I lapsed into a speechless stupor.

When she'd gotten herself situated, she sat gazing out toward the gulf, and I realized my eyes were wet with tears of amazement.

William smiled at me as I swiped them away with the back of my hand, and then he kissed me, and my heart nearly burst.

How could one night be filled with so much love and joy, and yet be overshadowed with such sadness?

I stared into his eyes, trying not to think about what tomorrow would bring.

Our summer had come to an end all too quickly, and I couldn't bear to consider what my life would be like with him away at college and me stuck at home for another year.

I looked back at our mama friend, determined not to ruin the time William and I had left together with fears of what might be. We sat in silence as she finished laying her eggs and secured the nest, and then she headed back to the water, leaving a trail of swept sand behind her.

William pulled me into his arms as he shifted to lay on his back, and I nestled my head against his shoulder and stared at the stars above us.

His chest expanded with his loud yawn, and I looked up to see him smiling down at me.

"Well, that was pretty cool, but we'd best get on the road," he said as he pulled me closer. "We've got a long drive back, and I'm already feeling sleepy."

"Not yet," I pleaded. "Please? Can we stay a little while longer?"

I buried my face in his neck and swallowed hard against the tears that burned my eyelids, so different from my happy tears of minutes before.

This was it.

This was our last hurrah. Everything would be different once we got back home. He'd move to Gainesville and into the dorm, and though he'd promised time and time again that it wouldn't change anything between us, I knew it would. How could it not? He was leaving me behind, and a whole new world waited for him on campus.

"Please, William. I'm not ready to say goodbye."

He tucked his thumb under my chin and lifted my face to search my eyes with his. "No one's saying goodbye, Catherine. It's only forty-five minutes from Ocala to the university. We'll figure out how to see each other. I'm definitely going to come home for the weekend of your birthday."

"But that's two months away! That's so long. I'm used to seeing you every day. Talking to you every day. Kissing you every day."

"Okay, well, we won't be able to do that, but I'm telling you, there's no reason to be all upset. Nothing is going to change my feelings for you. I love you. I love you with everything in me. We have plans, don't we? I'm going to school now, and you'll join me next year. And then when we both have our degrees, we'll get married and start our own farm."

"And we'll name it Turtle Crossing," I said, grinning despite the thick lump in my throat.

He rolled his eyes as he always did when I insisted on that name.

"We've been through this a hundred times. No one is going to see the name Turtle Crossing and realize it's a horse farm."

"Because it's not just a horse farm. You'll raise horses and nurse them back to health, and I'll rescue turtles and tortoises."

He shook his head as he laughed. "I know what we're doing, but that name makes no sense."

"It makes perfect sense. Please? For me? Just tell me we can name it that. It'll make me happy."

He leaned back to get a better look at me. "Oh, like everything else that happened tonight wasn't enough to make you happy?"

A warm blush crept into my cheeks at the memory of what I'd convinced him to do earlier, and I smiled, not wanting to concede so easily but aware that he made a good point.

"Then, let's just agree that Turtle Crossing isn't off the table, all right? It can still be considered."

"Agreed," he said. "Now, let's get on the road."

He moved to sit up, and I pushed him back down with both hands.

"No! Not yet. Hold me in your arms just a little bit longer. Just a few minutes more. Please?"

I couldn't hold back my tears any longer, and they flowed down my cheeks as he frowned.

"Oh, babe, please don't cry. Please. You know I can't stand to see you cry."

He cupped my cheeks in his hands and brushed away my tears with his thumbs.

"Then hold me," I whispered. "Hold me a little while longer. I'm not ready for this night to end."

He kissed me and pulled me onto his chest, wrapping his arms tightly around me as his heart thumped beneath my ear.

I never considered that we might fall asleep. It never even crossed my mind.

We'd been sneaking out at night for weeks, stealing forbidden moments while my parents slept. But we'd always made it back home in plenty of time for me to be safely in my bed before my father woke for his coffee.

When my eyes fluttered open to see the sky turning pink on the horizon, my heart filled with a panicked dread like I'd never known.

I'd been right to worry. Everything *would* change as soon as we got home, but in a more devastating way than I'd ever thought possible. Neither of our lives would ever fully recover from what we set in motion that night.

ORDER CROSSING PATHS TODAY AT YOUR FAVORITE ONLINE RETAILER!

A NOTE FROM THE AUTHOR

I hope you've enjoyed this story from Cedar Creek Families. I have several more books planned for this collection, including William and Cat's story (Crossing Paths—which is available now!), Piper's story, and more about Levi's sister, Rachel, who has a key role in The Glow in the Woods, the second volume in the Cedar Creek Mysteries.

All of The Cedar Creek Series novels feature recurring characters who live in this quaint community. While both Cedar Creek Mysteries and Cedar Creek Families are stories of love, laughter, family, and friendships, Cedar Creek Mysteries have the added elements of suspense, mystery, and a ghost or two.

For more information about future books set in the small town of Cedar Creek, visit www.violethowe.com to sign up for my newsletter or you can join my Facebook reader group, the Ultra Violets, for all the news about upcoming releases.

Happy Reading!

Violet

Love Romantic Mystery/Suspense?
You can find it in Cedar Creek Mysteries!

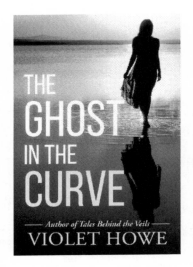

This lighthearted romantic mystery/suspense has a charming paranormal twist! Sloane Reid never believed in ghosts before she met Chelsea. Now she's trying to solve the mystery the young girl has struggled with since her death. But Sloane can't solve it alone, and before Levi's friend, Deputy Tristan Rogers, will help her, she'll have to convince him she's not crazy. Or a criminal. As they work together to unlock the secrets of the past, Sloane soon discovers it may be her own life that needs saving.

To purchase, visit http://www.books2read.com/GhostintheCurve

or www.violethowe.com.

Want more Romantic Women's Fiction?

Follow wedding planner Tyler's funny and poignant diary entries as she encounters crazy bridezillas and outlandish blind dates in her journey to find her own modern-day Prince Charming. Along the way, Tyler discovers that real-life love is often more complicated than the fairy tales she grew up believing. A lot happens between Once Upon a Time and Happily Ever After.

Learn more about the Tales Behind the Veils series at

www.violethowe.com.

ABOUT THE AUTHOR

Violet Howe enjoys writing romance and mystery with humor. She lives in Florida with her husband—her knight in shining armor—and their two handsome sons. They share their home with three adorable but spoiled dogs. When she's not writing, Violet is usually watching movies, reading, or planning her next travel adventure.

www.violethowe.com

Facebook.com/VioletHoweAuthor

@Violet_Howe

Instagram.com/VioletHowe

NEWSLETTER/READER GROUP

Sign up at www.violethowe.com to receive Violet's monthly newsletter with updates on new releases, appearances, prize drawings, and info on joining the Ultra Violets Facebook Reader Group.

THANK YOU

Thank you for taking the time to read this book.

I sincerely hope you enjoyed it! If you did, then please tell somebody!
Tell your friends. Tell your family. Tell a co-worker. Tell the person
next to you in line at the grocery store.

One of the best compliments you can give an author is to leave a
review on BookBub, Amazon, Goodreads, or any other social media
site you frequent.

#meetcute

Check out the other #MeetCute books from these authors:

Fifty Frogs by Tawdra Kandle

By Choice (A Playing Games Spin Off Novel) by Rene Folsom

What I Wasn't Looking For by Olivia Hardin

Ever After by K.S. Thomas

"O" Face by Heather Hildenbrand

Ready for Her Cameo by Sylvie Fox

Deuce of Hearts by Lyssa Layne

Fortune's Kiss by Anne Conley

Everything He Wants by Lisa Hughey

Coming Up Roses by Anie Michaels

BUILDING FENCES BY VIOLET HOWE

It Happened on a Tuesday by JK Rivers

Made in the USA
Middletown, DE
15 February 2020